SEIZE THE DAY

SEIZE THE DAY

EMPRESS BOOK ONE

J. V. Simms

Published in 2024 by Podium Publishing
www.podiumaudio.com
Podium

SEIZE THE DAY

Blood on the Field

Although his days of crawling through dangerous dungeons and trudging along on misery-soaked fields of battle were long behind him, Grandmaster Dask Thomlin still maintained a trim figure that he kept in fighting form. Even though he was now considered little more than an aging bureaucrat by the younger generation of adventurers that he presided over at the national guild, Thomlin still appreciated the value of always being prepared for an unexpected fight.

He was also well acquainted with the sight of soldiers who knew their cause was doomed, which was exactly the sight he beheld after he arrived at Fortress Starling. Everywhere he looked, the men exuded terror and hesitation. It seemed the only thing keeping many of them from outright fleeing for their lives was the self-discipline that had been drilled into them through years of rigorous training.

It was hardly the greatest welcome Thomlin had ever enjoyed.

"I'm afraid we've nothing much to laugh about today, my friend," General Aden Adler said by way of greeting after Thomlin was escorted to his office. Unlike Thomlin, Adler had let age and neglect steal away his once formidable and handsome figure, leaving nothing behind but a soft old man whose blotched nose told the tale of his rather severe drinking problem.

"It's a little early in the day for it, isn't it, Aden?" Thomlin asked as he accepted a cup of wine poured from a nearly empty bottle. "I haven't seen you in a state like this since the civil war. What's got you so distressed?"

"The long march south has been indefinitely delayed," Adler said in a quietly despairing voice. "First, we lost Fortress Rondale, and now Fortress Starling is in danger of being taken. If Oldstead succeeds in seizing it, our efforts will be set back by *years*. Many heads will roll for this failure, Thomlin, but mine will be the first."

"Things have really gotten that bad?" Thomlin asked, aghast at what his friend described. "The news back home has been nothing but golden, detailing inevitable victory for the kingdom. Have you all been lying to us?"

"Of *course*, we've been lying to you," Adler said miserably. He looked around the room with dazed, haunted eyes and spoke defensively, as though he could see the disappointed and angry faces of the people back home, "What choice did we have? Even if we told the truth, no one would bloody well believe us."

"Believe you about what?" Thomlin asked, now feeling concerned by his friend's erratic behavior.

"About *her!* About that monstrous creature! *The Empress*, she dares to call herself! Everly Graff Cruor! Who would ever believe that the greatest standing army on the continent could be defeated by a single deluded girl?"

"Everly who?" Thomlin asked. "I've never even heard of this person."

"You will. Once she finishes with us here, don't be surprised if Oldstead begins a long march *north*."

"Wait . . . wait a moment," Thomlin said in disbelief. "Are you really telling me that this random woman you speak of is somehow stalemating the advance of His Majesty's army?"

"Ha!" barked the increasingly unsettled Adler. "When did I say anything about us being *stalemated*? I'm telling you flatly that she's beating us back! We're losing, Thomlin. *Losing*. That rampaging bitch has been splashing the field with our blood."

Thomlin was shocked to hear this. "How?"

"Believe it or not, she's a *necromancer*. She calls the dead to her side, and they *obey*," Adler said. "It's like something out of a fairy tale. Do you know how hard it is to kill something that's already dead? Bloody things are *fast* too. Is that even fair? How can something be both dead *and* quick on its feet?"

"A necromancer? Aden, that's impossible. That foul art died out a thousand years ago, even before the founding of the empire."

"Oh, well, that's good to hear then," Adler said in a voice dripping with sarcasm. "The next time those monsters engage us, I'll have a message sent to my men informing them that their opponents are *impossible*. I'm certain that'll rally the lads to victory."

"Even if it really *is* an issue of necromancy, then surely the temple could deal with her—"

"As if. She smashes their holy knights aside and scorns the prayers of their priests."

"How can that be? The scriptures teach us that the undead have no power against the faithful," Thomlin said as he absentmindedly rubbed the temple chain he always wore for luck beneath his shirt.

"Is that so? Then tell *her* that. Go on, tell *Everly*. Let her know she's doing it wrong! Perhaps she'll bow her head in apology and allow us to kill her. Wouldn't that be a blessing?"

"Necromancy is just a form of magic. Even without the blessings of the temple, can't she be countered with a sufficiently skilled sword expert?"

"Thomlin, *please*," Adler said as he leaned against the back of his chair and closed his despairing eyes. "Everything you say is common sense, but this situation is *anything* but common. This woman possesses an immense command of magic like nothing I've ever witnessed. The land itself shatters at her approach. The dead serve her will. The sheer feeling of terror she exudes . . . "

"Adler?"

"I personally commanded the defense of Fortress Rondale, Thomlin. I barely managed to escape before its walls fell. We didn't have a mere sword expert among our ranks that day, we had a damn *sword king!* One of the Ten Blades."

Thomlin whistled at that. The rank of sword king was a title that only a select few ever achieved. It was the very pinnacle of the swordman's art. The requirements and training involved created a being that existed in the realm of the superhuman. The Ten Blades of Winstead were an elite brotherhood comprised of nothing *but* sword kings. They were considered the finest warriors in all the land, each one of them a veritable army unto themselves.

"Which one was it?" Thomlin asked.

"Willem, the Silent Storm," Adler replied.

"And how did he fare?"

"The Silent Storm has been silenced, *forever.*"

Thomlin was stunned into silence.

Adler laughed bitterly at his friend's reaction, then said, "Just imagine how I felt seeing it in person."

"I don't understand," Thomlin eventually said. "Sword kings are the absolute masters of *harada.* No matter how powerful a mage's magic, Willem still should have cut her down."

Adler leaned over his desk toward Thomlin, his eyes wide, his grin brittle, and said, "*The Empress* is a sword king as well, Dask! And a more powerful one than poor Willem ever was."

"Be serious, man!" Thomlin yelled, refusing to believe his ears. "Someone can potentially be a sword king, or they can be a mage, but it is impossible for them to be *both!* Such a being has *never* existed! Never!"

"HAHAHA!" laughed the maddened Adler. "And *now* you begin to see what I've been dealing with these past months. Have another drink, *please*," he said, as he refilled their cups with a shaking hand.

"Adler . . . is what you say the truth?" Thomlin asked his old friend quietly.

"It is."

"Why have you called for me?" Thomlin asked next, although he suspected he knew the answer.

"I wouldn't make this request if the circumstances weren't so urgent. Thomlin, please lend us the services of the Silver Lance."

"Aden, you *must* be joking. If this situation is as dire as you claim, then how can you possibly expect me to send in Winstead's only sky-ranked team? If anything, you should be sending for the other Ten Blades!"

"Thomlin, please, I dare not make that request. The Ten Blades are uncontrollable! Together they may very well destroy that woman, but the mayhem they'll unleash while doing it would be indescribable. Even the king can barely bring them to heel."

"And the temple won't send one of their paladins?"

"Another unacceptable risk! What if they sent *Sarah?*"

Thomlin had to admit that Adler made a good point. Sarah was not someone you could rely upon for restraint.

"Oh, for the love of . . . You're *really* going to put this all on me, aren't you?" Thomlin complained. "Adler, the Silver Lance is an irreplaceable treasure. Losing even one of them would mean the end of my career."

"If this fort falls, we'll lose our primary staging ground into Oldstead," Adler said, rubbing tenderly at his temples as he spoke. "Everly has been tearing our forces apart left and right. For the past month, the standing order for my men has been to retreat as soon as she's sighted. We just can't hold our ground before her."

"Do you really believe the Silver Lance could make a difference?" Thomlin asked.

"I don't know," Adler said bluntly. "But we *must* convince the men that we have a means of opposing that monster. We must help them to keep their hearts! They're terrified of her! She springs forth from nowhere, slaughters them by the dozens, and then saunters off the field to who knows where. Like it's all a game, but she's the only one who knows the rules."

"Are you saying you can't keep track of her?" Thomlin asked. "What's the use of those damned spirit wielders if they can't follow one girl?"

"Her defenses are *impenetrable.* Everything about her is a mystery to us. Thomlin, she may not even be human . . . "

"Adler, wait!" Thomlin said, now feeling a sudden burst of inspiration. "Have you tried paying her off? If she truly considers herself royalty, then she may be amenable to a few chests of gold. I haven't met a royal yet who could resist a bribe or ten."

"Of course we tried bribing her! We're not amateurs. She demanded far too much."

"How much is *too* much?" Thomlin wondered.

Adler described the amount, which in turn caused Thomlin's jaw to drop. "Is she *insane?*"

"She said that amount was a pittance compared to the value of her honor. Then she called us paupers for trying to negotiate."

They both sat in silence for nearly a minute and pondered the price of a madwoman's honor.

"All right. I suppose I'll have to rally the guild," Thomlin decided.

Adler was elated to hear it. "My friend, *thank you!*"

"Don't thank me yet. Sky-ranked adventurers are notoriously independent. Even if I put the call out, the Lance won't necessarily heed it. It'll take a bit of time to get help mobilized—"

"General Adler! News from the field!" shouted a young officer who burst through the doors, now out of breath from racing to deliver his message.

"Well, don't just stand there gawping for air, you little fool. Out with it!" Adler ordered him.

"Y-yes, sir! Uh, Sir Ian Kane has located the Empress and has directly engaged her!"

"WHAT?" Adler thundered. "Send orders telling him to fall back at once! NOW! NOW! Get out there and see it done! Tell the men to drag him back if they must! Send out our finest! No harm must come to the king's nephew!"

"Ian Kane?" Thomlin asked. "*The Dragon Slayer* is here?"

"Yes, Sir Ian bloody Kane!" Adler snapped. "The king's foolish nephew is running around the field playing at being a free knight! I gave him permission to assist with our efforts on his solemn word that he wouldn't place himself in danger! Damn him for this! Who's the one who'll lose his head if that armored witch slays him? Gods, I need a drink!"

But Thomlin wasn't so sure a drink was necessary.

Sir Ian Kane, although not a member of the Ten Blades, was considered one of the greatest swordsmen in the nation. He'd been the final pupil of the legendary Mountain Splitter himself, and it was said that his skill was equal to that of his teacher. Such was his ability that Thomlin had repeatedly entreated the young man to join the adventurers' guild.

I've seen him wield his blade, Thomlin thought as his heart surged with hope. *Sir Ian's talents are magnificent. He's a rare, once-in-a-generation genius! Perhaps he's exactly what is needed to put this villainess down. Fight on, Sir Ian! Fight on and win! I'll pray feverishly for your success.*

Yes, this could work. Sir Ian was the *Dragon Slayer!* Necromancer or not, who could possibly withstand him?

"I'm disappointed, Your Highness," taunted the Empress as her heavy blade collided with Sir Ian's, nearly driving him to his knees through sheer force. "Where did all your ferocity from earlier go? Is this how you planned to avenge your lost love?"

Everly Graff Cruor's distorted voice echoed with both malice and mockery as the two fighters continued their duel. It radiated supreme self-confidence and contempt for her opponent. A contempt that was likewise felt.

"Be silent!" Sir Ian Kane growled through his gritted teeth as he forced himself to remain standing. "I'm just getting started, murderer!"

"She put up a much better fight, you know," Everly said casually. "Nothing spectacular, but I admired the precision of her swordplay. She clearly trained diligently. Not an ounce of natural ability in her entire body, but she surpassed her limitations through repetition and sheer desire for strength. Admirable, truly admirable. Not that it saved her from *me* . . . "

The so-called Empress's expression could not be seen thanks to her intimidating ebon helmet. But beneath it, Ian could *feel* the witch's lip curling at him. "And to avenge her, you came running at me as soon as I appeared, like a little hero. You saw the great villainess and *knew* that justice was on your side! But look at how things have turned out! This isn't quite how you imagined your revenge would go, is it?"

"I said to *be silent!*" Ian roared back in response, his anger surging throughout his body, lending him renewed strength. "I'll hear no more of your poisonous words!"

"This world was steeped in poison long before my birth. A foul miasma known as *weakness*. I shall be its cure, but the taste *will* be bitter."

"You're a disease, Everly!" shouted Sir Ian. "A plague upon the land!"

"When I choose to be," she said tauntingly. "Does that upset you?"

As they crossed blades, Ian pushed forward into her guard. Then, with a sharp pivot as he stepped in, he drove his right elbow hard toward Everly's face, hoping to stun her long enough to make room for a swing at her neck. But Everly responded by holding out her hand to absorb the hit. Then she retaliated by thrusting her palm against Ian's clavicle, putting a sharp stop to his momentum.

Her strength was monstrous. Although Sir Ian was taller and heavier, he was dwarfed by the unnatural power she wielded.

As he grunted in pain, Everly backhanded him with a gauntleted fist that snapped his head back and had him spitting blood. Before Sir Ian could respond, Everly crouched low and swept forcefully with the flat of her sword, catching both of Ian's legs just beneath his knees to knock him painfully onto his back.

"No—" the young knight began to say before a boot planted itself firmly on his chest, holding him in place. When he tried to retaliate, the tip of Everly's sword was driven through his arm, causing him to scream with pain as he was forced to release his sword.

"Ah," said Everly. "So much for the great Dragon Slayer. I wouldn't wriggle around too much, by the way. You might accidentally sever your radial artery. I'd feel terrible if you bled out before I could finish gloating."

"I'm not afraid to die," Sir Ian said fearlessly.

In response, the Empress gave her sword an ever-so-slight twist that made Sir Ian howl once more with pain.

"Is that so?" Everly asked. "The problem with talented people like you, Ian, is that you've managed to avoid experiencing pain for so long that you never learned to properly respect it. That ignorance has stunted your growth. I think a little suffering would season you nicely."

"Damn you!" Sir Ian raged. "This isn't over, do you hear me? This isn't *nearly* over! Mock me all you like, but until you put that sword through my heart, I'll *never* stop coming for you! Not until you lie dead at my feet, traitor!"

"You've got a long way to go until that blessed day, Your Highness."

"*I don't care!* I'll stop you! I'll *find* a way to stop you!"

"I forgot how adorable your pouting face was."

"To hell with you!"

"Where was all this energy when we were together?" she wondered. "The sex could have been spicier."

"You're vulgar!"

"You used to love that about me."

"All I see now are my regrets!"

"Well, that's fair too."

"You can't stand against the entire kingdom, Everly!"

The Empress paused for a moment as though she were carefully considering the prince's words. Then she shrugged. "Well, if I can't stand against it, then I'll be *certain* to trample all ov—"

An arrow flew across the field and bounced harmlessly off Everly's helmet before landing at her feet. Everly seemed confused by its sudden appearance.

"What are those extras *doing?* How dare they interrupt me?" she said. Then an enormous fireball came hurtling at her. As it did, an aura of void-black darkness emanated around her armored body and swallowed the destructive surge of energy before it could harm her.

"Idiocy. That would have killed *you* as well," Everly murmured.

"I would gladly sacrifice my life to see you dead, witch!" Sir Ian boldly said.

"When will you grow up?" Everly wondered. Although her voice remained calm, her body language nakedly revealed her displeasure.

A force of thirty armored men on horseback came racing toward the two combatants with their weapons drawn and spells prepared. Soon, they were encircled.

"Release Sir Ian and surrender yourself at once, traitor!" ordered their captain.

"You interrupted me, just now. You threw off my line, and then you nearly killed my audience," Everly said.

"I ordered you to *surrender*—" the captain began to repeat before Everly raised her empty hand and made a swift slashing motion with it.

All around the circle, the members of the rescue party fell ungracefully from their mounts.

Headless.

"NO SCENE STEALING," seethed the Empress.

She then turned her attention back to Sir Ian and gave an embarrassed little laugh. "I apologize for that. I know they were on your side, but they had *no* sense of timing. I can't stand unnecessary improvisation. Mugging for screen time is *such* an ugly look. Now, where were we?"

"Wh-what?" asked Sir Ian.

"Before they interrupted us. You said . . . Shoot. Eris? What did he say? Oh, good, thank you. Okay, you said, '*You can't stand against the entire kingdom, Everly!*' Would you please repeat that?"

"What?"

"REPEAT. YOUR. LINE."

"You can't stand against the entire kingdom, Everly," Ian quietly repeated.

The Empress paused for a moment as though she were carefully considering her opponent's words. Then she shrugged. "Well, if I can't stand against it, then I'll be *certain* to trample all over it," she said.

After saying that, Everly gently removed her sword from Ian's arm and stepped back, allowing the prince to rise to his unsteady feet.

"What . . . what are you doing?" asked the confused Sir Ian as he nursed his injury.

"Isn't it obvious? I'm sparing your life," replied Everly.

"FOR WHAT PURPOSE?" Sir Ian yelled, outraged by her nonchalance.

In response, Everly began to wildly laugh; she was so delighted by Sir Ian's reaction that she couldn't contain her joy at the sight of his anger.

Her mockery continued until her sides hurt and her breath began to wheeze. When she finished and regained her composure, she said, "Isn't it obvious? *Personal amusement.* Sadly, though, I no longer have time to play with you."

"This is no game, Everly!" Sir Ian said angrily.

"You only think that because you lack the perspective gained with power," Everly replied. "Until you've overcome your limits and acquired *true* strength, you'll always be a bystander. A victim has no voice in the chorus, Ian."

"*I* am *no one's* victim!" he yelled.

"Then allow me to enlighten you."

Everly's sword swept across Sir Ian's face and left a deep furrow carved into it. The young warrior collapsed to his knees and covered his wounded face with his hands; blood seeped between his fingers.

On the ground before him lay his ruined left eye.

"If ignorance ever obscures your vision again, I'll come for the other one," warned Everly.

She then left Sir Ian behind to continue his helpless sobbing as she made her way to the gates of Fortress Starling.

As she walked, a bolt of lightning flashed across the sky in an unnatural red hue. From the ground beneath her feet, wretched figures—dressed in the battered remains of armor and bearing rusted, ancient weaponry—began to rise and fall in step with her as she approached the fortress.

Soon, a legion of them had formed.

A silent army of the dead awaited their master's command.

"She's here!" shrieked a panicked guard who stood watch on the wall. *"The Empress is here!"*

Everly smiled to herself, pleased that her title was now being recognized. They were finally starting to learn.

She thrust her sword toward the fortress. A terrible wave of motion and power erupted from her weapon and tore into the very substance of the Earth itself. The ground didn't just quake—it was *sundered*. Even the atmosphere seemed to shudder and crack. The air screamed as it was displaced by the forceful energies Everly unleashed.

The gates of Fortress Starling weren't merely knocked down. They were torn away, ripped aside like thin sheets of paper, as were the walls they were connected to.

With one attack, she had smashed half the settlement into ruinous collapse. "Their defenses are broken, my children. Go forth and reap!" commanded the Empress.

With the order now given, Everly's undead force ran through the breach to begin their bloody culling.

"Sound the order to retreat. Make no attempt to resist. Do what you must to survive," Adler commanded his adjutant, who hurriedly rushed from the room to fulfill his order, before turning back to Thomlin.

"Well, looks like I was too late in seeking your help, my friend. Get out of here, Dask. Remember what you saw today."

"Adler, what are you saying?" Thomlin asked him. "There's time enough for us both to escape!"

"No, I'm afraid there isn't," chided Adler. "I told you the crown will not accept failure. I'd rather die honorably here with my lads than cringe before those unforgiving bastards at court. My neck's so fat, they might have to drop the guillotine twice to properly execute me. I'd rather not experience that."

"Adler . . ."

"I had a good run, Dask. Far better than I deserved. Though I do wish sometimes that I hadn't let ambition tempt me into joining the military. I think the most fun I ever had in my life were those days I spent with you and the others, adventuring. Too bad we can't go back to that time, eh?"

"Those were great days for me as well, Aden. The best," Thomlin said softly.

"HA! Listen to us, reminiscing about times past, like those sad old men we enjoyed mocking in our youth! What a joke age makes of us. Get out of here, Dask. Get out of here and warn them. Warn anyone who'll listen."

"Aden—"

"JUST GO!" Adler shouted as he poured himself a final drink. When he looked up, Thomlin was gone.

"Ah, about time. He's a good man, he really is, but he always needed to be pushed into doing the hard part," Adler said to himself as he sipped his drink. "This world has never been kind to those too soft to act."

All around him, Adler heard men scrambling to escape. He also heard screaming, glass shattering, and the clattering steps of . . . *things* that shouldn't be walking.

The sound of his lads dying tore at him. Adler knew that as their leader, he should be out there with them. But he couldn't bring himself to leave his desk. He didn't want to see the bodies; he wanted to remember his soldiers as they were: well-trained, dependable, loyal, and brave.

He didn't want to see what the skeletons had made of them.

Speaking of which, the skeletons soon arrived at his office door and began filling the place, surrounding him on all sides. As one, they stepped toward him with their weapons held high.

"Well, that was life," Adler said to no one in particular. "I don't suppose any of you would care for a drink?"

When the skeletons completed their work, when the fighting had died down and the dying pleas for mercy were silenced, their master nodded her approval and sent her pets back to their rest. She then turned her back to the devastation she'd wrought and walked away into the night.

She soon vanished from sight in a flash of eldritch red.

Everly now stood before her ominous black tower, a fearsome place that existed within the chaotic planes of the astral realm. The massive building stood against a backdrop of endless raging storms, in a barren landscape filled with flame and crowned by darkness.

It was her home, her castle, her personal sanctuary.

And truly, it was dope as hell.

Everly entered through the front gates and approached a throne that sat in the center of the first floor. It was a twisted sight to behold, covered in detailed sculptures of screaming figures tormented by ferocious snarling beasts with snapping jaws that tore into their helpless flesh.

It was the sort of throne that might appear in the feverish dreams of an apocalyptic prophet—or on the album cover of a particularly cool metal band. Probably a German one. Those guys went hard.

After seating herself on her fearsome chair, the Empress silently reviewed the events of the day.

Then she sighed with immense satisfaction before gleefully kicking her feet in the air.

"That was boss level. That was absolutely *boss level.* Did you hear that line I said about Kane's eyes being veiled by weakness? Guys, I totally ad-libbed that! It just came to me on the spot!"

"I was observing through the viewing crystal, Your Majesty," said a sinister-looking goblin wearing a spotless white suit. "Your gift for improvisation is an absolute wonder to behold."

The goblin's name was Carter, and he proudly served as Everly's right-hand man.

"Appreciated," Everly replied. Her voice, although still distorted, contained considerably more cheer now that she was back home. "Improvisation isn't my forte; you know I prefer planning things in advance, but when inspiration strikes, you just gotta roll with it, right?"

That boy was a fool to cross blades with you, rumbled a voice into her mind that seemed to rise from the depths of the Earth. *The weak should know their place.*

"You never did like Ian very much, did you, Titania?" Everly asked with amusement.

He thinks too highly of himself. His prattling annoys me. Won't you please kill him, next time?

"Aw. You're hard to say no to. If you're nice, I promise I'll consider it."

Personally, I most enjoyed the moment when you left that foolish little prince on his knees in utter despair, came a second woman's seductive but venomous voice. *I could taste his pain. How deliciously cruel of you, mistress.*

"Well, what can I say? Leaving a sworn enemy with a gruesome reminder of my power felt thematically appropriate. True villains leave scars."

Wonderful. And I'm certain that particular scar won't heal for quite some time, Eris said with malignant delight.

"He should thank me for it," opined Everly. "His looks gave him too much confidence. Now, he has depth. No *depth perception,* but definitely lots of depth."

Everly Graff Cruor, the Empress, the terror of the battlefield and the self-styled ruler of darkness, reached for her helmet and removed it. Out from it spilled shimmering locks of bright golden hair, which framed the breathtaking features of the young woman they belonged to. So great was Everly's beauty that it could easily captivate the heart of any stranger who beheld her.

Only a closer look into her dazzling hazel eyes would reveal a glimpse of the mad fires that raged wildly within her; they were the eyes of a girl who worshipped destruction itself. One who happily shared her faith with others.

She was also frequently told she had a rotten personality.

"Woot! I killed a lot of dudes today. Makes it feel like a fried chicken sort of night, doesn't it?" she asked Carter.

"Does it really?" he replied, knowing better than to ask how killing anyone could make someone desire poultry.

"I think it does! Effort deserves reward. So, *I* deserve some *friiiiiiied* chicken!" proclaimed the Empress.

"I'll have your meal prepared at once," the goblin said with a bow.

"Don't skimp on the hot sauce! You know I like having some heat in each bite."

"I'd never dream of it, Great Everly."

"I love you, man. God, I'm *staaaarving*," she said.

When her food was ready, Everly followed Carter out of the throne room to the dining hall, removing bits of her armor as she walked. A pair of ghostly attendants followed behind her and patiently gathered each discarded piece for storage. When she'd completely freed herself of it, one of them handed her a robe to wear as she sat to eat her meal.

The chicken was very good.

"*Bitchin'*," she said with a satisfied smile.

"Oldstead sends you their fervent gratitude, Majesty," Carter informed her. "Their troops will soon take command of the remains of Fortress Starling."

"Yeah, gratitude. That's nice," Everly replied between mouthfuls. "More importantly, are they prepared to follow through on the deal?"

"Sadly, there's still considerable resistance to the idea of you becoming their monarch."

"Still? Which part of *obey or die* are they struggling with?"

"The prime minister believes that he can succeed in having you assassinated before you claim your rightful due."

"Aw, cute. Pin him naked to a wall where everyone can see him."

"Alive or dead?"

"Chef's choice."

"As my Empress commands."

The goblin left to fulfill his duty as Everly greedily continued to devour her food. After she finished her third plate, she pushed it aside and sighed in contentment.

Delicious food truly was a heavenly reward for a day's hard labor.

Coming to this world had been the best thing that ever happened to her.

She wondered what sort of fun tomorrow would bring.

CHAPTER ONE

The Racoon Conundrum

In the back alley of a bad neighborhood, two girls were having a fight.

"Let me go, you bitch! You better fucking let me go!" said the bigger of the two between her bloodied teeth after Kerri's arm snaked around her neck and completed the headlock that firmly held her in place.

Kerri found the other girl's reaction completely inappropriate. Didn't she realize the danger she was in right now? A properly cinched headlock could easily cut off blood flow from the carotid artery and induce unconsciousness in moments. That was one of the reasons why it was banned in most competitions. It was *dangerous*.

Potentially lethal.

The other girl was heavyset. She possessed a thicker and wider body, and she was nearly six inches taller than Kerri was. But her size wasn't what originally caught Kerri's attention. It was her aura of confidence and the scars she had on her hands. This was a lady with *swagger*, the kind you only developed after a lifetime of getting your way through intimidation and violence.

This was a girl who knew how to throw her weight around.

Her opponents must have all been terrible at fighting, though.

As soon as the fight began, the big girl had come charging at Kerri with a bull rush tackle, clearly intending to quickly bring them both to the ground, where she could use her weight to keep Kerri pinned beneath her. Kerri liked that the girl had a good instinct for what her strengths were. Too many times, other women would do something stupid like flail their hands wildly or pull at their opponent's hair. This chick just skipped the preamble and went straight for the takedown.

The problem was that her technique was awful. She was making a tackling attempt at Kerri's midsection, like this was a game of American football. The easier and more productive method would have been to aim at Kerri's lower body—specifically, one of her legs. There was a reason amateur wrestling placed so much emphasis on single-leg takedowns. Destroying your opponent's balance was the easiest way to get them on the ground.

Then again, as big as she was, maybe this girl was incapable of going lower? After all, the heavier you became, the more pressure you put on your own knees. Maybe her weight and lack of physical conditioning were holding her back? If so, that was a shame.

As the other girl closed in, Kerri stepped in and swung her knee up to catch her right beneath her jaw.

Clack! Her knee connected with such force that Kerri heard the other girl's mouth snap shut from the impact. That was another thing the big girl had done wrong: breathing out of her mouth. A costly mistake, really. Her jaw was now probably broken.

In the moment of blinding pain that her opponent was probably feeling, Kerri had placed her in a headlock, and that was the end of the fight right there. It was a disappointing conclusion. Kerri really thought she was going to be challenged this time.

Oh, well.

"Bitch, I said let go!" the big girl screamed. Now she was trying to punch Kerri in the side, but she didn't have the leverage to generate enough force for her swings. Kerri sneered and then tightened her grip. Then she began counting in her head: *one one thousand, two one thousand, three one thousand . . .*

The big girl was unconscious by the count of six. Kerri gently lowered her to the sidewalk and released her. Her opponent looked almost peaceful there, lying on the sidewalk with blood pooling from her open mouth. Like a wounded little angel.

She'd be in a lot of pain when she awoke. Kerri thought that was funny, so she laughed.

"Get her!" screamed one of the big girl's three companions, who had all been eagerly watching the fight, hoping to see Kerri get mauled. All three of them were now running at her, furious because of what she'd done to their friend.

This was something Kerri didn't quite understand about other people. How could you witness someone deliver such an effortless and humiliating defeat to another human being and still believe you'd fare better? Why was it so difficult to instill fear in others without the use of a weapon?

It was a real problem.

Kerri called it "the raccoon conundrum."

Racoons could be vicious, terrifying animals when provoked. When one hissed at you and went running at your legs, your instinct wasn't to stand your ground—it was to run. However, such behavior was completely illogical; even a small woman typically outweighed the biggest raccoon by nearly eighty pounds. Humans were also far stronger.

Capitulating to a raccoon was completely ridiculous. Why not simply kick the silly thing?

And yet the sight of a raccoon approaching aggressively was often enough to send a grown man running for safety. Maybe it was the fear of disease or the innate knowledge that agitated wild animals were fearless and would do anything to inflict as much harm as they could.

A sufficiently angry raccoon would do its level best to make you hurt regardless of how big you were. So people were cautious around them.

That caution was a sort of respect.

Why didn't humans give one another the same courtesy?

These girls had just seen Kerri destroy the biggest, strongest member of their clique. But instead of backing down and acknowledging her obvious superiority, they'd decided to attack her. Did that make any sense? It didn't, did it? And yet here they came, fearlessly throwing themselves at her. Real life was nothing like the comics and movies Kerri enjoyed. Real life operated on nonsensical principles.

They gave her less respect than a stupid raccoon would receive.

Kerri *hated* the raccoon conundrum.

Her first move was to sidestep the lead attacker's clumsy roundhouse and respond by thrusting an elbow into the back of her neck. This was another forbidden technique, for a very good reason. Although it was an excellent means of stunning your target, applying too much force to your blow could potentially leave the other person paralyzed for life.

The girl dropped to her face as though her body were boneless. While she lay helpless on the ground, Kerri kicked her in the face and sent a fresh spatter of blood across the sidewalk.

Good hit, she decided.

The other two attacked her at the same time. One grabbed her from behind and tried to apply a chokehold of her own while the other screamed, scratching and slapping Kerri's face. Again, not a very good technique at all. Where had these girls learned how to fight?

For the one trying to choke her from behind, Kerri lowered her hand and gripped her thigh just beneath the shorts she was wearing. Then she *squeezed* as hard as she could, which was very hard indeed, to the other girl's detriment. Kerri could feel blood welling beneath her nails as the other girl's skin was stripped away from her leg.

"Fuuuuuuuck!" the girl shrieked, finally releasing her grip around Kerri's throat so she could clutch at her shredded thigh. Kerri quickly delivered a back-thrusting kick, a move more famously known as a "mule kick," which caught her wounded target square in the gut and pushed all the air out of her, leaving her gasping for breath on the ground. That left only one other person standing. Kerri felt something warm on her cheek and carefully touched it.

Blood. The other girl's wild swipes at her face had drawn blood.

Kerri smiled and savored the stinging sensation when she pressed her finger into it. The wound hadn't been dealt fairly, but Kerri still gave the remaining girl a courteous nod for having managed to inflict it.

"Think you can do it again?" she asked her.

"Bitch, I'm going to fucking kill you," the other girl whispered menacingly.

The girls in this neighborhood really cursed a lot. Kerri liked that about them.

Kerri found it sad that she couldn't visit this place more often. She often had extracurricular activities that left her with very little free time in the evening for playing like this. But tomorrow was an extremely important day for her, which meant today would be the last time she'd ever get to come around.

So she'd decided to skip school and look for some trouble to get into.

"If you say you're sorry and kiss my ring, I'll let you go," Kerri promised while knowing the other girl would refuse.

"Bitch, I wouldn't let you go even if you kissed my ass," the other girl replied.

Kerri grinned and waded in with her fists up, knowing the time for talking had now passed.

What remained wasn't a fight so much as it was an execution. With no one else to jump to the other girl's rescue, Kerri began using her for experimentation. She got all kinds of useful data: How many headbutts a girl that size could take before collapsing. How hard you could punch a nose before it broke. All very practical information.

Kerri had to hand it to her opponent. Whether it was due to stupidity or sheer toughness, the other girl refused to stay down. She really had no quit in her!

"Why do you keep getting up?" Kerri asked her after she climbed back to her feet for the fourth time.

"Fuck you, this is my neighborhood," the girl spat out.

"*Whaaaaaat?*" Kerri asked, surprised and delighted by her answer.

"I said, '*Fuck you*, this is my neighborhood,'" the girl repeated.

So it was pride, Kerri thought happily.

Kerri understood pride. Sometimes it seemed that pride was the only thing she understood. Pride was the privilege of the strong and the capable. Pride was for the talented. Kerri felt a lot of pride in herself. She was good at a lot of things, and that meant she was better than a lot of other people.

But this girl wasn't like her. Her pride was different. She wasn't fighting to display her superiority. She was fighting because she loved her friends, and she loved her home. In other words, she was fighting in defense of others. Kerri had assumed the group had jumped her because they were sore losers about their friend being defeated.

But that wasn't the case at all. She realized that now. Their actions had been motivated by fear. Fear that she would hurt that big girl even more after putting her on the pavement.

They'd been trying to protect her. That made their actions selfless. No, it made them *heroic.*

Kerri loved heroes. She loved them more than anyone else in the world.

Loved hurting them, that was.

She grinned with malicious joy and continued destroying her opponent.

The attacks Kerri threw were delivered too quickly for the other girl to avoid. They were devastating open-palm strikes aimed at her opponent's ears, the hinge of her jaw, her injured nose, and her cheekbones—areas where percussive damage inflicted more pain than a simple punch would have.

A few moments of this barrage were enough to put the girl on her back.

This time, she didn't get back up.

Kerri knelt and kissed the other girl on her forehead. Then she patted her cheek affectionately and slipped back into her flip-flops. She had to go home now, and she'd have to make two transfers to catch the train that would take her back to her own neighborhood.

Aside from the scratches on her face, Kerri didn't look different from any other uptown teenager. Her skirt hadn't even been ruffled during the altercation. It was a shame, though; she would have loved to have gotten a few scars. The news said this side of town was filled with crime and violence, but so far, the worst she'd received while playing here had been scratches like these.

It was kind of a letdown.

It would have been nice if they had knives, she thought wistfully.

Knives probably wouldn't have made a difference with that group of girls, though. The sad truth was that they hadn't been good opponents. Bluntly speaking, they'd been trash. None of them had been enough to get her heart racing.

Well, except perhaps that last girl.

She'd been fun.

Righteousness had an allure that couldn't be matched. Genuinely good people drew Kerri to them like a moth to a lit candle. She wanted to see them, know them, and touch them. But mostly, she just wanted to hurt them. Physically, emotionally, spiritually—ideally all three at once, really. Heroic spirits brought out a powerful desire within her . . .

. . . to crush them.

She had her reasons, and they weren't good reasons at all. Her self-awareness made her happy. Knowing that she wasn't a good person was what made her feel comfortable in her own skin. A creature like her needed to exist in opposition to something. That was the only way it could survive.

But Kerri wasn't willing to settle for mere survival. She wanted to *thrive*.

She arrived home, kissed her parents in greeting, grabbed a snack, and then marched into her room to watch television.

Kerri was an intelligent girl who kept up on world events and enjoyed reading. She had a reputation for being quiet and studious. That's why it would have surprised many of the people who knew her at school to see her eagerly watching an old episode of the *Mighty Morphin Power Rangers*.

It was an absolute classic too. One of her favorites. It was the second season premiere when Lord Zedd first appeared and mercilessly destroyed the rangers' command center and murdered their Dinozord companions. Lord Zedd was a great villain, unlike the first season's Rita. He was a frightening monster with no redeeming qualities hindering his actions.

It was too bad that outraged parents, angered by how Zedd frightened their children, had complained to the network, demanding he be toned down. The writers complied by making him more bungling and comedic. It had completely ruined his character.

Kids ruined everything.

"Hey, pumpkin. Did you go to school today?" asked Kerri's father later that evening as they sat at the table to eat.

"Yeah. Why?" Kerri asked as she cut into her grilled steak. She preferred her meat rare and bloody. Her mother had once asked how she could eat something that undercooked, and she responded by saying, *I like pretending I can hear it cry*.

Her mother had stopped talking to her for a while after that.

"Are you being honest, young lady? The school called today to ask where you were," her father said with a frown.

"There's another girl in my homeroom named Carrie with a *c*. She didn't show up today. I think Mr. Rickson got our names mixed up," Kerri replied. She'd learned how to lie without blinking years ago and was very good at it.

It was enough to convince her father.

"Okay. Well, let's make sure we get this sorted. I tried to tell him that skipping class just isn't something you would do, but he was insistent. Tch, fella talked to me like I don't even know my own daughter."

You don't know me, thought Kerri. *You have no idea what I'm like.*

"My girl is on the student council and gets straight As. Does she sound like someone who'd play hooky?" her father continued with a disbelieving tilt of his head. "But I guess some teacher who only spends an hour a day with her knows her better than I do."

Hey, Daddy. Today I bashed a girl's face in for fun. I wanted to stick around and play with her blood, but I didn't have the time. I value nothing and respect no one. Tomorrow I'm going to do something terrible for no good reason. I'm already imagining what your face will look like when the reporters ask why you didn't stop me in time, and I'm doing my best not to laugh. That's the girl you raised.

"Daddy, be nice. Teaching is a hard job. I saw in the news that they aren't paid fairly for all they do, and our state government keeps making all these awful new laws that make things so much harder for them. It's *so* sad," Kerri said while wearing a compassionate expression on her face.

"I suppose you're right," her father said. "You know what, Kerri? I'm proud of you for thinking of others. You really are a good person."

Kerri gave her dad a happy smile and thought, *Fuck you, no, I'm not.*

Long after her parents had turned in for the night, Kerri sat on her bed, too wired to sleep.

Tomorrow was a big day for her—the most important day of her life. She couldn't fall asleep if she wanted to. So she decided to stay awake for as long as possible and focus on visualizing her goal.

Tomorrow really was a big day.

After all, that was when she'd decided to die.

She was *so* over life on Earth.

She had a plan . . .

CHAPTER TWO

Getting Results

What Kerri most wanted other people to know was that she understood how *silly* her fantasy was. She knew how immature it made her seem, how childish it made her look. It was all *very* embarrassing. Yet, despite now being a teenager, she still couldn't set her dream aside. She just loved the idea of being one of the bad guys too much.

She wanted to become an authentic *villain*.

Her desires weren't based on any sort of grudge against the world or anything like that. She was simply in love with the idea of becoming so powerful that she could live with impunity. *Impunity* was a wonderful word; it meant you never had to suffer any repercussions for your bad behavior.

Good people couldn't do that. They had to be polite and respectful and uphold the status quo.

But villains? Villains could say or do whatever they felt like. People expected it.

Villainy was where true freedom lay.

The appeal to her personality was obvious. Kerri had a nearly uncontrollable urge to troll society, but she didn't want to suffer any personal consequences for it. That was really all there was to it.

What was it that had spurred this strange fascination of hers? Perhaps it would have been easier to ask *who* it was. There were many culprits responsible for the inversion of Kerri's early moral education. Sauron. Darth Vader. Galvatron. Doctor Doom. Lord Soth. Too many to name, really.

Do you know what all those notorious fiends had in common? Aside from being fictitious? They had once been great heroes. But they were each manipulated by outside forces into becoming monstrous versions of themselves: corrupters bearing names like Melkor, Palpatine, Unicron, and the elder gods. Voices that whispered for them to embrace the path of darkness.

Those heroes would eventually give in to their temptations and complete their tragic falls from grace, which transformed them into merciless beasts who rejected everything they'd once proudly stood for . . .

To Kerri, that seemed *so* badass. She wanted to be like that too.

Growing up, she hadn't cared for virtuous protagonists who spouted their endless platitudes about honor and hard work. She detested the brave champions who struggled through adversity and built powerful bonds of friendship and love with their companions.

Who cared about any of that sanctimonious crap?

She much preferred the forces of evil. The Empire, the Decepticons, the Cylons, the void, etc.

Those were her people.

She didn't want to save the world; she wanted to help bring it to ruin.

Kerri had been much humbler back then. Before she truly realized her own worth, she had no wish to personally become a dark lord. Who needed the hassle of being in charge? She didn't enjoy bossing others around; it made her feel awkward. No, she had no ambition to be a leader of any kind. She just wanted to become the greatest singular servant of darkness.

Well, no, to be more precise, Kerri wanted to be *a black knight*. An *ace* of darkness itself.

She wanted to be the sort of powerful enemy champion who could have ended the heroes whenever she wished but never bothered to because they were beneath her notice. That secret boss fight you could only attempt on new game plus mode, at max level, with the very best gear you could get.

She essentially wanted to be the character game developers created as a raised middle finger to the players who thought their game was too easy. That one hateful encounter that would prevent anyone from getting a 100 percent achievement rating.

Sorry everyone, no platinum trophy for you.

Now die.

Hers was such a *specific* desire, wasn't it? Certainly, a much harder path to follow than a more traditional route. But it was all that Kerri's heart yearned for: to be an aimless but unstoppable evil.

She *had* to do it. It was who she was.

Some might wonder, though. Why be something as traditional as a black knight? Wasn't that just a little too old-fashioned?

It was. But it was also an issue of aesthetics. Who wouldn't look cool in dark armor with a huge black sword and a flowing cape?

Looking cool was very important to Kerri. She was a kid. Things like that matter to them.

The mad obsession had nested deeply within Kerri's heart, silently growing in intensity until she could barely contain it. She wanted to laugh maniacally whenever tragic news was broadcast on television and then ominously proclaim that the flickering light of hope could *never* match the awesome power of death.

She studied politics and world history to learn how the great tyrants of the past overthrew their leaders to seize power. She even learned of how organized crime manipulated the law and corrupted it to serve their interests. It was very enlightening.

To throw off any suspicions about her behavior, Kerri developed a gentle and friendly outward demeanor to disguise her true personality and swiftly became popular at her private school, even as she secretly sneered in contempt at her so-called "friends."

Meanwhile, in the basement of her home, she obsessively downloaded and studied medieval swordsmanship manuals and strove to master the intricacies of the sword. It was practically a requirement that all true black knights learned to use a sword. Everyone knew that swords were the absolute symbol of authority and strength in fantasy stories. That clearly made them the best way to dispatch any heroic fool who dared to bare their fangs at her.

Oh, the hours she spent sweating and toiling to master all aspects of the blade she'd convinced her parents to buy for her. Sometimes she practiced well into the early hours of the morning; that was how determined she was to become invincible with her chosen weapon. Just as a proper servant of darkness should.

After years of hard training, she became very confident of her ability to quickly kill with a sword.

She also convinced her parents to allow her to join an after-school mixed martial arts club. "To keep in shape," she explained. "It's like cardio kickboxing. I want to get toned. *Everyone's* doing it."

Her parents didn't need much convincing. Thanks to their money, Kerri trained relentlessly for six years and became very confident of her ability to kill with her bare hands. Her body also became well toned, but it was her new capacity for unarmed violence that she chose to focus on.

Sadly, though, life never presented her with any real opportunities to enjoy her hard-earned skills.

The problem was that life on Earth didn't really *require* the presence of a black knight. Did it?

Everywhere you looked, there was crime, mass starvation, slavery, constant pointless warfare, corruption, and selfishness in the highest offices. Didn't it seem as if scandalous betrayals of the public's trust were a daily occurrence? This wasn't even the end of days; this was just human civilization going through its usual weekday routine.

All the nations of the world were filled with injustice and hypocrisy. There weren't any heroes fighting to save the day and build a better tomorrow. No one to foolishly oppose Kerri's wicked designs, only to struggle in vain before she crushed them beneath her heel.

The world just didn't *need* any help in becoming an awful wasteland, and that meant nascent secret villains like her were automatically redundant.

Wasn't that pathetic? How could any aspiring fiend thrive in an environment as stale as this? Kerri supposed she could always become a private military contractor or something, but those guys all used *guns*. Guns were *lame*. Everyone knew wielding swords to slaughter the innocent was much cooler.

Sure, PMCs were immoral scum who profiteered from war, and that was an admirable thing. Kerri wanted to do that too! But their methods just didn't interest her.

As part of her training, Kerri taught herself how to meditate, and she often used it as a means of relaxation. She also hoped that it would allow her to one day connect to the great cosmic forces that surrounded us all so that she could fuel her insights with the unstoppable power of darkness. Meditation could be extremely potent; she had experienced some extremely wild visions after gradually altering her perception of reality.

Take the concept of light for instance. It was traditionally a resource for the good guys.

Through her intense mental training, Kerri taught herself to view the concept of *light means good* as arbitrary nonsense. Light was a neutral force that anyone could use and abuse. It wasn't just a resource for the heroes! It could just as easily be applied to destructive use. For example, skin cancer. That wasn't a very nice disease. And where did most people get it? From spending too much time under the sun.

Despite examples like that, people revered light as a symbol of holiness. Well, as Kerri saw it, turning on a lamp didn't make someone an angel any more than turning *off* a lamp made them the devil.

She envisioned a million different ways that light could be used to cause harm to others. She became very inventive with it. She prided herself on her cleverness.

But, as fun as those meditation sessions were, they didn't provide her with any solutions to her dilemma. Earth was just too corrupt to be corrupted. There was nothing she could accomplish here. No meaningful battles to fight. Modern human civilization was already as wicked as it came.

That made Kerri about as symbolically useful to this world as an appendix.

But then one day, in the deepest throes of despair, as she dramatically cursed her fate and struggled to get her homework done on time, the solution suddenly occurred to her. She thought she finally had the answer to her predicament.

The only way for Kerri to get an opportunity to participate in the unending war against the forces of justice and righteousness would be if she left this world behind. She had to pull up stakes and say *sayonara* to planet Earth so that she could find a home that was worthy of her. A place that would appreciate her talents.

Yep, there was no getting around it. She was absolutely going to have to kill herself.

If she ended her own life, wasn't there an excellent chance she'd be reborn in another world? That was what most of the popular media she consumed these days promised. Perhaps a self-inflicted *isekai* was her best option for happiness.

What did she have to lose? Life was meaningless. Why not try booking herself a passenger seat on *Truck-kun* and seeing what would happen?

Kerri felt that her reasoning was perfectly sane.

Kerri had no doubt that she could achieve her goal. Years of meditation and sword training had expanded her mental awareness to a cosmic level of *profound* insight. Her mind had become so powerful that she was surprised she wasn't already able to use the Force.

The Force, the one power, the will, the true magic—whatever you wanted to call it. She was sure it was out there somewhere, just waiting for her to connect to it. Once she did, she'd truly become the planetary menace she secretly aspired to be. She was certain of it.

She was a *very* determined kid.

But it wasn't going to happen on Earth. A place as lame as this could never lead to someone like her discovering an awesome power beyond all mortal reckoning. If magic had ever existed here, it must have withered away ages ago. Wasn't that sad?

Earth sucked. Kerri hated it.

Why was she stuck in such a dull place? Had a mistake been made . . . or was there *something else* behind it?

Had her coming been predicted by an oracle? Was there a secret prophecy she was unaware of? Had her enemies somehow removed her from the world she was *meant* to be born in and left her to waste away here, far from where she could cause them any harm?

That *had* to be the case. *Ha! Well played, you clever insects,* she thought to herself. But she refused to be denied! A true black knight would *never* let her ambitions be foiled by such petty schemes. *If you've rigged the game, then I'll just have to knock over the table. I'll use two open palms with one big upward sweeping motion! Watch me go!* she vowed.

She now knew *exactly* how to outplay her unseen foes. She would make those merciful fools regret not killing her when they had the chance by *killing herself instead.*

Sometimes even Kerri was stunned by her own capacity for brilliant planning.

Naturally, Kerri couldn't just throw herself off a bridge and be done with it.

Black knights *never* self-destructed. They had to be slain in battle or banished to the void. On the rare occasion that one was forced to take their own life, it was only so that their death would spitefully taint the hero's victory.

Ha, did you really think you could win without anyone dying? Grow up, you naive fool!

Something like that.

Rules were rules.

The correct way for Kerri to die would be by challenging a defender of order to life-or-death combat, then deliberately losing the match. Then, just before dying, she would ominously inform her opponent that their victory was meaningless because *this is only the beginning . . .*

Ominous warnings were an all-time classic.

Pulling one off would reek of villainous authenticity! She had to try it.

Sadly, Kerri's scheme didn't quite turn out the way she'd envisioned.

Once she was committed to her plan, Kerri decided to bring her sword to school. Since she was a member of the student council, it was easy to slip it in unnoticed. After all, who would ever suspect someone like her of smuggling a deadly weapon into class?

To be sure, it wasn't as though Kerri planned to harm any of her fellow students. She wasn't *crazy*. She just wanted a police officer to fatally wound her while she slashed away at him a few times, that was all.

After all, she was popular and well-adjusted. Only *losers* went on a pointless killing spree.

Unfortunately, once the police arrived after she pulled out her weapon and began threatening everyone, they kept trying to negotiate with her. It was so frustrating.

The way the news presented it, cops seemed to be shooting innocent people left and right like they were playing this year's *Call of Duty*. Yet here she was, giving them plenty of reason to open fire, but instead of lighting her up, they were trying to talk her down.

Weren't the police supposed to be *bad* at their jobs? Was this because her school was in a nicer neighborhood? Or was it because there were cameras everywhere, and they didn't want to look bad? Kerri certainly hoped it wasn't because of her ethnicity. Wouldn't refusing to shoot her because she was white be like reverse racism or something?

Things quickly escalated. Her impatience reached the point where she had to begin carving them up to get the results she wanted.

When she attacked, her speed caught them off guard. One moment, the young officer facing her was droning on about Kerri not wanting to do this, even after she had clearly indicated that she very much *did* want to do this. The next, Kerri became so exasperated with the officer's speechmaking that she severed his leg below the knee.

It had been an accident! She'd only wanted to lightly wound him. She just hadn't realized her own strength. Hadn't she mentioned that she practiced a lot? It was all about developing your grip enough so that contact with bone wouldn't rattle the sword out of your hand.

Kerri had *powerful* forearms.

"Oh, don't look at me like that. It's a clean cut!" she said defensively to the wailing officer. "Besides, I'm sure your insurance will pay to have your leg reattached. If not, there are all sorts of affordable prosthetics! You'll be *fine*."

Kerri wasn't worried about the officer's future. Didn't they say that nothing intrigued a woman like a man with a scar? Well, maybe there were also chicks who went cuckoo at the sight of an amputated knee. People had all sorts of interests. People were kinky at their core. There was no such thing as peak freak.

You just had to be willing to open yourself to life's possibilities.

Just her bad luck, though, the officer's partner tried to tackle her from behind. Why hadn't he opened fire? What was *with* these goofs? Why were they trying to minimize casualties? Did they really take their oaths of public service *that* seriously? Why weren't they behaving like they did on television, damn it!

Kerri found this behavior extremely annoying!

So, that guy, she disemboweled.

It was a complete accident; Kerri would have sworn to it on a stack of Bibles! The officer had tried to grab a twitchy kid brandishing a sharp sword from behind. Who *does* something that dumb? As soon as she sensed his presence, she performed a spinning slash to warn him to stay back, but the officer was committed to his tackle by then, so instead of jumping back to avoid the blade, he walked right into it and had his belly opened from left to right.

It was so gross. *Stuff* fell out of him and landed on Kerri's shoes.

It was *warm*.

"Wh-why?" the officer asked her in shock, before the pain kicked in and he started screaming and rolling around.

"Uh, how am I supposed to answer that?" she muttered.

So far, this attempted suicide by cop was turning into a complete hassle. Weren't there *any* loose cannons in the local constabulary? These guys were far too concerned with preserving life! Someone needed to tell these officers that no one became famous by caring about the public good.

Come on, people, let's see some grossly irresponsible behavior, thought Kerri.

As if in answer to her prayers, a rough-looking plainclothes detective rounded the corner with his pistol drawn. He seemed like a figure summoned forth from an '80s action film. He was even wearing sunglasses indoors while chewing on a toothpick! *Finally*, Kerri had someone she could work with.

"Drop the sword, or I'll drop you," the detective growled.

Oh, sweet, he wanted to put on a performance . . .

Kerri held her sword at the newly stump-legged officer's throat and said, "I have a better idea. You drop the heater, or this loser's neck gets some ventilation."

"You'll be dead before you so much as flick your wrist, Highlander," warned the cop.

"You want to take that chance? Because I'm feeling *luuuucky*," Kerri replied with a sneer.

This is so awesome! she thought. She had always wanted to banter with a good guy in a life-or-death situation. Who knew she'd be so great at it? Well, she'd kind of suspected she would be. She *had* spent a lot of time practicing her lines in front of a mirror.

"This is your last chance, kid."

"Yeah. My last chance to chop up some piggies."

"Why do I always have to deal with the crazy ones?" the detective asked himself before firing his gun.

The sound of the discharging pistol rang throughout the hallway. Then the detective said, "What the . . . hell?" He collapsed to the floor with blood welling from the wound that had appeared in his chest, staining his white shirt red.

Kerri was confused. Why hadn't the detective done a forward roll and taken another shot at her lower body? After all, hadn't it been *obvious* that she was going to use her sword to deflect that first shot? Hadn't the detective been setting her up for a feint?

Wait, what if he hadn't been?

"Holy crud, am I *too* good at this?" Kerri asked herself.

Irritated, she tossed aside her sword and pulled the cop's necktie off so she could use it to staunch his blood loss. She didn't want to kill anyone here! If that had been her intent, she would have just started hacking the faculty up left and right.

All she'd wanted was a stylish exit from this world!

"God, why are these idiots making everything so *complicated*?" she moaned.

It didn't look like the bullet had exited the officer's back, so Kerri assumed he'd be okay. Or maybe he was internally wounded and was slowly bleeding out where it couldn't be seen. Whatever. She had done her part. If the cop couldn't survive his own blunder, then that was *his* problem.

Kerri turned around to pick up her sword and had just enough time to grunt in surprise when some other chick she didn't recognize came running toward her and shoved the point of the weapon straight through her gut with the worst-looking lunge Kerri had ever seen.

She felt something inside herself go *pop* and instinctively realized she was finished. Warm blood began pouring from her wound and puddled beneath her as she slumped to the floor against a nearby locker.

She nodded gratefully at her killer. "*Finally*, someone makes a winning move! I appreciate this. Thanks."

The other girl stared at her in bewilderment.

I guess I can't blame her for being confused, thought Kerri. *This is an extreme situation for someone like her.*

"What are you talking about? Why are you thanking me?" asked the other girl.

Kerri laughed but then coughed up a mouthful of viscous red substance. Not much longer now, it seemed. "Don't worry about it. Congrats on being the hero of the day! Were you hiding in that restroom? And you came running anyway despite hearing gunshots and screaming? You're built different, aren't you?"

"I thought you were killing those officers," said the other girl miserably.

With a beaming smile, Kerri said, "I didn't! They're still alive. Just really messed up. All according to the plan!

Except not really.

"Mortal wounds sure freakin' hurt, though," she continued while grimacing in pain. "Nice sneak attack by the way. Your character class must be assassin."

"I wasn't trying to hurt you," the other girl said, as tears leaked from her eyes. "I just wanted to get that sword away from you. Wh-when you turned around, I panicked and—and—*and*—"

"Hey, hey, don't be like that," Kerri insisted. "Feel a little pride in yourself, okay? Your instincts took over. And you know what? They were the *right* instincts. If it helps, I'm okay with what you did."

"You are?"

"Yep. No grudges here."

The other girl sat beside Kerri against the locker, paying no attention to the blood now staining both of their school uniforms. "Aren't you on the student council? Why'd you *do* something like this?"

"Hee-hee! It's a *seeeecret*," Kerri said with a knowing smirk.

"You seem like a nice person. Couldn't you have talked to someone?"

"Probably, but they wouldn't have said what I wanted to hear."

"Aren't you scared of dying?"

"I think I'm more afraid of living in a world that doesn't need someone like me in it," she replied after giving the question a moment's thought.

"That's selfish. You have a family. You had friends."

"Yep. I'm a very selfish person," the dying girl said in agreement. "I always do whatever I want."

She shivered in pain. She was feeling a lot colder now. So very cold. She was surprised when the other girl held her hand and sadly said, "I really am sorry for killing you. I wish we'd met sooner."

"You seem pretty cool. I wish we'd met sooner too," replied Kerri, surprising herself.

Was she now feeling regret? Really? How interesting.

Sometimes I think I never understood myself at all, she thought to herself in bemusement.

Kerri quietly died a few moments later.

The girl didn't release her hand until the medics arrived.

CHAPTER THREE

Reborn

When she next opened her eyes, Kerri was now an infant in a crib.

Amazing . . . It actually worked! she thought gleefully. She'd managed to achieve the grand feat of reincarnating into a brand-new world!

She had to hand it to herself; she'd achieved something incredible here. Most people her age could barely force themselves out of bed for school in the morning, but here she was, traversing to a different dimension through pure force of will.

It had been a dangerous risk, but it had paid off. She'd even gotten to physically maim a few police officers and inflict a heavy emotional scar on a beautiful girl along the way. What a wonderful way to exit her former life and start over.

Yeah, she really was the best.

It wasn't very fun being an infant again, though. Having a teenager's intellect inside a baby's tiny body made certain activities feel far more awkward than they should. Take breastfeeding, for example.

When babies were hungry, they had to be fed. That's just how it was; it was a perfectly natural part of life.

And yet being held up to her new mother's exposed nipple was *such* a cringe-inducing experience for Kerri. Anyone else in her situation would have felt just as embarrassed! She always tried to get the ordeal over with as quickly as possible. It wasn't always easy, though. Sometimes it took a while to get the drip running, so to speak.

She hoped her hesitation wasn't too stressful for her new mother. She seemed like a kind person, and she knew feeding time was supposed to be a bonding activity for the two of them. But she'd still feel much happier when she was ready for solid food. Yes, that would be much better for them both. She was a normal person; she really had no interest in developing an Oedipus complex—or whatever it was girls got when they were down bad for their mothers.

Interestingly, she'd apparently been born into nobility. Unexpected, but not unwelcome!

Her new father held the rank of count, a title of considerable importance in this country. That meant he was a man of wealth and power whose children would enjoy a life of comfort and privilege. Even better, as the fourth child of the household, Kerri was considered little more than a potential replacement in case something disastrous happened to one of her more important siblings.

In other words, no one expected anything from her, and she'd be free to do whatever she liked. It was the ideal situation for a child who fully intended to one day become an enemy of the world. Food and lodging and lots of leisure time. What could possibly beat that?

Though . . . if she wanted to, she bet she could easily oust her brothers and take their place in the family hierarchy. The more she thought about it, the cooler the idea of being a count sounded. It was a noble ranking that had appealed to many grand doers of evil before her. Great men like Count Dracula, Count Vertigo, Count Neferia, and Count Dooku had each held that title.

All bad guys. All *legends*. Christopher Lee had played two of them!

Couldn't she do it if she wanted it badly enough? Was there really such a thing as being *too* ambitious?

Oh, who was she kidding? She didn't need some silly title of nobility in order to feel important.

After all, wasn't nobility just an ornamentation bequeathed to others by royalty?

That fact lessened a title's value in her opinion. Anything that was given could just as easily be taken away. Even worse, although being a noble made someone *appear* important, their rank was just a means of being controlled by the crown. The higher one stood, the more taxes they had to pay and the more soldiers they had to conscript for the king during times of war.

Out of their own pocket.

Really, the whole thing seemed like a scam. A way for the government to fleece its wealthier citizens for more gold.

Not interested, Kerri decided. *Also, I guess I'd be a countess. That sounds far less iconic.*

Gendered titles of nobility were so pointless. No one would ever call a female Darth Vader *Darthette*.

No, Kerri would gladly play the role of the useless spare part fate had so kindly prepared for her. Life held greater things in store for her than squabbling with her family over their social pecking order. She wouldn't be caught dead vying for such a meaningless thing.

Anyway, if she disguised herself adequately enough, no one would ever know her true identity. That meant if she ever needed to hide herself from the eyes of the law, then secretly being a worthless fourth child would be the *perfect* smoke screen.

Who would possibly suspect a notorious criminal of being a girl named Everly Vel Belsar?

She still wasn't certain how to feel about her new name.

Well, I suppose it sounds better than my old one, she eventually decided.

It wasn't as though she had a choice in the matter. Besides, since this was a new life, she may as well immerse herself completely within it.

Kerri was the past.

The future belonged to Everly.

The more Everly thought about it, the more it seemed like this world was *begging* for her to mess with it. Not only was she now a member of a noble household in a medieval-ish society, with all the assorted advantages that would surely come with being a part of society's upper crust, but she was also one of the chosen few who had access to *magic*.

That didn't come as a surprise to her. In her humble opinion, Everly had developed an extremely powerful mind in her past life. She was certain that she would have eventually developed superpowers if she'd kept at it. It was only natural that she'd excel in an environment infused with actual magic.

This nation's magic took the form of elementalism. It was the traditional fantasy package she remembered from countless books and shows like *Avatar: The Last Airbender*. Earth, water, air, fire, and spirit. If someone could use magic, then they would develop the ability to communicate with beings composed of mystical energy called *sprites*. Sprites were like little balls of light that followed people everywhere, but only their owners could see them.

For most mages, shortly after their twelfth birthday, they'd bond at random with one of these sprites, which then became their servant. If you were a man, the sprite transformed into an animus, which was male. If you were a woman, you received an anima, which was female.

The element their servant represented became the element their master could channel and manipulate. There were no limitations on which gender could control which element, but their level of strength could vary wildly. A huge man bonded with a wind animus might not have enough magical power to shake dew off a leaf, but a tiny girl with a fire anima might possess enough strength to put an entire city to the torch.

No one seemed to understand the reason for this.

What differentiated Everly from those who came before her was that she wasn't bonded to only *one* sprite. Instead, she was bonded with two! She had no idea why that was. The only reasonable conclusion she could draw was that she was the main character of the story, and therefore the rules that governed the lives of other people in this world didn't apply to her.

She was just better than everybody else.

Yes, that sounded about right.

Both her new sprites were very confused when she tried explaining the concept of a main character to them, but she paid no mind to their befuddlement. They'd catch on eventually.

Besides, she was far too busy gloating.

In this world, the younger you were when you bonded with a sprite, the more powerful you became as you grew. Your ranking corresponded with how old you were when you awakened to your abilities. Talented mages bonded with their servants at the age of twelve. Average ones usually awakened at the age of fifteen. Exceptional mages did it when they were eight or nine.

Legendary mages were empowered at the age of five. Those were the chosen elites who went on to make their mark in history as heroes.

Everly received her sprites when she was only *three days old*. And no one had ever heard of someone having two of them at once!

There had never been anyone like her in this world. Hers was a unique existence.

It felt good. It felt *very* good.

Everly gained all this useful information from her first servant. That one had a gift for stealing knowledge from other people, and she was always eager to share her findings with her new master.

Both sprites were extremely competitive with each other for her favor, which Everly found amusing. That was just how a villain's servants should be! Desperate to curry her favor and quick to stab each other in the back if it benefited them.

Everly decided to name the younger sprite "Titania." She was an earth elemental, which was considered the most common type. So common, in fact, that they were looked down upon by other mages. Everly could see that Titania had a chip on her shoulder because of that. Her low ranking made her eager to prove her strength.

Titania's older sister, Everly named "Eris." As a spirit type, Eris was the rarest of the rare. Having her as a partner was a lot like winning the lottery. Spirit elementals were considered etheric royalty and had the ability to manipulate the minds of mortal beings. She wasn't humble about her gifts either. In fact, Eris really loved rubbing her exalted status in Titania's face and provoking angry reactions from her.

It was cute. Everly enjoyed watching their little spats. Sibling rivalry made for some quality entertainment.

Everly's first order was to have Eris hide her presence from detection. She didn't want anyone else to know how special she was. Having an extra elemental would have to remain a closely guarded secret.

My lady, I don't understand, said Titania in her mind. *The element of earth is already scorned for being the weakest of the five. If you insist on hiding your powers, lesser mages will foolishly believe themselves superior to you.*

Why should we care about their opinions? Everly asked her. *Let them laugh at us! The real joke will be on them when we flatten them in battle. Instead of worrying about what others think, let's bask in the exquisite pleasure that comes with hiding our true strength in plain sight!*

Wasn't that a cool thing to say? It was, wasn't it? She felt like a shadowy over-lord giving guidance to an apprentice.

But why must I stay in the shadows, master? Eris whined. *I stand above all other elements! Why should I be forced to dim my radiance? It isn't fair!*

Don't be upset, Eris, Everly thought to her, soothingly. *Like I said to Titania, who cares what lesser beings think? All that matters is that I will know how glorious you are. No one else is worthy of beholding you. You're mine and mine alone.*

Really? Eris asked.

Really, Everly assured her.

Eris buzzed vividly with happiness and nestled against Everly's chest like a happy puppy eager to kiss its owner.

Wow, Everly thought to herself. *Some people are just that easy to please, huh?*

Everly couldn't immediately resume her physical training due to being so young, so instead, she spent most of her time training her new servants. Thanks to the spiritual bond she shared with Eris, she could send Eris and Titania miles away to the wilderness to slowly strengthen themselves, while still being able to observe them and give instructions.

How could an elemental become stronger? That was the riddle Everly now had to solve. She reasoned that an important part of it was a combination of the sprites themselves and the willpower of the master they bonded with. Titania and Eris were attracted to her because she desired an immense amount of power. That meant *they* wanted to be powerful as well. That was the common goal that united them.

Titania's desire for strength was easy to understand. She had an inferiority complex the size of a *kaiju* that made her feel like a loser. Low self-esteem was a desirable trait in a minion. It made manipulating them a piece of cake. Eris wasn't difficult to figure out either. *She* had a superiority complex and couldn't stand the idea of not being acknowledged for how incredible she believed herself to be.

It took a bit of experimentation to figure out how to make the sprites grow. There was a lot of trial and error. Despite all her potential, Eris wasn't much stronger than Titania. Neither of them was very impressive, really. But Everly had a vision for what she wanted them to become. She just had to devise a means of making it happen.

Guided meditation didn't do much for them. Since both sisters were comprised of magic, there really wasn't anything to be achieved by encouraging them to visualize themselves as floating beings made of energy. After all, they already *were* floating beings made of energy

They couldn't do any yoga stretches either. You needed a body for those.

Trying to teach them mental exercises quickly became a frustrating endeavor.

That was basically when Everly said *screw it* and forced them to use their powers until they nearly died from exhaustion, rested them up for a bit, and then had them repeat the process. Everyone received *much* better results that way.

It made sense from a certain perspective. When mortal beings lifted heavy weights and exercised, it made them stronger and faster. Surely that meant if a spiritual being were to use their power to the point of total collapse, recover, then do it again, they'd gradually become better at generating and controlling energy.

A human's ability to physically grow would always be limited by factors such as genetics, health, and age. Once they reached the limits of their body, they would eventually level off, then decline. But elementals weren't held back by mortal limitations. Their strength could grow without limit if the will of their master was equal to the task. And Everly certainly possessed a *very* strong will.

So she essentially placed her servants on a regimented exercise program. They hated it at first, but the results certainly spoke for themselves.

Deep in the heart of the gloomy forest that stood to the east of the count's estate, where there was no one to bear witness, the land constantly trembled and quaked as Titania flexed her mystical muscles. Her growth was astonishing. When she'd first come to Everly, she could barely make a doorknob rattle. Now she could knock over boulders, sunder stone, and shatter steel. It seemed she was reaching new heights every week.

Everly felt so proud of her!

It was such a shame that in her opinion, Titania was slowly turning into a fitness maniac. She *really* was. Titania was now totally that ultra-fit chick in the gym doing a million sets to failure with dumbbells while leaving her towels all over the equipment she wasn't even using. Except her version of dropping weights on the floor was knocking down redwoods.

Oh well, Everly figured. There was nothing wrong with a little focused narcissism if it fueled the need for progression. She had plans for Titania. As strong as the earth elemental had become, Everly wouldn't be satisfied until she was completely unstoppable. In the future, she would serve her mistress as her shield and chief enforcer.

But hey, she was on her way; that was what mattered.

Eris required more subtle training than that. As a spirit elemental, she was literally a creature of the mind. So Everly had her relentlessly practicing useful techniques that she remembered from all the *X-Men* comics she'd read over the years. Eris was essentially a telepath, right? That meant her wheelhouse included bodily possession, mind reading, casting illusions, and the ability to erase and falsify memories.

That was a broken skill set, wasn't it? That was why more people should fear telepaths. So hard to beat!

Just like with Titania, the more Eris was worn down with relentless training, the more powerful she slowly became. She enjoyed making things a little awkward, though. The more minds she visited, the more human she became. And the more human she became, the, uh, *kinkier* she got.

Oh, mistress. I'm so exhausted. You wear me down daily, forcing me to my very limits without mercy. And yet I cannot resist your commands! Push me HARDER. Scold me! Tell me what a worthless beast I am! I'll do ANYTHING you wish. I'll be ANY fantasy you want . . .

Jeez, Everly would think to herself. *She knows I'm still a baby, right? I mean, come on! Even if you accounted for the age of my mind, I was still only sixteen when I died.*

She wondered if this was how people normally behaved in this world. She hoped not. It sometimes felt to her like they were costarring in a television production of *To Catch a Predator: Narnia Edition.*

Hey, Eris? Everly later said to her.

Yes, mistress? Eris asked eagerly.

Tone it down a little, okay?

The recent history of the continent had been dominated by a bloody tale of two feuding brothers.

Not long ago, the great kingdom of Winstead, which Everly was now a proud citizen of, had been embroiled in a terrible civil war. It had lasted a full decade and ended just before her birth. The previous king had been a kind man who'd been blessed with twin sons, both of whom he dearly loved. He loved them *so* much, in fact, that he dithered too long on choosing which of them would be his successor.

Then one day he suddenly died without naming an official heir, leaving chaos in his wake.

As irresponsible fools often do.

It was a shame that this happened, because both his sons quickly declared themselves the new and rightful king before their father's body finished cooling. Naturally, the brothers strongly disagreed with each other, but rather than settle their differences with negotiation and compromise for the good of the realm, they instead conscripted thousands of soldiers and forced them to fight to the death in support of their individual claims.

The brothers' greed had plunged the realm into needless war entirely for each one's selfish benefit.

Everly couldn't be bothered to remember which prince had won. She did know that the loser's head had been snicked off with a guillotine, though. Now, after ten years and thousands of pointless deaths, Winstead was heavily in debt from money borrowed from other nations, many citizens were hungry and struggling under the burden of enormous taxes, and the losing army had degenerated into roaming mobs of bandits.

(Pay attention to that last part; it becomes plot relevant in a few paragraphs.)

Really, the entire situation was a *hopeless* mess. But that was royalty for you, wasn't it? The people with power always treated their subjects like toys in a sandbox.

But Everly didn't feel that she was fit to judge them. She was hardly better than those privileged twins had been.

She also enjoyed playing roughly with her toys.

One day, Titania informed Everly that a bandit group of thirty former soldiers had taken shelter in the woods that the elemental liked to train in. Titania was upset because their presence was throwing her out of her rhythm, so she asked her master for permission to dispose of them.

As a true and loyal subject of King Whatever-His-Name-Was, Everly couldn't possibly *dream* of letting such a golden opportunity to dispatch a remorseless gang of traitors and thieves pass her by! Obviously, she had to give Titania the thumbs-up to destroy those scoundrels. Wasn't that her duty as a servant of the crown? (She tried to, at least. Give a thumbs-up, that is. She had clumsy baby fingers, so it was difficult for her.)

That night, Titania struck the rebels *hard*. Her viciousness was impressive to behold. Everly had to give her kudos for her absolute lack of mercy because Titania *really* didn't believe in holding back. The first thing she did was viciously shake the Earth beneath the bandits' feet until she put them all on their backs. Before they could recover, she split the ground with a massive fissure that quickly sent half of them tumbling to their deaths, screaming as they plummeted to the depths below.

The remaining bandits began running for safety, desperate to survive, but Titania wouldn't allow them to escape. For them, she caused countless razor-tipped bits of granite to erupt from the soil they fled on. The sharpened stones easily tore through the worn leather soles of anyone unlucky enough to step on one, crippling many of the men outright and causing the rest to slow their flight to avoid injury to their feet.

Sadly for them, their caution gave Titania the time she needed to transmute the terrain into a massive pit of quicksand, which bogged down their movements and drained away their stamina. Before long, they were all ensnared up to their shoulders and too exhausted to offer resistance.

By that point, they had no chance to recover. Slowly, they were swallowed below to a dark and miserable ending.

All they could do was curse their fates before vanishing forever from the sight of the world.

"We've run afoul of a demon!" the last surviving man managed to scream before Titania brought a tree branch down on his skull.

Well, not exactly, thought Everly.

Still, it wasn't as though that poor fellow would have believed it if he were told the architect of his death had been an infant. Such a thing was impossible, right?

Common sense was a wonderful thing to hide behind.

The terrified cries of the bandits had been a delight to Everly's ears. Three of the men in that group had been bonded to elementals of their own, but their feeble magic had been nothing before Titania's overwhelming brute force. It was like comparing a pebble to a mountain!

Best of all, Titania was nowhere near the limits of her growth.

One day, she'd be an absolute terror. A tool worthy of enacting Everly's will.

Things returned to normal for a while, until another morning began with Titania angrily informing Everly about more bandits entering her forest. Apparently, this group had been tasked with locating their dead comrades from earlier. Titania asked for permission to give these new pests the same treatment as the others, but Eris objected. She complained that Titania had already gotten to have some fun and now it was *her* turn.

Everly saw the logic in her words and let her have her way.

That was a mistake. She'd made a mistake.

Just because she was conditioning herself to be a callous, black-hearted egotist didn't mean that Everly wanted to be completely *dead inside*. She was still human, after all. She reasoned that there should be limits to the sort of utterly messed up things a person might accidentally witness in their lifetime. It couldn't all be carnage!

Perhaps this moment was the birth of her lawful evil alignment?

Maybe reality needed a moderator?

But seriously, what Eris did to those men was bad.

It was *very* bad.

It was *what the heck is the Geneva convention, giggle-snort?* levels of bad.

Everly knew she was going to have nightmares because of what she saw Eris do to those men. And she did.

She still does.

Jeez, Eris, she thought to herself once she finished recovering from the shock. *Jeeeeeez.*

When Eris came to her later that night and happily asked what she thought of her performance, Everly was forced to have a difficult conversation with her servant about the sort of operation she wanted to run. She tried not to be overly critical and offered praise for Eris's . . . *creativity*, but she also set some firm ground rules.

Listen, we're going for stylistic evil above everything else, okay? she told her. *That means looking cool takes precedence over being sadistic. We want to be something that people can aspire to. They should fear us, but they should also want to BE us, you know? When they see us coming, their primary feelings should be overwhelming terror and envy. You understand, right?*

I think so, Eris replied. *So, we want to frighten them, but we also want . . . to make them feel insecure about themselves?*

Exactly! You're a very smart girl, Eris. Everly beamed at her warmly. *Now, with that in mind, the following is a list of things I don't ever want to see you doing again unless I give you permission, okay?*

Okay! Eris said enthusiastically.

Great! Now, here we go . . .

Eris's important guidelines for being a Much Cooler Villainess.
- No forcing parents to suffer visions of their children crying alone in a dark basement while a menacing, shadowy figure slowly approaches them.
- No forcing our enemies to self-cannibalize.
- No tricking someone into believing they're making love to their romantic partner, only to awaken and realize what they've *really* been having sex with.
- NO CLOWNS. NEVER CLOWNS. NO. BE <u>BETTER</u>.
- No whispers from deceased loved ones encouraging our enemies to atone for past mistakes with suicide.
- No causing anyone to go mad from the revelation.
- No convincing anyone they've made eye contact with an elder god.

It was a long list. They were at it for quite a while.

Eris was a diligent listener and took many notes.

Months passed since then. Eris and Titania continued to grow stronger, which in turn made Everly's magical abilities grow as well. Things were going great! She felt very happy for the two of them (and especially pleased with herself), but if she were being perfectly honest, she was also growing bored out of her adorable tiny baby's skull.

It had been far too long since she'd held a sword in her hands.

Outside on the estate training grounds, she could hear her father's men practicing with their weapons, and she desperately wanted to be out there with them. She wanted it so badly that it was driving her nuts.

She had once spent countless hours honing her skills with her blade. The idea of being forced to wait until her new body was big enough to pick up a training sword was unbearable. Just think of how much knowledge she was losing daily! Years of hard practice were going right out the window! Although meditation ate up a fair chunk of her day, it wasn't enough to keep her mind completely occupied.

Fortunately, for the sake of Everly's sanity, a solution soon presented itself in the form of an amusing little story she'd read as a child back on Earth. It was an enchanting novel named *The Silence of the Lambs*.

For those not well versed in the classics, *The Silence of the Lambs* was the captivating story of a tragically imprisoned former psychiatrist named Hannibal Lecter, a foxy, silver-haired gentleman who knew how to pose dramatically in the shadows. A trickster at heart, Lecter would often appear from nowhere to drop an absolutely *cutting* one-liner on anyone who behaved boorishly in his presence.

Everly thought the man was just *class* personified. The very embodiment of dignified cool!

Sure, he also enjoyed eating the people he killed, but that wasn't an important detail, was it?

After being caught and locked away for his supposed crimes against humanity, Dr. Lecter found himself burdened with endless amounts of free time, just as Everly now was. But, instead of going crazy(ier) from boredom, Lecter learned to pass the time inside his head, with the use of a famous mental exercise known as the memory palace technique.

Thank you, contemporary pop fiction, for once more giving guidance to a troubled young soul! she thought appreciatively.

The memory palace technique consisted of using your imagination to create new environments around yourself and storing your memories inside the spaces your creation contained. The stronger your focus was, the easier it became to immerse yourself completely within your palace, to the point that your imagination could feel as real to you as reality itself.

By placing her mind inside a memory palace, Everly would be able to perfectly relive any moment of her life that she chose.

That *included* her countless hours of precious sword practice and mixed martial arts training. She would reclaim every single moment of them.

Everly decided that her memory palace would be a massive black tower stretching upward toward a nightmarish red sky in a barren wasteland.

She'd built one exactly like it in *Minecraft* as her crowning achievement in that game. To hell with all creepers!

"Very impressive, mistress," Eris said to her as together they watched the tower slowly assemble itself from thousands of floating black bricks that gently drifted toward one another before merging into place.

"Thank you. I'm beyond pleased with it, myself," replied Everly with a smile.

Here, within her mind space, Everly's form now resembled the teenager she'd once been in her previous life. Just a normal-looking girl in athletic shorts, trainers, and a pink T-shirt bearing the Marvel Comics logo. At either side of her stood Eris and Titania, who'd joined her to observe the construction of the memory palace. They'd each taken a human form as well.

Titania appeared as a tall, lean beauty who wouldn't have looked out of place in the Roman Colosseum. She embodied health, rugged strength, and athleticism. To Everly's way of thinking, she resembled a member of a woman's soccer team. Probably the striker.

Eris was a harder thing to describe. She seemed familiar, but that familiarity couldn't be narrowed down to any one person from Everly's memories. She just looked . . . *familiar.* She could have been anyone Everly had ever met or a stranger who was completely new to her.

She guessed that was the point. Eris enjoyed defying easy description.

She just likes being difficult, Everly thought sarcastically.

It was thanks to Eris's power that Everly could visualize the creation of her memory palace so perfectly. The elemental's illusory gifts were incredibly useful. The mind was Eris's playground, which made it *Everly's* playground as well.

She had to love it.

The best part of all had to be Eris's ability to slow the perception of time in this place. It was an incomparable bonus. In the real world, time continued to pass at its normal rate. But here in the dreamscape? Eris's powers made it possible for a day to last a lifetime. Everly would be able to do months of training in the span of a two-hour nap.

That meant she'd lose none of the skills she had worked a lifetime to acquire and could only develop her abilities even further. It was just another great idea she'd gotten from watching old Japanese anime.

Man, television can teach you all kinds of useful stuff.

When the palace had finished construction, the trio entered its first level. This would be Everly's personal training ground. But instead of that lousy basement she'd had to use in the cold of winter and the sweltering heat of summer, here she envisioned a spacious dojo that had a solid hardwood floor on one side and a spacious section for grappling practice that was covered in tatami.

"Nice," she said happily as she reached for a perfect replica of the sword she'd used in her past life.

Next, she assumed a ready stance, then began practicing her lunges. Instantly, she fell back into her old training routine, losing all awareness of her surroundings as she repeated the exercises hundreds of times, then thousands, lost in the wonderful sensation of trying to perfect her movements while eliminating any extraneous motion.

She scraped away at all the unwanted rust until what remained was the purest steel.

Eris and Titania stayed for a while and watched, but eventually they wandered away to explore other areas of the tower. That was fine. Everly appreciated an audience, but training was always best when it was done alone.

Nothing else existed for her now. There was nothing but her and her sword.

Thanks again, Dr. Lecter! she thought with gratitude.

CHAPTER FOUR

The Mountain Splitter

It was now Everly's first birthday, and today she was the recipient of some unexpected and unwelcome news.

Today was the day she learned what a sword king was. They were a rare but extremely capable type of swordsman skillful enough to defeat a powerful mage in one-on-one combat. Eris informed Everly of this casually, after first wishing her a happy birthday.

Why hadn't she mentioned such a thing sooner?

Everly was a mage, after all. She'd been honing her mastery over the elements for the past year, intent on becoming invincible. The results thus far had been spectacular—truly beyond all her expectations. Titania had become so powerful that she grossly defied her status as the allegedly weakest element. Everly was now gradually introducing her to concepts related to the Earth, like magnetism, gravity, and magma.

Titania was an eager student too. As it turned out, the element of earth possessed a lot of practical and attractive qualities if one was willing to put in the work to develop them. If anyone thought all she could do was shake dirt and grow crops, then Titania had a few things to show them.

But, incredible as Everly's strength now was, what was the point if such power could be mitigated and ignored by some random jerk wielding a sword?

It was true that countering Everly's magic with a sword was something that could only be done by masters at the highest possible level of skill. Maybe one out of a thousand warriors were capable of the feat. But did that really matter? That number was still far too high. Everly needed her magic to be an absolute fact of reality. Like light and darkness, like life and death.

If *she* were to cast a spell, there shouldn't be the slightest chance of survival.

She wanted to be *inexorable*.

It was a matter of pride.

The challenge was now clear. Everly not only had to further increase her understanding of magic, but she had to master the highest principles of swordsmanship as well. With that in mind, she sent Eris out into the world to hunt for the strongest swordsman she could possibly find.

Everly needed a sword king.

It was very difficult to learn high-quality swordsmanship in Winstead. The most prestigious schools in the kingdom jealously guarded their secrets and refused to cooperate with their competitors. Intense rivalry was rife throughout the land. The only way to become a student of a particular style was to either be born into the family that taught it or be given a recommendation by a master.

Strangers were absolutely shunned. Even inquiring about becoming a student could endanger one's life. Such were the perils of seeking the way of the sword.

Naturally, the greatest styles were exclusively taught to the highest-ranked members of the nobility, with the allegedly strongest one of all, the imperial school, linked exclusively to the royal family. That felt logical to Everly; why shouldn't the king be the strongest fighter in his own country? It made no sense for the monarch to be weaker than his subjects.

Everly would have loved to learn the secrets of the imperial school, but she wasn't quite bold enough to send Eris to the palace training grounds to steal them. There was an excellent chance the royal family had spirit mages in their service, and Everly didn't want to risk attracting any unwanted attention. It saddened her to realize that she might never gain an opportunity to learn such an amazing-sounding method of cutting people up.

Luckily for Everly, Eris learned something *extremely* promising during her travels. Far away in the desolate, frozen north, living the remainder of his life in bitter exile, was the former sword instructor of the king!

"Specifically, he was the instructor for the king *and* the king's brother, years before the civil war began," Eris informed her when they met in the memory palace. "The royal princes loved him like a dear uncle, but sadly, the old man made the mistake of siding with the wrong brother during the war."

"Womp-womp-*wooomp*." Everly snickered. "Sounds like he had no talent for picking a winner. Are you sure this is the guy I want?"

Eris rolled her eyes and said, "Let me finish! After winning his throne, the king couldn't bear to have his beloved teacher executed, so he banished him instead."

"Now I feel even less interested," Everly said bluntly. "He sounds like a loser."

"Don't be so quick to judge," Eris chided. "Rumors say this old buzzard's skills are legendary."

"Is that right?" Everly asked. "*How* legendary?"

"*Capital L* legendary, mistress! His nickname before retiring was *the Mountain Splitter*."

Everly paused to let that little tidbit percolate in her head for a moment. "They really called him *the Mountain Splitter?*"

"They did!" Eris said eagerly. "Think about it! This world is crawling with monsters and magic and all that, so to get a nickname as menacing as his surely means people must have looked at him and thought, *Wow, what an absolute fiend this man is. I would certainly hate it if he killed me!*"

Everly listened carefully as Eris spoke. Her servant's enthusiasm for her discovery was infectious, even though her attempts to sound like a gossiping commoner weren't very good.

"He probably *would* kill us, wouldn't he?" Eris continued. "After all, he's the Mountain Splitter, right? Let's all agree never to anger him!"

Everly was convinced. Eris's acting was terrible, but her argument was sound. Everly *had* to have the knowledge this man possessed. If anyone could defeat magic with a sword, it would be this Mountain Splitter! With that in mind, she sent Eris off to the far north to find him, a mission the elemental accomplished with ease.

The old man's home was in the middle of a monster-infested forest, and he possessed only the bare necessities for survival. He had to cut his own wood and hunt his own meat. And he performed these dangerous tasks with aplomb because the old bastard was EVEN COOLER THAN EVERLY EXPECTED.

Through Eris's eyes, Everly observed the man standing before a snowbank in front of his cabin. Although the weather was freezing, he was bare chested. He was buff too, muscular in a way you only saw in lifelong fitness fanatics.

Daddy, thought Everly.

She didn't normally go for old meat, but this guy? He looked pretty good for his age.

In his right hand, he held an antique-looking saber raised above his head. It looked as though he were performing some sort of meditative exercise.

According to Eris, he had no elemental partner; he was just an ordinary human with a sword. And yet he stood there, perfectly poised, not so much as shivering. Then he suddenly swung his sword in a wide arc, the force of which sent all the snow flying away from his doorstep in a blinding white wave.

Having finished clearing his lawn, he went inside.

It seemed that Eris had been right. They'd found their man.

The day slowly dragged by as they waited for the old man to fall asleep. First, he put on a shirt, then he cooked himself breakfast, and afterward, he meditated in front of his fireplace for hours. When he was finished, he sat in his chair and read from a large book until dark fell.

Everly had a depressing feeling that this was the old man's daily routine. She couldn't imagine anything sadder than this. Everly was the sort of person who had to be kept occupied with meaningful work. Sitting around some drafty cabin waiting to die would have been torturous for her. She was very relieved when the old man finally fell asleep.

I can finally get what I came here for, she thought triumphantly.

Everly knew in her gut that someone with such a powerful, focused mind would resist if she and Eris tried to seize his knowledge while he was awake. But what if he were asleep? That was something else entirely. No one kept their guard up while they were sleeping. It was when everyone was at their most vulnerable, right?

So, after the old man passed out on his bed, Everly patiently waited until she was certain that her target was locked deeply into REM sleep. Then Everly sent Eris into his unconscious mind to plunder his memories for the knowledge they sought.

But her girl did even better than that. Instead of wasting time shuffling through separate memories, she copied his entire mind! They now had access to everything! Not only the years the old man spent as a teacher of the imperial style, but also the years he spent as an apprentice, learning from his own master!

Every moment the old man had ever spent sweating, struggling, and aspiring to absolute mastery of his blade now belonged to Everly.

This is so sweet! she thought happily. *Thank you so much! And don't worry, pops. I'm going to put your knowledge and experience to perfect use. Once I run wild in this country, if you're still around, maybe I'll set you free. Okay, I probably won't do that. I don't know. We'll figure something out. Later.*

When Eris finished imbuing her with the old man's knowledge, Everly closed her eyes and materialized inside her memory palace, where an image of the old guy awaited her. The man stood alarmed, with his sword drawn and pointed at his host.

"Who the devil are you? Where am I?" he demanded.

Oh, that's interesting, thought Everly. Apparently, Eris's copy of her new teacher's mind had some level of self-awareness. That was cool. *Kind of like a Siri or an Alexa. I can dig it.*

More importantly, by not being aware that he was a mere copy of a real person, he gave Everly the opportunity to practice some role-playing with him.

"It doesn't matter where you're at, sir," she told him. "What matters is that *I'm* in charge here. You don't have to call me *mistress* or *lady*. I'm not fussy about titles. Just acknowledge my authority and all will be well."

"Girl, I've survived too much in my life to bend my knee to an unknown upstart."

Excited by his defiance, Everly envisioned a sword in her hand. "There's a way we can settle this," she said eagerly.

"Oh, *please*." The old man snorted as he assumed a fighting posture. "You hold that oversize lump of steel like an amateur. Let me guess, you're self-taught?"

"Guilty! I could never find anyone to practice with back at home."

"This won't be practice, you little fool. I'm going to end your life."

"Prove it!" Everly laughed before dashing at him, swinging her sword as wildly as she pleased.

A split second later, the old man parried her swing and cut Everly's head off.

And that was how their encounters went over the next ten years of dream time. At first, Everly was excited to put her memory palace through its paces. What could possibly be more enjoyable than gradually improving her skills at a leisurely pace? This was the sort of training she'd always wanted to experience.

Or so she'd once thought, before the frustration of constantly being defeated began to set in.

Everly refused to believe that all the time she spent on Earth training alone in her basement had been a waste of time. Just because the old man often toyed with her like a cat with a mouse, and frequently killed her in the blink of an eye, didn't mean she was bad with a sword.

Didn't she possess reflexes sharp enough to deflect a bullet? She was crazy good!

The problem was that what was considered *good* in this world, with its systems of combat designed to fight monsters and magic users, was quite different from the standards on Earth. After all, the man she was fighting was the Mountain Splitter! Name one swordsman on Earth who ever had the power to split a mountain in half!

Obviously, the smart thing to do would have been to insert herself directly into the old man's memories as a background character and train gradually. After slowly improving her skills, she could then come back and fight this version of him once she was better prepared, as a litmus test of her skill.

But Everly didn't want to do that. She felt her pride was on the line. She'd also never seen *Inception*.

She didn't mind at all that she was continuously crushed like an insect. She found the challenge invigorating. And she really was starting to improve: timing when to strike, how to read an opponent's defense, knowing when to retreat, discovering the subtle nuances of body language. She gradually gained this knowledge by heedlessly throwing herself against the old man, again and again.

By doing this, without even realizing it, she slowly improved her fundamentals.

Martial artists on Earth liked to make big claims about how useful katas could be. Katas were a series of combat forms where basic movements of the style they were derived from were relentlessly drilled against imaginary opponents. Everly thought of them as a kind of regimented shadowboxing.

One karate practitioner had made the bold claim that if he trained one student with katas only and another with only sparring, the kata practitioner would win if the two ever fought.

To Everly's way of thinking, that was complete nonsense.

Martial arts were full of stupid proclamations like that. It wasn't that katas were useless. Memory exercises were never a bad thing, and they also provided fantastic cardiovascular conditioning. It was just that empty practice was empty practice, and fighting was *fighting*.

Had anyone ever heard of a piano player improving by *pretending* to play a piano? Did vocalists get better at singing by just humming? Could a lawn be mowed through visualization?

Practice was great, but experience was the best teacher.

Then again, most students of a combat art couldn't construct a memory palace, steal the memories of a grand master, create an exact mental duplicate of him, slow their perception of time to a near-infinite crawl, then fearlessly challenge him to an endless series of bouts to the death.

But didn't that simply mean that most students put no effort into their training?

With a lightning-fast motion, the old man cut Everly in half at the waist.

Heh, I feel funny, Everly thought to herself in amusement.

"Who the devil are you? Where am I?" the old man demanded to know as he quickly drew his blade and assumed a ready position.

Everly had stopped bantering with him ages ago. Instead, she held forth her great sword and assumed a ready position that matched that of her opponent. Then she silently ran to him and aimed a vicious downward strike at his head.

The old man parried the blow easily, just as Everly had known he would, but before he could respond with a thrust to the neck, Everly stepped into his counter, while swinging her blade in a low arc aimed at the old man's legs. As the old man made a quick sidestep to avoid the slash, Everly lashed out with her boot and caught him square in the belly with a powerful kick.

That kick accomplished absolutely nothing. Instead of pushing the old man back or injuring him, Everly was the one who bounced away at the contact and hit the ground hard, landing heavily on her head.

"Ha!" The old man laughed as she lay there stunned. "I see you have some talent, girl. But sadly, your education is incomplete if you believe speed and strength are all it takes to seize victory."

"Huh?" Everly asked him, still dazed by her tumble.

"My condolences for now ending your life so abruptly. But isn't that your own fault for challenging someone you weren't ready to face? Farewell."

And then, before Everly could finish recovering, he took her head clean off. Yet another brutal loss. But despite that, Everly felt ecstatic.

I think we're finally making some progress here, she thought giddily.

For ten time-dilated years inside the dreamscape, the old man would repeat the same things over and over. He would always mock Everly for being self-taught. Then he'd either kill her immediately, or he'd toy with her until he grew bored. Either way, Everly barely got the chance to make a few attacks before inevitably being slaughtered.

Everly would then stubbornly reset the clock back to the beginning and try again. But the results were always the same.

Death.

Death.

More death.

Even more death.

Endlessly on repeat.

But now, things had changed. Now he'd begun *complimenting* her before wiping her out.

It felt amazing. Progression was such a rush!

One of the things that Everly now realized was that in this world, a larger sword didn't have any inherent disadvantages against a lighter one. She'd been thinking too hard about it and basing her attacks on what she understood about fighting on Earth.

On Earth, a great sword was a slower, heavier weapon. You had to strike decisively, with extremely precise timing to succeed with it. Well, decisiveness and precision were still wonderful things to cultivate, but in this world, *magic* was also a factor in battle.

So who said a *mage's* weapon had to be slow?

Titania was an earth elemental. Swords were made from metal. Metal came from the earth. Therefore, by directly applying Titania's power to the weapon, Everly could make the sword in her hands as light or as heavy as she wished. Even the cartoonishly massive claymore she was currently wielding could move as lightly as a baton between a majorette's fingers, thanks to Titania's powers.

Everly stomped the ground, making it quake violently. The old man paid the trembling no heed, keeping his sure footing as he waited for Everly to follow through with her real attack. Everly didn't make him wait long. She aimed her sword at his neck and swung as quickly as she could.

When it was blocked, instead of following through with another swing, Everly jumped backward and willed a massive stalagmite spike to burst from the earth, which the old man barely managed to avoid. But as he jumped aside to avoid being skewered, Everly appeared in the air above him, bringing her sword down on the old man's defenseless head.

Everly was truly beginning to understand and master the concept of magical relativity. Regarding her sword's mass, not only could she make it as light as possible while holding it, but she could *simultaneously* make it as heavy as could be, relative to others.

From her perspective, her weapon weighed less than a feather, but if her attack connected with the old bastard's head, he would be crushed under the comparative weight of a large anvil. If he tried resisting the blow, his blade would shatter, and his skull would still be cleaved.

Got you, got you, finally got you, she thought happily to herself.

She was incorrect.

The old man still swept her strike aside with an effortless motion. When Everly's sword hit the ground, the ground shuddered beneath the weight of its edge.

How? *How* had he done it? He had no magic! It made no sense!

"What the hell?" Everly complained as she turned to face him. "How are you doing this? I had you. I know I did! What *is* that power you wield?!"

The old man laughed at her frustration, clearly delighted by his opponent's confusion and anger. "You challenged me without even knowing that much? You're an amusing little mage, but your arrogance is galling. I'm using *harada*, you ignorant fool."

"*Harada*," Everly said, mouthing the word slowly. It was the first time she'd ever heard it. "Is that the source of your strength? Teach it to me!"

"Don't be stupid, kid. For starters, I'm only permitted to instruct royalty. And secondly, you're a *mage*. A weakling who relies on an elemental as your source of strength. It's a crutch and an innate sign of inferiority."

"What are you talking about?" Everly asked him, annoyed by his condescending tone. "Are you claiming the royals have never used magic? That's nonsense."

"Not any of the ones who wish to master the imperial style. *Harada* and magic are incompatible with each other. Magic is power that comes from without. *Harada* is the power within. Developing it is a long process which must begin in your early childhood. The years you've squandered mastering your petty spells have already robbed you of your chance to learn."

"How old are most of your students when they can finally use this, uh, *harada*?" she asked him.

"The same age when most mages begin bonding with their elementals. Typically around twelve or so," he replied.

"Oh," Everly said thoughtfully as she considered his words. Then she said, "You do realize I'm barely a year old, right?"

"What?"

* * *

Harada. Also known as "sword aura." *This* was the power that Everly sought. The ability that allowed warriors to counter magic with willpower alone.

Now that she had a name for the power she desired, Everly began to seek it within herself. *Harada, harada, harada.* Within her memory palace, she walked in a perfect circle while meditating, her eyes shut tight in concentration, her heart set on nothing else but the awakening of this incredible ability.

Everly would have had an easier time of it if she'd just plucked the knowledge from the old man's memories. But her bouts with him had awakened within her a competitive urge to prove that she could be his equal. He mocked magic users; he called them weak and unworthy. Everly couldn't think of a more fitting reprisal than teaching herself the ability he prized so highly. A hated mage with a contemptible self-taught sword style who'd also awakened *harada?*

Ohhhh, he'd hate that, wouldn't he?

Everly continually reviewed everything she'd learned about the old man from the countless bouts they'd fought. First, he minimized his personal movements, only striking or parrying when necessary. Even when Everly violently shook the ground beneath his feet, he'd respond by settling into a deep stance and keeping his balance. His feet only moved when circumstances demanded it.

But when he *did* move, it was at lightning-fast speed. While reviewing her memories, Everly realized that the old man didn't run. He *never* ran. He leaped! He could jump so quickly that her eyes couldn't keep track of his movements.

His ability reminded Everly of a documentary she'd once seen about jumping spiders. Those were a tiny breed of arachnid hunters that were known for being light on their feet. Whenever they sighted prey, they'd jump at their target so quickly that it was as though they'd teleported. That was the kind of speed that Everly wanted for herself.

The old man always breathed in deeply and quickly exhaled as he moved. As Everly thought about it, she realized he also exhaled whenever striking his blows against her. Was that the nature of *harada?* Was it channeled through breath? She'd envisioned it as a persistent invisible force surrounding her body like mana did for magic users. But what if sword aura was more like a stream that could only flow in one direction at a time?

The old man said that *harada* and magic were the opposite of each other. Well, magic had to be directed forcefully. It had to be controlled. Did that mean *harada* could only be called upon instinctively? Was it the power of the unconscious mind? A *reactive* force instead of a directed one?

"Man, this is a real mystery, isn't it?" Everly asked herself after another slow day of limited improvement. It seemed the process of developing this power couldn't be forced. *Harada* could only be gradually coaxed out a little at a time. It was an excruciatingly slow pace.

Oh, screw it, she decided. Who had time for this? Well, she did. But so what? She wanted to get to the fun part already.

"C'mon, Eris," she said to her servant. "Let's crack this geezer's mind open and get to the good stuff while we're still young."

Eris was surprised by her decision. "But, mistress, didn't you say half the fun was in the pursuit? Aren't you just skipping steps?"

"Yeah, I know, I know," Everly replied. "I said I wanted to learn it on my own. But one of the best perks of being a villain is that we get to be awful hypocrites when the mood strikes."

"We do?" Eris asked.

"Yep!" Everly replied cheerfully. "And black knights are often the biggest hypocrites of all. We're utterly shameless! We're absolute rakes! Who'd ever trust scum like us to keep our word?"

"*I* trust you, mistress," said Titania without guile.

"So do I," said Eris just as honestly.

"Awww, I want to hug you both so much right now. Come here, bring it in!" Everly commanded them.

It was a nice moment they all shared. Hugs were wonderful.

Once it was over, Everly and Eris returned their attention to the secrets held by the old man. The time for playing was over. It was time to take what they wanted from him.

And Everly wanted *everything*.

CHAPTER FIVE

Stealing Inspiration

Now that Everly had finally gotten down to business, her talent for swordsmanship grew rapidly.

It seemed her father (the one from Earth) had been right about her. She really did enjoy playing around too much. Sometimes the best thing to do was not to avoid work. Sometimes it was best to just knuckle down and get the hard part out of the way. She'd have plenty of time to have fun later. The most important thing right now was learning as much as she could, as thoroughly as possible.

Inside the old man's memories . . . Actually, shouldn't she stop thinking of him as *the old man*? After all the time she'd spent trying (and failing) to defeat him, Everly felt she owed him a modicum of respect. He had a name, so she would start using it. He'd earned that much.

Inside the memories of Viscount Louis Parker, she found the knowledge of *harada* that she needed to complete her training. She discovered it through observing a series of intense one-on-one sessions Parker had with his own master, his long-deceased grandfather. A stern, humorless old buzzard who'd been even more ruthless than Parker would become later in life.

Once she fast-forwarded past all his embarrassing defeats, his exhausting struggle to gradually improve, as well as all the animosity and resentment Parker felt toward his grandfather (the two of them seriously needed a good family therapist) Everly eventually came to the moment of revelation, when Parker was sixteen and practicing alone in an open field during a ferocious thunderstorm.

This is so *hard-core*, Everly thought admiringly as she watched the boy torturing himself in the turbulent rain.

After another frustrating few months of practice where he once again failed to awaken *harada* within himself, Parker had pretty much forsaken his will to live. He planted himself in one spot with no food and just enough water to last a month and vowed to either become a sword king or die of starvation. *That* was how intense his resolve was.

When Parker had been a small child, his father died from a wasting illness, and now he was the final member of his line. His family had been the royal family's sword instructors for nearly two hundred years, but if Parker couldn't awaken *harada*, then that would be it for their illustrious history. It really didn't help that his grandfather was an unrelenting perfectionist who wouldn't stop pressuring him to succeed.

So, on that day, Parker began training fanatically.

He slept only when he had to, drank only when his throat was parched, and did nothing else but swing his sword. Everly thought he was amazing. The calluses on his hands were broken, seeping things that soaked his palms in blood. The wind and sun chapped his lips and burned his skin until the cold night air chilled him.

But Parker would not be broken. He refused to give up.

In a way, it was like he was dueling himself. He realized that he needed total commitment to finally achieve his dream and protect his family's legacy. For him, this was truly do or die.

And then it finally happened.

On the third day of the third week of his training, as an incredibly violent thunderstorm rumbled through the skies above him, covering the land in darkness that was barely illuminated by the occasional crashing bolt of lightning, something at the core of Parker's being began to awaken.

Startled by this development, his breath caught in his throat and triggered a painful coughing fit. Something was happening to him. He could *feel* it. He wondered if he was hallucinating, if madness had finally overtaken him, or if he'd simply had a stroke and was lying in the grass, dying . . .

As she shared this memory and felt the intensity of his confused emotions, Everly could only smile. No, Parker wasn't dying. If anything, this was the moment when he finally began to *live*. Because he'd finally done it. The dragon slumbering at the center of his being had fully awakened. He was no longer merely Louis Parker; he was the *Mountain Splitter*.

With *harada* flowing through his body, Parker leaped into the air, laughing madly as he flew. He slashed at a nearby boulder and splintered it instantly. The power raged in his veins, infusing him with strength that he'd never truly believed was possible, and now he laughed and laughed and laughed at his own ignorance.

Oh, and he also deflected a bolt of lightning that came straight at him with reflexes that surpassed those of a cheetah.

That was pretty dope too.

That night was probably the greatest of Parker's life. It was the ultimate reward for years of hard work and effort. It was the proof he craved that he was worthy of inheriting his grandfather's mantle. He now felt a glorious sense of continuation and a feeling of closeness with his family that he had always yearned to experience. His rapturous smile in the rain was truly a sight to behold.

So, you know, good for him, Everly decided. Awesome sauce. *Yaaaay team!*

Of course, Parker wasn't the only one who'd gotten what he wished for. This was a pretty good night for *Everly* too. Because by being inside Parker's memory of the event, she'd been able to not only experience his emotions but also the energy within his body. She could now perfectly visualize everything that he'd experienced as *harada* was unleashed within him.

And by doing so . . . *she figured out how he did it.*

Everly could now use *harada* for herself. No fuss, no muss, no standing in piss-soaked trousers under a raging thunderstorm.

Thanks, old man! Thank you so much! I promise to honor your hard work and the wonderful example you set for me as I set out to bring carnage and chaos to the entire world, she vowed with sincerity.

"Did you find what you wanted, mistress?" asked Eris.

"Hell yes, I did!" Everly yelled triumphantly. "Did you really say you'll only instruct members of the royal family, Parker? HA! Who are *you* to deny me anything? You should be grateful! I'll achieve things you could only dream of! And unlike you, I'LL NEVER LOSE! I'm the *greatest* pupil you ever had! YOU'LL WORSHIP ME!"

"Are you all right, mistress?" asked Eris with concern.

"I'm beyond all right! Laugh madly with me, Eris! *Laugh*, I said! MWAHAHAHA!"

It took some coaxing, but eventually, Eris joined in.

Too bad Everly was still a baby.

Oh, well, she decided. This just meant she had years of training left to enjoy. She'd practice relentlessly and forge herself to absolute perfection; and then, once she attained it, she'd train even harder until she reached a level *beyond* perfection.

When she eventually met the real Louis Parker, she wanted him to see the heights that the imperial style would reach thanks to her. She wanted him to stare at her with eyes filled with yearning and envy.

And then we'll become the best of friends. We'll enjoy each other's company and finish each other's sentences, and . . . do other things. Gosh, I already feel so close to him. In fact, I feel like I know him better than I know myself. And I totally dig older guys now too.

Oh, wow, I hope he doesn't think I'm clingy.

I just want him to like me. I want him to think I'm cool.

Wait, what am I even saying here?

Of course, I'm cool.

I'm the coolest chick on this fucking planet.
Right?
If he disappoints me, I'll drown him in his own blood, she vowed.

One month later.

"Who the devil are you? Where am I?" the old man demanded to know as he quickly drew his blade and assumed a ready position.

Everly smiled and closed her eyes before taking a deep breath and slowly exhaling. She'd been cultivating her *harada* relentlessly in the memory palace, seeking to understand this incredible power as thoroughly as she could. It felt like she'd been at it for centuries. Thirty days had passed in the real world—that was how enthusiastic she'd been about her training.

Now it was time to put what she'd learned into practice. It was time to face off with Parker once more. This wasn't just another training skirmish, though. She knew from his memories that if she could beat the old man fairly, one-on-one, she'd earn the right to call herself a sword king.

This was the equivalent of going for the rank of grand master. She wanted it *very* much. If she lost this bout, then, to penalize herself, she'd wait another thirty days before she challenged him again. That was how seriously she took this.

"Girl, I asked you where I was," Parker said threateningly as he stepped closer to her. "Don't make me repeat myself."

Everly smiled joyfully at him in response and held her great sword in a ready position that mirrored his own. "It doesn't matter where you are, Viscount. Why not enjoy this moment with me?" she asked him.

"You're a bit young to be challenging me, child," he replied with a frown.

"The young will eventually inherit everything, my lord." She smirked. "Why not begin today?"

Elation soared through Everly as she spoke. How freaking cool was she? All those hours she'd spent role-playing with Eris were now being rewarded! Here she was, a mysterious young fighter eager to test her mettle against a venerable and deadly master. It was the perfect backstory for a future bringer of chaos!

"I sense great potential in you, girl," Parker said reluctantly. "I can see you've trained hard. But it takes decades to truly harness the power of *harada*. Don't throw away a bright future over a youthful impulse. Your childish need for excitement could bring you to an unsightly end."

"Enough lectures, old man. Let me see the imperial style. Or do you *fear* me?" asked Everly with a bold sneer.

Judging by his expression, Parker didn't like having his bravery questioned.

"Tch, I offered you a way out," he said reproachfully. "But I won't suffer your arrogant discourtesy. I've killed too many to count on my bloodstained path to mastery. As much for my victims as for myself, I won't let you speak so lightly to a sword king."

"Prove it!" Everly eagerly shouted as she leaped at him, bringing her sword crashing against his in a titanic clash of screaming metal.

Parker's frown deepened as he struggled to parry her heavy steel, but she wouldn't allow him the room to push her weapon away. Instead, she pressed herself tightly against him, pushing him farther and farther back, before launching a heavy right hand that connected with his eye.

As he shouted in surprised pain, Everly followed through on her strike with a forward thrusting kick that, thanks to the *harada* pulsing throughout her body, sent Parker crashing backward through the air. However, Parker managed to avoid injury by pushing with his feet against the wall he would have collided with, canceling out his momentum and allowing him to land in a crouch on the floor.

"You fight like a brute," he said angrily.

"Ha! I fight like a *winner!*" Everly exclaimed with glee.

She filled her sword with power and swung it at him, whooping with delight as the area before her was demolished by the sheer force of her swing. Parker's speed allowed him to avoid it, though, and he counterattacked with a forward lunge that would have pierced Everly's throat if she hadn't sidestepped it, sending Parker stumbling past her.

With Parker now extended too far to react in time, Everly delivered a brutal downward slash that rewarded her with a splash of blood jettisoned from the wound she'd cleaved into his back. Parker gave an agonized cry and spun around clumsily with a weak slash that Everly easily parried before wounding him again, this time under his chin.

"Huh." Everly frowned to herself. Something was off. This didn't feel quite right.

"What's wrong with you?" she asked Parker. "You've never been like this before. Why are you moving so slowly?"

"What are you talking about?" he demanded angrily. "I've never met you before today!"

Oh, right. That was how this looping memory thing worked. Still, something was wrong. Although this had started out fun, it had quickly grown stale. Everly couldn't understand how. Had she somehow lowered the settings? Did the memory palace even come with settings?

What had *changed* here?

"What's wrong with your *harada*?" she suddenly asked Parker. "Why are you so weak?"

Perhaps asking that question had been a mistake. Parker's lips tightened as his frown became a ferocious scowl. A malicious hatred spiked with killing intent was now directed toward Everly with such intensity that it visibly emanated from the old man like a fog of poisonous fog.

Ohhhh, yeah, I definitely pissed him off, she thought to herself.

It only took a moment's consideration for Everly to realize why Parker was so furious. The viscount *hadn't* grown weaker since their last encounter. In fact, by the standards of this world, he was still considered incredibly powerful. (Not that long ago he'd been tossing Everly around like a straw doll!)

But that was only because he was considered strong by the standards of ordinary fighters.

The only advantage he'd ever possessed over Everly had been *harada*. Once she achieved it for herself, then spent time-dilated centuries surpassing his mastery of it, Parker had become nothing. It was like fighting a small child.

And that was the crux of the matter, wasn't it? It wasn't that the old man was too weak.

Everly was now too strong.

"Wow," she said, dazed by the enormity of her realization. "I really *am* amazing, huh?"

"Don't underestimate me, girl. You haven't got a tenth of my experience—" Parker began to say before Everly cut his legs out from beneath him, severed his arms, and then decapitated him.

From Everly's point of view, it seemed as though Parker's limbs were falling in slow motion. So, just to be petulant, she flicked him on the nose before his head finished hitting the ground.

"Well, all righty, then. I guess I'm a sword king now," she said smugly to herself.

Heh. A sword king. Why have I been so fixated on that silly title? she wondered. It all seemed so trivial now.

No title existed that could properly express the sum of all that Everly had become. What a fool she'd been for getting so caught up in things. Compared to the honor that came from simply being herself, being a sword king was a meaningless distinction. After all, *anyone* could achieve proficiency with a blade if they were motivated enough. What was so original about killing people with sharp pieces of metal?

Still, this hadn't been a complete waste of her time. *Harada* was an incredible power, and it was a welcome addition to her arsenal. With it, Everly could now dominate the battlefield with both magic *and* antimagic. She was now the complete package, able to adapt to any situation easily.

Also, the elementally neutral properties of *harada* meant that if she worked at it long enough, she'd eventually be able to combine its effects with the magic of her elementals, increasing their potency even further.

Suddenly, Everly had a *great* idea about what she could do with her new knowledge. Titania and Eris would hate it, but that was okay. They didn't have any free will, so their opinions didn't count.

Things are coming together so nicely for me, she thought. *I really hope these breakthroughs don't end anytime soon. Keeping occupied is important for my sanity.*

Wouldn't it be a shame if boredom drove her crazy while she waited to finish growing up?

Now that she thought about it, it had been a while since Everly had been outside her memory palace. It might be a good idea to check in on the real world and make sure everything was still as it should be. Not that she really had any clue about how things should be.

As the outside world slowly grew into existence, Everly saw she was still in her crib. Okay, no big changes there. But for some reason, a nicely dressed boy in expensive-looking clothing was staring down at her with an ugly expression of loathing on his young face.

In his hands, he held a large white pillow.

Before Everly even finished wondering what he intended to do with it, the little creep shoved it over her face and began pressing down *hard*.

CHAPTER SIX

Family

*A*ll *right, this is clearly an attempted smothering,* Everly decided.

Yes, this was certainly what *Webster's* would have defined as *infanticide,* the killing of a baby. This was a new experience for her. Everly had never been the target of an attempted murder before. Well, that was if you didn't count the time that beautiful girl at school panicked and skewered her with her own sword.

Perhaps that shouldn't count. By her killer's own admission, that had been more of an accident than anything else.

Everly briefly wondered how that girl was doing. She'd seemed nice. She had good bone structure too, so her smile was probably dazzling. Strange how Everly had never noticed her before that day. She'd always had an eye for the pretty ones.

Oh, well. Wasn't life filled with countless missed opportunities? What was the point of dwelling on what could have been? *C'est la vie* as the French said.

Everly then spent another moment wondering what sort of little psychopath would want to murder an innocent baby in her own crib. What were this boy's parents like? Did they not realize how depraved the child they spawned had become?

Maybe they just hadn't shown him enough tough love. Perhaps they were too afraid to assert themselves as the heads of their household. If so, that was a shame; overly permissive parenting could lead to children growing up without learning to respect boundaries. Everly knew that from personal experience, having once been a child who never respected other people's boundaries. And then a teenager.

(She also planned to continue being that way well into her adulthood.)

Yes, her behavior had definitely been all her parents' fault. You should always put the blame on your parents for why your life turned out wrong. That was not only good personal advice—it was also a sensible legal strategy.

Clearly, this misguided little tyke needed some one-on-one time with his father and his father's belt.

Well, if his old man was too afraid to do the necessary work with this wayward youth, then Everly would have to step in for him. How sad that it always came down to violence. Wait, sad or hilarious? Why couldn't it be both? After all, violence wasn't just a practical solution to most of life's problems.

It was also very entertaining.

With that decided, Everly lashed out with Titania's power of earth and sent her attacker crashing into a nearby wall.

"Aaaaah!" he squealed in a high-pitched mewling whine. After trying to stand, he collapsed with another shriek of pain. *Oh, no. I may have hit him too hard*, thought Everly, without sympathy. The boy's arm had been dislocated and now hung limply at his side.

Bless his little heart. Won't someone help him? His crying is annoying. I do wish he'd stop. He isn't stopping. Goodness, something might definitely happen to permanently silence him if someone doesn't come to collect him in five . . . four . . . three . . . two . . .

"Master Aiden, what's happened? What's wrong?" asked a deep, masculine voice that Everly didn't recognize.

Saved by the bell, you weak little bastard.

So, his name was Aiden, was it? He didn't look like an Aiden to Everly. He looked more like a Wesley. *Weak little Wesley, wah, wah, wah.*

A large man with a sword sheathed at his waist entered the room, followed quickly by Everly's mother. Because Everly didn't quite understand what was happening here, she decided the best thing to do was to start bawling loudly.

That's what babies did when they were upset, right?

"*Waaaah*," she wailed. It sounded unconvincing to her own ears, but it got the job done.

"Everly? Everly, what's wrong? What's happened to my daughter?" her mother asked as she swept Everly into her arms and began patting her soothingly.

Well, that whimpering little stain on the floor, whom you apparently invited into our home, tried to smother me in my sleep. Also, I need to be changed, but it's the smothering thing I'd like to focus on for now, was what Everly wanted to say but was unable to, due to her undeveloped vocal cords.

Meanwhile, the man, who appeared to be one of her father's household knights, attempted to get the murderous little brat to calm himself. He had his hands full with that task. The kid could not take the slightest bit of pain and kept on braying as though he were moments from death.

Well, technically, he had been. But he had no way of knowing that.

He was just being dramatic.

Serves him right, thought the vindictive Everly. *Son, when you take your shot at the queen, don't miss. Wu-tang.*

"What is that? Where did it come from?" her mother suddenly asked.

The knight and Everly both looked to see her pointing at the discarded pillow, which was now on the floor. A guilty look suddenly crossed the twerp's face.

Ha! Excellent question, Mom! Everly silently cheered. *Wherever did that pillow come from? Well, let's hear your answer, dummy.*

"I don't know. It was there when I came in," he lied poorly.

"No, it wasn't," said Mother. "I was in here alone with Everly before you arrived. I would never keep a pillow in a sleeping infant's crib."

"Yes, it *was!*" Aiden insisted with that ugly expression now back on his face. The one he'd worn just before attempting murder.

Everly was amused by his reaction. Spoiled children always became angry whenever their behavior was exposed. They even became genuinely offended if others refused to believe them, as though no one had any right to see through their fibs.

"Why were you in here anyway, Lord Aiden? You had no cause to be alone with my daughter," said Mother.

Now the boy grew very still. "What do you mean?" he asked slowly.

"I mean that if you've hurt my child, then a pulled arm is the *least* you'll deal with today, you little *bastard,*" she hissed.

It was an excellent thing that at that moment, no one in the room could see Everly's face, because it was taking all her willpower to hold back her laughter. *Damn, Mom, you're an ice-cold assassin! Get him! Whose house? Your house! Whose house? YOUR HOUSE!*

"You can't talk to me like that! You common-stock whore. Who are you? Just a concubine, that's all! How dare you speak that way to the family heir!" choked out little Lord Aiden.

"How dare *I?*" thundered back her mother. "You're the one who attacked your own sister!"

"My *sister?*" Aiden laughed at her in a disturbingly unchildlike manner. "You dare call that dirty blood, that nasty little nothing, *my sister?* My mother is right, you *are* reaching above your station!"

"By the light, did Lady Anne send you here?" asked Mother quietly. "Did your mother send you to kill a member of your own family?"

"I said that thing is *not* my family!" whined the murderous little brat.

"Get him out of here!" Mother said to the knight. "Get him out of here or so help me, I'll . . . Just get him away from my daughter!"

Aww, just when things were getting good. Was it already over? At this moment, Everly finally understood why her mother from Earth enjoyed watching daytime soap operas so much. This was the kind of juicy drama a girl could really feed on!

"A moment, ma'am," the knight said suddenly. He stepped closer to the pair of them, looming unpleasantly over mother and daughter both as he spoke. "Whatever you think may have occurred here, the fact remains that the count's firstborn son has suffered an injury in your quarters. Can you explain this?"

"Can I *explain* it?" Mother asked with growing outrage. "Of course I can't explain it! Except perhaps to say that the gods were defending my daughter from evil!"

Oh, Mom, stop. It's too much. I'm not a god. I'm just that *good.* Everly blushed.

"Have a care what you say, Lyona," the knight said. "Should you disparage my lord once more, I'll have no choice but to defend his honor."

To emphasize his point, the knight's hand drifted slowly to his scabbarded sword.

"Are we understood?" he asked her.

"Bastard," she whispered beneath her breath.

"I think it would be for the best if today's events didn't leave this room," the knight said. "Are we in agreement?"

"Just cut her down, Casten!" Aiden said. "Her and her bastard both. We don't need them here!"

"Such matters are decided by the count, my lord. Not us. I believe it would be best for everyone involved if he remained unaware of what's occurred. I'm sure if you apply a moment's thought to the situation, you'll find yourself in agreement."

"Are you saying that I don't think?" Aiden asked with a reddening scowl.

Everly was pretty sure Casten had just called Aiden stupid to his face. And that the boy had just proven him right by asking that question.

"Let's be off, my lord," Casten said.

The knight placed his hand on the boy's shoulder and gently guided him from the room. Aiden winced at the contact but allowed himself to be led away.

On his way out, he tried to give Everly and her mother an intimidating look of contempt but stopped with widened eyes when Everly responded with an absolutely *withering* glare of her own, which she delivered over her doting mother's shoulder.

That's right, big brother, her hate-filled expression conveyed to him. *I'm intelligent and self-aware. I KNOW what you just tried to do, but I'M the one who hurt YOU. And one night, when you're all alone, no one will come to save you when I return to finish the job.*

Sleep with the lights on, bitch.

Heh, demonic babies. That would screw with his head for a while.

Pretty slick, right?

Still, this incident showed that Everly needed to start paying more attention to circumstances in the real world. She'd spent so much time focusing on training inside her memory palace that she hadn't even realized her position in the family hierarchy wasn't as stable as she'd believed it to be.

She hadn't even known her mother was a concubine. That meant she wasn't even married to Everly's father, and Aiden had been right about her . . . She *was* a bastard. This was an upsetting revelation. Everly didn't like that word being applied to her. It meant she was *illegitimate. Violable.*

An embarrassment.

What an unsophisticated way of describing a member of your own family. She fumed. Back on Earth, no one cared if your parents were unmarried. Not unless you were an obnoxious puritan. And weren't people like that always exposed as being full of crap?

It happened all the time on television. The more loudly someone proclaimed themselves to be a guardian of public morality, the more likely they were to have a woman on the side. Or a man if they were *really* rocking that hypocritical self-denial.

Or maybe they were into hard drugs or were getting paid off by corrupt lobbyists. Whatever. People like that were as common as roaches in a Florida condo.

Everly needed to know more, so she sent Eris out to investigate her family for a bit. The news she brought back was more than a little troubling.

Apparently, Everly's family had participated in the civil war but hadn't fared as well as others. During one battle, her father was captured and taken hostage. Luckily for him, he was wealthy, and wealthy people didn't necessarily have to die just because they were facing the business end of a pike.

The good news was that he managed to pay his ransom and was set free. The bad news was that the cost had been *staggering.* Not only that, but opportunistic scavengers had taken advantage of her father's imprisonment and squeezed every drop of gold they could get from the Van Belsar estate during his absence.

What made all this a problem for Everly was that her father had been forced to sell off a large portion of his land to raise the necessary funds for his release, and consequently, that meant there was far less money to go around for his heirs.

That meant having extra children around in the background was an undesirable situation for his two official wives.

Everly hadn't been the only illegitimate child of the count. As it turned out, she'd had two other siblings born around the same time as her. Two younger brothers. Emphasis on the word *had.* A *mysterious illness* had apparently swept through the household and claimed both their lives.

Now Everly was the only baseborn child remaining.

Ladies Anne and Patrice, the count's two official wives, were waging a campaign against their unwanted competition. They were killing children. Anne was especially ruthless if she was willing to use her own son to do the deed.

I really seem to be in a precarious position, don't I? Everly asked herself.

What made the situation especially ridiculous was that Everly had no intention of relying on her father's name or wealth to make her way through life. She had no need.

The training she'd put Titania through had made the elemental so *powerful* that she'd gained an incredibly useful **[Transmutation]** ability that pretty much set Everly up for life. Anything that came from the earth could be altered by Titania into another form.

She could transform rocks into any sort of precious gem she wished. She could even change dirt into *gold dust*. Everly didn't need anything from her family.

Her wicked stepmothers were killing for scraps . . .

What a pair of fools.

And yet Everly couldn't help but delight in the awesome backstory she'd just been given. It really added to the flavor of her character.

Here she was, a hated, unwanted child, driven away by the murderous greed of her family in fear for her life, destined to live in miserable obscurity before being forgotten. A victim of this cruel and uncaring world, forsaken by all.

But instead of accepting the cruel fate that destiny had chosen for her, she chose to follow a darker path! Now, instead of becoming her family's victim, she would instead become an avenger with a heart blackened by tragedy!

Soon her campaign of vengeance against humanity would begin . . .

"Stop this, fallen one!" the hero would demand of her, during one of their confrontations. "Whatever misery you knew in your past cannot possibly justify the destruction you've wrought! The whole of humanity should not be judged by the cruelty of a few petty villains!"

"Hahaha! Such blissful ignorance! Truly, the love you were given has blinded you to the coldness of the human heart!" Everly would contemptuously reply. "You dare say I have no right to my vengeance? FOOL! *None* but I have the right to pronounce final judgment!"

"If you won't halt this path, then I have no choice but to stop you! Even if I must strike you down!" the hero would say with righteous conviction before drawing his shining sword.

"Your flowery words won't quell my wrath! Speak with your steel or NOT AT ALL!" Everly would yell before swinging her sword at him, and then their blades would clash as lightning flashed dramatically in the background, and then they'd have an awesome fight, which Everly would nearly win, but she'd let the hero drive her off at the last moment so they could do it again later.

Maaaan, being a recurring villain was going to be so much fun!

Everly dearly hoped the hero would be able to keep up with her. She was putting in a lot of work on her end, so it would be nice if the other guy was being equally as industrious with his time.

My mistress, these wicked mortals should be punished for daring to harm you. Say the word, and I will gladly torment them into utter madness, whispered Eris in her mind.

Yes, let her do that, and then I'll crush them into jellied gore, Titania said grimly. *These mongrels must be shown their error.*

Oh, you guys! I love you both, do you know that? Everly said to them. *But there's no need to rid ourselves of those people. They're helping me experience one of my favorite storytelling tropes. Imagine my luck, having an evil older brother AND a pair of evil stepmothers! How could I even consider disposing of such high-quality background characters?*

Mistress, are you certain? Eris asked doubtfully.

Trust me on this, Everly insisted. *Let's keep them around and see how things develop. I promise they'll add to the fun. All good stories need fodder like them.*

Eris understood what Everly meant, but poor Titania was a little slower to catch on. *Mistress, I don't get it. They killed your half siblings. Don't you want to avenge them?*

Meh, Everly replied. *I never met 'em. Why should I go around righting all the wrongs of the world? As a villain, when I take vengeance over something, it must be for petty and selfish reasons. Like not getting the girl I wanted or feeling slighted in public.*

Really?

Yep. Avenging some poor innocents with the powers of darkness is strictly anti-hero territory. I'm not interested in that sort of thing. Maybe we'll try it in the next playthrough.

But, mistress, they were your family. Shouldn't that matter? Titania asked her.

It does, Everly reluctantly agreed. *But the only ones I truly consider family are you and Eris. No one else matters. They're all just white static. Meaningless background characters.*

Even your mother?

What?

Is your mother also a background character?

Everly hadn't considered that.

Her mother now sat in the darkened nursery, holding Everly tightly to her chest while gently rocking her back and forth. Her lovely face was lined with worry, even as she sang sweetly to her babe. As Everly pondered Titania's question, she realized in that quiet moment they shared that her new mother genuinely loved her.

In her original life, Everly hadn't been very close to her first mother. Everly had been the younger of two siblings and had come to her parents much later in life as a surprise pregnancy. She believed her mother and father were kind people, but she had nothing in common with them. They were both old and always seemed so tired; she was often left to entertain herself. Everly hadn't felt much for her older sister either, since they were a decade apart in age.

Her family had never really known or understood her.

But here she was now, with this sad, beautiful woman who was trapped in a perilous situation but was determined to protect her child. Was this the ideal mother? Was she one of the connections Everly had always secretly longed for?

Maybe she was.

Titania asked surprisingly difficult questions.

CHAPTER SEVEN

Confrontation

Hours after the incident with Aiden, Lyona made the decision that she and Everly would no longer reside at the count's estate. She decided she would raise her daughter alone and insisted that she be allowed to move back to her place of birth, the small village her family had taken residence in after immigrating to Winstead.

Lyona was certain that such a place many miles removed from the reach of the count's wives would prove much safer for the two of them than spending another moment in that castle.

The count himself came to visit Lyona's quarters after he saw his son's injuries. Panicking under his father's scrutiny, Aiden claimed Lyona had attacked him. When he brought the boy's accusations to her attention, Lyona angrily defended herself by explaining what his son had attempted to do to the count's daughter.

The count listened quietly with no visible change in expression. After she told him of her intention to depart, he nodded and granted Lyona his permission to leave. Although they stood in the nursery, he didn't bother to check on Everly's condition. He simply left with no further words spoken.

He did, however, have the decency to place a guard outside Lyona's quarters, a competent one who obeyed only him. When the time came for Lyona and Everly to depart, he assigned five of his best knights to escort them safely to their destination.

Although it had been over a year since her birth, Everly still hadn't met her father. She hadn't even sent Eris to observe him and show her what he looked like. Why should she have to be the one to make such an effort? *She* was the main character, not him.

In her time in his home, never once did the count visit Everly or have her brought before him. While rocking her to sleep, Lyona would always whisper to her that her father loved her very much, but Everly could tell that she was just making excuses for him.

His disinterest didn't bother Everly in the slightest. If he didn't care, then neither would she.

A final incident occurred the night before their departure.

Well into the evening, after Everly had fallen asleep, Sir Casten appeared before Lyona. She'd spent a few quiet hours reading and was preparing to go to sleep herself. She had just changed into her sleeping gown when the knight's fist pounded on her chamber door. When she answered it, Casten was standing there, staring at her.

Lyona remembered his threats and was enraged by the sight of him.

However, she didn't fail to notice that the guard assigned to her was nowhere in sight.

"My lady, Countess Anne, wishes to speak with you. Come with me," he said.

"I have nothing to say to either of you. Good night," Lyona said in response to this unwanted summons.

But Sir Casten was insistent. "It could be perceived as an insult if you were to deliberately ignore my lady's request."

"Then I insist you think of it as an insult. *Good night*, Sir Casten," Lyona said archly.

"If I have to drag you to her by your hair, I'll gladly do it—" Casten began to say when a soft voice interrupted him.

"Manners, please, Sir Casten. A knight does not resort to threats when negotiating terms with a woman, even if she *is* a commoner."

Sir Casten immediately dropped to one knee in honor of the person who stood behind him. She was a beautiful red-haired woman with flawless porcelain skin and piercing gray eyes. She possessed a gorgeous figure whose curves were barely contained by her green dress, whose slit sides exposed her toned and lovely legs. Over her shoulders was draped a mantle of fur that trailed to the castle's cold stone floor.

Although Lyona knew that this woman was late into her third decade of life, it still surprised her to see how young she looked. Like a beautiful spring rose that would never wilt.

The only thing that detracted from her features was the detached expression she always wore. As though everything, and everyone, were beneath her.

This was Countess Anne. The count's primary wife and the only one permitted to share his title.

"Hello, Lyona," she said pleasantly. "May we speak?"

Lyona felt skewered by her gaze. Anne was not an ordinary woman, even for a count's wife. She was a daughter of the Godwell dukedom, a family that held influence and authority in Winstead that was second only to that of the king.

The Godwells were direct descendants of one of the five founding families of the kingdom. As mages, their power was legendary. Their lineage possessed an unheard-of success rate of over 75 percent for elemental bonding.

For centuries, their family had produced heroes, saviors, and saints. Anne herself possessed magic talents that rivaled that of a magus; sadly, that was not a title that women were permitted to possess in Winstead, due to the nation's powerful stigma against women serving in military roles.

Anne didn't care. She clearly knew how powerful she was. And she didn't mind demonstrating it to anyone who displeased her.

Lyona refused to be intimidated. "Sir Casten has my answer."

The knight was on his feet in an instant, his normally placid face now filled with a nearly feral anger. He reached for Lyona with hands that promised great violence and snarled, "You will *not* disrespect my lady, you commoner whor—"

Once more, he was interrupted by Anne. Not with words, however. This time, she backhanded him with such force that when he crashed into a nearby wall, the stone *cracked* on impact.

"Return to your quarters, Sir Casten. We will discuss your lack of decorum later," she said mildly.

Sir Casten slowly crawled to his feet and bowed before the countess. Then he quietly limped away, leaving a trail of blood in his wake.

Anne turned back to Lyona. "May I *please* come in?" she asked sweetly.

Now more frightened than she had ever been in her life, Lyona wordlessly stepped away from the doorway and allowed the countess to enter. Anne took stock of her surroundings and sniffed quietly. She removed the mantle from her shoulders and tossed it onto a nearby couch. Then she sat down and waited.

Lyona stood there for several moments, wondering what the other woman wanted, then realized she was waiting to be served.

"May I offer you a drink, Countess?" she asked her unwanted guest.

"Oh, yes. That would be lovely," Anne replied.

After being served a cup of tea, the countess explained the reason for her visit.

"I'm told you'll be leaving us soon, Lyona. I was sad to hear it. Having your presence in my home has been . . . a delight. May I ask what brought you to your decision?"

Lyona couldn't believe the gall of the other woman. "My lady . . . I believe you know very well why my daughter and I are leaving. Your son deliberately targeted her for murder."

"Murder?" asked Anne with a pained expression on her lovely face. "Oh, dear. I certainly hope that's not the language we'll be using to describe the horseplay of silly children. Aiden was curious about his new sibling and decided to introduce himself, that's all. Anything that would have come of his actions would have been purely accidental, I'm sure."

"You call smothering a baby in her crib *horseplay*?" Lyona asked incredulously.

"Legally, it would have been," Anne said matter-of-factly.

"GET OUT!" Lyona yelled angrily.

"Lyona, let's please not let histrionics derail our conversation. We have important things to discuss," Anne said.

"I SAID LEAVE!" Lyona shouted again.

Anne sighed in disappointment. "I had hoped we could be adults about this," she said.

"GET OUT—" Lyona began to shout once more, when in the blink of an eye, she was lifted and pinned against a table, held there in place by Anne's hand on her throat. Anne then leaned down so that her beautiful face was inches away from Lyona's.

She smiled at the trapped woman caught in her grasp.

A few locks of hair had fallen across the countess's face, obscuring one of her eyes, which somehow made her seem even more attractive. The eye that remained visible was now fully awakened and alert. It was the eye of a predator that had cornered its prey and wished to prolong the moment before making the kill.

"You really are beautiful, Lyona," she whispered into the other woman's ear. "I can see how you caught my husband's eye. You're a frail but fascinating thing. And so bold to speak that way to me! No one ever does. They used to, but then they learned why they shouldn't. I miss those days. I miss teaching decorum to those lacking it. You've gotten me *very* excited . . . "

Anne pressed her lips against Lyona's cheek and slowly dragged her tongue across it. "Oh, goodness. You even *taste* as sweet as you look. I think I could fall for you myself, Lyona. What do you think? Would you ever consider it? I don't know if it's because I'm falling in love or if it's because I hate you so much that it's affecting my judgment."

Her hand crept low to Lyona's thigh and lightly traced her fingers along it.

"What do *you* think?" she asked. "Love?" She gently caressed Lyona's face. "Or *hate*?"

She tightened her grip on Lyona's throat and squeezed until Lyona saw black spots. "I can't decide for myself. And that's why I've decided not to kill you."

Anne released Lyona and returned to the couch. She then resumed sipping from her cup of tea as though nothing had just happened.

Lyona coughed violently as she gasped for air. Then she climbed unsteadily to her feet, leaning on the table for support, and asked, "What do you *want* from me?"

"I don't know," Anne answered honestly. "I really don't. It's a confusing state for me. I'm normally very in touch with my desires. The way my husband's expression changes when he looks at you makes me feel *extremely* upset. But it's strange . . . I'm both jealous of you *and* jealous of him."

"What do you mean?" asked Lyona.

"I wasn't lying when I said you fascinated me. I value intelligence, bravery, and beauty, and *you* possess all three. I wonder, Lyona, do I want to be *with* you, or do I want to *be* you? I'm very unfamiliar with jealousy. Emotions are normally beneath my dignity as a Godwell."

Lyona stared quietly at the countess and said nothing.

Anne was peerless and unflappable. She was brilliant and influential. She was also so beautiful that even *the queen* was said to envy her.

But in those heated moments that they shared in her quarters, Lyona also knew as an absolute fact that Countess Anne Van Belsar . . . *was insane.*

Anne smiled at the expression she wore. "Oh, dear. Pretty little Lyona is *thinking things.* I wonder what sort of thoughts they are?"

"Please don't hurt my daughter," Lyona asked her.

Now Anne was displeased. "Stop that. Stop that right now. Don't *beg.* Dogs beg. Inferiors beg. Don't . . . don't taint my opinion of you by groveling, Lyona. I really couldn't stand it . . . Though I do admit that your distressed face excites me . . . *hmm.* Turn away from me, please."

"What?" asked Lyona.

"*Turn your back to me.* I need to finish speaking with you, and your . . . facial expressions are far too stimulating. It makes me want to pull your hair and pinch you. I'd enjoy that very much, but I doubt you would. As a child I broke my toys so frequently that I'd often be sternly scolded for it. I don't want to break you *too,* Lyona. Not until I understand you better. Now face away, please."

Reluctantly, Lyona turned her back to the countess. Suddenly, she felt Anne standing closely behind her. The other woman's fingers began to gently rake through her hair. "Just like spun gold," she said quietly.

"Say what you came to say," Lyona demanded.

Anne continued to stroke Lyona's hair as she spoke. "You're not wrong to assume that I had those other bastards disposed of. Their mother as well. However, you *are* wrong to assume that it was *completely* about avenging my honor. Those people were parasites. I'm bonded with an elemental that grants me mastery of water. One of my gifts is the ability to perceive bloodlines."

"You had *children* killed," Lyona whispered.

"Indeed, I did. I wonder why you find that so reprehensible. In nature, a lioness will defend her home from encroachment. Why should I be faulted for behaving in a similar fashion? Those children were *not* of my husband's bloodline. The whore he drunkenly slept with one night saw an opportunity to advance her status and lied to him. He was too stupid to have her claim verified and invited her and her brood into my home. When I inspected them and realized her deception, I acted decisively."

"You killed a mother and her children," Lyona said heatedly. "Their only crime was being poor and wanting more from life."

"Oh, yes. That *is* a crime, Lyona. A severe one. All nobles are charged with the primary duty of defending our sacred bloodlines. Those children could have potentially bred into a noble house and diluted them with their commoner seed. The ability to bond with the elementals is not a given. And one's chances are made slimmer the more muddled their genealogy becomes."

"And this excuses your cruelty?" Lyona asked bitterly.

"It does. Measures must be taken to protect our future," Anne continued. "You don't know how dangerous this world truly is. The diminishment of magic would be one of the greatest disasters to befall humanity. Those children died for a greater good. That their deaths happened to be a fitting punishment for their lying mother, before she joined them, was simply a happy coincidence."

"That is *madness*."

"Logic must seem like madness to those without the will to commit to it," Anne said.

"Why did you send Aiden to kill Everly?"

"I didn't. Everly is one of *us*. You didn't lie. But I was recently discussing the preventative measures I'd taken with Lady Patrice. Unfortunately, my son overheard and got the wrong idea. I wish you'd spoken to me first before telling my husband. His displeasure was *severe*. Aiden will be fortunate if he can walk without a limp for the rest of his life."

"Good. I'm glad of it," Lyona said vindictively.

Anne's grip on her hair tightened ever so slightly.

"Be careful. He's a fool. Too much like his father and not enough like me, but he *is* my son. His behavior can be corrected. It *will* be corrected. I will see to it," Anne said. "So there's nothing that you need to fear in the future. You don't have to leave, Lyona."

"Nothing I need to fear except *you*, that is," Lyona said softly.

Anne gently turned her around and looked her in the eye, with her hand on Lyona's cheek. "Lyona . . . do I look like someone you need to fear?" she quietly asked her.

"More than anyone else in this world," Lyona answered truthfully.

Anne stared at her for a moment. Then she smiled and said, "So brave."

Then Anne gathered her fur mantle from the couch and walked to the door. Before she exited, she paused without turning and said, "Goodbye, Lyona. I wish you happiness."

"Goodbye, Countess," Lyona replied hesitantly. Then she said, "I hope justice finds you one day."

Now the countess turned her head, and Lyona saw her cheeks were flushed red and her smile was as brilliant as that of a young maiden experiencing love and desire for the first time.

"Oh, Lyona," she said. "You're so sweet for thinking that word has *any* meaning in this world."

Then she was gone.

The following morning, so were Lyona and Everly.

CHAPTER EIGHT

Childhood

Time passed by. Days, weeks, months, then years.

Before she knew it, Everly was now eleven years old. She was glad of it too. Being a preteen was a *huge* improvement over being a helpless infant, and never having to be diapered again was a dream come true.

Everly decided that, overall, reexperiencing infancy hadn't been *too* awful, but it would be much better to seek out a means of immortality so that she wouldn't have to do it a third time. Three-peats were for the LA Lakers, not her.

"Everly, come inside please. I want to speak with you," her mom called to her as Everly sat in meditation in the backyard. They now lived in a comfortable two-story house in the central village of Anders, where Lyona had grown up.

Anders was a quiet and cozy sort of place, where there wasn't a lot of anything around, but the scenery was pretty. There were many trees to climb and a lot of nature to enjoy. *Flyover country*, they'd call it back in her old life, but Everly liked it. This was the ideal sort of home for a person like her, who'd grown up in a big city on Earth and had never gotten to visit places like this, outside of family vacations.

Honestly, it would have been perfect if only everyone hadn't been so jealous of her mother. They whispered about her all the time. They said the word *concubine* like it was a curse word and decided among themselves that Lyona was a hoity-toity harlot who thought herself better than she was.

Over the years, Everly had overheard more than one person mutter, "She isn't better than *me*."

"Man, that's a real catch-22, isn't it?" Everly asked Eris one day. "Most of those snobs at my dad's estate considered her too lowborn to live there, but these country mice out *here* think she's too fancy to ever be one of them. Mom can't catch a break, can she?"

Lyona is blessed above all others to have you as her progeny, mistress. Would you like me to flay the mind of any fool who dares to disparage her? Eris asked her.

"Not right now, but stick a pin in it, okay?" Everly said.

When Everly came inside, Lyona was waiting for her in the kitchen with her arms crossed.

"Everly, Mrs. Bellweather has just informed me that her son Samuel came running home with a broken nose and a missing front tooth. Would you like to explain to me how that happened?"

Everly was amenable to her mother's request.

"Well, he lost the tooth after he called me stupid to my face, when I was minding my own business in the clearing," she said mildly. "I think he felt safe because he had a few of his friends backing him up, but I showed him otherwise."

"Ah," Lyona said, while wearing a neutral expression. "And may I ask how he acquired his broken nose?"

"Well, he got back up after I told him to stay down. I felt disrespected."

"And what about his friends?"

"Well, you might be getting a few more visits from some other angry parents," Everly said honestly.

Lyona sighed deeply and told her daughter to go to her room. Everly obeyed like the dutiful child that she was.

Everly wasn't very popular with the other children in Anders. Since moving here, she'd picked up a reputation for being aloof and preferring her own company, which was 100 percent accurate. She wanted nothing to do with any of them.

It wasn't that she disliked them or anything. The reasons were more complicated than that. It came down primarily to two things: The first was that playing with those kids cut into her training time, which she found completely unacceptable. Why should she skip out on cultivating godlike power just to play tag or hide-and-seek?

That would be dumb.

The second reason was that, mentally, Everly was now aged twenty-seven. That made her far too old to hang out with those boring little thumb-suckers. She tried to be polite when declining their invitations to play, but many of the other kids interpreted her rejection of them as her being snooty.

So there went her reputation with the locals.

Most of the other children settled for complaining about Everly behind her back, but there were also dummies like Samuel Bellweather, a ten-year-old self-appointed champion of the people, who decided to strike back on behalf of those who felt slighted by Everly's maturity.

He did this by picking fights he couldn't possibly win and then whining to his mommy like a little bitch whenever Everly slapped him down.

"Jeez, that kid is getting to be a handful," Everly complained as she threw herself onto her mattress. "Eris, does Sammy have a crush on me or something? It's flattering if he does, but it's also awkward because the only thing *shotacon* about me are my front snap kicks, y'heard?"

I'm not entirely certain I do, mistress.

"It's a play on words. *Shotokan*, like the style of karate, and *shotacon*, which is Japanese slang for women who like young boys?"

I still don't get it, mistress.

"Meh, it's nuanced. Hey, send Sammy some terrible nightmares later, all right? Something lingering that'll have him begging to sleep in his mommy's bed for the next few months. That'll teach that little twerp not to be a snitch."

It shall be done.

"Awesome sauce," Everly said with mean-spirited satisfaction.

I think it would be cute if he did have a crush, Titania chirped in. *He's always trying to impress you with his paltry strength! He provides much amusement with his flailing attempts to overcome you.*

"Titania, you're being a bully right now," Everly said, smirking. "I like it."

Bullying others is fun. I've grown to enjoy it! I wish for more opportunities to indulge in it.

"Well, we'll have to wait until I'm older. Also, kids shouldn't be in such a hurry to experience romance! Why does everyone want to grow up so quickly? I'd blame it on social media if they had such a thing around here, but since they don't, it must be a cultural issue."

In this world, mortal lifespans are considerably shorter for the poor than they are in the world from which you hail, mistress, Eris said. *Courtships can begin as young as thirteen years of age and culminate in a legal marriage by the age of fifteen. Women who wait later in life to marry are generally those who can afford to do so.*

"Gross," Everly said.

Diseases are rampant, and deaths by war, misadventure, or monster predation are common. Once past the safety of a city or town, anything in this world can kill you. With that being the case, it makes sense for people to have children while young.

"Yeah, well, tell that to the FBI." Everly snorted.

Lyona ended up giving two silver pieces to the parents of each child that her daughter had injured. The money had been procured by Everly, using Titania's **[Transmutation]** ability. Lyona never questioned where it came from and simply assumed the count was providing for them. Everly saw no need to correct her assumption.

So long as her mother was happy and felt taken care of, why sweat the details?

Lyona also had Everly formally apologize to each of her victims. That seemed to settle things for now, but Everly couldn't help but notice the calculating looks that appeared on a few of the faces of the people her mother paid off.

Everly hoped for their sakes that no one was getting any ideas about breaking in later and attempting a robbery. Eris and Titania would both react negatively to such an ill-advised scheme. The two of them hated it when people didn't respect boundaries.

They were big sticklers for good manners.

That evening, Everly's uncle Tybalt and his son, Alden, came over for dinner. They did that a lot.

It wasn't that they were poor. They were simply gluttonous. Lyona liked to set a plentiful table, and Tybalt and Alden loved gorging themselves at it. Everly had a big appetite as well, so she appreciated having people around who enjoyed a good meal as much as she did.

Everly hated to cast shade on others, but she wasn't impressed at all by most of Lyona's other relatives. To her undiscerning eye, most of them were greedy, glad-handing losers who only visited because they wanted to borrow money.

It was an awful time whenever one of them showed up. They'd sit in the receiving room for hours, drinking tea and faking an interest in Everly's and Lyona's lives. They'd laugh loudly at their own bad jokes and talk about their personal hardships or their surefire investment opportunities and just drag things out for ages *until* they finally got to the point and begged for a handout, which Lyona would always give them.

"Mom, why not just drop some money out of the mail slot when they knock and spare yourself the ordeal?" Everly asked her one day.

"Because that would be impolite," Lyona replied.

"Okay. Well, then, why do *I* have to sit there and listen to all their nonsense? Surely, I don't contribute that much to the conversation?"

"I have you stay because you're a great source of comfort to your mother, my angel," Lyona said.

"What's that supposed to mean?"

"It means that if *I* must suffer, then *you* should suffer too. That's how mothers and daughters strengthen their bond."

"Jesus Christ."

"I don't know what that means, Everly, but I don't think I like the way you're saying it."

Her extended family's company was often a *brutal* test of Everly's patience.

After the last such ordeal, she'd begun to seriously consider sending Titania out one night to make a few accidents happen. No one would be able to trace it back to her, right?

Tybalt, on the other hand, was different from the rest of them. He was far more interesting.

He was Lyona's younger half brother, and like her, he'd traveled far beyond the tiny boundaries of the village and found work as a mercenary. He'd fought in skirmishes across the kingdom and beyond. He'd even taken part in the civil war. Tybalt possessed loads of experience and knowledge that others lacked, and he was an amusing guy to be around too.

Her cousin Alden was nearly thirteen years old. This summer, he was leaving with Tybalt to participate in the summer campaign, when so many of the country's nobles would temporarily set aside their petty arguments and grievances and work together to bring copious amounts of pointless violence and bloodshed to the Oldstead Republic, their neighbor to the south.

The ongoing war and the opportunities it provided had become the new driving force of Winstead's economy.

"My boy's going to do just fine, I think," Tybalt said proudly. "Oh, he'll piss himself a bit for sure, might even turn his trousers brown when he hears the cannons firing for the first time, but he'll adapt quickly."

"Ty, I wish you'd consider otherwise. Alden is such an intelligent child. He could do so much better for himself than becoming another mercenary," Lyona said worriedly.

"Well, what would you have him do instead, Lyss? Al's a good kid, but he's too ugly to be a concubine like you were!" Tybalt said, before roaring with laughter at his terrible joke.

"Gods, I really hate that word. It's all anyone ever focuses on when they learn about me," Lyona fumed angrily as she downed another glass of wine.

"Never mind the years I spent serving as a healer for the Medicaeus," she continued. "Never mind all the lives I saved and the impairments I restored! Because I had *one* meaningless fling with some titled landholder, all anyone thinks of me is that I'm a glorified bed warmer for the nobility."

"Lyss, you *did* move into his house," Tybalt said carefully.

"Only at his insistence! And he never told me I'd be sharing the space with his two official wives! That was the most uncomfortable year and a half of my life. Gods, the idea of those child-murdering harpies being so close to where my daughter slept, even now it makes my skin crawl!"

"Is that why you've been refusing his requests to visit?"

"He doesn't own me! The king's new charter guarantees citizens their right to liberty. The count never married me nor had his daughter legitimized, so he has no right to command either of us to do anything."

"That's harsh, Lyss. Noble or not, a man should be allowed to see his own child, shouldn't he?"

"Then let him come here! But I won't hop to obey when he snaps his fingers!" Lyona said bitterly. And that was the end of that conversation.

"Well, what about you, Everly?" Tybalt asked, turning to the girl. "Have you given any thoughts to your future? Let me guess, you want to marry a prince and become queen of a kingdom one day?"

"Tch, to hell with *that*. I'm going to raise an army of the damned and conquer the entire world," she replied proudly.

Everly had recently decided that being a black knight was too modest for her ambitions. She now had bigger plans, but she was still working on the details.

"Oh, no! You're still going on about that? I wouldn't try it! Surely a hero will arise to put an end to your mischief!" her uncle said with a perfectly straight face.

"Ha, I wish that fool would try. I'll skewer him on my sword and invite the crows to feast on his bloody remains," Everly said with perfect confidence.

"Everly, for heaven's sake, watch your language," Lyona said sharply. "And as for you, stop encouraging her silliness, Tybalt! I really ought to beat you with a stick! Thanks to you teaching her how to fight, she's always bullying the other children. That's all on you!"

"Now, Lyss, I only showed her a few moves, that was all. Believe it or not, little Everly has a natural talent for brawling!" Tybalt said in his defense.

I have a natural talent, huh? Everly thought wryly.

Tybalt hadn't shown her a single thing that she hadn't already known. But he insisted that all young girls needed to know how to protect themselves, and she found it fun pretending to be an ignorant student, although she'd been tempted more than once to knock him on his backside, just so he'd stop being so pretentious while coaching her.

She'd resisted the urge because she knew his actions were coming from a place of love.

"Children only learn what adults teach them," Lyona insisted.

"Not true, big sister," Tybalt responded. "You know as well as I do that our society is backward when it comes to the dissemination of military roles. I've been all around the continent, and I'm telling you, this country's taboo against female knights is ridiculous. We're depriving ourselves of an exceptional fighting force."

"That's utter dung," Lyona said.

"It's true! The prohibition would make sense if women couldn't use elementals to equalize their strength, but they can, so it doesn't! And even if you don't account for that, I've encountered women who could use *harada*! I barely survived one such she-devil destroying half a calvary charge by herself!"

Only half? thought Everly.

"Oh, not the Black Lioness again," Lyona said while rolling her eyes.

"Yes, the Black Lioness!" Tybalt said. "She carved us into nothing with that odd eastern sword she wielded! I counted the seconds in my head, Lyss. Ten of them! Ten bloody seconds to turn forty men on horseback into dog's meat! I was trapped beneath a dead stallion, wondering if this was the end for me as she came sauntering along to finish the job."

"Oh, that sounds so intense!" Everly said excitedly.

"Kid, you have no idea!" Tybalt chuckled. "She only spared me because I made her laugh!"

"You made her *laugh*?" Everly asked him.

"You're damn right, I did! She asked me if I was having a bad day. I said to her, 'Well, I sure as fuck have had better ones!' That set her off for nearly a minute."

"Tybalt! Stop! You'll have her cursing like a soldier if you keep speaking like that!" Lyona said angrily.

"I'm just telling her what happened," insisted Tybalt before turning back to his niece. "Listen, Sprout, I made the Black Lioness laugh *so* damn hard, she could barely breathe!"

"Really?"

"Really! In fact, she was so amused by my droll delivery that she ended up pulling me free and said I'd just bought back my life. Then she tossed me *this* coin and went off on her way. Presumably to slaughter more fighters on my side, but I didn't care. I wasn't getting paid enough to deal with a beast like her."

Tybalt reached for the necklace he wore around his neck and showed Everly the coin that hung on the end of it. He'd drilled a hole through it and pulled a chain through its center. It was a burned, blackened gold piece, the center of which held the image of a fiercely roaring lioness.

"Wow," she said admiringly. "Okay, that settles it. When I turn fifteen, I want to become a mercenary too. But just for a little while, Mom! I'll still attend the academy! I just want to see some amazing stuff like Tybalt so I'll have some funny stories of my own."

"Good for you, Everly—" Tybalt began to say, before Lyona stared him down with a blank but terrifying expression.

"Tybalt . . . " she said quietly.

Tybalt quickly cleared his throat and said, "Well, I mean, it's a very difficult path to follow, Everly. And, uh, like I said, our society is a little backward when it comes to women in frontline roles, you see, so, uh, it's unlikely any mercenary guild would give you any work—"

"That's all right, Uncle! I don't need to get paid. I just want to travel and fight," she told him.

"*Whaaaat?*" Tybalt said, his voice rising with outrage. "No niece of mine is going to stride the red fields of war for free! Mercenaries aren't heroes or *adventurers*," he growled while placing a very nasty emphasis on that last word. "We don't risk our lives for some paltry greater good!"

Everly was stunned. No one had ever taught her such a practical life lesson before! But Tybalt wasn't finished.

"*Always* make sure you get paid, sweetie. Even if it's just a copper penny, that's *your* goddamn copper penny, and if any bastard tries to keep it from you, stick him with a dull, rusty knife, then *twist it!*"

"Tybalt!" Lyona shouted angrily.

"Oh, uh, that is to say, go to school and then get married, sweetie. Such concerns aren't meant for a pretty girl like you," he finished feebly.

"How come she can't fight?" Alden suddenly asked.

Everyone turned to look at him. Her cousin was an extremely quiet boy who parted with his words as reluctantly as a dog would with a stick. To hear him speaking up was an unusual occurrence.

"Well, Alden, it just isn't appropriate," her mother said. "She's a count's daughter. Women of noble blood aren't meant for battle."

"Don't nobles become nobles to begin with because they killed a lot of people?" Alden asked pointedly.

"Yes, that's true, but it's still not something expected of a girl. A woman's place isn't in combat."

Everly rolled her eyes in embarrassment at her mother's outdated thinking. Why did people always resort to absolutism to justify their personal beliefs? Hadn't they just been discussing the Black Lioness? She alone was proof that what was true for one place wasn't necessarily true for another.

On Earth, Russia had fielded female tank pilots, snipers, and frontline soldiers to shore up their numbers during World War II. And what had that ragtag intergender army managed to achieve back then? Uh, they only killed a bunch of goddamn Nazis and chased the rest halfway across the European continent.

Yeesh.

Everly didn't care much about equal rights since she didn't think anyone else was her equal, but it really did hurt a little to see a woman as intelligent as her mother undercutting her own value due to social conditioning.

A killer is a killer, darn it! Don't sell yourselves short, girls. You can be murderers too, if you'll only let your hearts believe!

The argument continued across the table, but Everly tuned it out. It had grown boring.

Everly was amused that Lyona believed she could dictate to her what her future would be. Everly decided to let her mother keep that innocence for as long as possible. It was like letting a small child believe in Santa Claus or something to that effect.

But sooner or later, the time would come for her to leave. There was so much of this world that she wanted to see for herself. She wanted to gather as much information as she could, both for purposes of research and because she'd always wanted to travel on her own.

Plus, she wanted to fight! Everly longed to test her skills in genuine life-or-death combat. Her memory palace training had reached its apex. She could easily duel three copies of the Mountain Splitter at once and dominate them with pure skill. She no longer believed she could improve any further by using the palace as her only means of practice. The time was fast approaching when she would have to challenge genuine flesh and blood. To risk her life to prove her strength.

She was so excited by the idea that it practically made her tremble.

After dinner was finished, everyone gathered in the den to enjoy one another's company while having dessert. Alden and Everly played Kings and Crosses, while their parents discussed the latest events happening in the capital. Just pointless gossip, really. It was probably months out of date.

As the evening light began to wane, the time came for their guests to leave. Lyona and Everly walked them to the door. She gave Alden a hug and Tybalt gave her a kiss on the forehead, and then out they went.

After helping Lyona wash the dishes and put them away, Everly was sent off to bed while Lyona returned to the den to read. Once in her bed, Everly stared at the ceiling for a bit, then closed her eyes and quietly focused on her breathing until she once more left the confines of reality and returned to her memory palace.

There she once more assumed her original form, dressed in training clothes.

"Welcome, mistress," Eris and Titania said simultaneously, after they manifested physically.

"Is all well?" Eris asked, as Everly drew her sword and began her warm-up exercises.

"It's fine. Everything's fine. I'm just preoccupied with thoughts of the future," Everly replied as she began swinging her sword at illusory targets. "I think I've made a decision about how we'll be spending our time after I turn sixteen."

"Really? And what will that be?" Eris asked eagerly.

"How does life on the road sound to you?" Everly asked her.

CHAPTER NINE

Keeping The Faith

Far from the kingdom of Winstead, across a vast body of water, a city teetered at the point of collapse.

Riots had broken out everywhere. Many citizens had been enraged by an unknown force and driven into a maddened frenzy. They now rampaged throughout the streets, destroying everything around them.

Opportunistic criminals, the ones who hadn't fallen under the dark influence that compelled others to violence, still looted anything they could get away with. Random murders and other such indecencies were rampant. It was as though everyone had gone insane.

The city guard, although well-funded and numbering over a thousand members, was soon pressed to its limits, leaving many areas to fend for themselves.

The Stone Rose Monastery was located in one such area.

The monastery was a humble place built deep within the slums of the city to better allow the monks it housed to minister to the needs of the poor and destitute. It was a place of education for children whose parents could not afford their schooling. It was a place that fed the hungry and housed the homeless.

Best of all, it was also a house of healing for those who were turned away from the hospitals. The powerful holy magics wielded by the senior monks could heal almost any ailment, and they refused any form of compensation for the aid they provided. The greatest payment they could ever receive was the joy of knowing they had served humanity and, in so doing, served their faith.

To the adoring people who were served by it, the monastery was a place of love and acceptance. The pious brotherhood that resided there were cherished friends that the community would have gladly come to support. But the violence of the day left them with no choice but to stay in their homes to protect their families.

It was just as well. Today's battle would have been beyond them.

"Brothers! Prepare your hearts! Shield yourselves with faith and know that the light of the one is with us, always," said the abbot with his serene voice. "In this time of trial, he shall defend us. In this moment of darkness, he will be our light. Whatever fate now befalls us, know that all will be well. Be proud."

"We are proud!" shouted the brave faithful who sat facing the barred entryway with him.

"Be grateful," he said.

"We are grateful!" they shouted.

"I am glad. We are dearly loved. Never forget that—"

The entryway exploded. One of the massive wooden doors splintered beneath the force of the terrible blow that struck it. Into the prayer hall sauntered an arrogant figure dressed in the garb of the temple priesthood. But his defiled robe was so filthy and frayed from wear that it was nearly colored black.

A foul smell accompanied the man, as did a strange fog that seemed to rise with every step he took.

"Miasma!" said one young monk fearfully. "Demonic miasma!"

"Settle yourself, brother. It will not harm you," said the abbot calmly.

"He lies. Your faith will not protect you, boy. Unless you escape, you'll drown in poison and die with bloody froth on your lips. You're *so* young. Is this how your life was meant to end?" asked the invader.

"Those of us who die in service to the one shall know rewards greater than you can ever imagine, deceiver," said the abbot. "The one who should flee is *you*. Your endurance is remarkable to so withstand the power of this holy place. But how long will you last, I wonder?"

"I'll lassst long enough!" hissed the intruder, literally. A prehensile tongue now slithered from his mouth, leaking foul yellowish fluids on the monastery floor. "You know what I seek. Deliver it to me, and your lives will be spared. Refuse, and your *true* reward will be madness and death . . . "

"How sad it is that you genuinely believe that," replied the abbot, who shook his head in dismay at the intruder's demands. "The item we were entrusted with is not ours to give you. More importantly, the moment we swore ourselves to the service of heaven, our lives ceased to be our own. So, you see, we have nothing we can offer you, except our prayers for your salvation."

"So smug. So certain. I despise your kind so much," the ashen priest said. He flexed his hands, and his fingers became claws tipped with long bladelike talons. "We will now test the limits of your faith, old man. Let's see how long your serenity lasts."

"It will be longer than you think, fallen one," replied the abbot confidently.

"Oh? Do you mean to resist? Ha! I thought your kind took vows of nonviolence. Did that recently change?"

"No," said the abbot. "Fortunately for you, our vows to live in peace remain unbroken."

"Then how do you intend to—"

"Sadly for you, the templars who share our beliefs swear no such oaths."

"What are you babbling about—"

CLANG!

A war hammer was hurled with perfect accuracy at the fiend. It connected with the ashen priest's face and sent him flying backward like a rag doll. The hammer then vanished in a burst of blazing light and reappeared in the hand of its owner.

"SACRILEGE! BLASPHEMY! THIS OUTRAGE WILL *NOT* BE TOLERATED!" shouted the warrior who faced the intruder. His was a stout figure, barrel chested, with powerful arms and legs, wearing a gleaming suit of mail. His gray-streaked beard was massive and flowed from his chin to his beltline.

Such was the imposing strength he exuded that he seemed more solid than the stone floor on which he stood.

It was as though the power of the very mountains themselves had coalesced into the shape of a man.

He was also *very* short, standing no higher than five feet. Not that it mattered in the least.

"GROVEL BEFORE THE RIGHTEOUS, YE FAITHLESS DOG! PRAY FOR FORGIVENESS, AND IT SHALL BE GRANTED! ALTHOUGH I MUST STRIKE YE DOWN, YOUR FOOLISH SOUL MAY YET BE SAVED!" roared the warrior.

"Dark one, please allow me to introduce you to our esteemed visitor," said the abbot. "This is Lord Berjlot Gottbeard, a dwarven templar currently undertaking a sacred pilgrimage. Last night he visited us to sample the ale our monastery brews to raise funds for the services we provide. He sampled perhaps a little too much and decided to spend the night. Funny that should occur on today of all days, wouldn't you agree?"

"IT WAS VERY GOOD ALE!" shouted the dwarf.

"Thank you, Lord Berjlot. The approval of such a renowned hero is humbling to us."

"THINK NOTHING OF IT!" shouted the dwarf.

"*This* is your great defense?" sneered the intruder as he wiped his bloodied face. "A mere *dwarf* stands in my way? Stupid thing, you will *not* thwart me today. That little toy you wield won't save you—"

Clang!

Lord Berjlot did not wait for his opponent to finish speaking. Instead, he leaped across the room and smashed his hammer upon the false priest's face. Then, he swung mercilessly at his knee and shattered it with one powerful strike. As the intruder collapsed while screaming obscenities, Berjlot brought the hammer down three times in rapid succession on the back of his skull.

Clang! Clang Clang!

"DO NOT UNDERESTIMATE A DWARF!" shouted the dwarf. "DO NOT THINK LIGHTLY OF A DWARF! DO NOT PROFANE A SACRED PLACE OF WORSHIP WITHIN VIEW OF A DWARF! AND *ESPECIALLY DO NOT MOCK THE HAMMER OF A DWARF!*"

Clang! Clang! Clang!

Maddened by pain and humiliated by how easily he was being trounced, the intruder lashed out with his tongue, which wrapped itself around Lord Berjlot's arm, forcing him to drop his weapon. Then the intruder's jaw unhinged itself as his tongue began reeling the templar's hand toward his mouth.

This was a mistake.

For now, the dwarf was *angry.*

"EAT MY HAND, WOULD YE? NAY, FIEND! YE SHALL EAT *MY FIST*!" shouted the dwarf.

Holy light erupted around the dwarf in a brilliant and blinding aura that none in the hall but Lord Berjlot and the abbot could withstand. Even the younger monks had to shield their eyes, so intense was its glare. However, despite its radiance, the light caused no lasting pain to any who saw it.

No one except the demonic intruder, that was.

"It burns! It *burns! It buuuuuuuuurns!*" he shrieked in panic. He tried to retract his tongue so that he could escape, but Lord Berjlot would have none of it. His fingers sank into the meat of the tongue, and with one mighty heave, he dragged the demon toward him.

The screaming abomination landed at Berjlot's booted feet, where the dwarf stood towering over him with one fist clenched in anger.

"YE'D SKIP YER MEAL, WOULD YE? I SAID EAT MY FIST, BOY!" shouted the dwarf. "EAT! MY! *FIST!*"

The first two blows battered the intruder's face into unrecognizable hunks of meat. The third was driven deep into his mouth, all the way down his throat, where the holy fire that raged around Lord Berjlot flowed into the demon's body.

That light then exploded outward and disintegrated the foul creature completely.

Not even ashes remained.

"ENJOY ETERNITY, YE UNCLEAN BASTARD!" shouted the dwarf. "TELL THE PRINCES OF HELL THAT BERJLOT SAID TO WIPE YER ARSES WITH A THORNY BRANCH!"

"Lord Berjlot, *please,*" said the abbot disapprovingly.

"Ah, my apologies, sir," said the dwarf sheepishly. "I get a bit carried away. It's a flaw of mine; I need to work on it more."

"As long as you realize that, then there's nothing I need to forgive," replied the abbot. "Instead, on behalf of myself and my brothers, please accept my thanks. Although we were resolved to die, your intervention allows us to continue our service to this city. Thank you."

As one, all the monks gathered in that place rose and bowed their heads to the templar.

"There's no need to thank me, friends. Ye know as well as I that all happens as heaven wills," replied the humble dwarf.

"Even so, we're still very grateful—"

"Abbot! Abbot! Something terrible has happened!" shouted a young monk who came running to them in a panic.

"Remain calm, please. Tell me what has occurred," the abbot said.

"The gem . . . the gem was stolen! For some reason, Brother Fezra was found at the entrance to where it was hidden . . . He was dead! Oh, light, I can hardly describe the state of him. He was . . . he w-was . . . "

"Say no more, young one," the abbot said. Although his voice remained serene, his expression was now troubled.

"A brother of this monastery was slain?!" asked Lord Berjlot. "I apologize, sir. It would appear that I failed in my duty to protect all of ye."

"No, Lord Berjlot. There is no fault here. Fezra was a former member of our order. I recently had to dismiss him when I discovered he was stealing from us. Apparently, he gained a far greater knowledge of this place's purpose than I realized. I suspect the foe you dealt with was a distraction to allow for Fezra to lead the true mastermind to that which we guarded."

"Is that so? Then this Fezra . . . "

"Was given his due reward. Whatever tempted him to betray us in this manner has surely led his soul to damnation. I will pray for him. But first, I must inform my superiors, while you rally the city guards. Because a danger greater than we have ever known now approaches. I only hope we can prevent it before the worst comes to pass."

"The worst?" asked Lord Berjlot. "Worse even than this demonic incursion?"

"Indeed, my friend. Far worse. For I speak of *the apocalypse*."

Fires burned uncontrollably throughout the streets and homes of the populace, sending people scrambling for safety wherever they could find it. Among the panicked throng of humanity, one figure stood apart. A bald man in the tattered brown robes of a clergyman. Another member of the ashen priesthood.

The crowd, even in its near-animal panic, sensed there was something terrible about this holy man.

Something unnatural.

Without giving conscious thought to their actions, they parted before him like water, offering him a simple path to the lanes that exited the city. Although they didn't realize it, he was the source of the terror that had provoked all of this day's terrible violence.

The priest was pleased with the results his efforts had brought him. The fragile minds of humanity were so easily toyed with. Thanks to the weakness of the herd, he had procured a prize like no other.

With his fingers still slick with the foolish Fezra's blood, he held the gem before his eyes and grinned with malignant joy.

Suddenly, an arrow flew forth and struck the priest in the back of his neck. Rather than screaming in pain or dropping dead to the ground, he simply plucked it free. A long string of yellow puss drooled from the arrowhead as he examined it. He gave the tip a curious lick before tossing it aside.

Then, with surprising speed, he quickly ran away, slipping around the corner of an abandoned building to vanish from the sight of his attackers.

"Hurry! Keep on him!" shouted the armored young man who'd fired the shot; after tossing aside his bow, he raced after the priest while holding a drawn sword, running recklessly ahead of the others who followed him.

"Slow down, Kenneth!" one of them called.

"Run faster!" Kenneth yelled back. "We can't let the beast escape! He must be stopped!"

"We will! But we have to stay together! We need to send word to Lord Berjlot—"

"There's no time!" Kenneth shouted to him as he continued his chase. He was blinded by visions of the glory that would surely be his once this monster had been destroyed. "Keep up, lads!" He laughed. "This is our moment! This is our *moment!*"

As Kenneth rounded the corner that his quarry had passed, a hand snaked out of the darkness with serpentine grace and grabbed him by his throat. He was pinned roughly against a wall before his attacker's other hand thrust itself through the protection of his breastplate and easily pierced his heart.

The blow was delivered with such terrible force that it also bored a hole through the stone behind him.

"Your moment is as fleeting as your final breath, mortal," whispered the malefic voice of his murderer. Kenneth couldn't respond to the killer's taunt; the dead heard nothing.

"Nooooo!" screamed Kenneth's friend, his voice heavy with both sorrow and anger. "You bastard thing, die! DIE!" He ran toward the shadowy figure and swung a mighty blow with his sword, but his blade was unable to connect; the beast easily evaded his strikes and ran away, laughing in scorn at his foe's futile attempts to avenge his victim.

"Damn you, fight me! *FIGHT ME!*" the humiliated knight screamed as frustration and shame overwhelmed his fighting spirit. But the target of his wrath soon vanished from sight.

Quickly, the knight turned to an adjutant and issued a desperate order. "Seal the gates to the city. Seal *everything!* That demon mustn't escape! It'll be the end of us all!"

Despite his warning, chaos reigned in the burning city. At the portcullis that led out of the city, the guards assigned there had all been slain. Their faces were each frozen in a rictus of terrified agony. The portcullis itself had been completely destroyed.

Unholy green flames consumed it, sending choking black smoke high into the air, a brilliant conflagration that signaled the coming end of the age. A little way past the carnage, the pursuers found something. It was a smoldering circle heavy with a scent like burned amber. The remains of a circle of transposition.

The beast had teleported away. It could now be *anywhere.*

As he beheld his failure, the knight dropped to his knees, screaming his despair to the sky.

They had failed.

He had failed . . .

CHAPTER TEN

The Order

West of the burning city, in a place of great beauty built far from the prying eyes of common men, the choir of seers, with their beautiful voices, sang a song of fear.

There were nine members of the chorus. Each of them was a beautiful young maiden dressed in luminous white robes. They came from all walks of life, being of different social statuses, ethnicities, and nationalities. Three of them were even of different species.

The only thing they had in common was that they had each been blind since birth, and now the entirety of their world was the cavernous room below the massive castle-keep above their heads, where their natural gifts of prophecy allowed them to commune with the higher elementals and sing blessed songs that foretold the future.

Normally, their magnificent voices were blended in perfect harmony. For those privileged few allowed to witness their dazzling performances, the memory of the event would stay with them forever. Hearing them was almost like hearing heaven itself speak.

But today, a shrill note of terror disrupted their holy communion and warped their song with fear. Alec watched them as they stood, enveloped in white light, singing a discordant and despairing hymn of warning.

To see these dear ones so frightened pulled mightily at Alec's heart. He hated to see anyone experience such terror. *What are they seeing?* he wondered. *What frightens them so?*

Alec had learned through personal experience that the future was not an immutable thing. Even though the choir of seers saw many terrible things in their visions, they knew that such ordeals could be overcome with bravery and faith. They had never before expressed such stark terror.

For them to be so afflicted . . . Does this mean they don't believe there's any way we can win?

May the gods will that it not be so.

"My lord, the council awaits your presence," said an attendant who stood behind him.

"Of course," Alec said. Cool professionalism kept his face neutral, even as his empathy for the choir weighed heavily on his heart. Before he had become Lady Sylvain's squire, he had served as an assistant caretaker for the seers. He was barely older than the girls who comprised the current choir. He'd known all of them for years.

Trust in us, please, he asked them wordlessly. *Believe we can make a difference.*

One of them, Kelsie, turned her unseeing eyes in his direction. Although she couldn't possibly have heard his thoughts, she smiled gently at him as though he'd spoken to her aloud. Alec smiled in return, feeling some relief that the seers hadn't been completely overwhelmed by whatever it was they'd envisioned.

But he didn't allow himself to relax completely. The dire warning of the chorus was clear to all who'd heard it.

The very future of humanity was imperiled.

The grand meeting hall of eastern orthodoxy was filled with the usual collection of advisers, politicians, warriors, and their various attendants. Different arguments were being had across the room over one detail of the choir's song or another. Frustration was evident on the faces of many of the people there.

Alec wasn't surprised to see that the loudest debate involved the uncouth Lord Tyrnos and his lackies, who were shouting down his opponent's voice whenever he tried to raise a point. Tyrnos was a righteous man and a true believer, but by the gods, he could be so petulant! He loved having pointless, pedantic arguments about the verisimilitude of any topic that one could imagine.

He could waste hours debating the truth of anything!

Alec found it all so pointless and inelegant. It annoyed him to his very core. Why couldn't such an important man display more refined behavior?

"Enough, please," called out a gentle voice. Although far from a shout, it silenced the room immediately.

Excellent, thought Alec. *No sooner is she needed than she appears!*

The arch-templar of the Eastern Temple, Lady Sylvain, now entered the room, flanked by her loyal cadre of elite bodyguards.

Although her simple outfit—consisting of breeches, a forest-green tunic, and bare feet—could make her seem unsuited for her lofty rank, Sylvain radiated elegance and composure. To Alec, she was the very embodiment of graceful beneficence; she was one who worked tirelessly for the betterment of others.

And although her current garments hid certain aspects of her body from casual view, whenever Alec saw her, his mind couldn't help but drift to certain risqué thoughts about his beloved master. Nothing he would ever dare act upon, of course, but the desire was always there. It always would be.

He loved her. It wasn't something that would ever be acknowledged, but he still felt it all the same.

It's all right that it can never be, he told himself often. *It makes me happy, just knowing that there's someone like her who exists in this world. Just being near her, that's enough for the likes of me.*

Alec would never be worthy of someone like her. No man could be. Sylvain wasn't just anyone. She was half-elven and had lived a life that spanned centuries. With the continued blessings of the higher elementals, there was a chance she might *never* die. As the son of a farmhand and a mere soldier for the great cause they both served, there was nothing Alec could offer her except his continued devotion.

He only hoped his devotion would be enough.

Sylvain was not merely the leader of the Eastern Temple. She was also an important figure in their holy scriptures and the only one of the founder's apostles who still lived. When you spoke to her, you spoke with a woman who had personally known the blessed lord of radiance. She had laughed with, fought alongside, and eaten beside the child of the gods himself.

Her tears were the ones that had touched his forehead after the great betrayal.

Sylvain was *holy*.

Shortly before dying, the founder had bequeathed her his ability to commune with the higher elementals directly. They not only heard her voice, *but they also spoke to her directly*. This symbiotic relationship gave her tremendous power over the forces of darkness and charged her body with unheard-of energies. When she wore her regalia and armed herself with her shield and crackling sword of light, Sylvain was invincible.

A veritable goddess of war.

And Alec was her chosen squire. He'd been selected to serve as Sylvain's personal apprentice out of the thousands of aspirants who desired that role. Thanks to that, he'd also been gifted with the ability to draw in a portion of Sylvain's elemental power through the bond he now shared with her. He was closer to her than anyone else in the world.

He knew her resolve, her determination, and her sorrow.

He knew how much she had suffered over the centuries.

And that was why he loved her. Because she hurt, but she refused to give in.

With his mood now made melancholic by his somber thoughts, Alec recalled the day of his first battle. He'd been cut off from Lady Sylvain's side and been forced to stand alone as many came seeking him out for single combat. Since he was Sylvain's new squire, there were many eager to issue him a challenge—some for the thrill of battle and others with the hope that by killing him, they would settle old scores with his master.

Although he despised unnecessary violence, Alec refused to appear weak before anyone else. Sylvain had chosen *him*, and he wouldn't hesitate to show anyone else that she had chosen well.

Thus resolved, he mercilessly crushed anyone that dared impugn his master's honor by placing themselves in his path. That day, the new armor he'd been gifted was soon spattered red with the blood of the defeated.

No matter how many he killed, it never seemed to be enough. All of them, one after the other, kept coming. They relentlessly sought him out, eager to claim his life. It was *horrible*. Awful. The worst day he'd ever experienced. He finally understood what his veteran father had meant when he said that war was madness itself.

Eventually, the challenges died down, as did the challengers. They had all started out so arrogant, so confident of their victory over a mere boy. But they ended their lives pawing feebly at his boot, begging for Alec's mercy. He remembered his first two victims; one of them had been a particularly petty Venation man-at-arms, slipping on his own blood to sprawl on his back beside the body of his dead partner.

They'd come at him in tandem, working together to try to bring him down, mocking him when he begged them to stop, foolishly believing he was doing so out of fear for his own life, instead of from a reluctance to kill. When he realized that the only way to stop would be to claim their lives, he prayed sorrowfully for their souls.

Then he caved their chests in with his mace. The first one died instantly.

The second one . . . lingered.

Alec never forgot how terrible it had felt, watching that man die. The horror of watching his mouth open and shut as specks of blood sputtered from it with his every rasping breath. The relief he felt when that man's heart finally gave out . . . Why had it been so intense? Why had it felt more real than anything he'd ever before experienced?

At the very moment of his foe's passing, it felt as though a bolt of lightning had struck Alec in his head, forcing him to pull his helmet off and vomit in horror at what he'd done. Oh, gods. Oh, gods, why did people do these things to each other? All men had once been crying babies held in the arms of their mothers and soothed to sleep. They'd all been innocent once!

No baby had ever been capable of murder! No baby had ever wished for violence!

At the conclusion of the battle, Alec found a tree to lean against and sat there weeping, mourning for the dead and begging for their forgiveness. None of them would have done the same for him, but that wasn't the point. He'd been transformed that day into something he didn't want to be, and the implications of what he'd done now horrified him.

When Lady Sylvain came to find him, he ran from her, blaming her for what he'd been forced to do.

A few days later, after the cloud of sorrow finally began to clear from his mind, Alec realized what an awful thing he'd done. What right did he have to blame someone else for his decision to wield his mace? He'd been more powerful than any of the men he killed. It had ultimately been *his* decision to end their lives, no matter how much he sought to shift the blame to others.

And just think . . . Sylvain had lived for a thousand years. She knew this terrible sorrow more profoundly than any human being who had ever lived. She surely must have faced her own breaking point repeatedly. But she still served. She still believed in the cause. She still prayed for everyone.

She still believed in peace.

Bearing that in mind, Alec later approached her and offered her his sincerest apology. His reward had been her understanding, her forgiveness, and her smile.

He loved her.

He'd die for her.

That was what it meant to be her squire, he realized. Not to bask in the power her magic bestowed upon him. Not to enforce her will and kill her enemies. But to help carry the burden she had to live with. To support her. To do his part to make this world a place where Sylvain could finally rest and set aside war forever.

He would do that for her. He would be whatever she needed.

And that had been his role ever since.

"A prophecy of doom is upon us," whispered Sylvain. "The war we hoped to prevent will soon begin. This won't be another pointless clash of mortal against mortal over resources and greed. I almost wish that it were. What comes now will be the final battle. Mortal against *demon*."

The arch-templar's words swept across the room. Alec suspected that news of this magnitude was coming, so he managed to keep control of his emotions. But others lacked his steel.

"Lady Sylvain, you can't mean it!" said Lord Wembly, his thick chin trembling in terror. "Th-there are any number of ways the choir's verse c-could be interpreted! Why would the end times begin now? We haven't even begun the campaign to subjugate Winstead!"

"I wish I could assuage your fears with simple words, Wendel," Lady Sylvain replied, casually ignoring his title. "But destiny has caught us unawares. However, we must be thankful that we aren't completely unprepared, thanks to our seers."

Sylvain began to walk around the room, addressing each member by name. Some of them were officials who'd served the temple for decades and were now old men, but Sylvain spoke to them like they were children. Which they had been when they first met her, just as Alec had been.

"I've trained for this moment since childhood. I've prepared my heart for this, ever since my fellow apostles were betrayed and our savior's heart was stolen from his body. And I know that I've prepared all of you, my beautiful, faithful followers, for this eventuality as well. I've often wished that this day would never come. But it has. The people of this world are discordant, untamed, and unworthy. But they need us . . .

"We're all that they have."

Now Sylvain's voice began to rise with passion.

"And I *know* that the fine warriors of this honorable host are all perfectly willing to give their lives for our glorious cause. The mortal races *must* be protected! And we, the first and true Temple of the Holy Will, shall be their shield! Our cause is righteous, our hearts are pure, and our resolve is stronger than diamond and steel. Walk with me, brothers! Fight with me! Die with me if you must. But never forget that we were *called* to this purpose!"

As Sylvain spoke, silvery light began to emanate from her body. It flowed around her, forming a beautiful wave of radiance that soothed the fears of all who were touched by it, like cool water on a hot day. The boundless strength of the elementals surged from within her and awed all those gathered in her presence.

"The gods will see us!" she cried.

"THE GODS WILL SEE US!" the believers shouted in reply.

Sylvain smiled in gratitude and nodded. "Thank you, everyone. Your courage strengthens me far more than you know. Now that we've calmed ourselves, let us now plan how to proceed," she commanded.

"We have our experts studying the circle of transposition the false priest used to escape the city of An'Ara. They believe they'll soon be able to divine where the creature fled to. Undoubtedly, that very spot is where he will begin the ritual of summoning. And that is why all hands must be on alert. We must be prepared to deploy immediately once we have the location."

She gazed into the eyes of all those assembled before her, nodding as though what she saw pleased her. "I sense your resolve, everyone. Please lend me your boundless strength. Please help me save this poor world."

Tyrnos was on his feet immediately, with a fist held high. "For the order! *For Lady Sylvain!*"

Everyone else joined him, feverishly echoing his chant, but soon all mention of the order was dropped as they began repeating Sylvain's name, over and over.

"Sylvain! Sylvain! *Sylvain!*"

* * *

With his own heart swelling as well, Alec clasped his hands tightly together and held them prayerfully before his chest.

Lady Sylvain, he thought fervently. *I won't let anything prevent you from saving this world. I'll do anything to aid your success. And if anyone dares to approach you with wickedness in their heart . . .*

I will throw away my humanity and DESTROY THEM.

"ARAAAA ARCHOOOO!" Everly roared, after sneezing so hard that she hit the back of her head painfully against the tree she'd been napping against.

"Owww," she whined. "That huuurt!"

Mistress? Is everything all right? asked the concerned voice of Eris.

"I don't know. It's weird. I feel like a stranger just pointed a sword at me," replied Everly as she searched through her pockets for something to wipe her nose with.

Why would anyone do that? You're a wonderful person.

"I know, right?"

CHAPTER ELEVEN

Weight

More time passed uneventfully in the village of Anders. Everly grew older and was now a teenager and truly beginning to feel her oats, as the old folks in the Westerns might say.

On this day, the weather was much warmer than it had been, but it was still not yet spring. No matter. Everly was currently having no difficulties working up a sweat.

Are . . . are you certain you should do this? Titania asked, with concern in her voice.

"I'm doing this. I'm *doing* this! Give me a count. Give me a count, Titania!" Everly shouted aggressively.

You're at your limits, mistress! I'm worried about you. Even the slightest slip . . .

"What limits? No limits here! Give me a count!" Everly demanded. "Gimme a count!"

But . . .

"GIMME A COUNT!"

Ten . . . nine . . . eight . . . seven . . .

"RAAAAAAGH!" Everly screamed with vein-bulging intensity as she squatted low beneath the weight of the two-hundred-pound barbell she carried on her shoulders.

Today was leg day.

When Titania finally reached zero and the end of Everly's set, Everly let the weight roll off her shoulders and clatter to the forest floor. Then she began slapping her chest and roaring in triumph.

"YES! YES! HELL YES! WHAT?"

Now feeling extremely light on her feet, Everly began jumping into the air in celebration while crowing over her achievement.

"*Top of the world, Ma! Top of the world! No brakes on this crazy train! Do I even lift, bro?!*"

Mistress, what are you doing? Titania asked.

"I'm celebrating! A two-hundred-pound squat is pretty decent for someone my size," Everly said, before collapsing to the ground in glorious exhaustion. "I feel great about it! It's good to feel strong, Titania."

Mistress, two hundred pounds is a paltry sum compared to what you can achieve while channeling my strength. And even the usage of your harada *technique makes you considerably stronger than ordinary mortals. Why celebrate such an inconsequential benchmark?*

"Ha! It's different for you," explained Everly. "You're powerful *all the time.* I'm only powerful when I borrow your strength. Down here on the mortal scale, a two-hundred-pound squat is something to be proud of. It's something that can only be built toward gradually through strict self-discipline. Progression is an addiction, Titania! Setting a goal for yourself then accomplishing it feels unbelievable."

But what about your harada?

"I stole it," Everly said bluntly. "I rode someone else's coattails and plundered his sincere efforts to get what I wanted. I don't regret it in the slightest. Power is power, right? But doing something for yourself is also a pleasure, y'know? Teamwork makes the dream work, but self-reliance has its perks too."

You can always rely upon me, mistress. My power will always be yours to command.

"Ah! Ah! Ah! Don't set yourself up for failure, kid," Everly said chidingly while waggling a finger. "How did *X-Men: The Last Stand* end?"

Hmm? Oh. Lord Magneto was attacked with the antimutant cure and robbed of his powers.

"And how did *Superman II* end?"

General Zod and his companions were robbed of their powers and returned to the phantom zone.

"And what happened at the end of *Spider-Man III*?"

Eddie Brock was separated from the venom symbiote and depowered, and when he tried to retrieve it, Spider-Man murdered him with a hand grenade.

"All three answers are correct!" Everly said proudly. "I'm glad you've been watching all those old movies in my memory palace. So now you know what I must be prepared for as a villain. Heroes, you see, are powerful and highly skilled . . . but they're also fundamentally a bunch of chickenshit cowards."

They are? asked Titania. *Is that true for all of them?*

"Yeppers! Trust me. They *always* try to run from a fight if they can. And if they can't, they'll pull crap like depowering their opponents. Sealing away my abilities would be hero tactics one-oh-one. That's why it's important to know how to fight without always relying on them."

Your wisdom is truly profound, mistress. Your resourcefulness will surely confound all who dare oppose you.

"Ahhh, *praise*. My drug of choice," Everly said happily, as she reached for her towel.

Eris was currently training by herself, leaving Titania and Everly to hang out for the day. They were in the woods that stood north of Anders, where Everly had her elemental servant create a series of weights for her to use. She was now wearing breeches and boots, along with an old shirt that she'd had Titania carefully repurpose into a sports halter top for her.

Everly was now sixteen, and her body rippled with well-toned muscles that did not detract from her obvious beauty. Her form was compact, powerful, and aesthetically pleasing.

She also had abs for days, and that was cool as hell.

Mistress, said Titania's suddenly alert voice.

It's okay, I sense him too, Everly replied to her mentally. Then she sighed in dismay.

She knew exactly who was now trudging over the forest floor to see her. He was a large teenager, sixteen as well, but a few months younger than herself. He had medium-length black hair that he kept slicked back and a ruddy tint to his skin that made him seem like he was hot all day. Or embarrassed.

Everly knew him by sight because Anders was a small place and because he kept showing up wherever she was.

sammy freakin' Bellweather.

"What are you *wearing*?" he asked in shock. "I—I can see so much of you!"

"Then look away. You're the one encroaching on my personal time," she said coldly.

sammy was potentially the most annoying person Everly had ever met in either of her lives. He'd been an attempted childhood bully ever since she'd taken up residence in Anders. That was a life decision that had gone poorly for him; it had cost him a front tooth, after all—an injury he'd once tried relentlessly to avenge.

But ever since Mother Nature had arrived on the scene at the age of twelve and started peppering everyone with hormones, he'd been slowly transformed into something far more aggravating than a persistent punching bag.

He'd become an attempted suitor.

The lowercase *s* was deliberate, by the way. Everly thought of sammy as being such a nonentity that she didn't believe he deserved the dignity of a name beginning with a capital letter.

Capitals were for *closers*.

"So, sammy. What a *peasant* surprise," she said as he approached her.

"I think you meant *pleasant* surprise?"

"I know what I said. What do you want?"

Every time sammy opened his mouth to speak, he exposed the gap in his teeth she'd left him with. Even though she relished that memory, it still made for an unappealing visual. He'd had to work for months with his mother to painstakingly learn how to speak without whistling all the time.

"I'm *not* Sammy, by the way," he said. "I go by my given name now. Samuel."

"Thamuel," Everly replied.

"Thop that! I—I mean, stop that!"

"I'm thorry," she said insincerely. "I get carried away thumtimth."

"Just call me *Samuel*, please!" he insisted.

"Hmm," Everly said. "Maybe I should call you *Toot-Toot* instead?"

"Huh? Why?" he asked in confusion.

"Becauth. Thath the thound a whithle makth."

"What do I have to do to make you rethpect . . . respect me?!" he asked angrily.

"Say 'Solomon says shazam' three times in a row, and I might consider it," Everly offered.

"Ah . . . ah . . . Everly, would you please cover yourself? I . . . I want to talk to you, okay?" he said.

Shit. Well, there goes my workout, Everly thought darkly to herself as she pulled on her coat. She normally prided herself on her ability to plan ahead, but honestly, how does someone really prepare for an eventuality like sammy?

He was like a stye or a broken pinky toe. He was something that just *happened*. She sincerely wished that he'd go happen to someone else, for once.

Give the command and he's compost, Titania said to her. Although the elemental had once been amused by sammy's persistence, even she had grown intolerant of him; sammy was just one of those guys.

No. Not yet anyway. I don't want to interrupt Eris's training, and we'd need her to rearrange a bunch of memories to make people forget that I was the last person this idiot wanted to speak with before he died. Too much work; he's not worth it.

Very well, mistress. In that case, I shall return to the memory palace to resume my studies of your old movies. Please call if you need me—

Uh, hell no to that. You're staying right here with me!

What? But, mistress, what aid can I possibly offer in this situation?! whined Titania.

Silence! This is an important life lesson my mother taught me. Suffering should be shared with family.

Nooo! Your mother is a surprisingly cruel woman.

Yeah, don't I know it? Everly replied.

"Pretty is what," said sammy.

"Huh? What? What were you saying?" she asked him.

"I—I was saying how pretty I think you are," sammy stammered.

"Oh. Well, yes, I *am* pretty. Thank you for noticing. You really can leave now," Everly said.

"Everly, please! Why won't you listen to me?" he said. "I'm trying to give you my heart here."

"And I will literally take it from you, if you don't stop bothering me, sammy. I'm not interested, and your persistence is *not* appreciated."

"But why not?" he said stubbornly.

"Are you really going to make me go into detail?"

"Come on," he suddenly shouted. "This isn't fair! You . . . you have to give me a chance!"

Now Everly's temper was becoming frayed.

"Do I? Do I *really?*" she asked with a slight tilt of her head. She stepped closer to sammy, and now there was something baleful in her eyes. Something that warned him that he was now alone in the woods with her, and she *really* did not like him.

She reached a hand toward his face.

"Pleath . . . please!" he said. "I just wanted to tell you how I feel."

Everly paused before touching him. Then she reluctantly lowered her hand. With her eyes now tightly shut, she took a deep breath before opening them and saying, "*Fiiiiiine.* Okay, *Samuel,* let's try this. I'll ask you three different questions about yourself. You answer them honestly, and we'll see how things turn out from there, okay?"

sammy hesitated before answering. Then he nodded eagerly. Everly wondered if he thought she was finally warming up to him.

"All right!" he said enthusiastically. "Ask away!"

"First question: Do you like flowers?"

Oh, this was an easy one. "I love flowers," he said. "My mama loves growing them in her garden—"

"Too bad. I hate them," she said quickly. "Second question: What's your favorite hobby?"

"I've got two," he said. "I like hunting for quail with my dog, and I like listening to the weekly sermons in church."

"Wow, that's fucking *terrible,*" Everly said without mercy. "Last question: Where do you see yourself ten years from now?"

"Well, I'll be living with my folks still, helping to run my dad's farm."

"Yeah, I'm not living on a goddamn potato farm, Toot-Toot. Okay, sammy. You're oh-for-three. You tried your best. We're not compatible. Let's move on, okay?"

"Am I just a joke to you?" he asked her angrily.

"Do you want me to answer honestly, or do you want me to say no?"

"You know . . . you . . . you could be happier if you'd just learn to settle!" he suddenly yelled.

Everly stared at him blankly for a time. Then she said, "Screw it, I change my mind."

"What?" said sammy in surprise. "You do?" he asked.

"Yeah, but it's not what you're thinking of," she said as she raised her hand toward his face once more.

Suddenly a loud noise reverberated throughout the forest. With it came a strange, slightly sickening sensation that she'd never experienced before.

"What the hell?" she murmured.

Mistress, beware, warned Titania.

What is this feeling? Everly asked her.

Miasma. A demon is near you.

CHAPTER TWELVE

Mortal Peril

A demon . . . Everly thought to herself wonderingly. *Are you serious? There's such a thing as demons? Why am I just now hearing about this?*

It isn't a true demon, Titania said. *It's a corrupted human in the midst of apotheosis. His transformation isn't yet complete.*

All the same, should we go say hello? Maybe do some networking?

No. Their kind are beneath you, mistress. I would ordinarily recommend ignoring such a creature, but the levels of miasma it is generating suggests it is attempting a great magical undertaking.

Huh. I wonder what?

Whatever its purpose, I recommend you put an end to it before it is completed. Otherwise, Anders will likely be destroyed.

Pffft, like I care.

Lyona and all your personal belongings are there.

Oh, right. Hey, look at you, staying on the ball! You're good people, Titania.

Thank you, mistress.

Eris! Wherever you are, get back here. We've got a new neighbor, and we're gonna go say hi.

"Everly, where are you going?" asked sammy as she began to head in the direction where the miasma was strongest.

"Ah, forgot about you," she said. "I'm going to go check out whatever it was that made that noise. Be a dear and don't follow me."

"Everly, this doesn't feel right," he said urgently. "I don't think we should be wandering around right now. Something's going on!"

"Yeah, well, I'm doing it anyway. See ya," she said dismissively.

"Everly, wait!" sammy said. He took a deep, reluctant breath and clenched his fists as though he were resolving himself to act. Then he said, "Wherever you go, I'll go too, okay? I'll protect you."

Good god, this stupid piece of—

Mistress, you should frighten him away, immediately, Titania urged.

Why's that? Everly asked.

Demons strike instinctively at weakness. If sammy comes along, he'll almost certainly die.

Really? You're certain of that?

I have no doubt.

Everly turned to sammy and forced herself to smile at him, as though she were grateful to hear his unexpected offer. "Will you really protect me?" she asked him shyly.

"Y-yeah," he said in surprise, before hurriedly trying to sound more confident. "I mean, yeah," he said. "I will."

"Well, I'll be counting on you," Everly told him. "*Samuel.*"

Silence followed in the steps of the unhallowed man, like rain in the wake of a thunderhead.

Where his bare feet trod, stillness reigned.

The immense forest that surrounded him, filled to the brim with untamed and dangerous life, seemed to hold its breath in his presence. Animals of unquestionable ferociousness became meek as kittens as he passed, mewling in frozen terror thanks to his presence alone.

Should the unhallowed man linger too long in their midst, the enormity of their terror would still their hearts permanently, leaving them dead where they lay—and he *did* like to linger.

Joy danced like electric light in the rancid depths of his heart. Was there ever anyone else as blessed as the unhallowed man? Never. He was the voice of darkness itself, summoned forth to announce a renewal of the world. In the vast realms below that comprised the eternal kingdoms of hell, numberless legions of indescribable demonic horrors eagerly waited for him to speak in the voice of the Anti-God and triumphantly herald the arrival of the Seventh King: the future master of this and all worlds.

The unhallowed man wept purulent tears of stinking black fluid; to think that he, of all men, had been chosen for such a task. He'd once been a priest, a faithful member of the Temple of the Holy Will, foolishly wasting his life in slavery to the false gods who embodied justice and mercy.

He'd been a man of great faith in his youth, but age and illness had steadily eroded his conviction and over time replaced it with doubt and uncertainty.

When his final tremulous plea for healing had been ignored, when he'd become certain that his gods had truly forsaken him despite a lifetime of dedicated, self-less service, he turned his back on his former faith and chose to walk the dark path of malefic worship with the same fanatical zeal that had once defined his life as a priest.

He'd surprised himself with how easily he took to it . . . Indeed, it seemed he had been made for such pursuits! Murder, rape, the foulest rites of ritual magic, these became his new sacraments, replacing holy serenity with feverish rapacity. He'd become ravenous for all the pleasures society had always denied him.

He now delighted in the unholiest, most monstrous of deeds. At first, it was desperate self-preservation that fueled his relentless pursuits. Later, it was pure enjoyment, the race to redefine himself and to see how low he could truly fall. He rejoiced in the sights, the sounds, the blood, and the *chorus of screams.*

His mind had become a forsaken charnel house where no light ever dared dwell again; his soul, unquestionably damned beyond all hope of salvation, became a wicked seed within which germinated the antithetical lack of natural intent that could only be defined as demonhood. His very presence began to taint reality itself with the miasma of the unholy.

His real name now lost to antiquity, he wandered the world for centuries as the mad priest, the denier of faith, the devourer of the innocent.

He was the unhallowed man.

And now his greatest act of desecration was before him . . . For he had been chosen as the herald of Acedia, the Despairing—the seventh of the seven kings, the Lord of Sloth. The time of prophecy was now, when evil and good would begin their final fated clash. When hell would triumph, and the heavens would fall throughout shattered eternities.

The hour of the beast had arrived. And *he* was the flare that would ignite the firestorm.

Yes, this nameless forest, far from the sight of his enemies, this was where the unholy heraldry would begin . . .

The unhallowed man parted his septic lips and lifted the gem he had stolen from the monastery days earlier.

He then began his final prayer:

"Black Prince, beautiful wound, blinder of beauty, and denier of death. Come. Come. *Come.*"

As he spoke his horrid words, a hole began to form in the air itself, a growing rift from which shadowy figures tittered in horrifying triumph. Demons, one and all.

"Bring your legions of denial and despair, bring your locusts of disease and distortion. End this world. *Rape* this world. *Eat* this world. I beg thee, come, come, COME!"

The unhallowed man's eyes blazed with a sudden vision.

He saw a world much like his own. But in it there dwelt no magic, no grand mysteries. Instead, it was a place that operated on principles of science and logic and was filled with remarkably advanced technology.

He saw a handsome young man lying on a couch, staring at some of kind of viewing device in his hand. When the unhallowed man saw this, his heart raced with joy.

This was no mere boy—it was *him*! The Seventh King! The boy looked up, alarmed as the air around him became warped and distorted. Yes, yes, it was working! Soon his king would appear! He would arrive at this very spot, and then this world would BURN—

"Hey there, mister! What'cha doing?" asked the sweet voice of a young girl.

"Everly, what are you doing?" snapped another voice, this one belonging to the boy who accompanied her.

The unhallowed man ceased his incantation, and with a sharp wrenching sound, the portal to the abyss pulled itself shut, silencing the disappointed screams of the fallen legions therein.

Furious at the interruption, the demon priest soon glared his yellowed eyes at the two teenage mortals standing in front of him. The girl, a strikingly attractive thing, was smiling cheerfully at him as though he were about to offer her a piece of candy. The boy standing beside her looked as though he were about to die from terror.

How dare these worms disturb his sacred purpose?

"Hi!" the girl said again, while offering a friendly wave. "You're new around here, aren't you?"

"What fool interrupts the herald of hell?" hissed the outraged abomination.

"The herald of *what*?" shouted the boy.

"I'm Everly!" the girl replied, continuing to speak as though her companion hadn't said anything. "It rhymes with *Beverly*! I think that might be the only word it rhymes with. Unless you count the last two letters? In which case it also rhymes with *bee, gee, see, Christopher Lee*—"

"Cease your prattling, child. You don't seem to understand the situation you're in," said the unhallowed man. "You've committed a great sin by interrupting my work. That was a very foolish thing to do."

"Why do you say that?" asked the girl.

The unhallowed man couldn't believe this child's boldness.

Her hair was a windblown mane of blond curls. Her clothing was well-made, but dirty from hours spent outdoors engaged in some manner of physical labor. Worn leather boots covered her feet, and she carried an oak branch that she'd scrounged from somewhere to use as a walking stick.

She looked like a silly, energetic girl who enjoyed playing in the forest.

She also looked like a treat. Something he could spend a few leisurely hours hurting in the most unimaginable ways possible.

He could taste her fear-sweetened blood already.

"Don't question me, little songbird," the unhallowed man said.

"Songbird? Heh, you're funny! I'm not a *soooongbird!* I wasn't singing anything," Everly said with a delighted laugh.

"You will, though. You'll make a long and mournful cry, a special song that only *my* ears will hear. Your voice will scale to unbelievable heights. Come here. Come here and let me teach you the notes . . . "

"Everly. Everly, I really think we need to get out of here." Her companion sobbed as the fear began to consume him.

"No, boy. Stay with me. *Play* with me. Neither of you is going anywhere."

"Wooo," chittered Everly. "Wow, you're so *creepy!* You're a genuine stranger danger, aren't you?"

"You're far from the protection of your loved ones, little girl, and even farther from the grace of your feeble gods," the unhallowed man said in his unnerving whispery voice. "Choose your next words carefully; what you say next will dictate the course of the remainder of your life."

"I always say grace before eating supper." Everly snickered. "It's mostly because my mother makes me, though. I'm personally more of an agnostic than a true believer."

The unhallowed man stared at her quietly with a raised eyebrow.

"What?" said Everly defensively. "No one can really prove the existence of a god. If they're real, then they're not how we think they are. If they aren't, then it doesn't matter anyway. The only reasonable choice is agnosticism. I think most people pray just to play it safe, not because they really believe. It feels disingenuous to me."

"So . . . you question the existence of your own creators?" The unhallowed man sneered.

"Hey, if anyone created *me*, I think I'd have met them by now. I suspect I willed myself into being. I just can't remember how I did it," the girl said cockily.

"Not only ignorant but arrogant as well." The demon priest smiled. "Oh, I almost regret having to unknit you. You seem like you would have enjoyed being on our side."

"Say *whaaaaat?*" asked the girl with widening eyes.

"You are about to die in absolute horror and despair," the unhallowed man calmly replied. "You will be the first sacrifice of this, the final age! The time of the mortal races has ended! Now the Demonimachia will begin! With your agonized dying breath, you will witness their dread ascendency!"

"Oh, no!" cried Everly. "I think I'm in *bananas* trouble! sammy, take care of this bully!"

Suddenly the girl shoved her companion directly at him. The boy squealed in panic as he stumbled toward the ashen priest. For his part, the unhallowed man moved with incredible speed and had his hand around the boy's neck in an instant.

"sammy. No. Please, won't someone *saaaaave* him?" Everly asked in a poorly acted monotone. "How could you *dooooo* this?"

"There is no salvation for you or anyone else, girl," the unhallowed man said. "Soon the fires of oblivion shall consume this world—"

"Please stop. I was just being rhetorical. I really don't want to hear your manifesto," said Everly.

Was . . . was this girl *mocking* him? The unhallowed man couldn't believe it. Surely, she was just presenting a brave face. Many of his victims had, over the years. And yet everything she said, she said with a straight face. Furthermore, he didn't feel the slightest twinge of fear in her at all.

Why was she so calm? No child could contain their feelings in the presence of a true demon.

She really didn't appear to be bothered at all.

It was vexing.

"Stop your pretentious acting, girl. I'll *kill* this boy!" he said as he tightened his grip on the boy's neck.

"Would you *please?*" she said dryly in response. "Spares me the hassle."

"Stop bluffing!"

"Whatever. Listen, I normally enjoy these sorts of exchanges, but this isn't my scene, so have fun. I'd eat your snack quickly while it's fresh," she suggested, as she turned her back on the pair of them.

"Everly!" shouted the boy. "Everly!"

"Snacks can't speak, sammy! Get it right, silly."

"I'm about to open the very gates of hell!" shouted the incredulous demon.

"Cool. You do you, a'ight?"

"Bitch!" he shouted.

The unhallowed man threw sammy face-first at her like a screaming missile. She ducked.

sammy soared over her like a majestic bird whose piercing call sounded a lot like the name *Evvvvvvvvvvvverllyyyyyyyyy!* and collided with a nearby tree.

He . . . splattered. He'd been hurled with such momentum that the impact from colliding with the tree had utterly pulped him.

The demon laughed, certain now that this display of his might had finally shown the girl the lengths of her peril.

"Had you stayed in the safety of your little village," he whispered, "your friend would have lived just a little longer . . . Such a shame his life led him here to me . . . *all because of you* . . . "

"Because of me? Fuck you, *you're* the one who threw him." She laughed.

This wasn't going as he wished.

"Weep, child! Weep! Your friend has died because of your obstinance!"

"Heh, my *friend*? No. I need a friend like that like I need a polyp in my colon."

"YOU ENRAGE ME!"

"There's counseling available at the *chuuuurch*."

"Be silent!" the demon screamed, sending flecks of his spittle flying onto her face.

"Unbelievable," she muttered as she used the corner of her coat to dab at her face. "Here I am, being sociable to a new face in my neck of the woods. Not only being friendly, but also letting you indulge in some spontaneous oration! And what do I get for my kindly efforts? Facial spray! You really are a prick, huh?"

"*What* did you just say, you absurd little piglet?"

"I think you heard, Scabby. By the way, I find your self-confidence incredibly offensive. You keep acting as though I should know who you are, but you haven't done anything I would find memorable."

The fallen priest sneered at her. Over the long centuries of his blessed existence, he never tired of slowly, agonizingly instilling fear into the ignorant fools that occasionally appeared to challenge him. Saints, and heroes, and the odd knight-errant. Other demons and baser humans as well. He had faced them all, and by his own hand, brought them low.

Oh, how he would enjoy slowly defiling the flesh of this foolish girl. He would first break her mind, then her body, and then feed what remained by inches to the infernal horde waiting beyond the black gate.

He could already imagine her hysterical screams. What beautiful sounds she would make!

"I gave my name to the darkness long ago, little mortal. Now I am the unhallowed man, and to displease me is to invite ruin itself."

"Oh? Is that right? I gave up my old name too," Everly said thoughtfully. "What a surprising thing to have in common. Was yours as fair a trade as mine? You seem pretty satisfied, but I don't see why. You don't look like anything special to me."

"What are you babbling about?" he asked her, but the girl continued as though he hadn't spoken at all.

"This world is so much more interesting than where I came from. You really have no idea. I love it. I really do! Which is why, listening to you go on about how you're going to rape the land and devour the sky and stuff . . . I just find it disagreeable. I admit it: I lied earlier! I'm going to stop you after all. Also, I didn't want to say this in front of sammy, but you look disgusting."

"I . . . what?"

"Let me elaborate. I try not to judge others based on appearances, but your face looks like an anal fissure."

"*What* did you just say to me?"

"Your whole *Hellraiser* aesthetic—it's a tough sell for modern audiences. You know, pain and pleasure and demonic extremes, and all that crap; it's all very *niche*, isn't it? It really feels like nothing but diminishing returns. That's the problem with horror stories. They're over reliant on gore and jump scares. Once you get used to them, it's all *very* predictable."

Everly lifted her branch and slapped it against her palm menacingly while glaring at the demon. "By the way, did you really just call me a *little mortal?* Do you even realize how condescending you sound? Aren't you just begging for a proper kicking by speaking to me like that?"

"*What?*"

"Whaaaat? *Whaaaaat? Whaaaat?* Is that the only word you know? I just said you're a condescending old shit, and my mom is going to be laundering bits of you off my coat by tomorrow."

The unhallowed man didn't respond with words. With speed too quick to be detected by mortal sight, he vanished and reappeared inches away from the girl. His taloned fingers drove forth in a violent thrust that ended with them embedded in her chest. From there, he flexed his grip and pulled out his victim's heart through the hole he'd drilled into her.

Without sparing her another glance, the unhallowed man shoved her body away with such force that he sent it crashing into a tree. No, *through* the tree. He'd embedded her in it.

Savoring his treat, the unhallowed man began licking the blood off the heart, running his tongue over the exposed veins and the fresh, flavorful taste of its tender meat. Luxuriating in it, he rubbed it over his face before greedily stuffing it inside his mouth and slowly swallowing it, happily guiding the bulbous wad down his throat.

"Wonderful," he moaned, his eyes closed, lost in the pleasure of the squalid act.

"Was it *really*, though?" asked Everly wryly.

The unhallowed man opened his eyes just in time to see Everly's tree branch connect with his face. Like his victim before him, he was taken off his feet and sent careening through the forest. After finally skidding to a complete stop through the mud, he gingerly rose to his feet, frightened by his inability to sense the attack coming.

Dampness coated the unhallowed man's brow. He wiped at it and saw blood. That was nothing new. But wait . . . This was impossible. His face wasn't healing! It always healed! He was immortal. The whole point of his foul allegiances was that he couldn't be hurt! This shouldn't be happening!

"What . . . what *are* you?" he screamed, as Everly slowly approached him, still holding her branch.

"A perky little angel with a heart filled with honey," came the amused reply.

"I—I killed you!"

"*You* killed *me*? Do I look dead to you? Wow, Eris said your brain was buttery, but I didn't know it was *that* bad."

"Are you a paladin? An arch-templar? No mere champion of the gods will stop me—"

"*Blaaah, blaaaah, blah*," Everly interrupted. "Firstly, I'm not a champion of the gods. Didn't I just say I was agnostic? Please don't push your beliefs on other people in a public space!"

"How are you *still* alive?!" the unhallowed man demanded to know.

"Uh, duh? Because you never hit me? I only let you see what you wanted. Sorry about your hand by the way. I've talked to Eris before about making people self-cannibalize, but she's as pretty as a unicorn and as stubborn as a mule."

The unhallowed man looked down when a sudden pain flared in his right hand. He then saw that he'd bitten off a chunk of it, which included two fingers, leaving a spurting open wound behind in the absence of his flesh. That was what he'd been eating when he thought he'd swallowed the girl's heart . . .

"I will not be challenged by you!" he screamed, now made unhinged by rage. "I AM THE UNHALLOWED MAN—"

"Shortly to be renamed *the unhallowed corpse*." The girl snorted. "Hey, was that a good one-liner? It *was*, wasn't it? Don't be afraid to share your feedback. I'm not afraid of constructive criticism—"

The sound of ripping cloth filled the air as the unhallowed man transformed. His body distorted and extended as multiple arms and legs burst through his flesh. In mere seconds, where once was a man, a scuttling giant nightmare now appeared: a spider the size of a cottage, covered in shaggy gray fur, with corrosive poison dripping down its foul fangs. Demonic runes glowed around its obscene form as it prepared to strike.

"I know not where you come from, foolish warrior, but I shall make such a feast of you! This final futile defense of humanity ends now! Behold my glory and offer me your warm blood—"

A great hand of blazing stone burst from the earth and caught the spider in its grip. Massive though it was, the demonic arachnid was a miniscule thing compared to the godly fist that now held it tight. The monster screamed and wept helplessly as it was burned and crushed.

"No tears, please. It's a waste of good suffering," said Everly, directly quoting Pinhead.

The unhallowed man ignored her request and shrieked for what seemed like ages, before finally falling limp.

Once its corpse had been squeezed dry and nicely crisped, the hand flung it away to the treetops before dispersing back into the earth.

Now Everly stood alone.

* * *

Did I please you, mistress? Titania asked Everly as they began walking home.

"You were great," Everly said sincerely. "I loved it. A big hand for squashing a big bug. You're very practical."

He was nauseating, Eris chimed in. *Mortals who betray their own natures for an attempt at immortality are irredeemable. Such fools deserve a more terrible ending.*

"Yeah, I didn't like that guy at all. He may have been a fellow villain, but his aesthetics were repulsive. The pedo vibes didn't help either, yuck."

As you say, master. Those without style should be annihilated.

"Well, I never actually said that, but I like your enthusiasm."

So, what is Hellraiser, *anyway?*

"Something that worked better in the eighties when people were less open about their kinks."

Their idle conversation continued as they wandered along home.

Everly didn't remember about sammy until the next morning.

CHAPTER THIRTEEN

Disappointment

The Eastern Temple had many choirs that toiled in its service, talented believers in the light of the elementals, who used holy magic for a variety of purposes that served the temple's interests. The choir of seers, for example, existed to warn of dangerous future threats before they occurred.

The seers were so effective at their task that Lady Sylvain allowed knowledge of their existence to spread throughout the world as a deterrent for many of the temple's dangerous enemies.

After all, what fools would dare challenge the order if they knew their attacks would be predicted?

However, the seers were only one of the organization's many weapons. Another more utilitarian branch of the tree was the choir of sending, which used the incredible art of translocation. While there were only nine members of the seers, the senders numbered in the hundreds. Each member possessed a minor talent for teleportation that allowed them to summon and transpose small items through force of will.

By combining their gifts under the direction of Lady Sylvain, those minor talents became an essential tool for the order. By working together, they could send anyone anywhere in the world if the members were each able to properly visualize it.

Anywhere in the world.

Sylvain and Alec stood ready in their armor. Accompanying them would be Lord Tyrnos with twenty ordained knights and fifty men-at-arms, with many more on standby, depending on the needs of the battle. Reinforcements could only be sent gradually, to keep the senders from tiring.

The moment had now come. The seers had sung their final warning, and now it was up to them to respond.

The target was a legendary fiend known as the unhallowed man, an almost mythic figure of darkness that many disregarded as a mere folktale, a silly boogeyman of superstition. The fallen priest was destined to open the black gate and release an endless demonic wave to wash over the poor world.

Unfortunately, the unhallowed man was no myth, and he had every intention of performing a mass demonic summoning. He had to be stopped, no matter the cost. As a former member of the temple, he was also a stain on their honor that needed to be erased.

Tracking down a fiend of the unhallowed man's power was ordinarily an extraordinary effort, even for the order. Older demons such as he had long ago mastered hiding their presence from the eyes of their enemies. But even so, the order had a fresh trail to follow and the determination to stop him.

The temple's hunters eventually discovered his location.

Their spirit elemental users revealed that the unhallowed man hadn't moved for hours. Whether that meant he had started the ritual of unbinding or was merely taking a rest, this was the order's opportunity to strike!

Once the information was psychically relayed to the senders, they were ready to begin.

The castle and the choirs were prepared for a long, protracted battle. Many were ready to give their lives that day. Such was the price heroes often paid, sadly.

Sylvain turned to the conductor of the senders and nodded. "It's time."

The assembled priests knelt before her. "May the elementals light your path to victory, Lady Sylvain. Glory to mankind!" said their leader.

"Salvation to us all!" Sylvain said, concluding the ritual parting.

"All right, lads!" yelled the boisterous Lord Tyrnos. "Shields up, swords out! Time to be about our bloody business! Where we go, the very fiends of hell may have gathered against us. Let's show those evil bastards what a mistake that was, eh? GLORY TO MANKIND!"

"RRRRAAAAAAAARRRRRH!" his fighters screamed back with bloodthirsty zeal.

The fear was still in them, but now it was pushed back by their fondness for their cocky young leader and their desire to prove themselves worthy of him. Sylvain smiled in appreciation for what Tyrnos had done. As powerful as she was, the strength that Sylvain represented was beyond that which could be called *mortal.*

As such, she would always appear enigmatic to her followers, distant from them. Unapproachable to an ordinary person, no matter how greatly they admired her.

It was different with Tyrnos. He was a fighting man who'd earned his spurs from the lowest ranks. A son of mercenaries who'd climbed his way up the ladder of success, one rung at a time, through sheer force of will and charisma. Tyrnos represented the dream of countless lowborn: that they too could become a hero of legend and fight alongside the likes of Sylvain.

He showed that there were no barriers to advancement when one served the true temple.

Of course, that was all a carefully constructed fiction designed to inspire their lowborn followers.

In truth, Tyrnos was the result of hundreds of years of selective breeding. An ongoing experiment by the order to produce the ultimate human warrior. He was a fail-safe, designed to stand in place of Sylvain and the senior leadership if some crisis left them unable to perform their duties.

Some of Tyrnos's ancestors had been conductors, although he himself hadn't inherited the ability to bond with an elemental. Everything about him, from his rough-hewn mannerisms to that silly accent, was a deliberate affectation programmed into him since birth by some of the finest temple mages of the age.

He was a creation. A manufactured existence.

He didn't even know.

Sylvain was greatly troubled by the necessity of using Tyrnos and others like him in such a manner. But such deceptions were necessary for the greater good. If Tyrnos knew, he would surely agree.

She hoped he would.

"Forward!" commanded Sylvain, after everyone was settled into place. The chanting of the sending choir began to reverberate throughout the massive room. Large as it was, it could only contain fifty men at a time. Thus, it always took a while for an entire army to be dispatched, depending on its size.

The walls began to glow with bright azure luminosity, with images on them beginning to take mist-covered shape. Before long, the mists on the imagery pulled away, revealing countless trees . . . Perhaps a forest? Yes, exactly that! A large forest, somewhere in middle Winstead, here in the lower echelons of reality.

The sudden lurching in Sylvain's stomach warned her to close her eyes before a sudden flash of blinding light filled the entire sending room. When it passed, the warmer temperature of the air and the rich scent of the earth and trees told her they were now outside.

"Alec, with me!" she said, running forward with her sword and shield drawn. Her squire followed at once, easily keeping pace despite his heavy armor and massive spiked maul. The power of the elementals surged through them, transforming them from mere mortals to weapons of divine retribution.

This world did not belong to lowly man, nor the foul denizens of hell. No, it belonged to the elementals! All would kneel and be reborn in their divine glory. Those who refused would face judgment, but those who realized the truth would know salvation.

There would be peace, prosperity, and happiness for everyone, everywhere.

Just as there had been during the reign of her father.

This chaotic era of warfare, inefficient democracies, warring kings, and selfish oligarchs would soon be ended. The failures of the past would be swept aside, and the world would be returned to a more civilized time when the people were guided with strong but merciful leadership.

Once the true temple had completed their good works in the nations beyond this land, they would converge their forces on this continent, and as one united front, they would purge the false temple of light created by her treacherous sister and lead her deceived followers to the truth.

Then they would set mankind on the correct path. They would never fail in their obligations again. Humanity would be tamed, and the elementals would be venerated and given their proper worship.

But such glories were meant for the future. For now, the malevolent forces of hell had to be dealt with!

"For glory!" cried Sylvain as she ran forward and swung her sword, filling the clearing with pristine, natural light.

"Let's go, BOYS!" bellowed Tyrnos as his men stomped behind him.

They made for quite the sight: Sylvain and Alec in their gleaming regalia, the reverent knights who followed behind them, and the dozens of ordinary soldiers trying to keep pace with their masters. All gathered in place, prepared for the fight of their lives against . . .

Well, not very bloody much at all, eh? Sylvain thought.

The darkened forest they charged into was empty. A few trees had cracks and bent branches, and there was a distinct scent of burnt meat, but aside from that, there was nothing there. No demon lord. No portal to the infernal realms. No hellish army to combat.

Nothing.

"My lady?" asked Alec in confusion. "Were we sent to the correct place?"

Sylvain carefully studied their surroundings, somewhat confused herself. "I think so?"

Alec stared at her, bewildered. In all their time together, Sylvain had never appeared to be anything but utterly assured. Confident in all things. This was the first time he had ever seen his master confused.

"Hoy! Lady Sylvain!" called out Tyrnos, loud and irritated. "Dare I ask what the hell is happening here? Not exactly the legions of the damned me an' the lads were promised, yeah?"

"Calm yourself, Lord Tyrnos," Sylvain said, trying to keep him from breaking her concentration.

"Have the seers gone mental or something? Sending us out to the middle of nowhere? Should we replace them with fresher offerings? If so, I wouldn't mind recycling a few of them to warm my bed. If they can't do the one thing that they're supposedly good at, we may as well put them to better use—"

"Enough!" Alec said angrily to the knight. "This is Lady Sylvain that you address! Show her the respect she is due, or you'll answer to me!"

Tyrnos's face reddened at the squire's words. "So, the pup thinks he's big enough to bare his fangs, eh? Considering your power comes from her scraps, you're bold to make threats to a real warrior."

"You may be a real warrior, but your behavior ill suits the dignity of a knight," rebuked Alec.

"How much of a virgin *are* you, kid?" Tyrnos snorted. "Stop sucking up! She's not going to bite your apple no matter how hard you polish it, so piss off."

"You vulgar—"

"Both of you. Enough," Sylvain said to them.

Sylvain was slightly amused to see that Tyrnos's anger wasn't feigned. He was genuinely offended by being corrected by Alec. Sylvain had long suspected that Tyrnos was frustrated by his inability to use magic and jealous that he hadn't been selected to be her squire.

Although he'd achieved the rank of sword king, *harada* was a mortal power that paled in comparison to the blessings of the elementals. He could only destroy but never create, thus he would always be a lesser member of the upper echelon, no matter how strong he grew.

It was unfortunate, but such was his fate.

"Let him fight his own battles," Tyrnos snapped at her. "If you keep his hand tied to your apron, he'll never grow."

He was silenced by Sylvain gently placing a hand on his shoulder and applying light pressure.

"Tyrnos," she said gently.

Tyrnos stiffened slightly at the intonation in her voice, and he immediately backed down in embarrassment. Poor Tyrnos. He truly was dutiful, and his loyalty was without question. But despite the efforts of his teachers and martial instructors, his personality was like that of an aggressive dog. When his energy wasn't properly managed, he snapped at everyone.

Sylvain had once held high hopes for his future, but his difficult personality, combined with the elementals' indifference to him, made him unsuitable for greater responsibilities. His present posting would be the height of his career. She suspected he now realized this.

Poor, pitiful man.

Still, Tyrnos wasn't wrong to point out that a mistake had been made.

The unhallowed man should have been there; *a host of demons* should have been there. The choir of seers had never been proven wrong before. And yet . . . here stood the results. There was nothing here. Very disappointing. Very frustrating.

It would be a shame if they had to dismiss the current generation of seers, but the order depended on them for their accuracy. If they were wrong about as momentous an event as this, then they could be wrong about other things as well. If they weren't perfect, then the order itself would be endangered. Their greatest strength had always been their knowledge of the future.

How could any principle of uncertainty be tolerated if they were to succeed in their long-term goal of uniting humanity?

"I've discovered a dead body!" one of their spearmen cried out. After they rushed to his side, they saw the remains of what was barely recognizable as a young man. It seemed he'd been brutally smashed into the center of a tree.

"Just a boy, damn it," Tyrnos muttered, disgusted by this act of murder.

Sylvain walked forward, lost in thought, no longer paying attention to her surroundings, when suddenly Alec shouted, "Master! Above you!"

Startled, Sylvain jumped back as Alec ran forward and hurled his mace into the canopy above them. It spun forth, a deadly missile guided by Alec's unerring aim, and quickly connected with something on the tops of the trees. Something that must have been congested with unholy miasma. The instant Alec's holy weapon struck it, an explosive release of energy occurred that knocked the foul thing to the ground.

It was the charred remains of a gigantic arachnid.

"Did I kill it?" Alec asked, his voice raised in excitement.

Sylvain, her own sword drawn, cautiously stepped forward, poked the thing here and there, and perceived no motion in its body. "Peace, apprentice. It's already dead."

"Look!" said Tyrnos excitedly. He reached low and picked up a strange glowing gem. "Isn't this . . . It is! The summoning stone! The one stolen from the monastery!"

Sylvain held out her hand. After Tyrnos placed the gem in her palm, she closely examined it and saw that he was correct. "Interesting. The demon's entire scheme would have hinged upon always keeping this close to him. What could have so pressed the creature that it would have dropped it in its scramble to attack?"

"By the elementals," said Alec, as he studied the dead obscenity. "Mistress, the seers weren't wrong! This is an abyssal lord of the fifth rank! Look at the runes," he said, gesturing to the markings that coated the disgusting monster's fur. Sylvain stepped toward it, reading them as well.

Interesting. Truly, Alec's eye had been made keen by his studies.

"Indeed," Sylvain said. "Very good, squire. But that rune has been made incomplete by the wound this creature received. Observe." She knelt, grabbed a fold of the monster's flesh, and pulled it closer to the spider's ruined abdomen. When combined, the sigil no longer read *fifth*. It read *ninth*.

"A lord of the ninth rank." Alec shuddered. Even Tyrnos was startled by this revelation. It had long been suspected that the unhallowed man had begun to ascend to the greater tiers of demon kind, but to think he had gestated to the ninth rank while still dwelling in the material realm?

It was unthinkable.

"A mightier foe than we realized," Sylvain said quietly. "Well, Lord Tyrnos? Do you still believe the seers need to be dismissed?"

"This can't be true," the other man said stubbornly. "Demons always lie, even in death! There's no chance something this powerful could be running free without our knowing."

"There's only one way to truly know," Sylvain said reluctantly.

"My lady, there's no need for you to do this," said Alec after he realized her intention. "Lord Tyrnos is likely correct. There's no reason to put yourself through the pain—"

"Alec, my squire, I appreciate your protectiveness. But we *must* know how powerful our enemies are becoming. Any pain I now suffer will only contribute to the greater good."

Alec nodded respectfully and stepped back. Such a dear boy. So understanding. Her fondness for him grew daily. If only she could . . .

No. There was no point in wishing for something that could never be.

Sylvain began to pray.

"I invoke thee, the hidden master of this world, the god who stands above all other gods, who leads the faithful to perfection and strengthens those resolved to commit to thy will and thy way. Grant me the knowledge I seek, oh, lord of mysteries! Open my eyes to the truth of all things! Activate . . . [**Appraisal**]."

Sylvain turned her gaze to the dead demon and yelled in pain as knowledge began flooding her mind.

Name: ???
Race: Lesser Demon
CLS: Blood Druid
LVL: 9
ATK: 20 (v)
DEF: 15 (v)
MAG: 30
SKILLS: Silent Step
LV3. Unarmed Combat
LV2. Aura of Miasma
LV4. Advanced Shapeshifting
LV1. Advanced Cloak Presence
LV1 Dominate lesser LV2.

"Ahhh!" Sylvain cried out as she collapsed from the pain into Alec's arms.

Her heart raced in sudden fear. Doom had been far nearer than she'd realized! The unhallowed man really *had* been of the ninth rank! The truth was irrefutable. The eye of appraisal never lied. It was a gift from the master of the cosmos, the distant and all-powerful ruler of existence by whose design all life functioned.

This supreme being was a secret known only to the most senior members of the temple. Even his name was never spoken aloud for fear knowledge of it would disseminate to the common man and once more tempt his wrath.

The name of this god was *System.*

Sylvain rubbed a hand across her aching brow. [**Appraisal**] was an amazing ability indeed. But Lord System demanded a heavy price for its use. Of course, that was as it should be. Mortals should always hesitate to seek the knowledge possessed by heaven.

"I'm afraid I was correct. This demon was of the ninth."

Even Tyrnos was silenced by her words.

"I apologize, my lady," he said a few minutes later, after she'd recovered. "My ignorance shames me. To think our enemy had grown so powerful . . . It chills me to realize this. And to take the form of a spider as well? I can ill conceive of a more terrifying sight! In life, this monster must have been an absolute horror. Praise the elementals for destroying it."

"The elementals?" Alec asked in confusion. "What do you mean?"

"Use your head, boy," Tyrnos said scornfully. "Lady Sylvain would have had to summon her elemental lord in order to take on a beast of the ninth ranking. Surely, it would have been a battle like those fought in the imperial age, and even with you by her side, there would have been no guarantee of our victory."

"The elementals would have surely come to our aid if she requested their help," Alec said.

"That's what I'm *saying*, boy. It's obvious what happened here: The elementals intervened and dispatched this fiend on our behalf. *This* is a miracle."

Tyrnos turned to his men and raised his shield to them. "We are blessed! We are redeemed! We are honored! THE GODS HAVE SEEN US!"

Sylvain was uncertain of that conclusion, even as the voices of the men roared in jubilation.

Always with the cheers and screaming with that lot, honestly. Good for morale, bad for my sense of hearing. Fine, whatever. Placate them however you must, she thought to herself. *But I do doubt very much that the greater elementals intervened in this matter. It doesn't . . . feel right.*

No, we need another set of eyes on this. Someone more educated.

She knew exactly who to turn to.

CHAPTER FOURTEEN

The Minotaur

Simon Thelmar was one of the few mages who originated in Winstead that the Eastern Temple was willing to employ.

Those who wielded the power of the elementals without believing in their divinity were generally distrusted by the faithful. Such people were seekers of knowledge, but their actions weren't tempered by a belief in a power greater than themselves. They were frustratingly haphazard in their pursuits.

Unfortunately, they often refused to be corrected and reacted poorly to being told how misinformed they often were. That obstinance made them extremely dangerous. Sylvain sometimes worried that they would have to be purged when the time came for Winstead to join the true faith.

She hoped they would one day see the light, of their own volition.

Still, the skills they possessed had their uses.

Simon, for instance, could study the various energies that permeated the realms to determine their point of origin. He could even measure the level of strength of beings that wielded magic, though with nowhere near the accuracy of **[Appraisal]**. It was still a useful expertise for when you needed to know how dangerous the creatures you hunted were.

Simon had been sent along with Sylvain's group to provide them with a threat assessment of any foes they encountered in these woods. Even though there had been no fighting today, he could still provide an invaluable service.

After all, studying a corpse would be far easier than a living opponent in the heat of battle.

"Simon," Sylvain said warmly to him as she removed her helmet and held it at her waist.

"Ma'am," Simon replied, his voice thick with that odd accent of his. Simon was a strange man. He claimed one of his ancestors had been summoned to this world from a province of the realms beyond, called "Texas." He also claimed to be descended from a tribe of minotaurs, which he referred to as "Cowboys."

Sylvain found his fantasies of sharing a heritage with another world fascinating and enjoyed speaking with him. It was very rare to encounter someone descended from a spirit-beast ancestor who wasn't ashamed of his origins. He seemed so outwardly human too!

Did his hood hide his horns? Was he cannibalistic like many minotaurs were?

How had his maternal ancestors survived mating with bulls?

There were so many things she wanted to know! Ah, but now was not the time to indulge in such idle musings.

Sylvain needed answers to the questions that mattered.

She stood beside Simon as he inspected the corpse, noting that even his deeply tanned skin paled at the sight of the dead spider. He closed his eyes and held a hand before him, muttering incantations beneath his breath as he focused on sights that only he could see, images that only his disciplined mind could perceive. As he spoke, Sylvain noticed that the large gold watch he wore around his neck (a gaudy adornment in her opinion) began to lightly glow.

Ah, that must have been a focusing charm. Many mages developed them as a means of magnifying their personal strength. Winstead's mages were heretical, but they had developed many clever techniques to compensate for their lack of power in comparison to those sworn to the true faith.

Still, as fascinating as it was to watch him work, Sylvain wondered exactly what it was that Simon now saw.

Eris had been enjoying a peaceful slumber when she suddenly felt an annoying buzzing within her mind that disturbed her rest.

Night had fallen, and her dear master, Everly, was asleep in her bed. Titania, as always, assumed her place at their master's side, guarding her from any potential physical threats while she rested. Eris did the same, but her purview was mental or spiritual attacks.

Since her presence alone was enough to divert anything sensible enough to realize the dangers of angering her, Eris often had nothing to do and had also fallen into the habit of sleeping at night. Her mistress seemed to enjoy it, so Eris had decided to try it out for herself.

She liked it. She liked it very much.

She liked it so much that having it interrupted quickly ignited within her a murderous fury.

Eris was a creature of the mind. Unlike her patient younger sister, who embodied the unyielding strength of the Earth, spirit elementals were known for their emotional volatility. It took a powerful mind to calm them and keep them focused. With Everly asleep, there was no one around to soothe her anger at being bothered.

The annoying buzzing continued in her ears. It wasn't an actual fly; creatures of the flesh couldn't even touch her. Even so, verminous insects knew better than to go near Eris because she loathed them. Such life-forms had an innate wild instinct for self-preservation that many of the so-called civilized races had discarded long ago on their evolutionary paths.

No, this wasn't a gnat. Well, it *was*, but not a literal one. This was the telltale buzzing of a weak little mage attempting to scry on her location.

Scrying on the great Eris, proud servant of the even greater Lady Everly!

Honestly, did this opportunistic fool have any desire to live?

He must have somehow learned that Everly had recently experienced her first ranking advancement. That pitiful demon may not have been any challenge, but his death had allowed her mistress to advance beyond the first rank. She'd jumped directly to level three. No wonder she'd suddenly become so tired.

Tomorrow, when Everly awoke, she'd be able to draw upon much more of the sisters' power. Eris and Titania were very proud of her. Although Everly's control had been refined and perfected through countless hours of mental training, finally taking a life, especially one so potent with experience as that demon's had been, would allow her to begin unlocking her true potential.

But on this glorious day, while Everly rested, weary from her triumph, this coward dared to make a play against her?

This deserved a response.

A *firm* one.

"Sister, lend me the use of your power," she commanded Titania.

"For what purpose?"

"I need to teach someone a lesson, but our mistress has forbidden me from destroying any mortal minds without her permission."

"This won't get me in trouble, will it?"

"It'll be fine. Just our little secret. *Pleeease?*"

"Oh . . . all right. You do often know what's best."

"Yes, I do. Thank you for your help."

"It's nothing."

Eris smiled wickedly. Her adorable little sister was such an agreeable thing. What a terrifying place the world would become if she ever decided to think for herself.

Eris raised a hand, now imbued with Titania's incredible strength, then made a symbolic gesture by raising her middle finger. She then sent her curse racing to whoever had bothered her.

It wasn't the kindest response to an act that might have been performed in ignorance, but if you sought kindness from the likes of Eris, you clearly deserved whatever life sent your way.

That plus a swift kick to the genitals, for good measure.

After a few short minutes of whatever it was he was doing, Simon's watch flashed unnaturally bright, then burst into flame. And even as that happened, the hand he held out before the dead demon exploded in a shower of bone and meat.

"Holy shit!" screamed the Texan, as he rolled on the ground, attempting to simultaneously remove the burning piece of metal that was swiftly scarring his chest and neck, while also stopping the bleeding of his ruined arm. Sylvain was at his side immediately, pulling the watch off and tossing it aside, then healing his wounded arm with a quick application of elemental power.

He cried like a child in her arms; agony was stamped all over his face. She had him carried away by medics to rest and recover, bewildered by what she had just witnessed. His crying could be heard all throughout the area.

What the hell had just happened?

Later in the day, after he had sufficiently calmed down, she returned to Simon's side, determined to have her answers.

"Someone did this to me," Simon muttered. He was lying on a blanket in the dirt. He looked bad. He looked *very* bad.

It didn't escape Sylvain's notice that the burns she had healed were still raw and painful looking. Her elemental light should have removed even the slightest bit of scarring. Instead, it was all she could do to keep his skin pinched together. Sad as it was to say, this poor son of a minotaur had cast his final spell.

"It hurts so *baaaaad*," he moaned.

Sylvain gently stroked his forehead, smiling sadly at him, wishing she could stop his suffering. But also wishing he would get on with providing her with answers. Alec and Tyrnos stood at her side, each eager to learn as well.

"What were you doing, Simon?" Sylvain asked him softly.

"Nothing! Nothing that deserved . . . this! I was just trying to measure the level of the primordial . . . "

"What's a primordial?" asked Tyrnos.

Sylvain gave him an annoyed frown, before turning back to the dying mage and asking him herself. "What is a primordial?"

"It's a primordial elemental . . . *POWERFUL*. It must be ancient . . . It must be! Very . . . very strong. It combined fire and earth . . . No human mage alive could survive bonding with it . . . BUT SOMEONE DID! Could be them . . . COULD BE PANETHEONS! They have one! Incredible weapon. K-kills anything. *Killing me*," he groaned, pointing at his horrid wounds.

"And you suspect that the unhallowed man was slain by this . . . 'primordial'?" Sylvain asked carefully. This was the first she had ever heard of such a being. The most powerful elementals dwelled only in the astral realm. None with strength like he described could possibly exist in this world.

And he claimed a mere human had bonded with it?

What was a Panetheon?

Whatever they were, Sylvain suspected she wouldn't have learned that word if Simon's wits weren't so scattered by pain. Panetheons . . . could that mean the elves? It wouldn't surprise her. When it came to magic, her full-blooded kin had always known more than anyone else. But they hoarded their knowledge from those they considered inferior, like mortals. They even scorned their own mixed-race descendants.

The elves irritated Sylvain greatly. As the leader of the temple, she wielded more authority and power than any of them had ever known in their endless lives. But because she was *impure,* they considered her unworthy of it. Out of all the many races of the world, she considered them alone unworthy of the elementals' grace.

"H-had to have been. Nothing else fits. A spell l-like that leaves signs. I saw them. A-and I thought, if I used my astral sight, I c-could find them . . . find its master and replace him . . . "

"Why would you want to do that, Simon?"

"My ancestors aren't from this world . . . I wanted to see it! To see our true home! But I need power to do it! I knew it would be dangerous . . . but I had to take the chance. I had to! With astral sight, you can see things. You can learn the level of its power by counting the rings of it like a *treeeeeeeee . . .* "

He began to laugh then, despite his wounds. It was a groan at first, which began to rise in pitch until it became a hyena-like hysterical keening.

More of these fantasies about different worlds, Sylvain thought sadly. Simon had risked this much for such an insane delusion?

This poor, foolish man.

"Simon," Sylvain said, as she stroked his hair. "Simon, please control yourself. You said you could see the level of this being's power? Like rings on a tree. Is that right? Simon, please tell us! Simon? What level was it?"

A part of her dreaded knowing the answer to her question. Learning that the unhallowed man had been of the ninth rank was already a big enough blow to her confidence. If he hadn't been slain by this unknown force, there was a very good chance she would have died today. Still, she had to know . . .

"Simon. What. Level. Was it?"

Simon tittered madly once more, before finally screeching:

"Hands off! THIRTEEN! Hands off! THIRTEEN! THIRTEEN! THIRTEEEEEEN—THIRTEEEEEEEN— THIRTEEEEEEEEEEN!"

Thirteen? What did that even mean?

This primordial user or whatever, whom Sylvain had never even heard of, stood at the thirteenth rank? *Thirteen* was a level? That made no sense at all. Even she, the master of the true temple, who had dwelt in the presence of the radiant one and could commune with Lord System himself, even she could only cast miracles from the eighth rank of ascension.

That was power enough to shatter an entire city in a day, perhaps destroy an entire nation in a week, if she called upon her elemental lord. Yet there was someone out there who could control a power *five steps* above that?!

No. No, there was *not*.

"He's blinded by delusion and pain. End his suffering, Alec," Sylvain said, stepping away from the madman.

Startled, Alec looked from her to the dying man before quickly nodding. He raised his maul and forcefully brought it down on Simon's forehead, bringing the poor man the peace he desperately needed.

Sylvain nodded her gratitude to Alec.

"So, what was that about?" Tyrnos asked as they followed Sylvain outside.

"He cracked, simple as that," Sylvain said dismissively. "Power such as Simon described is a fantasy. Perhaps these . . . *primordial* elementals may exist. But if they do, they dwell only in the heavens as gods. It is blasphemous to believe a mere human could be bonded to such a majestic being. Ridiculous."

After all, if anyone would be permitted such power, it would be me alone. I am the daughter of the radiant one!

"But the demon was of the ninth rank—"

"What of it? That doesn't mean some celestial warrior happened to be in the area and swatted it away for the fun of it!"

"Then what destroyed Simon's hand and burned him?" the knight asked. "I mean, *something* reacted to him reaching out—"

"Tyrnos!" Sylvain shouted. Her patience with him had finally run out. "Do you realize how ridiculous all this sounds? Get ahold of yourself and use the logic we had bred into you."

"Huh?" Tyrnos asked in confusion. "What does that mean?"

Damn it, I'm reacting too emotionally. Sylvain fumed inwardly.

"I meant to say, 'Use the logic the temple has instilled in you.' If you think about this sensibly, you'll realize Simon wounded himself. That man always teetered on the brink of a mental collapse. Clearly, today was the day he finally succumbed to madness. We will pray for him, but we can't take his ravings seriously."

"Of . . . course," said Tyrnos, after he gave due consideration to her words. "Yeah, that makes sense."

"Good. Now focus. I have orders for you," Sylvain said.

"What would you have me do, my lady?"

"Kill any rumors that may arise from today's events. Kill them all as thoroughly as Alec killed Simon. Have the servants who tended to Simon's wounds gathered up for mental repurposing. This is a precaution in case he said any-thing not meant for them to know. Then I want you to seek out any of Simon's acquaintances that he might have shared his twisted theories with and do the same. The word 'primordial' dies today and shall never be spoken again."

"My lady, why go to such lengths?" asked Alec reluctantly.

"Because I suspect my sister has a hand in this, squire. Schemes like this would appeal to her cruel sense of play."

"Are you certain?" asked Tyrnos. "My lady, this seems so—"

"Do you feel overwhelmed by the mandate I have given you, knight?" Sylvain said in a voice heavy with scorn. "Such reticence ill suits your purpose! Stop questioning me and carry out my orders. Now!"

Tyrnos said nothing in response. He bowed stiffly, then turned to one of his men and began barking out commands of his own.

Sylvain paid him no further mind. Instead, she turned to her squire and said, "Alec, I need you to work on something for me. We can't stay in Winstead in these numbers, not without risking drawing the attention of the false temple. We'll soon have to withdraw. But I intend for you to remain here."

"What?" asked Alec. "B-but Lady Sylvain, my place is by your side—"

"Your place is wherever you are needed, Alec. And I need you *here*. I want you to investigate a nearby village that one of Tyrnos's scouts discovered. That's likely where that dead boy lived. I need you to discover what his connection to the unhallowed man was."

"But wasn't he just a victim of the beast?"

"Perhaps he was and perhaps he wasn't. I suspect there's a piece we're missing here. You shall be the one who seeks it out. Can I rely on you?"

Alec dropped to one reverent knee before her. "Anything you need, I will provide. My life belongs to you."

Sylvain smiled in gratitude at her squire's words.

Alec, her faithful servant.

Alec, her faithful dog.

CHAPTER FIFTEEN

Identity

One week later.

I t's the strangest thing," Everly said softly as she beheld her own reflection in the small mirror she held. "This is the first time I've ever noticed, but . . . when I enter the memory palace, I no longer look like my old self. I look as I currently am. I guess that means I really *am* Everly now. Kerri's gone."

"Why do you sound so somber, mistress?" asked Eris. "Isn't that a good thing? It means that you genuinely accept yourself as you now are. Not many people are fortunate enough to have such an unclouded self-image."

"You're probably right," Everly said. "But the thing is . . . I never really minded *being* Kerri. I think there was value in remembering how it felt to see things from her perspective. But she's gone now, first in body and now in spirit. I wonder if I'm still her reincarnation or if I'm just the thing that replaced her?"

The three of them were currently seated at a table in the memory palace. Everly, who was dressed in jeans and an old Pantera T-shirt, was joined by her servants, who'd manifested in physical forms of their own for the meeting she'd called.

Titania was wearing a white summer dress, which made her look like she was prepared for a Sunday picnic. Eris had manifested as an elven woman with blue-colored hair, wearing loose-fitting gray druidic robes.

She always has to stand out, doesn't she? Everly thought mildly to herself.

"I've always known you as Mistress Everly," said Titania with a shrug "But *Everly* is just the name your mother gave you. What matters most is if you've accepted that name or not. Are you Everly? Or is there someone else you yet wish to become?"

Everly had to smile at that. "Titania," she said. "Your deceptively big brain is occasionally terrifying."

"Why wouldn't my brain be as terrifying as the rest of me? I'm very powerful."

"Humble too."

"Thank you for noticing, mistress."

"This is such an interesting design," Eris said as she observed the large meeting room Everly had created for them. She'd envisioned it as a literal place among the heavens, with the Earth located far beneath them. "Very spacious. And the seats are extremely comfortable, mistress. That was a thoughtful detail to remember."

"I once read somewhere that the chairs used in team meetings for jobs in management are deliberately uncomfortable to force people to pay attention. I thought that sounded stupid, so I deliberately went out of my way to make these as pleasant to sit on as possible," Everly said as she swiveled around in her chair, which looked like a big fluffy cloud.

"Isn't that just like our mistress, to be so considerate of others?" asked Titania. "Comfortable chairs during an important meeting? That's just proof of her far-sightedness. No detail is too minor to escape her eye."

"Thank you both for the compliments. It's appreciated," Everly said to the pair of them. "But there's something I've been meaning to speak with you both about for some time."

"I'm all ears," Eris said as her ears literally perked up with interest.

"Please share your wisdom with us, mistress," Titania said eagerly.

"Well, we've known each other for well over a decade now, right?" Everly asked them. "I really do think of the two of you as my family. You're sisters to each other, but you're also sisters to me."

"You do?" Titania asked, dumbstruck. "We are?"

"That is . . . Mistress, I'd never hoped to hear such words from you," Eris said happily.

"Yeah, you two are definitely like kid sisters to me," Everly said with a nod. "Kid sisters who must obey my every whim and who empower me with copious amounts of magic that allows me to do whatever I want, whenever I feel like it. So you two are *better* than most kid sisters, actually."

"Yes," Titania said, nodding eagerly in agreement. "We are *far* superior to all others. No other selection could possibly compare."

"Indeed, little sister," Eris concurred. "Our mistress has once more proven that her perception and wisdom dwarf that of all others. We thank you for the godly praise you have lavished upon us. The pride we take in serving you is without limit."

"Okay, guys. Let me finish speaking, please," Everly said quickly. "I'm glad that you find no fault in me, I really am. That makes this next part easier: Eris, Titania, I have a request I want to make of you both that I would very much like you to accept."

"Give the word, great one," Titania said solemnly.

"Your every wish is my most sacred command, mistress," echoed Eris.

"Good, great," Everly said. "All right, here it is: stop calling me *mistress*."

"What? Why?" asked Titania.

"Would you prefer another title?" asked Eris. "Wait, of *course* you would! Heh, *mistress* is far too paltry a term. Your greatness must be expounded upon! How does *Your Magnificence* sound?"

"Oh! I like that! I like that a lot! Wait, what if we also called her *Your Divinity*?" asked Titania.

"Little sister, you are, on occasion, a *brilliant* thinker! What a perfect description of our leader," Eris said warmly.

"Thank you! Our mistress just recently relayed to me her admiration for the terror my brain instills within her."

"A finer and more discerning eye simply does not exist in this world."

"I fully agree—"

"STOP! BOTH OF YOU, STOP RIGHT NOW!" shouted Everly in exasperation. She then took a deep breath and slowly exhaled to regain her focus before speaking.

"Guys. Addressing me as your mistress makes me feel uncomfortable. That wasn't always the case, but the three of us have grown much closer over time. I've also gradually realized that the way elementals see the world differs greatly from how humans do and that hierarchy and respect for authority are very important to you."

"A leader must be obeyed," both sisters said at once.

"And that's fine! I'm *very* comfortable with being your ultimate authority," Everly said. "I don't mind that you worship me. In fact, I deserve it! I'm incredible, and there's nothing wrong with being acknowledged for it."

"Then what's the problem?" asked the confused Titania.

"The problem, Titania, is that you're my family, not my *property*. You're not just tools to me—you're also my partners and my collaborators. You're my *friends*. And friends don't address each other like serfs or slaves. Call me *Everly*, just as I call you *Titania* and *Eris*. You two are a part of me. My *favorite* parts! Naturally, I still expect your absolute obedience in all things, but no more of this overt kowtowing. Okay?"

"So . . . " Eris began to ask. "What you'd like is to form a more equitable alliance with the two of us?"

"No, Sister. What she's saying is that she desires to share her authority with us, as three equal parts of a triad!" Titania said, with eyes that nearly sparkled with helpless adoration.

"No. No, no, no, not in the slightest. That was completely wrong," Everly said firmly. "*I'm* the one in charge. *Me.* Always and forever! I get the final say on all decisions—never question that. NEVER! I just want you both to call me *Everly* from now on, without any unnecessary honorifics. You'll do it if you really love me, won't you?"

"If that is truly what you wish, then it shall be done . . . *Everly,*" said Titania hesitantly.

"Yes, because *Everly* has decided that it shall be so," said Eris, with a slowly dawning grin.

"Do you know what? I really like this. I *like* just saying *Everly,*" said Titania with a grin of her own.

"*Everly* is our leader, but also our friend. *That* is who *Everly* is," said Eris. "Is that not so . . . *Everly?*"

"You two are doing great; I don't hate this," said Everly with a smile.

"We have pleased Everly!" Eris said happily. "Behold our greatness!"

"Once more we have proven our devotion! Once more we have demonstrated our value to Everly!" Titania shouted, with a raised fist. "All others stand beneath us! Let those that would attempt to displace us in her heart be crushed by our unyielding might!"

"No usurper shall ever surpass us! Those who dare make the attempt shall die screaming!" said Eris in agreement.

"Yeah. Okay. All right. Thank you, girls. You can stop now," Everly said neutrally.

"Of course, *Everly,*" Titania said with a nod.

"If that's what you want, *Everly,*" said Eris with a wink.

At that moment, Everly realized she was going to have to start paying greater attention to her elementals. It had never before occurred to her that in their own way, they were just as mentally cracked as *she* was. But now that the idea had taken root in her mind, it was a little scary.

Actually, it was terrifying.

Oh, well, she decided, after giving it a moment's thought. *You get the family that you're born with, not the family that you want.*

That was true for everybody, even the bad guys. Besides, even if they were possibly crazy, at least the two of them were *fun.* Her family back on Earth had been the dullest people imaginable. Her older sister had enjoyed reality television and old romantic comedies featuring Sandra Bullock.

She'd obviously been a complete monster.

"So, what have you summoned us to discuss, Everly?" asked Eris.

"Yes, how may we serve?" asked Titania.

"I'm glad you asked," Everly said as she leaned back in her chair. "Guys, I'd like your feedback about how things were handled with sammy."

"Satisfactorily, in my personal opinion," said Eris.

"I most liked the part where he was smashed into the tree." Titania smirked. "It was wonderful."

"Yeeeeah, he was pretty annoying, wasn't he?" asked Everly.

"Oh, he was a horrid little toad. I can't believe you let him live as long as you did," Eris said.

"Truly, you exercised the patience of the Earth. And I *am* the Earth, so I would know," Titania agreed with a nod.

"The thing is," Everly said reluctantly. "I just—I don't feel like I resolved things correctly."

"What do you mean? He's dead, isn't he?" asked Eris.

"Last I checked, he was," said Titania. "Oh, do you think I should have stepped on him, just to be certain? Maybe I should have mashed him up a little more."

"No, there was no need," Eris said. "Even if he'd still been alive when we left, he was obviously fatally wounded. That just means his remaining ragged breaths would have been hideously painful. So, again, I'm not really seeing the problem here, Everly."

"Wait . . . You're not feeling *guilt* over letting him die, are you?" asked Titania. "You're not, right? Please say you're not."

"What?" Everly asked. "Oh, be serious! No, him being dead has been great. I can finally spend some time outside without having to worry about him popping up and bothering me. His silly family still desperately searching for him while slowly losing hope that he's alive has been a treat as well. Didn't we all attend that special service they held for him at the church, just so we could watch his mother cry?"

"Ha! *Yeeeeeah.* She asked everyone there to please pray for his safe return. It was pretty funny." Eris snickered.

"Yeah, that was a good time," agreed Everly. "I got to be *very* edgy that day, which is always nice. That new usher they hired was cute too. But there's something a little off about him, isn't there? He seems so uptight! What was his name, again?"

"I believe it was Alex, or Alan, or something like that," Eris said. "I didn't pay too much attention. He seemed boring."

"He wasn't boring," said Titania. "He was just *shy*. I wonder why? With a face like that, he shouldn't have any issues attracting a mate. He just needs to be a little more ostentatious to catch someone's attention."

"What do you mean?" asked Eris.

"Well, he should wear brighter colors and make an aggressive display of his virility in front of other people. What better place for that than a church?"

"*Peacocking?*" asked Everly incredulously. "You think the new guy should try peacocking in front of the altar to get a girl?"

"It's the best place for it. Everyone would see him," said Titania mildly.

"Human women are a *little* more complicated than that. It takes more to attract them than behaving like a very fancy bird," Everly informed her.

"Ha! It's funny that you really believe that." Titania smirked.

"Okay, let's get back on topic. Now, despite the laughs we've enjoyed thanks to him being gone, I still don't think I handled things correctly with sammy. Guys, I want to be a villain, but I *don't* want to be a *psycho*. I don't want to be the kind of antagonist who kills because of a mood swing. That's off-brand for my character, yeah?"

"I think so?" said Titania.

"Great. But that's the problem, isn't it? sammy's death was *satisfying*, but it was also petty as hell. I don't feel as though my actions reflected the kind of person I'd like to be."

"What kind of person *do* you want to be?" asked Eris.

"Well, that's what we're here to decide," Everly said.

The door to the room opened, and a familiar-looking man entered and took a seat at the table.

"Ladies, I'm sure you recognize my old sword instructor, Viscount Louis Parker. Viscount, please allow me to introduce Titania and Eris, my elementals."

"Ah, the so-called Mountain Splitter," said Titania, who liked mountains and resented those who split them. "How strange it is to see you walking around without Everly's blade jutting from your neck," she said in a poisonously pleasant tone of voice.

"Have you still not recovered from the trauma of losing the war, your precious king, and your reason to keep on living?" asked Eris casually. Unlike Titania, Eris had no personal grudge against Parker. She just enjoyed being unpleasant to others for no particular reason. "No? Oh, that's wonderful. Keep at it. Failure breeds character!"

"Who *are* these *devils?*" snapped Parker angrily.

"They're your exact moral opposites," said Everly. "Which is exactly why you're here, old man. Today, the four of us are going to sit here and properly decide my moral alignment. You'll be representing good and lawful, Eris will be evil and chaotic, and Titania will be neutral everything. Fair warning: I'm not picking *good*, but I'm open to arguments about being lawful."

"I have no idea what you're even speaking of," said Parker irritably.

"I just told you. I'm picking a life path today. It's to better . . . Actually, Eris? Could you just place knowledge of the alignment chart directly into his mind and save us a few steps? I hate repeating myself."

"Done," Eris said at once.

Parker fell from his seat to the floor and began screaming in pain as the information he needed was inserted into his mind.

At this, Everly frowned and asked, "Eris? Was it really necessary to make it so unpleasant for him?"

"No," Eris said.

"Well, at least you're honest." Everly shrugged.

Once Parker finished recovering, they began.

CHAPTER SIXTEEN

The Decision

It didn't take long for things to descend into petty bickering.

"Darth Vader was *not* lawful evil!" Parker shouted at Eris. He was so angry that the cords on his neck had bulged out as he furiously attempted to make his point. "Lawful evil is defined by a strict code of conduct that includes honoring your word, never telling a lie, and avoiding harm to children. Lord Vader violated *all three* of these central tenants, therefore he's NOT! LAWFUL! EVIL!"

He pounded his fist on the conference table three times to put emphasis on each word.

Everly was impressed by how completely Parker now understood pop culture references from Earth and could use them to reinforce his arguments. Eris had done a very thorough job of instilling such knowledge in him. Everly could also see that she'd been right to select Parker to represent the alignment of lawfulness.

As it turned out, he was a *very* pedantic man.

"In what way?" Eris demanded. "Stop acting like you've won and provide some actual examples, you bloviating old goat!"

"That's *easily* done, you insufferable harridan," Parker said smugly. "First of all, Lord Vader *personally* murdered all the younglings during the siege of the Jedi temple. Strike one! He also allowed Moff Tarkin to destroy the planet Alderaan, causing the deaths of millions of loyal noncombatant imperial citizens. That's strike two! And finally, in Cloud City on Bespin, he broke his deal with Lando Calrissian, thereby violating his given word. Strike three! *Not* lawful evil. END OF DISCUSSION. I WIN!"

"He didn't break the deal—he *altered* it!" shouted Eris. "He could have altered it further!"

"IT'S *STILL* LYING!"

"None of your precious three tenants were broken if Vader was acting as a law enforcement figure!"

"*What* law?" scoffed Parker.

"*Imperial* law!" Eris said triumphantly. "Emperor Palpatine was the supreme legal authority of the galaxy. He was Darth *I will make it legal* Sidious himself! Therefore, every command he gave to Vader was a *legal* command, which made Vader an agent of justice!"

Eris rose from her seat and began to circle the room as she made her case.

"Yes, Vader killed those younglings. So? They were indoctrinated mutant terrorists! And yes, he let Tarkin blow up Alderaan. What of it? Tarkin had permission from the emperor! Alderaan was a hotbed of seditious activity. The unfortunate loss of civilian life was collateral damage inflicted in the pursuit of lasting order!"

"You call billions of dead people *collateral* damage?"

"This discussion isn't about scale! Now, for my final point. Yes, Lord Vader deceived Lando Calrissian. *But* Lando was colluding with the rebels! What's more, law enforcement is permitted to deceive criminals when in the pursuit of justice! Everything Lord Vader did was a legal exercise of the authority vested in him by the state. Therefore, he *was* lawful evil! You lose again, Parker! You lose again!"

"Do I? I wonder . . . " Parker sneered before springing his final trap. "Because there is a *fourth* pillar of being lawful evil that you haven't even considered! *Strict adherence to hierarchy!* Darth Vader colluded with his son to overthrow the emperor and seize the throne for himself! He was a traitor! Lawful evil characters do not turn against their organizations; hence, Vader was *not* lawful evil!"

When Eris didn't immediately reply, Titania began to snort in laughter. "Heh, heh, I think he got you!"

"Oh, what's that?" taunted Parker. "Nothing to say? Well, then, I seem to have won after all, haven't I? Go ahead and admit it, you caterwauling banshee!"

Eris was furious. "L-Lord Vader was merely exercising his right to religious expression! As a member of the Sith order, there was an expectation for him to overthrow his master and assume control!"

"Lawful evil characters give *no* consideration to the exercise of religion." Parker laughed. "Unless you can prove that being a member of the Sith cult is an essential aspect of also being an imperial citizen, then that argument has no traction. Give it up, child. In fact, doesn't a standing commandment to assassinate your teacher PROVE DECISIVELY that the Sith are incapable of being lawful at anything? Face it: you lose, I win, and *that's* the duel."

Parker resumed his seat, while Titania clapped in approval until Eris glared at her.

"You wretched mortal filth!" said Eris to Parker. "Do you know what I could do to you with my thoughts alone?"

"I don't know, what? Lose another argument?"

"I'LL KILL YOU—"

"Eris," said Everly.

"Did you hear how disrespectful this little simulacrum of an actual person was *being* to me? I'll OBLITERATE HIM—"

"*Eris*," said Everly once more.

Eris sat angrily at the table and crossed her arms, refusing to look at the smirking Parker.

"I think the Joker is neutral-neutral," said Titania.

Just as Eris was about to begin screaming at her, Everly called for a break. Eris stormed out of the room, dragging Titania with her, leaving Everly alone with the old man.

"I'm beginning to think that choosing a moral path to follow, based on a role-playing game, was a stupid idea," she moaned, as she rested her chin glumly on her hands.

"Of course it was a stupid idea," Parker said, as he sipped from the mug of ale he'd been provided with. "As clever as this Master Gygax was in designing this system for his game, genuine morality has far too much nuance involved. Too many moving pieces that change every day. No one's true character can be ascertained by a static chart. If anything, all that does is encourage baseless stereotyping and false assumptions."

"That's so annoying." Everly grunted. "So far, treating everything like a game has worked out splendidly for me. Why is it failing now?"

"Oh, that's easy to figure out, you horrid little back-blade," Parker said without humor. "Treating other people like objects to be toyed with is normally fun for a monster like you. But now you've discovered that applying the same standards by which you judge others to your own behavior makes you feel empty inside."

"What . . . ?" Everly asked him in surprise.

"You heard me," Parker said. "That's why that boy's death bothers you so much. The way you let him die has exposed your true nature, and as it turns out, *you don't like yourself,* do you?"

"Bullshit! I love myself more than anything else," Everly said.

"Then why'd you call your little gang together for this silly discussion? It's because you understand yourself so little that you're hoping someone else's opinion will offer you some insight into your own character. You're a hopelessly ignorant fool."

Everly said nothing in reply. Instead, she stared at him, confused, her mouth agape.

"Hey . . . do you really think I'm horrid?" Everly asked him, after they'd sat in silence for a few minutes. Her cheeks had turned rosy with an embarrassed flush, and a shy smile had formed on her lips.

Every time she tried to look at him, her eyes would pull away.

"Of course I do," Parker said sharply. "Your mind parasite of an associate did me the unkindness of letting me know what my existence has been for the past fifteen years, you wretched thing."

Parker took another sip before continuing. "Not only am I not a real man, but I've also spent all this time as the thrall of a villainous little doll who's been torturing me for her own edification and cruel amusement. My fate is . . . unbearable. You aren't just a horrid person, Everly. You're a nightmare folded in flesh. I wish nothing but the worst for you in all things, ever and always."

The flush had grown to encompass Everly's entire body, and she shivered in delight with a blissful expression on her face. As she hugged herself tightly with giddy pleasure, the Mountain Splitter looked upon her in bewilderment.

"What the hell is wrong with you?" he asked her.

"I'm sorry. I'm sorry, it's just, no one's ever *encouraged* me like this before," Everly replied. "Do you . . . do you really think I'm a nightmare?"

"I think that you're an irredeemable piece of filth who should burn in the darkest, hottest pit of hell that the demons can stuff you in—STOP SMILING AT ME! By the gods, has your feeble mind cracked?" yelled the disturbed swordsman.

"Parker, *stooooop*." The flustered Everly giggled. "I'm not *ready* for this! Just—just not now, okay?"

Parker could only stare at her in horror. He was unable to muster another word.

Everly faced her chair away from him and tried to regain her composure, but it was difficult. Her bad habit from her prior life on Earth had flared up within her like wildfire. If she didn't keep a tight rein on herself, she was going to lose it.

It was all she could do to stay in control.

To keep seated.

To not throw herself at him.

To hold back the powerful urge to tear him apart and daub her face with his blood.

Parker had been an important figure in Winstead's civil war. Participating in it had been a principled decision based on his desire to achieve the greatest possible good for the people of the land, not just the king he served. He was a beloved champion who'd saved many lives and sacrificed everything for what was ultimately a doomed cause.

His life was a cacophony of triumph and sorrow.

He was a legend. An exemplar.

A . . . *hero.*

Everly's mouth began to ache from the pressure her demented smile exerted on it.

He's not a real person, she thought. *And besides, I could just erase his memories, make it like nothing ever happened. So there's nothing wrong with me turning around and HURTING HIM. He's so handsome, and stalwart, and fearless, and I JUST WANT TO BREAK HIM IN HALF. I WANT TO MAKE HIM CRY . . .*

It would be easy. It would be *so* easy . . .

But Everly refused.

He might not have been a real person, but he existed because Everly had created him. As his maker, she held certain responsibilities toward him. It was true she abused him daily in training, but there was no justification for going beyond that into . . . further extremes.

In a way, he wasn't just her creation. He was her *subject.* And a ruler had a responsibility toward those they ruled.

Even a villain like her.

Everly's eyes widened as she suddenly realized what she wanted to become.

At that moment, Eris and Titania returned. "Now do you understand how neutrality works?" Eris asked her sister irritably.

"No," Titania answered.

"Sister, why are you even participating if you don't understand what it is we're doing?" Eris asked her.

"I just enjoy spending time with everyone. You always say such interesting things," Titania replied.

"Well, I suppose that's true," Eris conceded reluctantly.

The sisters then noticed Everly's expression and abruptly stopped.

"Everly?" asked Eris slowly. "Is . . . is everything all right?"

"Hmm?" Everly asked, as she snapped out of her reverie.

"I was asking if aught was amiss," Eris said. "Your expression was slightly . . . foreboding."

"Was it?" Everly asked.

"Uh, fucking *scary,*" Titania said bluntly. "That's the same look you gave that demon when we were slow roasting him."

"Oh, sorry. Sorry," Everly repeated sheepishly. "Viscount Parker just gave me some excellent advice, and I now feel that the matter of my alignment has been settled. Honestly, it's a relief."

"Really?" asked Titania. "Which one did you choose? You went with neutral evil, right? I had a *feeling* that neutrality was going to win out! There's just something about it. It seems very reliable."

"Mmm, close, but not quite," Everly said. "Let's call my new path *modified* lawful evil. Honor is a pointless irrelevancy, but for reasons of personal aesthetics,

I've decided I'll abide by a certain code of conduct. I won't be doing any more pointless killing."

"Awww, that sounds moralistic," complained Eris.

"It's not!" said Everly. "I've just decided I prefer to reserve my greatest wrath for those who dare to oppose me. I want to keep this endeavor pure, y'know? If I wanted to slaughter the little people at random, I could have just stayed on Earth. I'd have been good at it. I was cute too, so they'd eventually have made a Netflix documentary about me. But I wanted bigger things than that."

She rose from her seat and gestured at the land below them.

"No, I came to this world because I wanted something *better* for myself. I've also decided that I'll deceive others whenever I feel like it. Because you know what? Lying is fun! Deception is like a thong on a sumo! I wouldn't be me without it. Of course, naturally, my greatest focus shall go toward establishing my absolute dominion over everyone and everything on this planet that's weaker than I am."

"Hey, isn't that *everybody*?" asked Titania after giving it a little thought.

"Why, coincidentally, *yes*. Yes, it is! So, hey, funny how that works out, right?" replied Everly.

"In what possible way is this lawful behavior, modified or otherwise?" Parker demanded to know.

"BECAUSE *I* ALONE WILL DECIDE WHAT THE LAW IS!" Everly shouted, with a voice that roared like thunder.

The sky around them became covered with storm clouds, and the light slowly faded into darkness in which only their table was illuminated. The change didn't disturb the elementals, but Parker was frightened. To Everly's eyes, he seemed far less sure of himself than he ever had in the past.

Eris's revelation of his purpose had unsettled him. Was he now questioning his very humanity?

He now seemed so vulnerable.

So very, very vulnerable . . .

Eris, I want to try something here, Everly said to her elemental through their shared link.

What would you like me to do? Eris replied.

I want you to make Parker more susceptible to my words. Make him more vulnerable to my suggestions.

Why bother? I can just reprogram him to behave in any manner you wish.

No, no, that's not the same, Everly insisted. *He has to have his free will. What he decides next, I want him to do of his own volition. I just want my words to appear more compelling to him than they'd otherwise be. Can it be done?*

Of course it can. I will never fail you.

Awesome.

"This world needs direction, Parker," Everly then said to him. "Isn't your own life a perfect example of why? Principles, duty, honor, and love—you lived with those ideals as your guiding light for your entire life! But where did they take you? What do you have to show for all your great deeds?"

Images began flashing across the sky. Memories she'd taken directly from him. His defeats. His frustrations. His exile. One after another, they appeared before him, a parade of endless shame.

"You were a good man, Louis," she said compassionately. "A good man doing the best you could in a corrupt world . . . but the bad guys won! They always do. Because good people like you lack the tools necessary for true victory. You didn't have the heart to *commit*."

"That isn't true!" Parker yelled furiously. "I did everything I possibly could!"

"Except *win*," Everly said. "And isn't that what mattered most?"

"I had greater considerations than mere victory," he said haughtily.

"And thanks to those considerations, your life is over. If you'd only had the courage to cast them aside, who knows what could have been?"

"So, you're saying I should have abandoned my principles and acted with abandon? That I should have just thrown my honor away?" he asked her belligerently.

"If it was holding you back . . . yes. No one can keep their head held high while they're drowning, Louis."

"What you're saying isn't true!" Parker insisted.

"Isn't it? Then why is your king dead? Why does his murderer reign? Why does war continue against Oldstead? Why is your true self languishing in exile, cut off from everything and everyone he ever held dear? Because this world is *broken*, Louis. It's broken, and it needs a firm hand willing to do the necessary work to repair it."

"And I suppose that's you? A monster like *you*?" he scoffed.

"Of course!" Everly laughed. "Monsters respect only *strength*, Louis. They value nothing except absolute power. So, in a world overrun with them, you don't want a saint like your beloved dead king at the helm. They'd have eaten him alive! No, you want something far worse to keep the others in check. Something that can instill *fear* in them. You need someone like . . . me. In fact, the entire *world* needs *me*."

Give us a little showmanship, girls, she ordered the sisters.

Eris and Titania dropped to their knees and bowed their heads reverently to Everly as she spoke.

Nice, she said to them.

Do you want us to say anything? asked Titania.

No, this is good. Stay exactly like that.

"Louis . . . Put your trust in me," Everly urged him. "Do it, and I'll fix what was broken."

She rose from her seat and approached the startled Parker. He tried to shake his arm free when she put her hand on it, but she held him firmly in place.

"*Listen* to me. I'll make things fair, like they always should have been. Under my guidance, the right people will be put in the right places to affect the greatest possible good. We'll toss aside the corrupt and venal, then set others in their place. We'll repair this broken machine called *Winstead*, and once we've done it, we'll share my vision with the other nations of the world. Can you imagine it, Louis? Can you imagine a world of peace, prosperity, and joy? A world where no one will ever again have need of a sword?"

The entire notion is complete bullshit, of course, she thought with amusement. *No one can imagine a world that ideal. It just isn't sustainable! But you WANT to believe in it, don't you, Parker? You WANT to believe in this lie. That's why you're going to join me . . .*

"It can't be done . . . " Parker said miserably. "People . . . we just don't have the capacity for such greatness."

"Louis," Everly said urgently. "If you can't believe in yourself, if life and disappointment have taken that much away from you, then why not believe in *me*? If you can't find it within yourself to be great, then shield yourself behind *my* greatness! If you can't walk to paradise, then let me carry you."

"But . . . but you said you were *evil*," Parker whispered.

"I am. I'm a *necessary* evil. But I'm also the path to peace. Don't you want to believe in me?"

" . . . Yes."

"Then *do it*."

" . . . I'm scared," he said weakly.

In response, Everly hugged him. Like a daughter comforting her father, she embraced him lovingly and placed her cheek against his chest. "You've lost so much. *They've* taken so much from you. You deserve better, and now you'll have it. There'll be no fear in the world I'll create for us. None at all, except for those who deserve it. Isn't that what you want?"

" . . . Yes."

"And do you believe I can give it to you?"

" . . . Yes."

Everly raised her head and looked him directly in the eye. "Then there's only one thing you have to do, Louis," she said gently.

He understood.

And with that, Parker joined Eris and Titania in their kneeling and swore himself to her.

Everly, what did you just do? Eris asked her through their mental link.

What do you think? I just scored a Darth Vader of my own, she replied giddily. *Check me out with my corrupting influence!*

Haha! Look at you go! Well, if he's your Vader, then I guess from now on, we should call you the Empress, *right?*

Everly didn't respond.

Everly? Hey, Everly! Are you listening to me? Hey, say something!

Eris, Everly finally replied. *Eris, I think you may be on to something . . .*

CHAPTER SEVENTEEN

The Rat Room

One week later.

Too bad sammy's dead. In a way, it's thanks to him that I have my newfound focus in life. It's a shame I can't show my gratitude," Everly said one day after meeting with Titania in the memory palace.

"Why not?" asked Titania.

"Because he's dead, silly," Everly said.

The two of them were sitting in the dining section of a Wendy's, one that Everly had enjoyed frequenting back on Earth. Titania was now enjoying her first taste of American fast food, which was naturally the greatest fast food in the world. She liked it immediately and was now determined to sample everything on the menu.

"What's that got to do with anything?" she asked, between mouthfuls of her hamburger.

"Titania, when someone's dead, they're no longer capable of *anything*. That's what being dead means. You're gone forever. You ought to know that," Everly explained patiently.

"Dead meat's just meat. It's all replaceable," Titania said. "I could fix 'em."

"What are you saying? You can just bring someone back to life if you want?" Everly asked.

"Only if they're composed of materials that come from the earth. Which is, like, *everything* in the material world. So, yeah, sure. I could patch him up. Fix him good as new. Why would I, though? sammy *sucked*."

"Yeah, sammy *did* suck," Everly agreed as she dipped her fries in some honey mustard. "But you know what? This isn't about how much he overwhelmingly sucked, which he did, greatly. This is about defying the natural order and doing something really *cool!* Titania, if we could bring the dead back to life, we'd practically be gods! That level of blasphemous affront isn't something we should avoid committing just because our test dummy was an actual dummy."

"Hmm. I don't know, boss," Titania said reluctantly.

"Pleeease? You help me restore that idiot to life, and next time, we'll do something *you* like! Anything you want!"

Titania's ears perked up immediately. "Really?"

"It's a sacred promise," Everly said as she held up her fist.

"Yay!" Titania said happily as she bumped Everly's fist with one of her own.

"So, what all do we need?" Everly asked eagerly.

"Well, it's been a few weeks, so we'll need a bunch of fresh meat to replace all the rotted tissue. I mean, *a lot* of meat. I can coat him in it and convert it all into new muscle and bone and other stuff that's harder to pronounce."

"Ewww, meat magic!" Everly laughed.

"Yeah, basically," Titania said as she sipped her soda. "The real problem's gonna be his mind. Recreating a body's easy, but I can't restore a mind."

"Shoot," Everly said. "There's no point in remaking him if he can't convince others of his identity."

"Now, hold on! I can't do it, but Eris could. It'd be easy-peasy for her."

"I doubt she has a copy of sammy's mind lying around for us to borrow, Titania," Everly said glumly.

"Boss, I think I'm about to surprise you!" Titania said with a wink.

"What exactly is this?" Everly asked her later, as they descended into the deepest, darkest layers of the memory palace.

"Ah, this is cool. You're going to like it," Titania said cheerfully as they went farther down the stairs. "This is where Eris goes to let out some steam when she's mad about something, which is, like, *all* the time. Heh, she's fiery! But she really does have some great ideas, and this is one of them."

Now they appeared before an iron door. From beneath it, Everly could see crimson stains covering the ground. Curious, she knelt and scraped at the floor a bit, then held her hand before her face as she rubbed the substance between her thumb and forefinger.

It was coagulated blood.

"Titania? What *is* this place?" she asked her.

"This is the rat room!" Titania said.

"And . . . what do you do in the rat room?" Everly asked, although she suspected she already knew.

"Heh! You feed the rats, silly," Titania said before pushing the door open.

It was . . . exactly what one would expect. There were a lot of people in there, chained to the floor. And there were a lot of rats as well.

Eating them.

"Ahhhh," Everly said in a carefully neutral tone of voice. As she looked around, she recognized more than a few faces. These were all people she knew. "Titania?"

"Hmm?"

"Why did Eris build a rat room?"

"Oh, well, see, you're always telling her to hold back and not kill people who annoy her. But, heh, Eris *really* likes killing people! But she'd never disobey you, so instead, she makes copies of their minds and then plops them in here to, y'know, suffer for all eternity! She says it takes the edge off."

"Jesus Christ."

"I know, right? I told you, she's good at stuff! That mind of hers is amazing. Hey, look, I found sammy."

It was indeed sammy. Well, mostly his head and torso.

That was what the teeth of the rats had reduced him to.

"Gross," Everly said. "Look at him! We can't use this."

"Sure we can!" Titania said. "He'll regenerate at dawn. Eternal torment, remember?"

"Ah. Well . . . I guess it is what it is," Everly said reluctantly.

However, the more she thought about it, the more comfortable she became with the situation. This really wasn't so bad. No, in fact, this was perfectly fine! They could just iron out any little issues involving sammy potentially having post-traumatic stress disorder if it came up down the road.

The important part was having material to work with.

"This is going to be so awesome," Everly said happily. Then a thought occurred to her. "Hey, Titania. There aren't any copies of *me* in here, are there?"

"What? Why would Eris do that?" Titania asked as she scratched her head. "She says you're the only real person in the world."

"Oh. Well, good."

Just to be certain, she later came back and checked.

How the subject of rewarding a dead person veered so quickly into a mission to conduct actual necromancy, Everly didn't quite know, but now that they were actually going to do it, she quickly became eager to get on with it.

Necromancy. Of all the dark powers that existed in fantasy, the ability to raise and command the dead was considered by most to be the darkest one of all. Only the most fiendish of villains would dare to violate the sanctity of the grave and enslave the deceased for their selfish purposes.

It sounded amazing. Everly was totally down.

There was only one small issue.

"I can't remember where we left his body," she told the others.

Everly, Titania, and Eris had gathered once more in the meeting room to discuss the operation they were soon commencing. Parker had joined them as well, but shortly after arriving, he informed them that he would no longer answer to the name of the person he'd been modeled after.

"I'm Grail now," he told them.

"Why 'Grail'?" Everly asked him out of curiosity.

"Yeah, why pick *Grail*, of all names? I don't get the significance," Titania said.

"He probably just liked the way it sounded," Eris said dismissively. "Didn't you, Parker?"

"It's *Grail*," he repeated.

"Whatever you say, Parker." Eris smirked. She had been irritable upon learning that Titania had informed Everly about the existence of the rat room. She'd been very reluctant to depart with her copy of sammy, but Everly had managed to convince her.

"I *said* my name is Grail—" Grail began to say once more, when Everly cut him off.

"Okay, whatever, it's Grail. I like it. Stay on topic, everyone! I still don't remember where sammy's corpse is," Everly said impatiently.

"No worries, boss. I know exactly where it is. I remember the location of every place I've ever been to," Titania said.

"Oh, that's helpful!" Everly said. "Would you be a dear and go fetch it? Hide it behind my mother's garden shed."

"Can do, will do, am doing!" Titania said cheerfully as she momentarily vanished from sight.

Everly smiled as they awaited her return. When had Titania developed such a lighthearted personality? Everly liked it. It suited the elemental perfectly. Over time, she'd gradually become very enjoyable to be around. Eris was great too, but she was more of an acquired taste. If you didn't know her very well, she could come across as off-puttingly severe.

And cruel.

And unempathetic.

And sadistic.

And bloodthirsty.

And vengeful.

Yeah, they were both great kids.

When Titania returned, however, her smile had vanished. "Uh, bad news, Everly. sammy's body, uh, it's—"

"Missing? It's not missing, is it?" Everly asked. "Damn it! Did a bear find him? Oh, that's so irritating."

"No, no, that's not it. It's weirder than that," Titania said. "Someone *buried* him. Dug a hole and placed him inside with a sheet over him."

"Someone *buried* him?" Everly asked in surprise. "But no one in the village knows he's dead! Or if they do, they haven't shared that knowledge with anyone else. But why would they do that? It makes no sense."

As she pondered this strange development, another thought suddenly occurred to her. "Titania?"

"Yeah?"

"Is that spider still there?"

"What spider?"

Everly rolled her eyes. "The *big* spider? The demon? That idiot? Remember?"

"Ohhhh! Hold on," Titania said before disappearing once more.

When she returned, she shook her head. "Nope. He's gone."

"Was he buried too?"

"Nope, just gone."

"Damn it!" Everly swore. "Well, this is a complication."

"Do you think he survived somehow?" Titania asked. "And buried the kid before leaving?"

"Sister," Eris said archly, "*why* would a giant demonic spider bury one of his victims instead of eating him?"

"I don't know. He was dressed like a priest, wasn't he? Don't priests do stuff like that?" Titania asked.

"In this case? *No*," said Eris firmly.

"Lady Titania," Grail said. "Was there anything strange about the boy's body? Aside from the cloth they covered him with. Were any objects left behind?"

"Umm," Titania said. "Actually, yeah! There was! Someone left this behind." Titania took her sister's hand and said, "Show them for me."

Eris traced her finger through the air, and soon an image appeared before them. It looked like a flat metal disk that had been shaped in the form of a sun. Everly had no idea what it symbolized, but Grail's breath caught in his throat.

"Tch. It figures they'd be involved," he said gruffly.

"Who?" Everly asked. "Don't skimp on the details, please."

"That's the sigil of radiance," Grail said. "It's the symbol of the Eastern Temple of the Holy Will. Is this the correct color, Lady Titania?"

"Yep."

"Light silver. Like those carried by a templar. Well, that explains where your spider went."

"I thought the name of the organization was the Temple of the Sacred Heart?" Everly asked.

"It is on *this* continent. There was a schism in the organization centuries ago. No one knows why. Not dissimilar to our own civil war, each temple claims to be the one true order and the other a pretender. Members of each group get along about as well as you'd expect."

"Ahhh," Everly said in understanding. "Yeah, there've been more than a few disagreements based on similar reasons back on Earth."

Well, if you wanted to call centuries of recurring persecution, war, and genocide a simple disagreement. Which *technically* it was.

"So, this Eastern Temple swiped my bug, huh?" Everly said. "Well, no big. I didn't want it anyway. But why'd they bury sammy? Why would they care?"

"Whoever did it probably considered it the right thing to do," Grail said.

"Huh. What a peculiar concept," Everly said without interest. "I wonder why they were there, though? Didn't you say they were based on another continent?"

"The Eastern Temple has access to rare magical resources," Grail said. "I've encountered them more than once over the years. They can appear out of nowhere when you least expect it. Literally out of thin air."

"Teleportation? *Sweet!*" Everly exclaimed. "Oh, I wish I could do that."

"So do many others. However, they're unwilling to share the knowledge," Grail said. "The loyalty of their members is ironclad. Even when under question by spirit elemental wielders, they don't break."

"Sounds like they don't know the correct way to make an inquiry," Eris said in amusement. "It's all in the approach."

"Still, this raises an important question," Grail continued without acknowledging Eris, which visibly annoyed her. "Did the person who buried the boy *leave?*"

Eris snorted. "Why wouldn't they? If all they came for was the spider's corpse, then what reason would they have to stay?"

"Ignorance," Grail said. "Sheer ignorance."

Eris began to frown as Grail continued to speak.

"If this demon was powerful enough to prompt a response from the Eastern Temple, then that means they're going to have questions they'll want answered. Questions like . . . who could possibly be strong enough to kill such a thing single-handedly?"

"No one's made any attempt to reach out," Everly said. "I haven't noticed anyone attempting to track me either."

"Track you?" Titania said, as though she were trying to remember something. "How would they go about doing something like that?"

"They have hounds of their own," said Grail. "Gifted mages who can use their magic to scry for knowledge from a corpse."

Titania's eyes widened. "Hey! Hey, Eris, didn't you say someone was trying to scry on Everly last week?"

Eris's face reddened. "Shut up—shut up—*shut up*," she hissed while punching Titania in the shoulder.

"Eris?" Everly asked her in surprise.

"It was nothing, Everly. Nothing at all. I've already dealt with it."

"*Eris*," Everly repeated as she began to frown.

"It's taken care of! Some insignificant wretch went poking around, so I swatted him. Whoever he was, he's quite dead, I assure you."

"You *killed* their tracker?" Grail said flatly.

"Don't say it like that!" Eris said defensively. "We have no way of even knowing if he was one of them—"

Titania vanished from sight.

Moments after returning, she said, "There's a second body buried out there."

"God DAMN IT, Eris!" Everly cursed.

"No, no, listen. I'm not to blame. He was *disturbing my sleep*—"

"*That's* why you killed him?!" Everly yelled. "Why didn't you at least tell me about this?"

"It was hardly worth your attention—"

"THAT ISN'T FOR YOU TO DECIDE!" Everly screamed as her eyes flared red with anger.

In an instant, Eris was on her hands and knees, trembling. "I'm sorry. It won't happen again. I promise."

Everly said nothing. She continued to glare at Eris without speaking as her hands clenched into fists. "Fail me like this again, and the next one to spend time in the rat room will be *you*. Am I understood?"

"Yes, Everly," she said.

"Yes, *mistress*. When you apologize for screwing up this badly, you call me 'mistress.' Got it?"

"Yes, *mistress*." Eris quavered. "I'm sorry."

"Good," Everly said. Then she held out a hand and helped Eris to her feet. "Well, no biggie! Mistakes are why pencils have erasers. Seems like we might have a problem on our hands, though, huh?"

"Yes," Grail said after silently giving Eris a hateful smirk. "Thanks to this, they'll certainly have sent someone here to seek you out. Still, in a village this small, there are only so many suspects it could be. If any strangers have recently arrived, they'll most likely be the spy—"

"It's Alec," said Everly.

"It's Alec," said Eris.

"Yeah, it's definitely Alec," said Titania.

Grail paused. "Who's Alec?"

"The new usher at the village church," Titania said. "Eris said he was *boooring*. Does that count as another screwup, Everly?"

"Oh, shut up!" snapped Eris.

"Hee-hee!"

"All righty," Everly said decisively. "We'll just wait until night falls and then go pay our little church mouse a visit. Sound good?"

"No. That's exactly what we *shouldn't* do," said Grail suddenly.

"Huh? Why not?" Everly asked. "Trust me, if this guy is weak enough to think that silly spider was a heavy hitter, then we won't have any problems handling him."

"That's not it," Grail said. "The problem is that if he's a warrior of the Eastern Temple, then he'll be more of a danger than he seems."

"How so?"

"He'll be backed by the choir of seers," he said starkly.

"The choir of what?" Everly asked.

"I'm unsurprised by your ignorance. Your education is sorely lacking, Majesty," Grail said.

"Watch your tongue!" Eris snapped. "You're being far too forward with your opinions, Parker."

"That *isn't* my name," he growled as he stepped angrily toward the elemental. "My name is *Grail.*"

Eris grinned at his reaction. "I think your name is whatever *I* decide it is. Don't think that just because Everly has graciously allowed you to join us that I'll hesitate to discipline a disobedient dog that doesn't heel at my command. *Parker.*"

At that last taunt, Grail's patience was at an end. Before Eris could react, his hand was at her throat, lifting her easily into the air and squeezing. "The only one of us who needs disciplining is *you!*" he said furiously.

"HEY! Let go of my sister!" Titania said as she began to stomp toward the pair, but Everly's hand on her shoulder restrained her. "Everly?" she asked confusedly.

"Let them sort it out," she said. "A wolf pack will naturally balance itself."

"B-but—"

"Titania," Everly said, letting her voice trail off.

"Oh, fine. I was just trying to help him out, anyway. What sort of fool attacks a spirit elemental in a place like this?"

"Hmmm," said Everly sagely.

Although she'd adopted an insightful tone while giving her order to Titania, in truth, Everly didn't know the slightest thing about wolf-pack dynamics. She just wanted to see the two of them slug it out.

The bitter clone of a famous sword king versus a homicidal telepathic narcissist? Are you kidding? LET THEM FIGHT! her inner child screamed into her mind.

A flash of violet light surged from Eris's body and threw Grail back, sending him flying to smash into a wall. "You *dare* to raise your hand against me? I can see I've been lax in my duties," she said reproachfully. "I'll just have to put you in your place so thoroughly that you'll never even *dream* of opposing me again!"

"You condescending witch," Grail said. His sword appeared in his hand, drawn so swiftly that only Everly's eyes could follow it. "The only thing I've been dreaming of is doing exactly *this*!"

Grail's sword then swept through the air, generating a wave of pure force that sundered everything before it. Had it connected with Eris, her body would have been halved, but she held forth a hand that deflected it, negating Grail's attack entirely.

"Oh, my. How breezy," she said as she casually examined her fingernails. "Maybe I'll have you converted into a ceiling fan. Ruffling my hair appears to be the limit of your ability—"

Grail appeared suddenly behind her and slashed at her back. The smug grin immediately vanished from Eris's face as she took a stumbling step forward and clutched at her injury. When she raised her hand to her eyes, her palm was covered in vivid red blood.

"What . . . ?" she asked herself in shock.

"You're so used to being invincible, aren't you, witch?" Grail said to her with a cruel sneer. "So used to walking through this life untouched and pristine. You like looking down on others, don't you? But this isn't the outside world, is it? Here, in the realm of the mind, I'm your *equal*. Not only can I hurt you, I can also *kill you*."

Ooooh, shouldn't have told her that, bud, Everly thought to herself with a sad shake of her head.

He'd been doing so well too.

Oh, well.

Eris's face became pale with fury. Now too angry to speak, she simply glared at Grail.

And destroyed him.

Countless chains appeared from nowhere—descending from the sky, sprouting from the ground and walls—all around them. They were large rusting heaps of crude iron, tipped with razor-sharp hooks that moved so quickly, and in such quantity, that even Grail couldn't avoid them all.

Soon, dozens of them pierced his body and tore into his flesh, immobilizing his limbs and holding him so tautly that even the slightest bit of incremental pressure would have instantly quartered him.

I really shouldn't have told her about the Hellraiser *movies,* Everly thought to herself.

She and Eris had recently watched the first two movies together in the memory palace. Eris had been curious about the films ever since Everly mentioned them during their confrontation with the unhallowed man. Everly had never enjoyed them very much; they just weren't very interesting to her.

But Eris had been enthralled. And apparently, she'd taken notes.

"You'll kill me, will you?" she whispered, as she approached her immobilized victim ensnared in her web of chains. Her hair began to float behind her as though her body were submerged in water.

Eris's hand gently stroked Grail's exposed chest.

Then her fingers curled into claws that tore into him as she began to peel away his skin.

Grail screamed in agony.

"Once I've finished playing, I'm going to wear you like a *robe*," she said to him with a maniacal grin.

Suddenly the sound of a loud clap echoed throughout the room.

"All right, all right," Everly said briskly as she stepped between them. "Grail, Eris holds seniority over you, so please speak respectfully when you address her. Eris, Grail is a treasured member of our organization. Please address him by the name he prefers to be called, and refrain from flaying him when he upsets you."

With a disappointed sigh, Eris snapped her fingers. The chains popped out of existence and Grail dropped to the floor and landed on his face. Eris turned her back on him and began to walk away when Everly loudly coughed.

"Now, now! We're all teammates and friends here. Shake hands, please," she insisted.

With a disdainful expression on her face, Eris turned back to Grail and shook his hand.

"One day, witch . . . " he said quietly to her.

"I'm looking forward to it, *Grail*," she whispered back, before lightly biting the lobe of his ear.

"Anyhoo, you were telling us about the choir of seers?" Everly asked him.

CHAPTER EIGHTEEN

The Message

Five years later.

The last of the sending choir had been killed after sending the remaining faithful to this, their final refuge. They had no means of escape and nowhere to flee to, even if they could. The Temple of the Holy Will was finished and had no more resources. Their forces now numbered less than a thousand, and supplies had to be strictly rationed.

All they could do in this new desolate landscape was hope that they'd finally escaped her.

They hadn't. Despite their base's supposedly secret location in the farthest, most remote corner of the world, she found them anyway.

Within a month of their arrival, the Empress came for them.

The seers huddled together miserably as the sounds of battle continued to echo throughout the keep. Outside the doors of their final refuge, they heard the brave templars of the eastern order shout their battle cries before fearlessly engaging the intruders.

They also heard those same brave knights screaming in pain and begging for mercy as one by one they were cut down.

Although each of the nine seers had been blind since birth, their gifts still allowed them to perceive the world around them. They knew what the color of blood was. They knew what dead warriors looked like.

And most of all, they knew that they were soon going to join them.

Their two remaining guards stood before the entrance to the seers' quarters, rigid with tension. Their hands gripped their weapons tightly, prepared at any moment to give their lives in defense of those they'd been charged with protecting.

Their opportunity soon arrived.

A fist knocked on the door, pounding an unfamiliar tempo into it.

Dun-dun-du-du-dun! Dun-dun!

"Stay behind us. Everything will be well," said the first of them.

"Announce yourself!" shouted the second one.

"I've heard tell there are seers here within. So, now that I've knocked, won't you please let me in?" asked a young woman's voice.

The seers recognized it at once and began to weep. One of them shrieked in nearly mindless terror.

"I said *announce* yourself!" repeated the second guard.

"Darkness has come, and a wolf's at your door; the battle is over. I *win*. First, I knocked once, now I'll knock twice. Knock-knock-knock, *let me in*."

"Begone, devil! You won't get by us!" the first guard said defiantly.

"I'm very delighted that you'd like to play! Now I'll huff and I'll puff, and I'll brutally *slay* . . . you both. Sorry, continuous rhyming is hard."

The seers heard the door smash open. Then they heard the guards charge ahead toward someone.

Then . . . they felt something wet spraying upon them.

"Whoops. Got them all over you, didn't I? Sorry about that, ladies," said the woman who'd invaded their home. "You know, in a situation like this, you ought to be grateful for your blindness. If you knew what you looked like right now, you'd probably vomit."

The seers next heard a wooden chair being dragged along the stone floor and placed in front of them. Then they heard the woman take a seat in it and sigh.

"Ahhh. Sorry, I hope you don't mind if I take a load off. Ha, your templar guardians fought like wild beasts today! Goodness, they really gave proof to the saying 'nothing's more dangerous than a cornered animal.' Your boys had nothing left to lose, and they proved it!"

The woman paused for a moment, and the seers heard her taking a large swallow of water before she resumed speaking.

"I really should have brought live soldiers so your side could have killed a ton of them and gone out in a true blaze of glory. But, you know, the undead are *so* cost-efficient. And they always get up just when you think you've put them down. Still, from my lips to your ears, your men did well for themselves. Well, except for *these* two idiots. Sorry, I couldn't be bothered giving them a heroic send-off, so I just misted them."

"Are you going to kill us?" one of the seers asked.

"Oh, sweetie, it's a little late in the day for a question like that, isn't it? Of course I'm going to kill you! That's why I've been hunting you for the past five years. That's why I tracked down your families, your friends, and finally, *you*. It's funny. I kept telling the templars that they didn't have to die. All these years they kept sacrificing themselves for your sake, and they really didn't have to. I'll never understand a heroic mindset!"

"Why are you doing this? Why won't you leave us alone?" asked another.

"Because it's fun?" the woman said.

"No, no, no! Please, I don't want to die! I don't want to die!" another seer sobbed.

"If that's the case, you shouldn't have gotten in my way," the Empress said.

"We're no threat to you! We never were. You have no reason to do this!"

"Of course you were never a threat to me," the Empress said scornfully. "But that doesn't mean I have no reason to do this. Quite the contrary. I'm giving a spirited demonstration of the consequences that result from *fucking with me*. I'm doing this to thoroughly convince you of what happens when my desires are impeded."

"You've done it! I swear you've done it. We'll never cross you again, we'll never—AGH!"

The voice of the pleading seer vanished, and more warm mist coated those who remained.

"Too. Late."

"You were going to kill Alec!" one of them suddenly shouted.

Her name was Eliza, and although she was the youngest of the seers, she was the fiercest among them. She refused to spend the remainder of her life cowering before this monster. She shook her arms free of her sisters and stood defiantly before their tormentor.

"Oh? Look at this. A mouse that roars like a lion!" said the amused Empress.

"We did nothing wrong! We had every right to defend our sworn brother! It's you who's escalated everything to this level and you alone!" Eliza said boldly.

"Okay. What's your point?" asked the Empress.

"What?" asked Eliza in confusion.

"I asked you what your point was. Okay, so I'm clearly the aggressor here. I've escalated everything to this ridiculous extreme, and now I'm about to have you all tortured to death. So what? Do you believe that pointing out that I'm clearly in the wrong will make any difference? Pardon my crude language, but you're still boned."

"But you don't have to do this if you know it's wrong . . . " Eliza said.

"Lady, you're still not saying anything I don't already know." The Empress sighed. "Listen, I can see you're struggling with this a little, so I'm going to lay things out as clearly as I can. I've driven you from refuge after refuge, killed your allies and defenders, and cornered you in this little backwater castle for one reason and one reason only: because you *spoiled* my fun."

Eliza couldn't believe what she was hearing. As she opened her mouth to ask if the other woman was being serious, she was quickly cut off.

"Oh, I can see you're about to say something! Do yourself a favor and *don't*. Let me finish. I've ruined your lives and crushed your precious temple for the most *pedantic* of reasons. Because I'm a petty and selfish woman, and I NEVER forgive a slight. And you, my dear songbirds, have slighted me. You sang your little song, warned your precious Lady Sylvain, gods rest her soul, and she had Alec snatched away before I could get my hands on him."

"But you were going to kill him," Eliza said.

"I STILL KILLED HIM!" the Empress yelled. "Don't you get it yet, you little fool? It took me a year, but I got him! A year after that, I got Sylvain too! That moron Tyrnos tried his best to hold things together, but news flash, he didn't do a very good job! He's the only one of your order's leaders I *haven't* killed, by the way, but I very much assure you, he really does wish I'd just let him die. He's constantly making requests for it!"

The seers heard the chair creak as its occupant stood up and angrily walked back and forth across the room.

"You . . . can't . . . stop me. You can't stop me! You little brats can see the future, so you should have realized what I'd do! But you still got in my way, and that just . . . *Ohhhh*, I hate people like you! I hate you all so much! You're spoilers! You people are *literally* walking spoilers! Your entire purpose is to see the ending of everything and ruin it for everyone else!"

"Our purpose is to protect the world!" Eliza shouted.

"And now you know you can't!" replied the Empress. "You irrefutably cannot. All your interference amounted to was an irritating delay of the inevitable! And because of your poor decision-making . . . Well, why get into it again? You know what I did. And you also know what I'm *about* to do. A message must now be sent."

Now the seers heard something, or rather, some *thing*, entering their chambers. A repulsive smell of rot and filth accompanied it, along with the sound of its horrid breathing. Although they were all blind, they could all *feel* the thing sweeping its eyes over them. They could hear its teeth gnashing and knew that it *hungered* . . .

"What is it? What *is* that thing?!" Eliza asked as her courage finally began to fail her.

"*This* is the messenger," the Empress said coldly.

Whatever the creature was, it now began to scuttle eagerly toward them.

"Please . . . please don't do this," Eliza begged. "Please, we're sorry. We're very sorry!"

"I suspect you are," said the Empress.

"Listen . . . listen to me! We can be of service to you! We can! We can offer you . . . the future itself!"

"Yes! Yes, please! Let us serve you! As we once served Sylvain!" said another seer.

"Hmm," said the Empress as she considered their offer. "I won't lie, that does sound *very* tempting."

She idly drummed her fingers against the back of the chair before asking, "Would you really be willing to do that? To tell me whatever I wish to know of the future?"

"Anything! Spare us, and we'll do anything you say!" said another through sobs.

"Wow. You know, I'd be a real fool to say no to that. All right! Your offer is accepted. Now, I'll expect your absolute obedience and stringent adherence to my commands. Give me the slightest reason to doubt you, and I needn't explain what happens next, yes?"

"Yes! Yes! Thank you, thank you, Your Majesty!" said Eliza.

On their knees they crawled to her, clutching at her feet and thanking Everly for her mercy. Thanking her for sparing their lives.

"Well, thank goodness we got all this unpleasantness out of the way," the Empress said in a magnanimous tone of voice. "I look forward to working with each of you."

She then turned her head toward the beast and said, "You may kill them now."

It began tearing into them at once—claws slashing, teeth shredding, seers dying.

Chewing. Swallowing. Repeating.

"Why? WHY?! You said you'd spare us!" Eliza wept. "You said you'd let us serve you!"

"Sweetie," the Empress explained patiently, "I can't use you as you are. Doesn't your choir need nine members to function? I've got things to do and zero interest in finding someone to complete your set. No, my decision to spare you is genuine, but it's not *for* the 'you' that I'm speaking with right now."

"You—you mean . . . "

"That's *riiiiight*. I'm addressing the choir of seers five years ago, who are seeing what's become of you and now have a decision to make. Save Alec and provoke my lasting enmity, or stay silent and accept my mercy. In one future, everyone they love will still be alive, as will the seers, and all they need to do is look at one another and say '*shhhhhh*' and nothing else."

"No, no, no," Eliza cried.

"Yes, yes, yes," Everly replied. "That's the big weakness that comes with seeing the future, kid. It only matters *if* and *only* if, you can affect *lasting* change. If you can't, all you'll do is paint a target on your back. Have you enjoyed these past five years? I bet you haven't. But *I* have. And I'll enjoy them all over again if I must! It's nothing to me, but it's *everything* to you."

Now the beast had its claws sunk into Eliza's flesh. After it pulled her head between its jaws, the last thing she ever heard was the Empress saying, "I hope you'll choose wisely."

Five years earlier.

One by one, the seers awoke in the darkness of their sleeping quarters and silently wept. The last of them to do so was Eliza. Made emotional by what they had endured, the nine of them came together and clung tightly to one another, sobbing quietly in relief at being alive and knowing that those dearest to them had yet to suffer as they had foreseen.

Everyone was safe.

Everyone except Alec.

With their new knowledge of the future came the need to sing and give their warning to the temple. To save their precious, trusting friend. It was a powerful urge, one deeply instilled in them through years of relentless training, and not easily ignored.

They wanted to help. They wanted to, so desperately . . .

But they couldn't bring themselves to break their silence. Because in that moment, fear trumped loyalty.

Fear and the desire to survive.

Standing in their circle, crying their silent tears, each of them held a finger to her lips and quietly said to the others, "Shhhhh."

Meanwhile, in the village of Anders.

Inside Everly's memory palace . . .

"Wait, they can see the future?" Everly asked after Grail finished explaining. "Seriously?"

"I'm afraid so," Grail said. "That's why the Eastern Temple isn't easily crossed, Majesty. Whatever move we make against them, they'll anticipate and have contingencies in place."

"That's so *irritating*," Everly groused. "Do you know what they sound like to me? Walking, talking *spoilers*! God, I *hate* people like that! Bastards like them ruined *Deathly Hallows* for me! I swear, if they get in my way tonight, I'm *really* going to hold a significant grudge."

"But, Your Majesty," Grail pleaded, "if you go after Alec, you'll expose yourself to the seers. The entire Eastern Temple will become aware of you. It'll be a war!"

"So?" Everly said bluntly. "Grail, do hurricanes exist in this world?"

"Sea storms? Yes, of course they do," he said.

"Then you already know. When a hurricane comes, you either hide or you flee. You don't attempt to fight it. If these seers are as talented as you claim, then they already know better than to *irk* me."

"But . . . Everly, how can you be certain that they'll stay silent?"

Everly smiled at him. "Grail, isn't knowing what will happen with certainty the very definition of foretelling the future? If that's really their gift, then the matter was settled as soon as I made up my mind. If they cross me, I'll kill their loved ones, then I'll destroy everything that ever made them feel safe, and then I'll kill them. I'll hunt them relentlessly until they have nowhere left to run. Then I'll take my time butchering them."

Are you listening, seers? she thought silently. *NO SPOILERS, okay? That's your only warning.*

Everly rose to her feet and stretched as she prepared to awaken in the real world.

"So, now that we've gotten *that* out of the way, let's go play with Alec," she said with a mischievous grin.

CHAPTER NINETEEN

Pain

Alec wondered when this awful duty would end.

Gaining employment as an usher in Anders's only church had been easy enough. Even those who worshiped at the false temple that dominated this nation could sense the holiness that lay within him. The greatness that came from being Lady Sylvain's hand.

A community church was the perfect place to gain the knowledge necessary for his mission. He soon discovered the identity of the young man he'd buried in the woods. One Samuel Bellweather. As befitted Lady Sylvain's squire, he'd personally laid the boy to rest and blessed his grave so that no animal would disturb it in search of a meal. It was the least he could do for the youth, even though he'd been raised to worship at the wrong temple.

It saddened Alec to have to pretend to believe in their false faith. He longed to correct the misunderstandings of the local priest and lead his flock to the correct path, but unfortunately, his mission required deception.

So he stayed silent and observed them.

He also *endured*.

Mrs. Bellweather, Samuel's mother, came to the church daily to pray for the salvation of her son. "Bring him home, bring him home, *please* bring him home," she begged daily at the altar. Her pain tore at Alec's heart. He wished so very much that he could just tell her the truth. If she knew of her son's fate, then she could properly grieve for him and eventually move on with her life.

But he couldn't.

And so she continued her daily pleas to heaven.

And Alec was forced to bear witness.

* * *

He awoke in the middle of the night when he heard people speaking in the sanctuary.

It had been difficult for him to fall asleep. Just as he was about to turn in, a wave of extreme pain flashed through his head. He'd never felt anything like it before. It hurt so much! There was nothing he could compare it to; it was like nothing he'd ever experienced before.

"What the hell was that?" he asked himself, after the pain finally subsided.

Troubled by whatever that had been, and hoping it wasn't anything serious, he eventually drifted into sleep. But now it had been interrupted by the arrival of these strangers.

What was going on? Evening services had ended hours ago, and morning services wouldn't begin until much later. What were these people doing here?

It wouldn't surprise him if they were drunk. The people of Winstead didn't seem to properly venerate their places of worship as they should. No wonder the presence of the gods was so diminished in these lands.

"I'm sorry, friends. Services won't begin until after dawn," he said regretfully to the hooded pair who sat in the foremost pew, after he entered the sanctum. "I'm afraid whatever business you have here will have to wait until then . . . "

He came to a stop when the cloying combination of earth and blood reached his nose. These strangers smelled filthy. Not only that, but they'd been wounded as well!

"Are the two of you all right?" Alec asked immediately, moving to examine them. "Show me where you're injured," he said to them.

"It's hard to say," said the taller of the pair, with a strangely familiar voice. "It's mostly my head, but I kind of feel it all over, I think. Isn't that weird?"

"Did you recently fall?" asked Alec. "Did you receive any kind of injury to your head?"

"Yeah, funny you should say," the stranger replied.

"What happened?"

"Well, a man I thought I could trust, a man who likes to present himself as kind and caring . . . heh, he basically bashed my damned skull in with a big hunk of steel."

Alec gazed at the face beneath the stranger's hood and scrambled backward so quickly that he fell to the floor.

The ruined face that smiled back at him belonged to Simon Thelmar.

"Being hammered to death doesn't sound so bad," said the second person, who Alec now realized was a teenage boy. "I got smashed into a tree. Hurled face-first right into it. It *compacted* me. It hurt so much that I wanted to die. So I did. But it still hurts. How come it still hurts when I'm dead?"

The boy was Samuel Bellweather. His injuries were . . . *terrible.*

It was all Alec could do not to vomit at the sight of him.

"I hear you, kid," Simon agreed. "It's nothing but pain, isn't it? And it's so damn cold! Why didn't the temple scriptures say anything about how cold being dead got?"

"I don't know. I thought if you weren't bad and did no evil, you'd go to paradise when you died. This ain't paradise. It's awful. No light, no joy, just darkness and pain," Samuel said miserably.

"My head really hurts, Alec. By the gods, it hurts *so* much," Simon said. "Why'd you do it, man? Why'd you kill me?"

"Simon, please, I swear I didn't want to," Alec said. "But you were suffering. You were suffering so much, and Lady Sylvain said to put you out of your misery."

"What about my parents? What about *their* misery?" asked Samuel. "My mother comes in here every day. You *see* her! You see how she hopes for a miracle, but you won't tell her the truth! She blames herself. You're letting her torture herself! What kind of a godly man are you?"

"He's not, kid," Simon said. "There *are* no gods. If there were, why would they let us suffer like this?"

"I'm so cold all the time," Samuel said sadly. "Until my parents let me go, I can't move on. The voices in the dark say it's warm where they're at. They say if I go to them, there's fire everywhere. I'm so cold . . . "

"That does sound pretty good, kid," Simon said. "I'm sick of being cold too. Some unending flame sounds like exactly what we need."

"What if it's worse than this?" asked Samuel.

"Who cares?" replied Simon. "Even if it is, it's not *our* fault. We aren't to blame for our fate. Alec is."

"Yeah," Samuel said. "Yeah, you're right. We're going to hell, and it's *all* Alec's fault. He couldn't save us. He can't save *anyone*."

"Please," Alec said desperately. "Please, I'm sorry. Please, don't go! Please!"

The two phantoms rose from the pew and began walking to the exit. The two doors slowly opened themselves, revealing an endless blazing fire that raged just beyond them. The unyielding heat of it saturated the sanctuary and brought sweat to Alec's brow as he beheld the dead men walking toward their eternal doom.

"Wow, kid. Do you feel that?" asked Simon. "It's so *warm*."

"Yeah," Samuel said. "It's paradise, compared to this. Let's burn forever."

Side by side, the two of them walked forth into the inferno.

"*Paradise*," Samuel said once more.

"Yeah," Simon said in agreement.

Then the two of them began to scream.

"NOOOOOO!" shouted Alec. He ran to save them, enduring the terrible heat as best he could, but before he could reach them, the doors slammed shut. When he hurriedly opened them, all he saw were the quiet homes of the sleeping villagers, accompanied by the chirping of nocturnal insects.

They were gone.

"Alec," said a woman.

He turned and saw none other than Lady Sylvain herself standing before the altar.

He ran to her, sobbing, tears streaming down his face like a terrified child, wanting only to be comforted, wanting only to be assured that he wasn't a bad person. In that moment he needed her assurance that he really *had* done the right thing. On his knees, he clung tightly to her leg, begging to be forgiven.

"Alec," she said once more.

Now he felt something wet drip onto his scalp.

When he rubbed his palm against it, he saw that it was blood.

"What?" he asked in bewilderment. Then he looked up.

Lady Sylvain's eyes had been gouged out. From the black depths of her empty sockets, she wept tears of blood that landed on Alec's upturned face.

"You really *can't* save anyone," she said.

Then she smiled at him.

Alec awoke screaming in the dark.

He was on his bed in the small room the church let him use as his private quarters. He ran his fingers through his sweat-soaked hair and held his head tightly as he wept. What an awful nightmare that had been. What a horrid dream.

It had felt so real. A perfect encapsulation of everything he'd been feeling these past two weeks. The guilt of not letting Mrs. Bellweather know the truth about her son's death. The even greater guilt of taking Simon's life.

He knew that his actions served a noble and holy purpose.

He knew they had been necessary.

But if so, why did he feel so conflicted? He didn't feel like a hero.

He didn't feel like a defender of the righteous.

He felt like a murderer.

He felt like a sick voyeur who had gorged on a perverse lust for the suffering of others.

What sort of man was he? Why would any god accept one such as he?

You really can't *save anyone, Alec.*

There are no gods . . .

Why had it felt so real?

With his head bowed in misery, Alec wiped at the sweat on his brow. Then he froze in sudden, overwhelming terror.

His fingers were slick with blood.

"No," he whimpered. "No, no, no, no . . . "

Frantically, he ran to the church sanctuary and saw that the floor had been dirtied with footprints and droplets of blood. He also saw that the front pew was similarly coated in dirt and gore.

"No . . . this can't be," he said frantically to himself. "It was a dream, it was a dream, it was a DREAM . . . "

Desperately, he grabbed his traveling cloak and ran from the church.

He ran in the direction of the only place that could prove he wasn't losing his mind.

Deep in the forest north of the village, Alec dropped to his knees in despair.

The graves were empty.

"I'm sorry," he said. "I'm sorry! I'm sorry! I'M SORRY, I'M SORRY, *I'M SORRY!*"

"I guess you really are, huh?" asked a young girl.

He turned and recognized her from the village. She was a pretty thing wearing a spring dress. Beautiful, even. According to the gossiping attendees of the church, she was an illegitimate child of some regional noble. What had her name been? Emily? Amelia? No, no.

"*Everly*," he said. "Everly . . . why are you here?" he asked her.

"Waiting for you," she said perkily.

"What? Why?" he asked.

"Gosh, Alec. You're slow to catch on, aren't you? No wonder you can't save anyone."

He stared at her with eyes that slowly widened in shock. "What did you say?"

She smiled prettily at him and stepped closer. "I said, 'You can't save anyone.' That's what Simon and sammy said, wasn't it?"

"How do you know about them?" he asked her.

In response, she smiled even wider and lightly tapped her finger against the side of her head.

"*You . . .* " he said as anger slowly rose from within him. "Who *are* you?"

"A concerned citizen worried for her community. Didn't you hear? There's a *murderer* running lose."

"I'm not a murderer," Alec said.

"I hear he's a rabid dog who attacks his own allies," she continued merrily. "A pathetic worm who'd kill for a treat from his mistress. He'd spill anyone's blood for a pat on the head!"

"Shut up!" he yelled furiously.

"How did it feel?" Everly asked him. "Watching sammy's parents, I mean. Keeping a secret like that must have been difficult! Was it thrilling to watch them suffer, while knowing you could end it whenever you wished? Did it make you feel important? Did it make you feel as *powerful* as those silly gods you pretend to believe in?"

"You've been inside my mind," he realized.

"Yep!" she said brightly. "How's your headache been?"

"Everly . . . " he began to say.

"*Mmmm*, listen to him. Saying my name like *that*," she said with her eyes closed. "Oh, it's like verbal honey."

"You've violated a sacred space! Only the gods may see into our souls," Alec said in outrage.

"I don't disagree," Everly said to him. "Not in the slightest! I suppose that must mean I'm a god."

"You've gone too far!" he shouted.

"Ha! Oh, Alec. I'm afraid that's where our opinions diverge. You see, *I* don't think I've gone *nearly* far enough."

"How did Samuel Bellweather die?" Alec demanded to know.

"Poorly."

"Were you the one who burned Simon with your magic?"

"Eh, *technically?*" she said with a shrug.

"Everly," he said. "I need you to come with me. In the name of the Temple of the Holy Will, I will have you put to the question. Any sins you've committed, any affronts you've given to the gods, these you will answer for."

"Oh, is this how you want to do this?" she asked him. "Are you a god cop now? Working the street on a heavenly beat? Shoot, I bet Fox already has a show like that in production. They'll air like three episodes before canceling it."

"What are you babbling about?"

"I'm just being meta. You don't approve?" She pouted.

Instead of responding to her baiting, Alec focused inward and called upon the holy power that dwelt within him. Soon his holy armor and blessed mace would appear, granting him the superhuman prowess he would require to subdue this madwoman.

Nothing happened.

"What have you done?" he asked her after she flashed another knowing grin.

"It's a minor application of *harada*. Nothing special. I'm sure *anyone* could do it. *Maybe.*"

"You can use *harada*?" he asked in astonishment.

"Mm-hmm. I can project it too. If you're not already channeling your magic, I can cut you off from it before you can. In my presence, you're nothing special, Alec. I don't see a holy knight. All I see are joints I can bend the wrong way and blood vessels I can pop. Want me to show you?"

She darted toward him suddenly and caught his jaw with a spinning kick that sent him tumbling to the ground. Rising quickly to his feet, he tried to retaliate with a straight right punch that she lightly brushed aside, before slamming her right elbow against his cheek.

Stunned by the ferocity of the blow, he began to fall backward, but she quickly caught him by the front of his cloak and held him firmly in place.

"Is this all you've got?" she asked him, before slamming her forehead into his nose. "Can't you do anything on your own?"

She released him and let him fall onto the dirt.

Alec sputtered angrily as blood trickled down his throat. After getting back to his feet, he hurriedly grabbed a rock lying on the ground and was preparing to charge at her with it when he realized she had vanished from sight.

Where had she gone?

"You're *slooooow*," she whispered into his ear from behind.

As Alec spun around in surprise, she swung her arm in a lazy backfist that connected with his ribs.

And shattered them.

"AAAAARGH!" he screamed before dropping to all fours.

"And *crunchy*." She laughed.

Alec tried to rise to his feet, but the pain of his new injury was agony itself. The slightest movement forced him to gasp desperately for air, of which there didn't seem to be enough.

Gods, oh, gods above, did she collapse one of my lungs? he wondered deliriously.

Meanwhile, Everly began to sing.

"Puppy, puppy, at my feet!
Puppy, puppy, want a treat?
If you do, then raise your paw!
Puppy, puppy, now say aww!"

Everly knelt low so that she was level with Alec's head. Then she scooped up a handful of forest soil and shoved it into his mouth and nose. She ignored his struggling and clamped down hard once she'd forced him onto his back. Alec wheezed desperately and tried to push her hand away, but he didn't have the strength.

Instead, he could only stare helplessly as darkness overtook his vision.

The last thing he saw was her expression of serenity.

She looks so happy . . . he found himself thinking.

When he awoke, Alec discovered that he couldn't move.

Above him, Everly loomed.

"Hello, there," she said. "Did you sleep well?"

"What happened?" he struggled to ask.

"Nothing much. I just had you take a nap while I made a few adjustments that you're going to need for the long haul. You'll *barely* notice them."

"W-what?" he asked. Why was it so difficult to speak? It was like there was something in his throat.

There was. Some sort of tube had been inserted down his esophagus. It garbled his words, but she could still understand him.

"Hey, Alec?" Everly suddenly asked. "Alec, may I tell you a bad joke? Please? I swear you'll like it! *Pleeeeease?*" she pleaded.

"What did you do to me?" he asked her.

In response, Everly reached to her side and picked up two objects. In each of her hands, she now held an amputated arm.

"Alec," she said with a childish grin. "Wave goodbye to your arms!"

Then she began waving at him with them.

"RAAAAAAAAAAAAAAGH!" he screamed in a moment of sheer animal panic.

His arms were gone.

His legs were gone.

He was a torso in a grave, connected to the earth through a series of strange vines that were now running throughout his body.

"Haha! I knew you'd love it," Everly said merrily, before tossing his arms into the hole with him. Then she sat down at the edge of the grave and cheerfully kicked her legs out as she spoke to him.

"Now, listen. You're going to be fine, okay? Those vines are going to bring you air, water, and nutrients. They're going to be your umbilical cords, connecting you to Mother Nature herself. Doesn't that sound nice? And worry not—you won't be lonely either."

She crooked a finger, and Alec saw something emerge from the dirt beside him.

It was a rotting corpse.

"See?" Everly said. "It's your friend Simon. Remember him? You're going to be roommates!"

"Why are you doing this to me?" he asked her.

A shadow seemed to cover her face before she answered. "Because you should have minded your own fucking business," she said sweetly.

"People will look for me. I'm Lady Sylvain's squire. PEOPLE WILL LOOK FOR ME!" he shouted.

"No, they won't. Will they, Alec?"

"Why would they? I'm right here," said a familiar-sounding man who sat down beside her.

It was him. He was looking down at himself. Or was he looking up at himself?

His duplicate smiled at him as though he knew exactly what Alec was thinking, then shrugged as if to say, *Who knows?*

"Alec, this is Alec," Everly said. "I feel silly introducing you because it's like you've already met. You know, when people think of necromancy, they mostly think of it as animating a dead corpse. Skeletal warriors and rampaging zombies and the like. They rarely think of the more interesting applications for it. Like this . . . ”

She gestured toward the duplicate as though she were showing off a new item for sale at the market. “Converting a few kilograms of protein into a new living form and then sculpting it to appear like someone else. ‘Meat magic,’ I like to call it! Amazing, isn’t it?”

“It’s a feat like no other, Everly,” said the Alec at her side. “An astonishing achievement!”

“Oh, goodness! Feel free to praise me more,” she said demurely.

“You’re an incomparable beauty, Everly. My heart longs for your angelic smile, and my soul thirsts for your affection. Why did I waste even a moment of my life longing for that hag, Sylvain, when a goddess like you was within reach of my arms?”

Everly blushed in delighted embarrassment and lightly slapped him on the shoulder. “Oh, *you*! You’re such a charmer.”

Then she turned back to the original Alec.

“I know what you’re thinking. He’ll never fool anyone! Except he will. I’ve been inside your mind, remember? He knows everything you know; he’s exactly like you, except he’s a far, *far* superior product. Faster, stronger, smarter, and *extremely* devious. You see, I’ve been thinking about your precious temple, Alec. I think there’s a lot of potential there. But not for all this nonsense of dillydallying around, trying to save the world. How pointless is that?”

She turned an affectionate gaze toward the duplicate and lightly tousled his hair. “Alec here is going to scout out your senior leadership. Then he’s going to gradually help me replace them, one by one, just as we’ve done with you. I’d say by next summer at the latest your order is going to be under new leadership. I’m sure Lady Sylvain will understand.”

“No . . . ” whimpered Alec.

“Oh, yes! Say hello to the new management, my friend. But Alec . . . I’ve got to be honest with you. As your new supervisor, I don’t believe your current level of output will be able to match the expectations I have for the team. Sadly, I’m going to have to let you go. This shouldn’t surprise you, though. You’ve already been given your *severance*.”

“Don’t do this . . . Please don’t do this,” he begged. “I only wanted to help people. That’s all I ever wanted to do . . . ”

“So far, you have been,” Everly said as she and the other Alec rose to their feet and brushed off their clothing. “You’ve helped me out a great deal. I’m really looking forward to poking through your memories and studying how this so-called ‘holy magic’ works. That’ll be fun! Maybe once I’ve mastered it, I’ll have your temple venerate me as a new saint.”

“*Saint Everly*. To my ears, your very name evokes divinity itself,” the other

Alec said as he reverently kissed her hand. "Please allow me be the first to worship at your feet."

"Do you love me?" she asked him.

"More than life itself," he assured her. "You are my *everything*."

"Oh, my. I'd better get you back to the temple before you get me in trouble." She giggled.

"No, no. Don't do this! NO," begged the true Alec, feebly.

"You'll be fine, Alec. I'm sure you will! Just hang in there," Everly said to him.

Then she paused as if realizing an important detail.

"Oh, wait. You'd need arms for that, wouldn't you?"

"THEY'LL FIND ME! SYLVAIN WILL FIND ME—" Alec howled before he was silenced by the earth that now covered him.

"It's more likely that she'll join you." Everly smirked.

Then she turned to her companion. "Well," she said. "Didn't he seem sweet?"

CHAPTER TWENTY

Guidance

Everly, I'm confused about something," Alec said as they walked back to the village.

"Oh? What's that?" she asked him.

Everly had been a little lost in thought as she pondered today's success. Crushing the original Alec hadn't been quite as fun as she'd hoped it would be, but the psychological torment she'd inflicted upon him after the fight—*that* had been beyond amazing!

She would have given the look of terror and defeat imprinted on Alec's face a chef's kiss if she didn't have her dignity as a burgeoning evil overlord to consider.

"Well, I was wondering, Everly. Why didn't we just kill the poor wretch? I mean, sure, leaving him alive to suffer was wicked fun too, but wouldn't it have been more practical to just snuff him out?" Alec asked. "He seems like a loose end."

Everly had to hand it to him—that was a surprisingly good observation for something she'd assembled from a pile of unusable leftovers she'd had gathered from a tannery. She'd made this creature well.

His name was kind of a pain, though. She kept wanting to call him Alec II, or New Alec, or even Nu Alec. It was difficult to think of her creation as being anything like that broken thing she'd left buried in the forest.

"Hey, when it's just us, from now on I'm calling you *Nalec*, got it?" she said to him.

"Ah. I take it that's a portmanteau of the words *new* and *Alec*?" he asked her.

"Why, yes, it is! You really do catch on quickly." Everly beamed at him.

"Well, thanks to you having had a hand in my creation, my thought processes aren't nearly as muddled as those of my inferior predecessor," Nalec said. "I pity him for not having you in his life."

"Nalec, I enjoy you quite a bit," Everly said to him. "But I must warn you, my appreciation of your shameless fawning does have its limits. Just speak to me normally, please."

"I wasn't fawning!" Nalec said in a wounded tone of voice. "It's just that in your presence, I feel compelled to share the passion you inspire within me."

"*Nalec*," Everly said evenly.

She hadn't raised her voice in the slightest, but at that moment, the insects that surrounded them ceased their chirping.

Nalec quickly cleared his throat. "Ahem! As you say, Everly."

"Wonderful," she replied with a pleased smile. "Now, to answer your question, Alec isn't a loose end. He's a tie that binds. Specifically, we'll be using him to bind the choir of seers tightly to us. One day, perhaps out of some desperate need to atone for their complicity, the threat of my displeasure might not be enough to keep them quiet."

"*Ahhh*," Nalec said as he nodded in understanding. "So you're going to use their fondness for him against them?"

"Precisely!" Everly said. "Alec is still alive, but he's hardly safe. The vines keeping him alive can also be used to trigger a fatal anaphylactic shock in his respiratory system. If anyone attempts to remove him from his prison, Titania will know in an instant and kill him in a flash. Anaphylaxis is a *terrible* way to die, Nalec. Ask anyone with a peanut allergy."

"It sounds like it," he said. "But will that really be enough to keep those blind little mice under control?"

"His life will be considerable leverage," Everly said. "One of the seers has it *particularly* bad for him. I saw it in his own memories! The poor fool was too fixated on his precious Lady Sylvain to notice."

"Wait . . . " Nalec said slowly, before realization quickly dawned on him. Then he gave a cruel laugh and said, "*Eliza?* Noooo. That can't be right! Really?"

"I'm afraid so," Everly said smugly. "Goodness, the poor thing was so clumsy and overt about it that I'm shocked he never noticed. It makes me feel bad for her.

"Hmm," Nalec said thoughtfully. "You know, as I think about it, she's really quite fetching. If her virginity is chaffing her so much, I could probably offer some assistance."

Everly frowned at his words and shook her head. "Gross," she said. "Not happening."

"Why not?" Nalec asked with a sly expression on his face. "Hey, the experience might be good for her. Unless . . . You wouldn't happen to be feeling *jealous* of the idea, would you, Everly—"

Everly backhanded Nalec through a tree.

Not against one.

Not into one.

Through it.

"Nalec," Everly said to him mildly as he lay bleeding before her. "There are rules governing how the seers function. There must be nine of them, and they have to be physically *pure*. As in untouched by the hands of man. For some reason, those heavenly types in the realms beyond prefer their oracles to be virgins. *I* don't know why. It's a god thing—they're way too fixated on details like that. It's pretty gross."

"Okay," Nalec groaned from his position on the dirt. When he looked up, she saw fear in his eyes. "That really hurt! You didn't have to hit me."

"Yes, I'm afraid I did," she said in annoyance. "Because *I* learned of those details by perusing Alec's memories. And since I instilled those very same memories into *you*, for you not to realize something so important must mean you haven't been studying them. That displeases me, Nalec. I'm disappointed in you."

He flinched after hearing her say that, as though she'd struck him again.

That made her smile. The conditioning she and Eris had devised during Nalec's creation appeared to be a success.

I told you it would be, Eris said proudly. *Does this please you? Am I forgiven for my lapse in judgment?*

Not quite. But this does *go a long way toward getting you there*, Everly replied.

How wonderful!

Everly reached down and gently guided Nalec back to his feet.

"Arrogance is an admirable trait, and I don't dislike that about you," she said. "But make certain that your carefree attitude doesn't get you *caught*. You were made for a purpose, and if you fail to achieve it . . . then what's the point of having you around?"

She then held out a hand and said, "Handkerchief."

Nalec quickly pulled one from his shirt pocket and handed it to her.

Everly licked a corner of the cloth and began to wipe away the blood and dirt that now covered his face. "Look at you. Your first day of existence, and you're already so messy! You're a silly thing, aren't you, Nalec?" she asked him.

"Yes," he said unhappily. "Yes, I'm very . . . silly. I don't mean to be."

"I know you don't," she said softly. "Please don't make me do that again. I like you. You've got potential. But potential alone doesn't guarantee success. You're very replaceable, and you're not even a real person. You're just an idea I had."

"What? No, I'm *real*," he began to whine. "I am! I'm real, aren't I?"

"No. You're not. Not unless I say you are," she said to him gently. "If you really want my acknowledgment, don't fail me. Prove you weren't a mistake. Don't be a *loser*. I don't like losers, Nalec. For me, they just don't exist. Do you understand?"

" . . . Yes," he said sadly, with a trembling lip.

"Good," she said to him. She stuffed his handkerchief back into his pocket. Then she suddenly pulled him into a tight hug. "I want to feel proud of you. Can you do that? Can you make me feel proud?"

"Yes," he said, as he buried his face into her shoulder. "I can do it. I can make you feel proud. I swear I'm real. I'm a real person . . . "

"We'll see," Everly said as she patted his back. "Do you love me?"

"*Yes*," he said, weeping "You really *are* my everything."

"Good," she said. She lightly pushed him away and resumed walking home. "*Everybody* should love me."

One day they all would.

The survivors, anyway.

CHAPTER TWENTY-ONE

Departures

The safe return of Samuel Bellweather was considered nothing less than a miracle by the good people of Anders.

After Mrs. Bellweather arrived at the church shortly after the midday service, to resume her lonely daily ritual of begging her child's safe return, it seemed that her prayers were finally answered.

Her husband had given up the previous week and urged her to do the same. To accept reality. But she refused. She'd never been a particularly pious woman before her son's disappearance, but her faith in the teachings of the temple had grown equally with her desperation to see her child returned to their home.

So she spurned her husband's advice and continued her vigil.

"Please bring him home, please bring him home, please bring him home," she quietly begged. Behind her, she heard the doors to the sanctuary opening, but she paid it no mind.

All her energy was focused on pleading with heaven.

"Mama?" said a weary young voice behind her.

Her eyes widened at the sound of it. She turned around, and who should it be that stood before her?

Her boy. Her boy returned to her at last!

"Mama!" He sobbed. His clothes were dirty and torn, and he was pale and sickly looking. The very sight of him told her immediately that wherever he'd been, her boy had suffered.

Her poor, poor boy!

But that didn't matter anymore. He was home at last!

"SAMMYYYYYY!" she shrieked as she climbed to her feet and raced down the aisle to cover him with kisses and hugs. The new usher, Alec, came running into the sanctuary, alerted by the noise Mrs. Bellweather was making, but as soon as he heard the name being shouted and beheld the boy she was embracing, he quickly understood.

"Glory to the light!" he shouted dramatically. "This is a MIRACLE!"

Alec fell to his knees and shouted praises to heaven for the mercy of the light and so on and so forth. The sanctuary became so loud between his celebratory yelling and Mrs. Bellweather's ecstatic bellowing that soon, alarmed strangers began coming in off the street to make certain that everything was all right. Once they too realized what happened, they joined the din and offered cheers and congratulations of their own.

"PEOPLE, LET US GIVE PRAAAAAAAISE!" Alec said in holy jubilation. "I *said*, 'Let us give PRAAAAAAAAAAAAISE!'"

And that was exactly what the people did.

Over his mother's shoulder, Samuel gave a slight nod to the usher, who returned it with a wink and a nod of his own.

Things moved quickly after that.

Samuel explained to the curious people that he didn't know where he'd been. "It was a dark place," he said. "That's all I can remember. I hurt all over, and I couldn't see, and I was *so scared*. Wherever it was, I thought I was going to die . . ."

"Oh, my baby boy." His mother wept.

"But then . . . one day, I don't know how, it was like I could *hear* my mother's voice calling to me. And in that moment, I knew . . . I just *knew* that I was going to be all right! Like heaven itself was guiding me home! So I crawled up from wherever it was . . . and . . . *and* . . ."

He began to silently cry. "And I just followed my mama's voice! Oh, Mama, I'm so glad you prayed for me! I'm *so* glad!"

The two of them embraced once more to the cheers of the crowd, and that was that.

Shortly afterward, Alec resigned from his position. He told everyone that he'd been so moved by the miracle he'd witnessed that he felt compelled to study at the central temple in the capital and spread word of the power of hope and belief.

It was a shame. He'd been quite popular with the community and would be dearly missed.

In the Eastern Temple, Alec knelt before Lady Sylvain and gave his report.

After weeks of silence, that morning he'd signaled for pickup from the choir of senders and was swiftly whisked back home. After arriving, he'd immediately gone to consult with his mistress.

"I apologize, my lady, but in the end, the village of Anders was a place of no consequence," he informed her. "The people there are a simple, good-hearted folk, but nothing beyond that. I've begun to suspect that Lord Tyrnos was correct in his assumption. The defeat of the unhallowed man must have been divine judgment."

"How can you be certain?" Sylvain asked him.

"Because nothing else makes sense," Alec answered confidently. He then rose from his bent knee without permission, which Sylvain found surprising. Normally, he would have waited for her to bid him to rise.

"My lady, perhaps it's time we put this matter behind us. You have greater responsibilities than the matter of what struck down some filthy demon. The work of the gods demands your focus."

"I *know* what the gods require of me, squire," Sylvain said curtly.

"Please forgive me if I was being presumptuous," Alec replied smoothly. "I simply wish to be of greater assistance to you. I think it's time I truly settled into my role."

"Oh? Do you?"

"I do. I've realized in my time away from your side that . . . I haven't been as committed to our cause as I should be. I've let doubts plague me. I've questioned our methods and the sad necessities of the war we wage against evil. I realize now how selfish I've been. Lady Sylvain, I'll be that way no longer."

Suddenly, he stepped closer to her and took her hand into his own. He boldly kissed it and gazed into her eyes with such intensity that even *she* was startled.

"Alec!" she said in surprise.

"I will do *anything* that my lady wishes of me. I am but a tool in her hand, and whatever she wills of me, I shall do it without hesitation. This I vow," he said to her without breaking eye contact.

"Well . . . well, good. Excellent. I'm pleased by your renewal of commitment," she said as her skin flushed. "Uh . . . We'll speak later. I must soon consult with the choir of seers."

"Excellent," he replied. "Perhaps we could do so over dinner?"

"Y-yes, that sounds lovely. A nice meal between the two of us," Sylvain agreed.

"I look forward to it," Alec said. He then departed after giving her an elegant bow.

Once she was alone, Sylvain took a moment to collect herself. Goodness, when had Alec become so . . . self-assured? It seemed his time out in the world had matured him.

She smiled softly as she remembered the feel of his lips brushing against her fingers and decided that she liked these changes.

She was looking forward to dinner.

* * *

Nalec strutted down the halls of the great temple, greatly pleased with himself.

So far, his performance had been flawless. Everly would be pleased, and knowing that made him very happy.

She would soon see what he could accomplish. He would prove himself the greatest of her creations!

She would see. She *would*.

As he continued on his way, he saw the choir of seers being carefully guided to where Sylvain awaited them.

He found them all so very strange. Despite being blind, they seemed to be able to sense his presence. Wasn't that interesting?

Most of them had turned their heads away in fear. All but Eliza.

He smiled and raised a finger to his lips as they passed each other.

"Shhhhhhh," he whispered to her.

Everly decided it was time she got moving.

The country was still months away from the seasonal summer campaign against Oldstead, but she figured she could find lots of different ways to keep herself occupied while on the road. All that mattered to her was getting out there and seeing the world she would one day rule, with her own two eyes.

It was time. She was ready.

It was a shame that Lyona was putting up such a fight.

"Everly Vel Belsar, turn around *right now* and get back in the house this instant! You're not going anywhere, young lady!" she yelled at her daughter.

Oof. Everly had hoped their parting would be on friendlier terms than this.

In the years they'd spent together, she'd genuinely grown to love her new mother. Heck, she didn't even think of her as *New Mom*, anymore. To her, Lyona was just *Mom*. Everly didn't want to make her worry.

But as much as Everly cared for her, Lyona's role had basically concluded. At this point in time, she wasn't needed, and Everly had no intention of sticking around the house until it was time to be sent to the Imperial Magus Academy that all magically gifted nobles were required to attend at age fifteen.

Her testing had been performed the previous year. Two examiners had arrived in the village with a strange orb they claimed could measure one's affinity with the elementals. By law, all those descended from nobility were required to be tested to see if they possessed any capacity for magic.

Naturally, Everly had barely passed. According to them, she was a minor talent, but still possessed *just* enough ability to be worth instructing. So, in four months' time she'd be sent off to the capital.

Everly refused to even consider squandering the remainder of her free time doing nothing. Sure, she was looking forward to beginning her time at the academy since adventures at magic school were a hallmark of all the best *isekai* adventure stories she'd read back on Earth. But first, she wanted to take a trip.

The idea of languishing in boredom in Anders, just so her mother could feel better by knowing where she was at all times, was out of the question. It was pure nonsense! Everly wasn't ungrateful for everything Lyona had done for her, but it was now time she began asserting her independence.

"Mom, I'll be fine. I promise," she told her. "When I arrive in Baseland, I'll meet up with Tybalt and Alden. There really isn't anything for you to worry about."

"Everly, if you don't stop this nonsense at once, so help me girl, I'll—" Lyona fumed.

"Lyona. I *said* I'll be fine," Everly said more firmly this time. "I love you, and this won't be the last time we meet, I promise. I'll be back eventually, but for now, I'm *going*. Please stop making this awkward. I don't want our neighbors gossiping about us."

Everly didn't know why her words set her mother off so badly. She thought she'd spoken *very* respectfully to her, but from the way she reacted, you'd have thought she'd called her the c-word. Lyona stomped down the walkway to her daughter, raised her hand, and gave her the grandmother of all slaps across the cheek.

Everly let it connect. Hopefully, Lyona now felt a little better.

"Are you finished?" Everly asked her.

"Get back inside!" Lyona yelled as she raised her hand to deliver another slap.

Jeez, so unreasonable, Everly thought. This time she caught Lyona's hand at the wrist. She didn't apply any pressure to her grip. She didn't want to injure her mother or make her feel afraid. She merely held her hand firmly in place to let her know how much stronger she was.

"Let go of me!" Lyona demanded.

Everly realized in that moment that there was nothing she could say that would convince her mother that she'd be safe. Everly couldn't understand her reaction. She'd been telling Lyona for months in advance of her intention to leave, so it wasn't as though she was springing this out of nowhere.

Why hadn't Lyona believed her? She was a *very* honest person!

Seeing now that she had no other choice, Everly tapped into Eris's power of spirit. Then she gazed into her mother's eyes and gently entered her mind; she did so carefully so that she wouldn't accidentally cause her any mental harm. If she pushed in too forcefully, she'd crack Lyona's brain like a quail's egg.

With their minds now connected, Everly gave her mother a series of commands that she would be unable to disobey. *I'm leaving to study in the south for a bit. You're very happy for me. I'll be back next year before I head off to school. You love me very much. You're not worried in the slightest. You're so proud of me.*

"I'm so proud of you, Everly," Lyona said as she reached forth to give her daughter a tight hug. "I love you very much, and I'll miss you every day that you're gone. Write to me constantly, do you hear? And when you see your uncle and cousin, give them my best and tell them not to do anything dangerous."

"I will, Mom," Everly said with a smile. "And like I said, everything will be just fine."

"Of course it will," Lyona said with a dazzling smile of her own. "You're a *very* capable person!"

Using a Jedi mind trick on poor Lyona . . . Honestly, Everly didn't feel *great* about doing it, but at least now she wouldn't worry unnecessarily. Everly really wished she could have parted ways with her mother without having to resort to such methods, but what could she say?

Man maketh plans, but the devil laughs.

Mom will be fine. I'll have Titania and Eris check in on her every day. Unlike Everly, her elementals could traverse thousands of miles in mere moments. If anyone tried anything funny just because Lyona now lived alone, they'd die an ugly death for their folly.

Leave my mother alone, assorted opportunistic scumbags of Winstead, thought Everly. *If you think I'm joking, then fool around and find out. Ask Alec! This has been a PSA for people who wish to keep their limbs attached to their torsos.*

Although she could have had Titania whip up a new carriage for her and Eris could have mind-buzzed a few wild horses into pulling it, Everly chose to exit Anders on her own two feet so she could better enjoy the feeling of finally being out in the world on her own.

This was a pleasure she'd never gotten to enjoy in her old life on Earth. *Complete autonomy.* She was finally free to do whatever she wished, whenever she wanted, and there was no one around who could stop her. Although, in the interests of accuracy, there technically hadn't been anyone capable of stopping her from doing whatever she wanted since she'd been a newborn.

Yes, the possibilities were endless. Nothing left to do now but enjoy the happy life of a wanderer.

"Whore's child. Hey, whore's child! Where're you going? Hey, I'm *talking* to you."

With her musings now interrupted, Everly turned to see a shabbily dressed trio of men approaching her. She was now on the outskirts of Anders, on her way to the King's Road that would take her south. Her route to it had taken her past the less desirable area of town. She'd been so caught up in her thoughts that she hadn't even noticed.

"Well, look at this. The whore's child is wearing herself a pair of trousers and a damn nice coat. Why're you dressed like that? Hmm? Someone could mistake you for a boy, you silly thing. Did your whore mom teach you to dress that way?" asked the first of them, a wiry-looking idiot with a mouth full of yellowed teeth that were slowly rotting away.

Ugh, thought the displeased Everly. *I get it already, fantasy world! These guys have troublesome values. Do we really have to go all grimdark with it, though? I was having such a nice walk.*

"Hey, I asked you a question," the man said, while his friends laughed their heads off.

Their rude behavior was making Everly angry.

They reminded her, in a way, of that idiot who had transformed into a spider. Everly had a powerful, singular vision for how she wanted her career as a future monarch to proceed. There were milestones she wanted to hit and moments she wanted to experience.

But dealing with "realistic situations" wasn't one of them. She loathed this sort of confrontation!

These utter wads had no place in *her* story. They weren't worth a moment of her time.

So she turned her back on them and resumed her walk.

"Haha! Look at that, Will! She's just as stuck up as her mama!" Another member of the trio laughed.

"Then maybe we need to teach her some manners," the third one said with a disgustingly *moist*-sounding voice. "Little whore wants to act like a grown woman. Maybe we should treat her like one. Look at her. She's old enough."

"Friends, I think you're right," agreed the one who had spoken first. "Let's have some fun with that sweet little body. But I get to go first with her."

"You always go first!" complained the second voice.

"I don't mind," breathed out the third. "I like it when he warms them up for me."

The three of them broke out into laughter and quickly began to follow her.

Oh, for god's sake, Everly fumed. *This body's sixteen years old! Nope. Uh-uh. Not having it. I can only put up with so much Westeros-ing! I was walking away, you all saw it, and then that shithead went and said what he said. I am completely without fault! Not that I care about fault or anything, because, hey, I'm a goddamned dark lord!*

It was time to show these goat lickers exactly what that title meant.

She turned around and began marching toward them.

"What'cha doing, girl? You hear something you didn't like?" Rogel asked with a leering sneer. "I said, 'Did you hear something you didn't'—*hsk!*"

Everly didn't respond to him with words. She responded with a sword. A sword in his throat, that was. If it were a medical condition, perhaps they'd call it a sword throat?

You know, like a *sore throat?*

Fine, don't laugh. Everly still thought it was funny.

"Not anymore," Everly said sweetly as she pulled her blade free after giving it a nice twist.

Blood came jetting out of Rogel's ruined throat. It gushed out so quickly that Everly wondered if it had been waiting years for an opportunity to escape his nasty veins. Who could blame it? Why be trapped inside that depraved loser's circulatory system if it could be helped?

"*ROGEL!*" screamed one of the dying creep's friends. He grabbed a heavy branch from the ground and came running in like he believed he could achieve something meaningful with it.

Everly found his loyalty touching to behold. She rewarded his concern for his friend's safety by sidestepping the oaf and using the magically enhanced sharpness of her blade to cleave through both his ankles with one clean slash.

The sight of a man attempting to run without any feet was not one Everly would quickly forget. Nor hearing that same footless man hysterically squealing like a dying swine. Very musical. He could have been a singer with a falsetto as refined as that.

The last guy was smarter than his friends had been. He stayed quiet and snuck up behind Everly with a dagger. When he was close enough, he dragged it across her throat with a crude slash. It was a good attempt. Compared to those other idiots, she would have awarded his effort a five-point-five out of ten.

However, as soon as he touched her, she projected a defensive aura of *harada* around her body. It was only half an inch thick, but it provided her with more than enough protection from the dagger's edge. Before he noticed that his attack failed, Everly stabbed her sword down through the top of his boot.

"Aaaarrrrgh!" he screamed.

I guess being stabbed through the arch of your foot is extremely painful, thought Everly.

Wow, who knew?

Next, she borrowed some of Titania's strength and elbowed her assailant in his gut. So forceful was the blow that he was sent flying backward for several meters. But wasn't that a good thing, since his foot had been pulled free? Sure, it was now split in half and flapping like a slice of greasy roast beef, but it was still free, right?

Take your blessings where you get them, folks.

"Whyyyyyyy?" He sobbed as he desperately tried to staunch the bleeding.

"Why?" Everly asked him out of disgusted curiosity. "Why what? Why did you say all that nonsense about my mother? Why were you bothering me when I wanted to be left alone? Why were you and your friends behaving like such complete trash? I don't know, asshole. Why don't you tell me? *Why? Whyyyyy?*"

The fool said nothing else. He just lay there sobbing and suffering.

Everly found the sight of his misery gratifying. She would have been okay with just leaving him crippled in the dirt, surrounded by his dead friends. The injury she'd given him meant his foot would soon have to be amputated, and she quite liked the idea of him spending the rest of his life maimed.

He'd stare at the mutilation Everly had dealt him and always remember this day with pain and fear.

The thought pleased her. Sadism suited her personality quite nicely.

Sadly, she couldn't do it.

A coward like this only remembered his place at the point of a sword. As soon as Everly was gone, he'd transfer his anger from her to her mother. Over time, he'd slowly regain his courage, and then he'd round up some other dirtbags who were sympathetic to his story.

Then they'd venture out one dark night to Lyona's home to seek revenge . . .

Naturally, the moment they tried, Titania would go full wood chipper on them. But Everly didn't want her mom to see that. So she decided it would be best to skip a few steps and just get rid of him now.

"Titania," she said.

At your service, Everly, rumbled the elemental in her mind.

"Clean it up," she said as she sheathed her blade and resumed her journey.

Kell couldn't understand what had just happened.

One moment he'd been sharing a bottle of fire-swill with his two best friends, and then along came strolling that little noble bitch, casually walking her way through their part of town in that fine red coat and breeches, like she owned the place.

Everyone knew her mother, Lyona, was a slut. They had a fancy word for it. Was it *cucumbine*? Was it *conkerbine*? It was something slick sounding that was hard to pronounce. But it didn't matter what it was; she was just a whore. Willem had been obsessed with her for years, ever since she'd returned to town. He insisted that she just needed a *real* man to put her in her place and that he was the one for the job.

Of course, he'd never made a move against her because everyone knew she was Tybalt Skolder's sister. No one dared to cross Tybalt. The reputation he'd earned as a mercenary, that was to say a *killer*, was well-earned. Laying a finger on his family was the same as slitting your own throat.

But Tybalt and his son had left months ago for the summer campaigns. And everyone knew how dangerous mercenary work was. There might come a time when he would never return to Anders. And if that were the case, miss fancy noble whore would be left all alone.

Willem had been talking about paying her a visit more and more often. He'd also been working Brader and Kell up to it as well, talking about how there was sure to be money in that fancy house, maybe jewels and other wonderful things, but mostly he'd just wanted the woman.

And then along came that girl, and it seemed like they were finally going to get to have some fun. But then, in a few brief moments, it had all gone to shit!

"Bitch," Kell said hatefully to himself. "You evil little bitch. You think this is the end of it? I'll get you! You just wait and see if I don't! We'll pay your mama a visit first, though. Think you can kill *my* friends and get away with it? Just you wait! Just you WAIT . . . Wait! Wait! Oh, gods, please wait! Please wait! Please, I'm begging you. Wait—"

The ground around Kell had begun to tremble. Dirt and rocks began coalescing and combining until, finally, above him loomed a giant hand connected to a massive arm that rose from the ground like the tip of a mountain.

Kell instinctively understood that the owner of this massive arm served the girl he'd just threatened and cursed. And it had also heard every word he'd said.

"I'm sorry," he said, so terrified by his predicament that a dumb, dazed smile was now plastered on his face. "I really am sorry," he repeated. "We weren't going to hurt her. We just got carried away—NOOOOOOOO, GOD, PLEEEEEEASE—"

Splat!

The giant's hand came down like an avalanche and landed with full force on Kell's body as he desperately tried to crawl away, pancaking him instantly. Now embedded in the earth was a very flat humanoid shape surrounded by a vivid splash of red.

Moments later all three bodies were dragged deep into the Earth, never to be seen again.

All traces erased.

It's finished, Titania informed Everly, as she made her way down the King's Road.

So soon? Eris asked her. *You really should have drawn it out longer, Sister. I would have made his dying screams last an eternity. They would have served as a warning to anyone else considering behaving as they did.*

Our leader commanded me to end his existence, Sister. So that's what I did. I didn't enjoy his wretched company so much that I'd put up with it longer than necessary. Besides, I'm certain that his final moments seemed an eternity, thanks to the miserable ending I dealt him.

Whatever. I still would have done it better, Eris insisted.

As you say, Titania replied in a bored tone of voice.

I do say, Eris said.

All right, then, Titania replied without resisting.

Stop doing that! Eris said irritably.

Stop doing what? Titania asked.

Stop agreeing with me!

Okay.

Are you mocking me?!

Everly laughed at their exchange. Titania had gotten much better at dealing with Eris's forceful personality over the years. Everly felt proud of how confident she'd become. She didn't win arguments with her sister very often, but when she did, they were crushing victories.

Very appropriate for an earth elemental.

"Calm down, you two. Everything's fine," Everly said. "Titania, you did excellent work. Eris, I'm certain you would have also done a fine job. Instead of focusing on losers like that prick, let's instead enjoy the beginning of our new adventure! What do you say?"

Of course, Everly. Your words ring true with wisdom! said Eris.

Yeah, what she said, Titania concurred.

"Awesome sauce," Everly said with a smile.

And thus did the Empress abandon the path of morality to begin her journey in these strange new lands. Although she was a tormented and miserable soul, a sad misfit who had never known true comfort or joy, she would soon begin gathering like-minded comrades who had also been rejected by society.

Many would surely flock to her sinister banner!

Then, after years of enacting secret plans and honing her incredible abilities, Everly would wage war against all who dared deny her ambitions!

"Beware, oh foolish world!" Everly declared. "For soon the darkness shall overtake you! And *I* shall be its guiding hand!"

How thrilling! exclaimed Eris. *That was an excellent delivery!*

It was, wasn't it? Everly preened.

Wow, that's a fat squirrel. Look over there, Everly. See how fat that squirrel is? Titania cooed.

Everly turned to look.

Oh, she's right, she thought to herself. *That* is *one fat squirrel.*

That darn thing is adorable.

It really was.

CHAPTER TWENTY-TWO

The Venerable

I was talking about you with Brenton Rode the other day," Norris Grain said, as he took a swallow of beer from his mug. "I was saying, 'Mister Rode, when you come into my shop, I'd prefer your eyes roamed over my wares, and *not* my daughter's body.'"

"You did *not*." Nellie chortled. Her pretty brown eyes widened in merriment. "Dad! You can't go around shaming all the young men! Do you want me to stay unmarried forever?"

"Well, I wouldn't mind it." Grain laughed in response. He was home for lunch with Nellie, a ritual that he looked forward to every day. She had her late mother's talent for cooking and could make a kingly feast out of anything if she had enough flour and butter. He'd starve if it weren't for her. He might have had a knack for hammering out tools on his forge, but preparing an edible meal was a skill he'd never had.

Of course, it wasn't merely the food that made him enjoy his daughter's company. Nellie was the light of his life. He sometimes found it difficult to believe he'd had anything to do with creating someone like her. She was a lovely girl, the prettiest in the village, and a good friend to anyone who needed one. She also possessed a blistering tongue that could lash a fool's hide like a whip, which she'd inherited from her mother; but her fearsome temper was evened out by her father's patience. She was a wonderful blend of her parents, truly the best of both worlds.

She'll be the village head one day, Grain thought happily. *Might make it a family tradition. The light above knows she's got the sense for it.*

Nellie was collecting their plates for cleaning when a knock at the door drew her attention, and she left to answer it. When she returned, she wore a stricken look on her face.

"Dad," Nellie said. "Wesley came from up the road to pass a message. He says there are people waiting for you at the shop."

"Oh? Who's that, peach?"

"Wesley didn't know, Dad." She paused, seemed to steel herself, then continued. "But he said they looked fancy. Said one of them was wearing armor and a templar's white cloak."

Grain stared at his glass of beer for some time. Then he muttered a curse under his breath and quaffed it. "Well, no sense in drawing this out," he muttered. "What can't be helped can't be helped."

"*Dad,*" Nellie said. She wrapped her arms around the big man and hugged him as tightly as she could.

"Now, now, girl. No need for fear. We'll get through this. I did nothing wrong, and the facts will redeem me. There might be a penance headed my way, but I'll endure it. It was worth it to keep you and the others safe."

Norris returned his daughter's hug and then set out on his way, hoping he seemed confident to her. Inwardly, he was quite frightened.

Grain had known for a while that this day was coming. The village had chosen him as its headman because he could keep a cool head and make hard decisions when the situation called for it. Last year's winter had been a brutal, lingering affair. Seemingly without end. The supplies they had stored would not have lasted long enough to see all of them safely to spring.

People were beginning to go hungry, and a wave of deaths would have swiftly followed if Norris hadn't made the decision to dip into the money set aside as their yearly tithe for the temple. With it, they'd been able to buy desperately needed supplies from Peacevale, enough food and medicine to carry them through the worst of that harsh long season of cold.

Grain's decision wasn't without its detractors, but desperation eventually convinced them. The choice between warm bread or a slow death from starvation was no choice at all. When spring finally arrived, many took him aside to thank him for what he'd done. Everyone seemed happy they'd escaped harm, except the tithe collectors when they came for their annual visit.

They warned Norris that the faith poorly regarded those who spurned their obligations.

Grain refused to be intimidated. Instead, he vowed to pay them twice next year what was owed today. The collectors were displeased with his decision but had no other choice but to accept his compromise. The village worked hard to make good on Grain's word, and it seemed as though the light above approved of their resolve, for the harvest they collected next was *abundant*.

They had a huge reserve to sell, which brought them plenty of coins. Grain's promise of a twofold return for the faith was kept, while still leaving the village with plenty of food for the following winter.

Hadn't everything worked out for the best? Surely the temple would be pleased with how things had transpired.

What cause had they to be upset?

"Expect a visitor soon," the collectors warned him when they next returned. "Present yourself when you are called for and make no attempt to flee. May the light above illuminate you."

"God's light on you both," Grain replied, stunned.

Now the time had come to give them his accounting.

I did what was right, Grain thought stubbornly. *It was a choice between dead children and a few measly coins for the wealthiest temple on the continent. What else could they expect of me? What could they expect of anyone placed in that situation?*

But Grain knew the answer to that question.

They expected their money.

Grain saw the strangers standing in the field that his workshop overlooked. One was tall, the other short. They both wore armor but carried no weapons. Interesting. As he neared them, Grain nearly snorted out a laugh. *Who under god's light is this?* Grain thought to himself, amused.

The girl looked like a young noblewoman playing in costumed armor, the sort of outfit her lord father might gift her with for a masquerade ball. She was beautiful, true, but she looked so silly! She wore expensive-looking white boots that ended just below her knees, thigh-high stockings beneath them, and a short skirt that left some of the skin of her thighs exposed.

On her torso she wore a gleaming silver breastplate, gauntlets, and a pristine white half cape that reached the middle of her back. Lastly, she wore her auburn hair in pretty ringlets that surrounded her face.

And what a face it was! Her eyes were a guileless, entrancing shade of green that radiated wholesome energy. Her pink skin radiated health and vitality. There seemed . . . there seemed to be such a *light* that emanated from her. Pure and wholesome, just as she was. Who was she?

"Hello," the girl said. Her gentle and melodious voice was just as beautiful as the rest of her. "Would you happen to be the village headman?"

Grain coughed to clear his throat a bit before speaking. God above, to think he'd been bragging to himself earlier about what a beauty his Nellie was! Showed what he knew. "I am," he said. "A-ahem! I'm called 'Grain' around these parts, Lady . . . ?"

His question amused her, as though she couldn't remember the last time someone had failed to recognize her on sight. "I'm Sarah," she replied. She didn't offer a family name. She didn't need to; a girl named Sarah who wore silver armor and radiated light?

Grain knew *exactly* who she was!

Surprise couldn't begin to describe what he felt. This was Sarah Godwell! One of the four invincible champions of the faith: *a paladin.* He knelt at her boot, his earlier thoughts swept away by a wave of awe and respect that washed over him. "The light's blessings upon you, great lady," he said with sincere reverence.

Sarah smiled. She gestured to the man who stood beside her, a tall eye-patched fellow wearing simple traveling clothes beneath a battered-looking chest plate. His face, which was framed by unkempt black hair, had a hungry, vulpine quality to it, made even seedier by his unshaven stubble.

Grain didn't like the look of that man. His eye patch, and his pervasive aura of malevolence, made him seem a sinister figure. He looked better suited to plundering a village at night than assisting a holy knight in her sacred duties. What could someone like *him* be doing in service to a paladin?

The one-eyed man bowed to Sarah and began walking toward the village. As he passed Grain, she gave him a knowing wink. Grain blinked in puzzlement. What was *that* about? Well, it didn't matter. He turned back to Sarah and said, "My lady, I am honored that you've come so far to see me. But why *you*, great one? This is surely beneath the notice of one of heaven's chosen."

Sarah's eyes sparkled with impish merriment. "Why, Mister Grain, *your* surprise surprises *me*." She gestured for him to rise before continuing. "Paladins are more than the guardians of the faith, Mister Grain. They are also servants to the people. *All* the people—high and low. From the splendor of the capital all the way to the most remote and rustic locales, such as this. And what a pleasing place this is! The beauty of it—it *soothes* me. Living here must be wonderful, isn't it?"

Grain nodded in agreement, his face breaking into a smile. "Aye, it is, my lady! A wonderful place! A hard living at times, but a worthy life all the same! It's the peace that brings us here. A chance to raise our families as we see fit—"

"As you see fit, but *still* trusting in the loving guidance of our faith, yes?" Sarah asked sweetly.

"O-of course! Of course!" Grain said enthusiastically. "'Tis the creator that guides us, who binds us, who—"

"*That leads us home*," Sarah finished for him. "I'm glad, Mister Grain. I'm very glad. It may shock you to learn that many remote villages, far removed from the vigilant eye of our mother church, have begun to develop some rather disappointing views regarding the absolute necessity of obedience."

Her eyes narrowed as she spoke. Her voice became hard with anger. "They begin to see a false equivalence between that which is false and that which we *know* to be true. There is only one way in life, Mister Grain. The correct one. And our faith *is* that path. I'm sure you agree?"

Grain swallowed nervously at the sight of her anger. God, she might *look* like a young girl, but the aura of bloodlust emanating from her—that told a different tale. Her ringlets and that silly armor might make her seem like a child playing at being a knight, but he could *feel* the power radiating from her, like heat from his forge.

It was said that paladins were strong enough to crush stone with their bare hands and could kill by speaking a single word. They were walking weapons, each one far mightier than a mage or a sword king. They were humanity's dreaded trump card and the ultimate defense against the void and its devils.

Standing this close to one in the flesh, Grain believed it. He didn't doubt for a moment that her presence alone could burn the faithless with holy fire. It awed him, but it was also terrifying.

I need to be careful with this one. Very, very careful.

"Yes, you do," Sarah said, in response to his thoughts.

"What?" Grain gasped in surprise.

"Oh, don't be so shocked, Mister Grain. The thoughts of a wicked man like *you* are easy enough to read. Your mind is terribly *open*, you know. You think I look like a child? 'A girl playing in toy armor.' That's what you thought when you saw me, yes?"

After removing one of her gauntlets, Sarah reached out and rubbed at his chest. Grain was a strong man, his body made fit from years of hard labor. The firmness of his pectoral muscles seemed to please the girl. To his extreme discomfort, Grain watched her face twist into a lascivious leer as she touched him.

"What are you thinking of *now*?" she asked him in a knowing voice. "Oh, you're a bad one, aren't you, Mister Grain? Is that anyway to look at a servant of the temple?"

She stepped closer to him, her face inches from his.

"What are you doing?" Norris asked.

"I'm curious about something."

Sarah had to stand on her toes to kiss him. There was a sweetness to it that he hadn't expected, a pleasure generated from contact with her lips that enveloped him in the exquisite warmth of her light.

But Sarah's teeth lingered too long on his lower lip; then they bit firmly into it. Grain tried to pull away, but her hands held his face firmly in place. She was *strong*. Like a mother gripping an unruly infant.

Blood welled from his wounded lip, and Sarah's tongue eagerly lapped up.

"*Wow*," she said. "You taste . . . *sinful.*"

"What?" Grain asked, frightened.

"You'll understand soon," she said. She gave him a playful flick on the tip of his nose, then released him. "Bandon!" she called out. "Bandon! Are they ready?"

"They are, my lady," a man called out in reply. "If you'll but come this way."

Grain heard voices in the distance then. Some were shouting, others crying. What was happening here?

"Penance, Mister Grain," Sarah said, once more reading his thoughts. "*Penance.* Follow me, please." Sarah led the way to the village center, walking ahead of Grain excitedly, pulling at his arm like a child leading her father to a toy seller. Her enthusiasm terrified him, which seemed to delight her.

"Watch, Mister Grain! Wait until you see. *Wait until you see!*"

CHAPTER TWENTY-THREE

Cruel Mercy

When they reached the center of the village, Grain saw what she meant. The villagers—every single one of them, including Nellie—were kneeling in the muddy ground, surrounded by a group of hard-looking men in armor. In his youth, Grain had spent a fair number of years in conscripted service. He knew full well when he was in the presence of a killer, and that was precisely what each of these men were: killers.

The one-eyed man he'd met earlier must have been Bandon. He stood among the frightened villagers and gave Grain a friendly nod.

What is happening?

"Surprise, Mister Grain!" Sarah laughed delightedly. She spun around, happily dancing this way and that. "Do you like it? I thought long and hard about this, didn't I, Bandon?"

"You did, my lady," replied Bandon, now affecting the mannerism of a proud uncle.

"Wasn't I *so* clever?" she asked him happily.

"Your wits are sharper than any blade could ever be."

Sarah clapped her hands once, pleased by his words. "Thank you!"

"What—what is this? What's going on?" asked Grain. His voice had grown higher in pitch as fear began to set in his heart.

"Silly Mister Grain. I *told* you already," came Sarah's chiding reply. "This is penance! Did you think you could get away with your villainy? That your sins had escaped our notice? No, no, no, no. Justice has *found* you, Mister Grain! You and all these people who benefited from your petty selfishness! You stole from the temple! Oh, Mister Grain! *Poor* Mister Grain! Don't you understand what that means?"

Sarah looked from left to right, holding her hands over her cheeks, as though she were about to say something naughty to a friend and didn't wish to be overheard by her chaperone. She crept closer to Grain and whispered, "That means you stole from us. That means you stole from the *temple!*"

She looked at him with wide-eyed dismay, like a small child who'd just heard someone swearing.

"I don't understand!" Grain shouted. "It was *one* winter! We needed to *eat!* We made reparations! Didn't they tell you? We delivered twofold what we took to survive! *Twofold!*"

Sarah chuckled at his words. "Bandon! Did you notice? He said *twofold* twice."

"You're very observant, my lady. That was quite humorous."

"It was!" she agreed. Then, turning back to Grain, she said, "What you must understand, Mister Grain, is that your so-called reparations do nothing to make amends for what you've already done. Haven't you realized? The money you spent didn't belong to you! You're a thief! Repay it a thousand times if you like— it doesn't matter! The seeds of sin will always sprout *more* sin! You're so silly for not realizing that! Isn't he silly, Bandon?"

"I'm afraid so," the one-eyed man agreed. "Very silly."

Sarah closed her eyes and took a tremulous breath. "Do you know what I'm afraid of, Mister Grain? I'm afraid that others may become inspired by what you've done. They'll start thinking that they can pay their tithes when it's convenient for them, instead of when the temple requires it. Oh, can you imagine, Mister Grain? Can you imagine it? Oh, what a dreadful possibility!"

"How can—" Norris began to ask before she cut him off.

"Chaos, Mister Grain! Rampant selfishness! Who benefits most when the faithful are in disharmony? Only the archfiend himself! Oh, Mister Grain, don't you know what he'll do to you? What he'd do to *any* of us in an instant? Oh, such violations of the flesh, such torment of the soul!"

Tears sparkled in the paladin's eyes, as though she now envisioned herself enduring the horrors of hell itself. "Imagine what he'd do to *me!* It's scary! I'm afraid to even think of it! Bandon, I'm so afraid!"

Sarah turned to Bandon and hugged him tightly; she appeared the very image of a frightened girl seeking solace from a dear friend. Only the grimace of pain on Bandon's face, and the creaking of his armor, gave away how much pressure Sarah's embrace exerted on him.

Now Grain understood why Bandon's chest plate was so dented.

When she released him, the one-eyed man gave a quiet sigh of relief.

"My lady, wait. Please wait," Grain said desperately. "I'm sorry. I'm *so* sorry for what I've done. B-but the fault is entirely mine! It was my decision, and the others just followed along. I wouldn't let them say no! I love them all as I do my own family, and I wanted to save them! Please, please, I'm *so* sorry!"

Sarah closed her eyes. She stood there, as though weighing the sincerity of his words. Then she opened her eyes, smiled, and said, "I believe you, Mister Grain. I believe you're being sincere. *You* are feeling *contrite*."

"Yes," said Grain. "Yes, yes, that's exactly right! I'm feeling contrite! Please, *please* accept my apo—"

Sarah held up a palm, cutting off his words. "Ah, but what you fail to understand, silly Mister Grain, is that contrition without penance is . . . why, it's like toast without jam! Can you *imagine* toast without jam? Could you, Bandon?"

"Would life be worth living, my lady?"

"It would not!" she yelled ferociously, her face now twisted with anger, her hands clenched into tight fists. She took a few moments to breathe deeply and collect her emotions before continuing.

"It's not enough to be *sorry*, Mister Grain. Not *nearly* enough. As charming as your little village is, you're still guilty of putting its needs ahead of the requirements of your faith. Only now do you begin to understand what a dreadful mistake that was. You've stepped on some toes, Mister Grain. You have *stepped on some toes*."

Sarah gestured toward the kneeling villagers. Then she pointed at Grain and said in a voice heavy with judgment, "You claim you love them as you do your own family, yes? Then you are guilty of putting your family before your faith!"

"No, it's not like that," moaned Norris helplessly.

"Yes, it is!" insisted Sarah. "You are guilty of eating well when the *truly* devout would have happily starved! You were clearly being tested, Norris Grain! And you *failed!* You failed due to hubris! Yes, *hubris!* By giving in to your fear, you've proclaimed yourself an existence on par with our creator!"

Grain's jaw dropped in dismay. Mad! This woman was raving *mad!* "I—I did no such thing, my lady! I wouldn't! Never! H-how could you say that?"

Sarah's beautiful smile seemed to envelop her in radiant light; she was now the very image of a blessed angel. Only her eyes hinted at the malice roiling within her.

"When you chose to *eat*, Mister Grain, you put the creator *second*. By placing him second, you declared that you were above him, that *your* needs mattered more than his. You have chosen your ephemeral flesh over your eternal soul, Mister Grain. You have *SINNED*. The mark of it hangs over you, as indelible as black ink. It's perfectly logical. Isn't it, Bandon?"

"As insightful as the scriptures themselves, my lady," Bandon confirmed.

Grain collapsed to his knees. Oh, light, why? He'd been denounced by a paladin. Not just any paladin—Sarah of the Godwell family! He'd be burned alive for this. But *why*? He'd only been trying to save his village! Why wouldn't Sarah understand?

"Dad!" came the cry of his daughter. Nellie ran to him, wrapped her arms around him, and wept into his hair. Oh god, Nellie would be alone now!

This couldn't be happening. It couldn't!

"My lady. My lady, *please*." Nellie wept. "My dad, he works so hard; he only wanted to protect everyone! He didn't mean it! He didn't mean any harm! Please, there must be some way we can make this right!"

Sarah's smile became even toothier. "Well, look at you. A dutiful daughter filled only with love, fearful for her foolish father's fate." She knelt and reached out a hand to gently cup Nellie's chin. "There, there, Sister. Why do you weep? Your father's predicament is his own doing. Why concern yourself with what becomes of a sinner?"

Nellie cried even harder. "Because he's my *dad!* Please, I beg you, I beg you, I *beg* you." Her voice swelled with emotion until she could no longer speak, only cry and clutch at the paladin's boot.

Sarah closed her eyes, her expression now rapturous. She turned her face upward to the sky and nodded, as though the heavens had communed with her and she agreed with their decision. Then she stood, patted the girl on her head, and said, "This is so beautiful. Devotion of this magnitude cannot be ignored. Child, you will perform a service for the faith. Yes, *you* will atone for your father's trespasses, and in so doing, you'll clear his slate. Will you accept this task? Will you intervene and save your father's soul?"

Nellie stared in mesmerized wonder. The way Sarah spoke was entrancing. Her beauty, her conviction; she couldn't refuse the demands of this angel. "Wh-what would have me do, my lady?" she asked.

Sarah gestured to her men, and it seemed to Nellie that they were holding back cruel laughter. Their knowing smirks were very unpleasant. Sarah smiled at her discomfort and said, "My men are committed servants of the greater good, the *greatest* possible good, prepared at any moment to throw their lives away in battle with the enemies of humanity. Isn't that wonderful?"

"Y-yes," Nellie stammered in reply.

"Obviously!" Sarah continued. "They serve, knowing that what they do, they do not only in the service of our kingdom but in the service of our *faith*. Knowing that, how can my heart fail to be moved by such nobility? If only everyone were as committed to service as they are! But happily for us, now your fellow villagers will have an opportunity to prove their devotion as well!"

"My lady, I don't understand. What do you mean?" Nellie asked.

"*You*, my dear girl, will atone for your father's misdeeds by choosing which of your fellow villagers will join other volunteers for a long journey to the north.

You see, the temple has recently come into possession of a *mithril mine*. Can you believe it? Isn't that exciting? It is, isn't it, Bandon?"

"Beyond thrilling."

"That's what I think too!" Sarah said. "Sadly, harvesting mithril is dangerous, daunting work, and labor is in short supply. The condensed mana in the ore attracts all manner of dangerous monsters. But I'm sure a hardy group of robust villagers like *you* won't fear such things!"

"Why are you doing this?" Nellie asked quietly.

"What?" Sarah asked her with a dumbfounded expression. "Do you think I'm being unfair? I'm not! I'm really not! Since your father placed *his* community's needs ahead of the faith, then it's *only* fair that we get to use them too! Worry not. Any injuries your friends sustain during their service will reflect favorably on their character. Suffering proves *devotion*."

"Wha—" Nellie tried to say.

"And listen, this is the good part! If any of your friends die during their service, you have my *word*, my absolute *guarantee*, that they'll wake up in paradise, all sins forgiven! Pretty good deal, right? *Right?*" asked Sarah with a wink and a nudge.

Nellie's face once more flooded with tears.

"Oh, men, look how she weeps! What joy she must feel to be of *such* use! Isn't that wonderful? This is how you make a difference in someone's life!"

"*YOU CAN'T DO THIS!*" bellowed Grain. "I won't let you hurt them! I WON'T LET YOU!"

Bandon rolled his one eye in sarcastic amusement. "Oh, dear. You really said it now, didn't you, you provincial twit?"

Sarah didn't share Bandon's amusement "What? What did you say, Mister Grain? You won't *let* me? You say I *cannot*? Is that what you said? Is *THAT* what you said?"

Sarah's face slowly grew terrible to behold. Whatever beauty it held was now masked behind a twisted mix of childish confusion and seething rage that made her seem almost fiendish. Fearful as it was to see, she never stopped smiling, although the corners of her lips twitched spasmodically.

"Why did he say that? *Why* did he say that?" she asked Bandon. "I was just joking. It was a jest! We wouldn't do anything like that. We're good people! Why is he looking at me like that, Bandon? Did I say something I shouldn't have?"

Sarah kept blinking repeatedly as she spoke, her body shivering in the afternoon light, although no cold wind blew.

Several of her men who stood behind her began backing away.

Slowly.

"Did I do something wrong? I didn't, did I? DID I?"

"Lady Sarah, how could a chosen of heaven like you do *anything* wrong? It makes no sense," replied Bandon.

"But then why did he say that, Bandon? He said I can't. He said I can't! *Bandon.*" Sarah sobbed, shutting her eyes in distress.

"My lady," said Bandon with a shrug, "*I* say you *can.*"

"*OF COURSE I FUCKING CAN!*" Sara howled with animal fury.

Sara's gauntleted hand lashed out in a brutal swipe that smashed into Grain's face, crushed his cheekbone, and knocked out most of his teeth. The force of that powerful blow sent him skidding onto his back, where he clutched at his ruined face and shrieked in agony.

"Penitent," Sarah ranted as she walked toward him. "You're a *penitent.* You don't talk back to me! You don't talk back to *me*! I do what I want, and *you do what I say*! Look at me! *Look at me!* Bandon! He isn't looking at me! Why isn't he looking at me?"

"Some men are lost in self-absorption, my lady."

"I hate being ignored!"

"Why would anyone ignore you? You're such a good person."

"Right! Exactly! That's absolutely correct! He's a stupid old man, just a *stupid* old man! Aren't you, Mister Grain? *Aren't* you? *ANSWER ME! ANSWER ME, I SAID!*"

Sarah jumped on top of Grain and mounted his torso just above his waist, using her strong legs to lock herself in place and keep him from squirming away.

Then she raised her fists and rained terrible blows down on his defenseless head.

It wasn't just the gauntlets she wore that caused him such terrible damage. Sarah's strength was simply beyond that which ordinary flesh could endure.

She existed on a level that few beings ever attained, and the sheer power behind each of her merciless strikes pulped Grain's face, spattering his blood and brains on her armor and face. Muscle was shredded and bone was powdered with each punch she delivered, and still they continued to rain down.

All the while, she chanted, "*Stupid old man, stupid old man, stupid, stupid, stupid…*"

Grain stopped resisting before long, then stopped breathing shortly after that, but the enraged Sarah continued to punish him. She wasn't content with merely killing him for questioning her. It seemed she wanted to erase him from existence itself through her unrelenting, unstoppable violence. Her desire was the annihilation of his physical being.

Stupid old man! Who was he to question her? So judgmental! So arrogant! *Who* did he think she was? Nothing, that was what. *NOTHING!*

SHE WAS A GODWELL!

With a final terrible punch from Sarah, Norris Grain's head came apart like a rotting melon tossed from a window. Sarah screamed in bestial frustration at his weakness. *Look at him falling apart like that. Couldn't even take a few punches. Couldn't handle a little chastisement.* Where was his sass now?

Weak. *So* fucking weak!

Sarah still wasn't satisfied.

She rose from her victim and stalked toward his daughter. She grabbed the screaming girl by the sides of her face with her bloodied hands and stared into her eyes with her piercing gaze. When Nellie tried to pull away, Sarah held her firmly in place, then said, "He did that. I didn't do that. *He* caused it. I had to save you."

She pressed her forehead against Nellie's and whispered, "He was a bad person. It's *okay* now. I'll take care of you."

Nellie's mind couldn't take anymore. She fainted.

Sarah grinned at her unconscious body. Silly. Silly girl. Sleep didn't make you safe. It just made you stationary.

She turned to Bandon and said, "I've changed my mind. I've *changed my mind!* A third of these people won't be *nearly* enough for this village to properly atone. Not nearly enough! Oh, Norris Grain was such an awful man! He was! *He was!*"

Sarah shook her head; she did it with such force that her ringlets whipped violently against her face, as though she were trying to dislodge an insect crawling in her ear. After a few moments of this, she resumed speaking.

"I'm keeping Nellie for myself. I feel close to her. I think we can be friends. I love her."

Bandon's raised eyebrow caused Sarah to frown in annoyance. "Oh, stop that! I'll take care of this one, you'll see! I'll feed her and bathe her and give her pretty clothes to wear! She'll love me back. She'll see I was right!"

"Questions will be raised over the disappearance of an entire village, Lady Sarah," Bandon said.

"I don't care! Blame some goblins or something! Just burn this hovel to the ground! Chain up all these awful people. These wretched *sinners*. Have word sent out that this place was heretical. Crawling with evil. *Filthy with it.* We've cut out a cancer, Bandon. Root and stem, haven't we?"

"Steady as a barber's blade, my lady."

"Exactly! Exactly!"

"But are you certain this will be overlooked?" Bandon asked carefully.

"They wanted laborers. I got them laborers! I did my best! Leave me alone!" she replied with tears of stress in her eyes.

Bandon nodded and walked away to give her some space.

Sarah lay down beside the unconscious Nellie and stared wistfully at the sky. Work was so difficult.

"I didn't do anything wrong, I really didn't," she said to her new friend. "You understand, right? Your father attacked me. He attacked *my principles*. Why is everyone always so mean to me?"

All around them houses were burned, and the villagers, young and old, pleaded for mercy as they were hauled away to the cages.

"People should be kinder," she insisted. "It doesn't cost anything to be civil. I'm trying my best. I really am."

CHAPTER TWENTY-FOUR

Rescue Pet

Life on the road was an enjoyable experience. So far, Everly found she liked it quite a bit.

It wasn't surprising when one considered the advantages she possessed. Most vagabonds didn't have it as good as she did.

Each night, Titania would build Everly a comfortable shelter to rest in and would also capture food for her to eat. She would pluck fish from a stream or strike down a game animal, prepare it, season it with wild herbs, then spark fire over wood to cook it. The meals she prepared always tasted delicious; Everly sometimes wondered if Titania had missed her calling in life as a chef.

Whenever Everly tired of walking, Titania also made a carriage to carry her. Then she'd create two clay golems, which Eris disguised as a pair of horses, to pull it, which allowed Everly to kick back and enjoy the scenery.

For entertainment, Everly either trained her swordsmanship, meditated, or recalled one of the thousands of movies or television shows she'd seen in her previous life and watched them on a conjured screen in her memory palace. Sometimes she listened to music and did nothing else.

She'd just lie on her back and calmly enjoy her idleness.

Everly felt bad for anyone who didn't get to spend any time by themselves. Sometimes being alone was the best feeling in the world. Life always demanded so much from everyone. Time, effort, energy. Didn't it sometimes feel like all anyone ever did was live their life for the sake of someone else?

Living life in service to a master was no life at all as far as she was concerned.

Well, that was unless *she* was that master, she supposed.

Everly, something is happening on the road. There are many people gathered nearby, rumbled Titania's voice into her thoughts.

"Is that right?" Everly asked. "Oh, could they be highwaymen? Are we being held up? That would be *awesome.* I've always wanted to kill a bunch of bandits!"

You've already killed many bandits, haven't you?

"Not personally!"

It's not that much fun. They mostly run around panicking instead of putting up a fight. Slaughtering them feels like a chore more than anything else.

"Yeah, from *your* perspective!" Everly said. "But I just love that old storytelling trope where a mysterious stranger shows up out of nowhere to thrash a gang of thieves. I'll leave one alive to tell the tale, and years later, long after we've conquered the world, he'll recognize me from a distance and fearfully tell everyone he knows that he once barely survived an encounter with me. Everyone will call him a drunk and a liar and shame him for trying to get attention. Or they'll hang him for admitting he was a thief. Either way, it'll be great."

Wow. You're planning things this far in advance? asked the impressed Titania.

"Of course I am! When it comes to demonstrating my awesome prowess, I'm always ready to put on a performance."

Pardon my interruption, but I don't believe these people are thieves, Eris cut in.

"Really?" Everly whined. "That sucks! There I was, getting worked up over nothing."

Oh, I'm sorry to hear that, Eris said apologetically. *But you know there's nothing preventing you from attacking those mortal clods anyway. As the future ruler of all, you are entitled to slay whomever you please!*

"Eris! Stop. I'm not *psychotic.* I'm not going to go trampling on the peasantry just because I feel like doing it. That's not true villainy! Remember, one of my goals is to deceive the foolish masses into loving me so that they'll never suspect I'm secretly their greatest enemy."

Once more, I apologize, my lady. Your machinations are beyond my scope as always, said Eris contritely.

"No need for apologies, my friend," Everly said with magnanimity. "I operate inside wheels within wheels. I'm a real spinner. Now let's look at what's got these yokels so worked up."

Everly stepped outside the carriage and saw a large group of people gathered in a circle around something. She then proceeded to squeeze her way into their midst to see what the big deal was.

Little cousin! Titania said in dismay as she beheld a small fat green creature with a beaked nose and floppy bat-like ears, hissing viciously at the crowd and trying to escape their encirclement. Every attempt it made was rebuffed with a sharp weapon or a vicious kick. The crowd laughed whenever it was struck. Even children joined in to mock the poor creature.

"Kill it!" someone said. "Kill the dirty goblin!"

"Yeah, kill it! I hate these stupid things!"

"Kill it, kill it, kill it!" someone else said in an obvious attempt to get a chant going.

"What's going on over here?" Everly asked a nearby woman.

"Can't you tell?" she responded with a haughty sniff. "This dirty goblin was caught wandering outside on human lands. Stupid ugly things know they're not wanted where civilized folks can see 'em, so now it's time it learned its proper place, isn't it?"

Everly found that odd. Goblins, as far as she knew, were shy creatures who hated being anywhere near human settlements. Probably because attacks like this so often occurred.

"Why'd he come running out this way?" she asked the other woman.

"Hmph. Probably running away from the hunters, I'd expect."

"Raaaagh!" yelped the pitiful-sounding goblin as someone stabbed it in the back with a sharpened stick to the raucous cheers of the crowd.

Everly, this greatly displeases me. May I please destroy these horrid people? Titania asked angrily.

My brutish sister makes an excellent point, concurred Eris. *This deliberate mistreatment of our kin is infuriating to see.*

Oh, shoot, thought Everly.

She'd forgotten that elementals and goblins shared a common ancestry. They were both etheric beings descended from the realm of spirits. While the elementals embraced and embodied the various aspects of nature, the goblins had slowly transitioned into a mortal race.

Despite those very distinct differences, the two races still considered themselves kin to each other. So much so that the deliberate mistreatment of goblins and any other magical race was banned by a centuries-old royal decree. It was a wise decision because such abusive behavior greatly offended any elemental that witnessed it.

Just like now.

Guys, there's really no reason we should get involved. It's just one little goblin, Everly tried telling them.

Wrong is wrong, Everly, Titania said stubbornly. *This must be stopped.*

If you don't end this offensive display at once, I'm going to peel their little minds open and let the bad things crawl inside to play, Eris calmly said.

And there you had it. What choice did Everly have? Her elementals would ordinarily never dream of disobeying her, but some things were ingrained too deeply into their core to ignore. The protective instinct for their "kin" was one such thing.

So, like it or not, she had to step in.

Oh, well, she decided. *Part of being a good boss is making sure your subordinates are happy.*

"All right, all right," Everly called out to the crowd, making herself heard over their shouting. "Everyone back away. I *said* back away!"

She pushed her way past the people and stepped in front of the injured creature. "Show's over. You've had your fun, now go away."

"Huh? Who the hell's this?" asked a large man with an ugly-looking pimple on the tip of his nose.

"Yeah, who're you to tell us what to do?" asked another guy with . . . *brown* teeth.

"Hold on, look at how she's dressed," someone said. "That's a noble. Listen to what she says."

"I don't care if she's a noble. That goblin is our rightful prey, and she's got no right to meddle with our hunt," Zit Nose said stubbornly. "Hey, tell us why we shouldn't just knock you on your ass and finish killing that little beast?"

Ohhh, Everly thought with excitement. This was turning into quite the scene, wasn't it? Oh, did she ever love having an audience!

"My name is Everly Vel Belsar, daughter of Count Marcis Van Belsar, the ruler of Belsar County. You can knock me down if you'd like, but my father would make quite a nasty example of you if you did! Wouldn't it be nicer just to listen to what I have to say instead of being so aggressively rude about things? Or do you disagree?"

The people began murmuring among themselves after taking in her words.

"A count's daughter? That's damned important, isn't it?" asked one.

"I feel underdressed now," said another.

"What's she doing on the King's Road alone? Someone should offer her some hospitality!" demanded another.

But one of them was not impressed.

"*Vel* Belsar, did you say?" asked one of the members of the crowd with a derisive snort.

Everly saw that this man wore the black-and-purple robes and white skullcap of a temple scholar. "How very, very amusing. Are you sure your lord father would be fine with you running around dropping his name like this, little girl?"

"What's that supposed to mean, sir?" a confused teenager asked him.

"Pay attention in your schooling, Riken!" the scholar said irritably. "The nobility in our country possesses four officially recognized family ranks. Van, Vae-es, Vae, and Vel! *Van* means you are a titleholder, such as a duke or a baron. *Vae-es* means you're an official heir. *Vae* means you're a direct descendant of the main line and a potential inheritor."

"But she said she was a Vel! What does *Vel* mean?" asked the boy.

The scholar gave Everly an unpleasant smirk before answering. "Well, Riken, *Vel* is what you are when your father is nobility, but *you* are not."

"Huh?" asked Riken. "But how can her pa be a noble without her being one too?"

"Because, my dear boy, her parents weren't married. She's a *bastard*. *Vel* simply means that he acknowledged fathering her. Quite a lucky break for her ilk. Her mother was undoubtedly a concubine."

The scholar said that last part with a knowing sneer that quickly began spreading among the others.

"Ha! So, she's just some uppity bastard trying to lord it over us, huh?" someone asked.

"That's so sad. She's lucky enough to have a rich daddy, but she also wants to be treated like a princess. Talk about *desperate*," chided one girl to her tittering friends.

"Why's she wearing trousers anyway? What gets into these people? All the money in the world but not an ounce of common sense."

"Oh, who even cares? Step aside, girlie," said Zit Nose. "That little green rat needs to die now."

Titania, knock these idiots on their asses, please, ordered Everly.

Titania was only too happy to obey.

The ground surged in motion as a sudden quake tore through the earth beneath the crowd and sent them tumbling off their feet. A second tremor shook them so violently that a few of them nearly *bounced*.

Everly was now the only person on the road still standing.

She took a quick moment to bask in her glorious sense of superiority as the fools before her cowered in fear. Then she said, "Hmm. You know, I'm not entirely certain exactly what the status of my legitimacy has to do with what we were discussing, but thanks *so much* for sharing your opinions. Now I'll share a few of *mine*."

God, that was a killer line delivery! Listen to how *cold* she sounded! How could any audience fail to enjoy such a performance? Who wouldn't be impressed by the way her razor-sharp sarcasm cut straight to the chase?

I'm so awesome at this, Everly thought. *I'm the very picture of a no-nonsense nobleman! Er, noblewoman. Whatever! I'm just great!*

"It is general knowledge among the *educated* that goblins, gnomes, pixies, fairies, and any other being descended from the spirit realm must be left alone," Everly informed them. "Most of them are completely harmless. What's more, the elementals consider them their beloved relations. As you've just seen for yourselves, the elementals are *very* defensive of those they consider family."

"Harmless? You say those freaks are *harmless*?" yelled the scholar. "A mob of those goblin miscreants just raided a village of farmers far to the east of here! They killed half the people living there and burned the place to ashes! The Western Temple dispatched Lady Sarah herself to take in the survivors!"

"Huh?" Everly asked in confusion. "I don't know anything about that."

"Of course you wouldn't! Why should the daughter of a wealthy nobleman give a damn about the ills that plague the common man? This is further proof of the nobility's arrogance *and* their ignorance! Look at her, throwing her orders around and telling us to submit to the presence of evil spirits! The time of revival is coming soon, I tell you! A time when the temple shall reassert itself as the true authority in Winstead!"

"Amen! Preach!" someone shouted enthusiastically.

"We will not bow our heads to demons!" cried another.

Titania immediately responded by knocking them off their feet again.

She *really* didn't like being called a demon.

"People, please," said Everly. "I'm not here to discuss politics or religion. I'm just telling you what's what. There's obviously a strong elemental here who's been displeased by your behavior. Back away and leave the goblin be, or you're just asking for needless trouble."

"Armor yourselves in faith, brothers and sisters! Do not heed the honeyed words of a heretical noble!" the scholar cried out.

This time, instead of merely knocking him down, Titania pulled him by his feet into the dirt; she pulled him down up to his nose, leaving his mouth buried. Although he could still (barely) breathe through his nostrils, he was now unable to speak.

He talks too much, Titania growled.

The locals quickly got the hint and dispersed. A brave few remained behind to dig up the scholar, but other than them, it was now just Everly and the goblin. She would have been happy to leave things at that, but Titania and Eris insisted that she take the wounded thing with her.

You guys are joking right? she asked in disbelief.

Everly, he's wounded and tired. Let him rest in our carriage, Titania pleaded.

Look at how small and weak he is. How could we possibly be so neglectful? Eris asked.

He smells like moldy cheese, Everly whined. *I don't want that stench getting on my clothes.*

He just needs a bath, Titania insisted.

Guys! I don't want a goblin, okay?

Everly! they both said at once.

Jeez, what could she possibly say in the face of that overwhelming pressure?

Fine! If you two want a pet so badly, you can have one. But you're the ones who'll care for him.

You won't regret this, boss! Goblins are so clever and very loyal. Just you wait and see. It'll be like having a third elemental around! Titania said enthusiastically.

Well, I wouldn't go quite that far, but my sister is correct about one thing. A goblin's loyalty, though rarely earned, comes with many benefits. This could pay off nicely in your future, said Eris.

Benefits? For Everly? Derived from keeping a goblin around? Yeah, sure, okay.

Yeah, yeah, whatever you say, she muttered to Eris.

Man, being in charge can be tough sometimes, Everly groused.

Later that night, Everly once again entered her memory palace to train with her sword.

It felt like a productive session. Lately, she'd been experimenting with how to combine *harada* with her magic to enhance her attacks. It had been slow going at first, but lately her progression had sped up nicely. Soon, she'd grow even stronger.

Her studies with holy magic, however, weren't going as well. Everly had no issues with the standard application of elemental magic. She enjoyed destroying things, so it came easily to her. For some reason, holy magic seemed to require a desire to aid other people. For it to be fully effective, you really had to want to help.

It was a real puzzle to her. Why would anyone want to do that?

No, there was a trick to it hidden somewhere. She'd figure it out eventually. She had plenty of time.

She couldn't wait until the summer campaigns began and she could finally put all her hard training to practical use.

The summer campaign might be a deadly war for the common fighters being forced to slug it out for the glory of their uncaring lords, but for Everly, they were a long-awaited session of playtime and experimentation. But to keep any curious eyes from looking too closely at her, she would have to settle for letting everyone see perhaps a tenth of what she was truly capable of.

Thanks to Winstead's silly taboo against female knights, she would have to disguise herself and enlist as a foreign mercenary, like the Black Lioness or the Fury. Maybe she'd even hide her gender. That way she'd be free to run wild.

But only up to a point. Obviously, Everly wouldn't be able to show off the *full* extent of her powers.

She'd let them think she was incredible, but not beyond the scope of mortal potential.

For now.

However, when the time came for her to dominate the battlefield, *that* was when she'd show the world how rife with weakness it was and how futile it would be to challenge her. That was when she'd reign as the very embodiment of hopeless despair and crush the ambitions of any fool brave enough to clash blades with her.

It was going to be so sweet! She was already looking forward to all the monologuing she'd get to do.

Public speaking was an important aspect of being a supreme ruler. You never knew when you'd be called upon for some spontaneous oration, but you always had to be prepared to deliver on the spot because *everyone* craved the villain's special insight. That was why Everly had recently begun ending her training sessions by practicing her speeches.

Today's theme was adventurers who invaded her castle seeking to bring her to justice.

"Hahaha!" She laughed coldly as she imagined the defiant faces of her would-be challengers after they boldly declared their intention to take her down. "It would appear that some rats have managed to sneak into my home and now dare to bare their fangs at me."

"You'll pay for your misdeeds, dark one! Your evil crusade ends tonight!" their leader would say.

"Insolent child. You're just another fool blinded by his precious light of justice," Everly would reply with withering mockery. "Come, then. I welcome your challenge. Let me show you what terrors the darkness has in store for you!"

She would then raise her fist and make a slicing motion through the air. If she'd been wearing a cape at the time, it would have been thrown back, revealing the hilt of her sword as she prepared to do battle.

Everly paused to assess her performance. Then she nodded to herself, pleased with how she'd done.

"Yep, killed it again," she said with a satisfied smile.

Suddenly, the sound of someone clapping echoed throughout the room and filled the air with its enthusiasm. Confused, Everly looked around but didn't see anyone else. Titania was controlling the carriage and keeping watch over her body, and Eris was in her rat room, doing . . . *things.*

So who was the one making all the noise?

A moment later, the goblin stepped out from behind a pillar.

"Graheha eha rera!" he said with a goofy smile on his oddly shaped face.

"Huh? Hey, how'd you get in here? This is a memory palace. *My* memory palace. This is all supposed to be inside my head."

The goblin responded with more annoying gibberish. Everly could see this getting old very quickly, so she sent a command to Eris to translate his words for her, which the elemental promptly did, allowing her to now understand the creature's strange language.

"Great one, Skiddz was invited into your glorious demesne when you accepted him into your household. Skiddz desires to be your faithful friend and your humble retainer! Please allow this unworthy one to repay your mercy with a vow of eternal service!"

"No," Everly said firmly.

"No? Great one, why? Skiddz is clever and will learn quickly. Among goblinkind, he is considered wise and well traveled! Anything you need of him, he will do! Allow him to show his appreciation! Please, let Skiddz be your servant!" the little goblin begged.

"Oh, I wasn't saying no to you being my servant, little guy," Everly said. "I was saying no to your *name*. No offense, but I kind of hate it. I hope it's not reflective of your identity or cultural values or anything, because it's got to go. *Skiddz?* No, that won't do at all. You need a better name. A *cooler* one."

"You . . . want to rename this unworthy one?" asked the surprised goblin.

"Yes. And no more speaking in the third person, okay? If you're going to be my fancy goblin butler, I'm going to require correct diction from you, plus a certain level of stylistic chill. How would you feel about speaking with a posh British accent?"

"Skiddz does not know what that means, great one."

"No worries, we'll get you caught up! But, before we do, tell me how you got into my memory palace. You're a creature of flesh like me. How did you physically enter this place?"

The soon-to-be ex-Skiddz did his best to explain. And Everly had to admit, the implications of what he told her blew her mind. Soon, she would have another massive advantage in her quest to be the best.

As it turned out, Eris was right. Coming across this little goblin had been one of the luckiest breaks of Everly's new life.

CHAPTER TWENTY-FIVE

The Tower

Sometime later . . .

Shortly after taking him into her service, Everly renamed the goblin *Carter*. Wasn't that a much more dignified-sounding name than *Skiddz*? To Everly's way of thinking, Carter was the name of a proper right-hand man for a secretive dark ruler. That was the name of a fellow who could be trusted to sort her laundry, clean her home, and quietly dispose of anyone she deemed a risk to their organization.

Seriously, just look at how naturally that name flowed from a conversational standpoint! *Carter, fetch me the mail. Carter, refill my glass. Carter . . . they know too much. Silence them!*

God, I'm feeling downright gleeful right now! This feels like a complete win! The team is gradually coming together so nicely, thought the jubilant Everly.

Carter was confused at first, but that was fine. Everly had Eris begin filling his mind with the information she deemed necessary for a majordomo to perform his duties. Like how to meticulously maintain a butler's pristine white uniform and how to affect the proper fancy English accent that best suited his role. (For his accent, she selected Received Pronunciation, the official accent of the British royal family.)

Everly personally handled Carter's combat training. He didn't like it very much at first, but he quickly grew to enjoy how rigorous it was. As a goblin, he didn't possess enough physical strength to challenge his opponents head-on, but he was quiet, light on his feet, and nature had gifted him with excellent reflexes. To Everly, that signaled he had the makings of a very effective assassin.

Ah, her very own sneaky butler-ninja. Who'd have thought the day would ever come that she would experience such joy?

Dare to follow your dreams, kids. They can take you anywhere in life!

For today's training session in the memory palace, the setting was an immense dark forest. Carter's opponents were a squad of five pikemen led by one armored knight. Everly called this scenario *Predator*. It was based on the classic 20th Century Studios movie of the same name. Ever seen it? She loved it to death.

The premise was simple: eliminate the targets before any of them could escape.

It seemed to her that Carter was really enjoying himself.

"Hold on a moment," one of the soldiers called out to his fellows. "If I don't have a piss now, I'll soil my trousers."

"Never stopped you before," one of his companions said with a rough-sounding laugh.

"Oh, go to hell," snapped the first one. He stepped behind a tree, undid some straps, and sighed in relief as he began emptying his bladder.

"Ahhh, been waiting to do that for a while, I have," he said to himself.

Suddenly, a shadow darted out from behind a bush and launched itself into the air, then collided with the back of the soldier's head and slammed his skull viciously against the tree he was urinating on.

As the soldier lay dazed on the ground, the small figure quickly slit his throat with a vicious-looking curved dagger, then clamped a hand over his victim's mouth to stifle his gurgling as he slowly bled out.

"I've been waiting to do *this* for a while too," the killer quietly whispered into the dying man's ear.

From a small viewing room constructed especially for the occasion, Everly and her companions gathered to watch Carter's performance. This was the first time he'd be left to his own devices in training, and Everly was eager to see how he'd do.

Also, she wanted to show off her high production values to the others.

"Gods, Harven, what's taking you so long?" bellowed an impatient voice. "We need to get a move on—OH, SHIT!"

One of the pikemen checked to see what was taking his companion so long and was shocked to discover his corpse. "OY! We need help here! HELP!" he called out.

"What the hell's happened here?" the knight asked coldly as he examined the body. He turned to the man who'd discovered the body and stepped directly into his space "You, peasant. Are you responsible for this?"

"Wh-what? No! Harven and I were friends. I'd never do something like this!"

"You were friends, you claim? Right," said the skeptical knight. "You hovel rats are quick to turn on each other over the smallest thing. What happened? Did he owe you coin? Did he sleep with your sister? Speak up, worm! Admit your crime! You slit this poor fool's throat, didn't you?"

Everly was glad she'd written the knight to be such an untrusting snob. She felt that adding social commentary to a story helped make it more relevant for viewers. Something could be both entertaining *and* hard-hitting! That was what the youth of today demanded!

"I said I didn't do it!" the innocent man insisted.

"RAAAGH!" screamed another soldier. When the others turned in the direction of the scream, they saw him lying on the ground, squealing in helpless pain.

He'd been disemboweled.

"I did that to someone once!" Everly cheered. "It was *so* nasty! It got on my shoes!"

"Shhhh," said Titania. "Quiet up front!"

"Oh, sorry!" Everly said.

"Why am I here?" Grail wondered aloud.

"God's precious light!" shouted the knight. "What happened? Who did this to you, man?"

"It's in the trees!" the dying man gasped. *"It's in the trees!"*

"I can *seeeeeeee* you," Carter whispered from above to the frightened men.

It went on like that for quite a while. Everly had to give herself credit for the quality of the writing; this really was a thrill-a-minute adventure/horror story that would have easily entertained most audiences. Carter, for his part, perfectly played the role of the fiendish, inhuman stalker who mercilessly whittled down the intrepid fighters one by one. No matter what traps they set or how hard they fought when he cornered them individually, he took them out one after the other.

Really, what more could be said? The role of a relentless murderer suited the little guy brilliantly.

Everly wasn't concerned in the slightest about Carter's depraved enjoyment of killing humans. He was just having a little fun, that was all. Why wouldn't he want to cut loose after years of being oppressed?

Besides, Titania and Eris watched out for her while she slept.

Seriously, there was nothing for her to worry over.

Nothing at all.

Now the untrusting knight was left all alone. His sword was drawn, he was frightened but resolved, and his opponent now stood before him: a short little goblin in leather armor, dual wielding two very nasty-looking daggers and wearing a skull mask.

"What is this? You expect me to believe a bloody *goblin* did all this?" he said in disbelief. "Not fucking likely!"

"You may believe anything that you'd like, Sir Knight," Carter replied with elegant disdain. "The fact remains that you will soon join your friends in the grave."

"Will I? I think you'll find a true knight is a different thing entirely than a handful of pikemen, you arrogant little toad," the knight retorted.

"Meat of a higher grade is *still* only meat to the butcher," said Carter as he began to scrape the edges of his blades against each other, sending sparks flickering with each slicing motion he made.

It was at that moment that Everly's heart exploded with pride. She hadn't written that line. Carter had ad-libbed it on the spot. AND IT WAS BRILLIANT!

Everly quickly looked around to make certain no one was watching and then quickly wiped a tear of joy from her eye. Carter understood his role so perfectly! Yes, he was the absolute embodiment of Everly's perfect vision.

His success was *her* success, and taking credit for his talent felt so natural and *right*.

Could this be how the parents of a successful child actor felt?

She loved this little goblin.

Wait, she was missing the fight! Yeesh. What a sentimental thing she was becoming.

The knight wielded his broadsword and delivered controlled and powerful strikes, but it was clear that he was at a disadvantage in this duel. His heavy armor provided excellent protection, but he was only a common sword wielder; he possessed no magic to cast spells, nor did he have any *harada* to empower his attacks or increase his stamina. The longer the fight continued, the wearier he grew.

What position did knights like him occupy again? Third rank, wasn't it? That meant his title was essentially honorary. Men like him came from landed families that had access to better training and equipment, but unless they possessed enchanted weaponry, they were only a threat to ordinary men.

Knights like this one were chiefly used as junior officers to bridge the gap between the more exceptional warriors of the second rank, who held the titles of mage or sword expert, and the far rarer and infinitely more dangerous elites that occupied rank one.

Those were the men who'd ascended to become archmagi or sword kings.

Compared to his faltering opponent, Carter had plenty of energy to spare. Not only was he unencumbered by the weight of chain mail, his natural speed and agility was perfectly enhanced with the *harada* he'd been trained to harness.

That was right! That little green monster was bristling with sword aura!

Carter could have slaughtered that squad at any time, but he chose instead to drag things out just so he could instill terror into his victims, all for the sake of his sadistic enjoyment.

Everly found him absolutely precious.

Everly had originally been excited when she discovered that Carter could use *harada*. She'd always assumed it was a method of cultivation unique to humans alone, something humanity had developed to fight evenly with magic users. Neither Eris nor Titania could use it, after all. They couldn't even understand the *concept* of it, no matter how hard Everly tried to share it with them.

But then it had occurred to her . . . What if *harada* was something that a being completely composed of ethereal energy couldn't learn because they weren't conventionally alive? They didn't breathe, and they didn't have a physical form, both of which were prerequisites for cultivation.

Didn't that mean the only requirement for learning was that you had to be a creature of living flesh? If so, then didn't beings like goblins qualify? As it turned out, they *did*. And they were so much better at it than humans that it blew Everly's mind.

Realizing she was weaker than a goblin had been a humbling moment for her. Shortly after she'd shared her knowledge with Carter, his capacity for it exploded at a rate she found astonishing. If she hadn't discreetly placed a mental block in his mind to limit his growth (just a sensible precaution any dark lord would take to keep from being surpassed) Carter might have become a threat to her!

Everly had been certain that she was the greatest master of *harada* on the planet! She'd been training it up since *infancy*, for god's sake! How could this silly little goblin possibly be better than *her*?

It wasn't right!

Fortunately, Everly kept a cool head. Instead of childishly lashing out in jealous anger, she instead observed the methods by which Carter generated his power. She obsessively focused on his breathing methods, his heart rate, and his state of mind as they focused on his training. These were helpful things to observe, but then she decided she wanted to kick things up a notch and see what *really* made the goblin tick.

With that in mind, Everly began using Eris to create living duplicates of Carter's body. It was the same method that Eris had once used to recreate Grail. After thoroughly examining Carter's body, she could easily replicate copies of him in the memory palace that were indistinguishable from the real item.

Duplicates Everly repeatedly dissected to further her studies of *harada*.

Heh, it felt like she'd cut open a million Carters in her fervor to learn more. In her little lab, she'd slice them open over and over, bathing in blood and viscera until she finally gained a complete understanding of his goblin biology.

It was both enlightening *and* stress relieving!

Naturally, Everly kept her experiments a secret from Carter and Titania. Eris had been reluctant to keep helping, but Everly managed to convince her that duplicates didn't count as living beings. They weren't the *real* Carter, just little study guides she needed to use for self-improvement.

What they were doing was fine.

Just fine.

What? Progression is a difficult road. Being squeamish would only deny her the opportunity to grow stronger.

Speaking of squeamish . . .

Once Everly felt she had gained sufficient knowledge of how Carter's body worked, she had Titania and Eris make some slight surgical modifications to her internal organs.

Okay, that was a lie. She had them make *extensive* modifications.

In addition to being an act of blasphemous self-entitlement, renovating a human body so that it could process more internal energy than should be naturally possible was a complicated procedure. There were many bloody bits that had to be cut out, resized, or tossed aside and replaced.

With Eris deadening her nerve endings to suppress the pain, Everly was able to stay conscious and direct the entire procedure. She learned a lot about herself that day. In fact, it wouldn't be a lie to say she now knew herself inside and out.

There was no need to go into any gory details.

Even though the details *were* extremely gory.

That had not been a pleasant month of recovery.

Ah, but the price Everly had paid in suffering had been well worth the reward!

She couldn't believe she'd ever considered the Mountain Splitter a master of *harada*. Hell, she now spat at the very concept of what she'd once considered a sword king. What a joke! With the corrections she had made to her body she could now generate roughly four times the power she'd been capable of before.

Four freakin' times!

This confirmed something Everly had begun to suspect after seeing how powerful Carter had become. *Harada* wasn't something humanity had created for itself. No, far from it—it had been a technique developed by an otherworldly race. And based on their comparatively crude methodology, humans hadn't been *taught* the secrets of *harada* . . .

They'd stolen them!

But who had been the originators? Who had been the first sword kings?

It couldn't have been any of the races she already knew of. Not the dwarves nor the elves. Not the goblins nor the gnomes and so on. Certainly not the orcs. Those beasts were so unbelievably hostile and destructive that even the elementals couldn't tolerate them.

Who were they? Were they some unknown civilization that had vanished long ago from the annals of history?

Or were they hiding, waiting for their moment to step back onto the world's stage?

Everly supposed it didn't matter. Whoever they were, whatever their plans, they were just background exposition. Supplementary to her tale. Unless they acted, they were nothing except unlikely variables. Just something to keep in mind, like running into a spider in a dusty basement.

No, less than that. They were *flavor text*.

What really mattered was that thanks to this discovery, Everly was now more powerful than she'd ever been. Certainly, far more powerful than *Carter* (not that she had been worried about him in the slightest).

In fact, with this fresh infusion of knowledge and power, she'd even go so far as to say that she was humanity's *only* true sword king. The rest of them were all ignorant fakes, and the poor fools didn't even *know* it.

Man, life could be such a gag sometimes, she thought to herself.

Truly hilarious.

Eventually, Carter grew tired of playing with his toy and nimbly rolled past a downward swing of the knight's sword, then sliced at his opponent's knee from behind. With a shout of pain, the armored warrior collapsed, which allowed the goblin to hop onto his torso, raise the visor of his helm, and stab the point of his dagger through the knight's eye and into his brain.

Yeah, that was certainly one way to ring a bell, wasn't it?

"Did you enjoy my performance, my lady?" he asked Everly.

"Carter, that was cooler than the other side of the pillow," she said to him while applauding.

Later, after making camp for the night, Carter himself prepared their evening meal. It was a delicious rack of lamb alongside roast vegetables. Everly didn't know where he'd found a lamb, but she lowkey hoped it had died painlessly when the goblin caught up to it.

It probably had, but you never really knew with the little guy.

"So, tell me again how you entered my memory palace," Everly asked him once more, after they finished eating. It was something she'd been obsessing over for a while.

Her memory palace might've *felt* real, but it wasn't. So how could someone just step in and out of it with their actual body as though it were perfectly natural? It made no sense!

Carter shrugged. "To me, it feels no different from any other demesne that a tribal chieftain could create," he answered. "What I find far stranger is that you project yourself into it mentally, rather than entering it personally like I do."

"You've mentioned that term before," Everly said. "What exactly *is* a demesne?"

"You truly don't know, great one?" Carter asked in surprise. "Hmm. I suppose even a mind as powerful as yours cannot know everything."

Easy, Cousin, said Titania with a warning rumble. *There exists nothing beyond the scope of our leader's vision.*

Indeed, concurred Eris. *Don't be quick to forget how easily she uplifted you from your squalid condition. Those who are ungrateful can just as easily be returned to the muck, "Skiddz."*

I have no opinion on any of this. Why do you keep including me? Grail muttered.

"Whoa, whoa, guys, none of that!" Everly said as she waved her hands back and forth. "Our newest teammate just shared an honest opinion, that's all. And he's correct. I *don't* know everything. That's why I'm so reliant on all of you to fill the gaps in my education. For our goals to be met, we have to work together."

Our leader is wise, Titania said approvingly.

Obviously! That's why this world will bow before us, agreed Eris.

"Truly, I meant no offense, my great cousins. My only wish is to serve our master faithfully in whatever manner she sees fit," Carter said placatingly.

Everly thought he sounded pretty smooth there. Maybe a little *too* smooth?

Oh, what if Carter were a potential traitor? A ruthless schemer lying in wait for his opportunity to strike and usurp her position? He had an English accent, didn't he? *Everyone* knew all the best bad guys in fantasy films were played by the Brits!

Damn, how cool would that be? Every respectable villain had their very own rebellious minion out to undermine them. It not only kept them on their toes, but it was also a symbol of status! Palpatine had Vader, Megatron had Starscream, and Bush had Cheney.

Could Carter be Everly's?

I'll have to keep an eye on him, she thought.

Oh, sweet! "She'd have to keep an eye on someone." Lines like that were *such* a supervillain cliché!

She really *was* living the life!

"A demesne is a portion of the astral realm, the source of all spiritual existence, in which dwell beings of extraordinary will," Carter continued. "Depending on the strength of the one who created it, many beings of spiritual origin are capable of dwelling within one."

"Make it simpler," Everly told him.

"Huh?"

"Dumb down the exposition, please."

"Ah, yes, right," Carter said apologetically. "Um, how to put it? The astral realm is the sea of souls. A place where imagination itself is power. A demesne is a portion of the astral realm that you've claimed for yourself. The land upon which your home is built, so to speak. The stronger your mind is, the greater your demesne becomes."

"Ohhh, so is mine very strong?" she asked him eagerly.

"What?" Carter asked, now genuinely baffled. "Your demesne is *immense!* The largest I've ever seen! You've built a massive tower over an entire desert wasteland!"

"That's not normal?"

"*What?* No! No, that is far from normal! A goblin chieftain would only be able to create a murky cave den that would barely fit fifty of us in it. Yours could easily accommodate entire armies. By the sky, you could even build a city with what you have! Is this a test? Are you hazing me right now?"

"No. No, Carter, far from it. What you're saying is startling to me," Everly said. "This is a hard concept to properly process. You're basically telling me that my imaginary training ground is *real* and that it exists in a separate dimension. It's just taking me a minute to really accept this as a fact."

Everly's memory palace, which was lovingly cultivated from everything she considered essential about the interests that made her who she was, was a real place. It existed, not only inside her mind, but as an actual area in the cosmos, a place that she could physically enter and *touch*.

She just didn't know how to do it.

It was maddening. She wanted to go there, not merely project herself there psychically; she wanted to be *inside* the damn place! It was hers! No, more than that, it was *her!* It was her and she was it, and—and—and . . . damn! It was so hard to describe this sudden yearning.

Dracula! Not the historical Romanian king or the boring character from that old novel, but rather, the badass figure from the *Castlevania* games! He was the best explanation for the feeling that had come over her.

In his stories, Dracula was the great lord of vampires who returned from death once every century to terrorize the world! His immortality was due to his incredible castle, which was also a living embodiment of chaos itself; it lovingly resurrected him after each of his defeats, making him an indestructible force of darkness.

Dracula and his castle were a dear inspiration to Everly.

Normally, she detested vampires as a story concept. She thought they were all disgusting, disease-spreading corpses whose very existence was unhygienic to its core. Did sex-obsessed blood-sucking necrophiles sound like someone you'd want to have dinner with?

Nasty!

But Dracula . . . Dracula was different. He was elegance personified, a refined and intelligent man who'd only become a vampire because he *felt* like it. He could manifest himself as anything he wished—he only chose vampirism to annoy his enemies!

What a mad genius!

Dracula was a *true* dark lord, and Everly bowed before him. He was truly an inspiration.

The thought of having a *Castlevania* of her own was maddening. She wanted it. She wanted it right now. She wanted it *here.*

Come to me. Come to me right now, she demanded. *Let me see you in the flesh. I demand it! I want you! I need you! Please, come to me!*

Had anyone ever begged for their lover as desperately as Everly begged for her tower?

It was doubtful.

What a rewarding moment it was when her desperate pleas were answered.

"Majesty? What's happening?!" Carter cried out in alarm as the land began to quake.

Everly, I feel strange . . . Titania said.

I do as well, Eris said. *What are you doing? It's . . . it's unnatural . . . It feels so WRONG.*

Wrong? Ha, no. No, that was incorrect. Silly thing . . .

What was *wrong* was what Eris had just said. No, *this* was *right.* It was *so* right. It was a combination of sickness, horror, and release. Like when you were about to vomit, feeling nauseous up until the moment your face was over the toilet and you were letting all the bad things pour out of your system.

In that moment when you were puking your guts out, all you felt was *relief.*

That's exactly what Everly felt when her memory palace came bursting out of the earth to loom above the landscape in answer to her summons.

There it stood, a huge and foreboding tower. She'd constructed it, brick by brick. It was comprised of everything she held dear. She had finally found her home, and now she could finally envelop herself within its walls and feel wanted and safe.

She felt grateful. She felt *so grateful.*

The two massive doors at its center opened as she approached, welcoming her entry.

"You . . . you've pulled an astral locale *into the waking world,*" Carter said in shock.

"Hell yeah, I did!" Everly whooped. Then she entered the tower.

Her tower.

CHAPTER TWENTY-SIX

The Brave Quartet

Leaving the tower was one of the hardest things Everly had ever done.

She'd felt such contentment being in that place. Like she was finally somewhere she belonged. Have you ever experienced anything like that before? The sensation of finding your place in the world and knowing that you now had a home of your own?

It's difficult to walk away from an attachment as powerful as that.

Something Everly had always desired more than anything else was to live in a place where she could be free from obligation and societal pressure. She'd lived in two different worlds, and in both, there were people who wanted her to be one thing or another, who wanted her to do this or do that and be grateful for their unwanted advice.

Everly felt that such people were always quick to judge her. She could sometimes feel herself suffocating under the weight of their selfish expectations.

No heed was ever given to what *she* wanted.

Thinking she'd been a disappointment made Everly feel horrible. She hated it! And after a while, she began to hate the people who made her feel that way.

That was the trap of society, wasn't it? People would set up their arbitrary rules, which they made up as they went along, all so they could treat others poorly and berate them for not understanding what they'd done wrong or for daring to follow their own ambitions.

Everly found it all so frustrating. Life could be such a rigged game.

No wonder she wanted to be a villain.

Say what you will about the forces of darkness, but at least they let you live your own life and make your own mistakes. That was what Everly believed. Finding her own path was what mattered most to her.

Freedom to fail. That was what everyone deserved. Unless Everly decided they didn't. After all, a big part of being a black knight was punishing people for failure. Okay then, freedom for *her* at least. And if the only way she could express her freedom was by denying it to others, well, that was perfectly fine.

Life was what you made of it.

No, life was what *she* made of it.

But it was cool, no worries. She'd make sure everyone benefited when she was in charge.

That was a dark lord pinky promise.

The next morning, after a wonderfully restful night of sleep, Everly sent the tower back to the astral realm.

As noted earlier, it was a hard thing for her to do. But her journeys throughout the world had just begun. She couldn't just skip to the end and recline happily in paradise while there was still so much work that needed doing. After all, she had a reputation to build up.

This was no time to kick back and take it easy!

Farewell for now, Black Tower, she wistfully thought. *Your master will return sooner than you think. And it's not like I won't be stopping by anytime soon. I'll still mentally project myself into you for my daily training sessions. I just won't return in the flesh for a while, that's all.*

Anyway, just wait for me, okay?

Meeting a group of adventurers for the first time was a slightly disappointing experience.

Two days after leaving the tower, Everly dismissed her carriage so she could walk on foot for the pleasure of it alongside Carter. They were an hour into their stroll and enjoying a bit of idle chitchat, when they met a team of honest-to-goodness, guild-minted, totally official adventurers, who were riding to the north.

These adventurers were certainly moving in a hurry. There were four of them, all racing down the road on horseback, moving at a much faster speed than the other travelers. But after he noticed Everly, their leader—a roguish-looking fellow in black leather—raised a hand and signaled for the rest to slow down. Then he trotted his horse over to Everly, while checking her out in a manner she didn't appreciate.

Not for the first time since hitting puberty, Everly wished strangers would stop giving her *the look*.

Which look was that? You *know* which one.

Everly often wondered if she was now being punished or something for being slightly skeevy in her previous life. Was this a judgment from the collective unconscious for all the people she'd secretly given a thirsty side-eye to when they weren't paying attention?

If that was the case, ladies and gentlemen, Everly was sorry!

So she liked beautiful people. Was that such a sin? Who didn't? But she never acted entitled about it. She never hit on anybody who seemed vulnerable or stalked anyone online, and she certainly never forced her company on any who didn't want it.

She just liked taking an occasional look.

A lot.

All the time.

Everybody did it!

She was a growing girl!

Jeez, why even dress like that if they didn't want to be noticed?

Okay, that last one was terrible, and Everly felt bad for even thinking it.

Everly knew that if she wanted to truly grow as a person, she was going to have to stop objectifying women. And guys. But mostly women. And a lot of guys. Well, *everybody*, really. And probably orcs too because those stupid Peter Jackson movies had given her an orc fetish, and she was down bad for them.

Why did Rule 34 about porn exist? Easy. So that girls could pretend to fuck orcs. *Looks like Everly's back on the menu, boys!*

But yeah, she really had to stop pretending she stood apart from the crowd just because she had novel tastes. Sure, she liked pale redheads, but that didn't mean she wasn't guilty of turning into one of the brides of Dionysus whenever a BTS song started playing on the radio.

Damn, those boys were pretty.

But hey, just because *she* was a letch didn't mean she wanted to be subjected to lechery!

Was that a double standard? Yes!

Did she care? No!

Everly understood why others were interested in her; it was pretty obvious. Her new body was hot. She wasn't going to deny it. She'd recently done a full review of herself back in the tower in front of a conjured mirror. She had a head of flowing golden hair, gorgeous hazel eyes, and an athletic, well-proportioned body with nicely toned muscles and lush curves.

Yes, that's right, she had *lush curves*. She called them that because that's what they were—get over it!

But what Everly especially liked about herself were the pale scars all over her skin below her neck from the *harada* modifications she'd performed on herself. They looked like sword wounds and were a startling contrast to the rest of her.

She loved the dichotomy of her marred skin.

She cherished her savage imperfection.

It wasn't like Everly's appearance was surprising; her mom was a total fox, so it was perfectly natural that her offspring would inherit that trait as well. The problem was that her face attracted loads of attention but not an iota of respect.

Lots of courtesy, sure; people were always courteous to a beautiful woman, but no one ever looked past that to see the mortal hazard she represented.

It was a little exasperating. She appreciated the attention, but she also just wanted to kill people and break shit. Did no one understand the heart of the modern youth? No wonder society was at odds with itself.

Winstead's stuffiness was probably the main reason Everly preferred dressing like a guy. Her usual outfits consisted of pants, boots, a cotton shirt, and her favorite red coat. She also kept her hair tied back in a practical ponytail. It sort of made her look like a British soldier from the eighteenth century but so what? Those guys had *style*.

Being stylish was *always* where it was at.

"Hello, fellow travelers," Everly said politely as they approached her. "Anything I can help you with?"

"Well, isn't that a coincidence? I was wondering that very same thing myself!" the rogue said with what he clearly assumed was an endearing smirk.

"Ha, ha. That's *so* interesting. Seriously, though, what do you want?" Everly asked again.

A second adventurer, this one clad in heavy armor, spoke up. "We've been dispatched to investigate rumors of a mysterious black tower suddenly appearing to the north of here. You may have passed it during your travels. Did you perhaps see anything like that?"

Everly held her chin and faked a thoughtful expression as she pretended to consider his words. Then she said, "I'm sorry. Nothing seems to come to mind. What about you, Carter? Did you see a big black tower recently?"

"I'm afraid not, mistress," Carter answered promptly.

"Is that a *goblin*?" the third member of their group, a fellow mage by the looks of her, said delightedly. She was a pretty brunette only slightly older than Everly. "And it can speak the common tongue? Where did you find this thing?"

Carter's eyes narrowed slightly at the mage's words. Everly was amused by the other girl's poorly developed survival instincts. Weren't adventurers supposed to be professionals?

Then again, mages were made up almost exclusively of nobility. The ones who became adventurers tended to belong to families that had hit hard times and hoped to restore their fortunes by striking it rich raiding a dungeon or slaying dangerous monsters.

The thing about nobles was that a lifetime of privilege tended to make them immune to common sense.

"Miss," Everly said politely, "this goblin's name is Carter, and while he's only recently come into my employment, I consider him family. Please refrain from using such hurtful words to describe him. He's just as intelligent as I am."

And far more intelligent than you, dumbass.

"Are you certain that thing's not just mimicking words like a parrot?" the mage asked with a condescending sneer.

Hmmm. It appeared a lesson needed to be taught.

"You may be right," Everly said. "Let's find out! Carter, would you please use the word *amputate* in a sentence?"

"Certainly, my lady," Carter promptly responded before turning to face the mage. "Dear woman, if you refer to me as an '*it*' or a '*thing*' one more time, I'm going to amputate two of your limbs without an anesthetic. How was that?"

"A flawless effort, Carter," Everly cheered. "What did *you* think, adventurer?"

An ugly look crept over the mage's face as her three companions began laughing at her. *Awww*, thought Everly. It appeared that she didn't have much of a sense of humor. That made her anger even funnier.

"I think some tart dressed like a man, accompanied by a *freak*, should know better than to—" was what she *started* to say before Carter had her off her horse and on her back with the tip of a dagger pointed at her face.

"It may be difficult to complete that sentence without your tongue, miss," Carter said in a poisonously polite tone of voice. His pupils gleamed red with murderous intent as his blade drew near the mage's mouth.

"Whoa, whoa!" said the final member of the group. He looked . . . familiar, somehow. Everly had never met him before, but she recognized the cloak he wore. She remembered the symbol stitched into it. That weird old man from a little while back, the rude one who'd turned into a spider.

He'd worn one just like it.

Jeez, is he going to turn into a big bug too?

This man was a cleric of some sort, probably their healer, and he seemed a good deal more sensible than the mage or the rogue. He dismounted and stepped toward them with his hands raised placatingly.

"I apologize for my friend, Mister Carter," he said to the goblin. "You've got every right to be offended by her words. But I still ask that you not harm her. Believe it or not, she's a good person behind that fiery temper."

"I shall release her only under the condition that she does not belittle me or my master again," Carter replied. "If she can agree, then I'll be satisfied with what I've already done."

"Understandable," the cleric said. "I accept your terms on her behalf."

"So granted," Carter said with a sniff. In a flash, he stood beside Everly once more with his hands behind his back, looking unflappably calm without even a hint of his prior bloodlust showing.

The mage hadn't enjoyed that exchange at all. "What are you doing, Bryce?" she shouted angrily. "You can't just let them get away with treating me like that!"

"Bree," Bryce said slowly and patiently. "I realize you're newer at the adventuring game than the rest of us, but you really must learn how to appraise someone's strength without relying on a tool. Make it a priority."

"What's that supposed to mean?!"

"It *means* that the goblin you seem so dead set on provoking into violence is strong enough to kill all four of us."

"Ha! Are you serious?" The mage laughed.

"Deadly serious," replied the cleric.

"Well, why don't we test him out, then?" the mage asked as power from her elemental connection flowed into her body. Brilliant flames sprang to life around her hands as she prepared to attack. It appeared the girl was bonded to a fire elemental. A decently strong one too.

Strong by *mortal* standards, that was.

"Let's not," Everly said while snapping her finger.

She directed a wave of *harada* into the mage's core, cutting her off from the source of her power, which doused her flames as thoroughly as if someone had dropped a large bucket of sand on her.

She stared at her hands, stunned. "H-how? How did you do that?"

"I *could* tell you, but then my goblin would have to kill you," Everly said sweetly.

Bryce laughed at that. "Well, it looks like Mister. Carter isn't the only one we have to look out for."

"Hey, was that *harada*?" the rogue asked excitedly. "That was amazing! I've never seen it used that way before."

"Are you a sword expert?" asked the armored knight. "That's incredible! You're not only a girl, you're so young! You must be a prodigy."

"Who is your master? Is he accepting new students?" inquired the rogue eagerly.

Oh, shoot, thought Everly. *This* was a sudden problem.

Everly still hadn't bothered coming up with an explanation for her abilities. Obviously, if she were a sword expert, that meant she had to have an instructor, right? But she couldn't just drop old man Parker's name, even though he had technically been her teacher, because it was common knowledge throughout the kingdom that he'd been banished by the king since before Everly's birth.

Even worse, she used the imperial style, which was reserved exclusively for the royal family. How could she explain that?

The answer was obvious.

She couldn't!

After racking her brain, trying to come up with a plausible-sounding lie,

Everly sighed in defeat and prepared to give Carter the order to eliminate them all. Before she did, however, she was rescued at the last moment by the knight.

"Tch! As if a reputable sword master would pass along the secrets of *harada* to a future assassin!" the big man said. "*I'd* make a far better disciple."

"The last I checked, sword masters prefer students who can *use* swords. You're just a flea's brain in an ox's body, Guyner!" retorted the rogue. "Go hide behind your shield and let me finish speaking with her."

"I'm an ox that could *easily* crush *you*, Eric!" Guyner yelled with a snarl.

"I'd love to see you try!"

"Why didn't either of you idiots back me up with that goblin?" interjected Bree.

"Do you want us to wipe your ass too if you can't find any leaves?" replied Eric.

"Everyone, please—" Bryce began to say.

"Shut up!" the other three yelled at him.

And just like that, everyone continued arguing.

Loudly.

Whenever Bryce tried desperately to calm the others down, they'd gang up on him and tell him to piss off and mind his own business, before turning back on one another, which in turn made him angry as well. Now they were all screaming. At some point it stopped being about Everly and Carter and became about who contributed the least to the group and which lazy bastard was refusing to follow Bryce's chore wheel.

After a few minutes of that, they began delving into even older grievances and hurling *deeply* hurtful insults that made even Carter's eyes widen.

Even Everly was stunned by some of the things they said.

"—and that's why I'm glad your little brother has epilepsy!" said Guyner.

"At least I *have* a little brother! And real parents too, you adopted piece of shit!"

"Only the incestuous spawn of a pair of cousin-fucking hicks would be proud to call those monsters his *parents*! That's why the gods hate you, Eric! That's why they *hate you*!"

"My father would have you whipped for speaking to me like that!" shouted Bree.

"Well, it's a good thing he died in that debtor's prison, isn't it?"

"WHEN THE ARROW TOUCHES YOUR NAME, YOU *WASH* THE FUCKING COOK POT! CAN ANY OF YOU ANIMALS *READ*?!"

"By the darkness below, great lady," Carter murmured to her. "What manner of savages *are* these people?"

"Adventurers, I guess?" replied the stunned Everly. Then, unable to watch any more of this madness, she and Carter slowly backed away, eager to escape the furious quarreling before it escalated even further and got them caught up in it.

And that was how Everly first met the Brave Quartet.

Of course, that was only their first name. On the day they added their final member, they changed it to something else. Something more fitting for their noble purpose.

The Silver Lance.

CHAPTER TWENTY-SEVEN

Needs

Hold on, Carter. What exactly do you mean by *demon kings*, plural?" Everly asked him as they stopped by the side of the road to enjoy a light lunch. "There's more than one? This is the first time I've ever heard that."

"Really? That surprises me, great one," Carter said as he bit into a tasty-looking ham-and-egg sandwich. "I would have thought a person aiming to be one of the world's top villains would have heard of them ages ago."

"No, never. I get most of my information about the world through Titania and Eris. They've never mentioned such beings before."

"Oh, well, there it is, then. Elementals *despise* demons. They'd never bring up the names of the seven kings willingly. They're quite unpopular with that crowd."

"Really? Why's that?" Everly asked him as she took a sip of water. "If elementals and demons both descend from the astral realm, wouldn't that make them related?"

"Technically yes, but that's an unpleasant comparison to make, master. Just as we lesser spirit folk diverged from our great elemental cousins, the elementals themselves broke from demonkind. Irreconcilable differences, I'm afraid."

"Ohhh, sounds like a juicy story. Please go on."

"Well, there's really not much to it," the goblin said as he finished his sandwich off and reached for another.

Goblins really did have impressive appetites for such small people.

"Demons used to be beings composed of energy and will like the elementals. But they were forced into physical form when they were cast down after losing their great war."

"Holy smokes, Carter. Are you telling me there was an actual *war in heaven?* Oh, that is cool! See, that's the kind of awesome high-fantasy backstory I've been wanting to immerse myself in ever since getting reborn into this world," Everly said enthusiastically.

"Well, I don't know about heaven *per se*, but yes, in the realms beyond, the elementals went to war among themselves. A war that changed everything throughout creation. And the losers who were cast down were renamed "demons." Most of them now comprise a mortal race not dissimilar to humans, minus certain distinct features."

"Such as?"

"Superior physicality. Long lifespans that dwarf even those of elves. And, of course, their exclusive foul magics."

"Foul magics? What makes magic foul?"

Carter grimaced in distaste before continuing. "True magic is done in accordance with the balance of the world. An elemental will provide their power in conjunction with mortal will. Two equal forces working in tandem: the eternal and the ephemeral. Even lesser spirit beings such as I exist within that delicate framework. But demons don't respect that. They just *take*. They seize power wherever they can and abuse it however they wish with no regard for the consequences."

"What kind of consequences?" Everly asked.

"Their lands are a desecrated waste. The air is toxic and spreads disease, and no crops will take root. The water itself is noxious and poisonous. They're forced to live in massive domed cities to survive, and their entire nation exists in a permanent crisis of resource deprivation."

"I thought you said they had massive lifespans. Why haven't they figured out a solution?"

"Because they don't *want* one. The easiest method of improving their situation would be to stop using their twisted sorcery that drains the very Earth beneath their feet of life, but their leaders find it more convenient to simply purge their population of excessive numbers through generational massacres, rather than cast off their preferred methods of empowerment."

"Oh," Everly said, now less interested in the conversation. She leaned back against a tree and put her hands behind her head, basking in the warmth of the sun. "That's disappointing to learn. I hate people like that."

"You do? But don't you intend to become a demon king yourself?" Carter asked.

"I'm going to become a *dark lord*, Carter. Not a demon king. There's a big difference," corrected Everly.

"I'm confused. Shouldn't you be more interested in seeking the greatest possible rank? Wouldn't you be interested in working alongside them?"

"Uh, absolutely not! From the way you describe them, these demon kings are raging morons, flailing their arms around. No vision, no daring, just stupid traditionalist brutes afraid to lose what they have. True monarchs empower their nations, they don't make them weaker. The idea of purging your own people instead of conquering other countries is so pathetic, I could cry."

"Demonic magic *is* potent, ma'am."

"No, it's *easy*. It's a shortcut to real power. There are about a million different stories in my old world that warn of the consequences of shortcuts. One of my favorite franchises has this thing called the dark side of the Force, which is basically magic that makes you awesome at everything, but it'll drive you insane and make you look like a rotting corpse if you rely on it."

"That sounds terrible!"

"Well, it *does* make your eyes look really cool, but cool eyes alone aren't worth the risk."

"But, great one, if the dark side is too dangerous to use, then how would you be able to function as a villain in that universe? Aren't you required to use dark powers in order to do evil?"

"Well, I'd figure out a way to do bad things without it," Everly said gleefully. "See, if you don't use the Force *itself* to hurt people, the dark side can't touch you! Like, if I Force choked you to death, that's dark-side points. But if instead I turned you over to the authorities knowing that they'll execute you for your crimes, I'm not only in the clear, I'm also *the hero*."

"Really?"

"Oh, yeah! There're all these games out there that prove it. Even better, if I kill someone in self-defense, that's *still* killing people! But if I don't instigate the fight, then no dark-side points! So I'd just be a stickler for the rules. I'd follow the letter of the law, put logic ahead of feelings, *never* cut anyone a break, and be passive-aggressive as hell. Oh, man, I'd cause so much damage, Carter! It'd be a hoot. Good guys draped in righteousness make some of the best villains ever."

"You are a *profound* monster, my lady," Carter said as he bowed.

"Awww, no need for that, pal. I just like to put a little thought into things, that's all."

Everly smirked at the thought of those pathetic demons hiding in their enclosures, so afraid of losing everything that they never tried anything new. What lame opponents they would make.

"But, you know, even if I did use the dark side, I'm sure I could still control myself. I've got a pretty powerful mind, y'know," she said airily.

"Surely, it's not as simple as having mere strength of will, master," Carter said. "The very nature of magic can at times be insidious."

"Strength of will is what it *always* comes down to," Everly replied dismissively. "A strong mind is the basic building block of mastering magic. Mastery of complex abilities begins with first mastering the fundamentals of your chosen art. Combat styles basically boil down to swinging a weapon or throwing some punches and kicks a few million times until you can do so perfectly. Magic's no different."

"There's no difference at all?"

"None! It's merely the act of gradually strengthening your will until you can force reality to submit to your vision. Even people without magic can do that if they want it badly enough."

"Is such focus possible?"

"Of course it is. But if you haven't mastered the basics and developed a little self-control, of course, you're going to become a worthless mana addict who can't see past your own baseless lust for power. Those demons you spoke of sound completely inferior. I doubt I'll ever be able to do business with them."

"Oh, but their kings are entirely different from their mortal subjects, master."

"Really? How so?"

"They alone among their race have retained their immortality and their power of old. They are among the most terrible and fearsome beings in this world."

"Really, now? I wonder why that is," Everly wondered.

"There exist seven of them. Seven who reign over the seven principal flaws that mar the mortal spirit. Pride, wrath, lust—"

"Carter? I'm sure you think this is a profound revelation for me, bud, but I'm going to stop you right there. I *know* about the seven deadly sins. Everyone in my old world has heard of them! To be honest, I think it's kind of sad that this world couldn't come up with something a little more original. It's a really played-out concept."

"Such notions are above my head, my lady," Carter said, after giving the matter some consideration. "I will instead trust in your leadership and power."

"That's exactly how it should be, Carter. If you're ever in doubt, just remember that *I'm incredible*, and I can make *anything* happen."

Carter laughed and said, "Well, our side certainly doesn't lack confidence! But I have been wondering, Majesty. Why are we heading to the southern border of the kingdom? Participating in these seasonal campaigns seems beneath you. I don't see what you'll gain from the experience."

"Honestly?" Everly asked him. "I just wanted to be on my own. You have to understand, Carter. Despite this body's age, my mind is nearly thirty years old. If you count the time dilation I use while training in my memory palace, I might even be centuries old! I'm a grown-ass woman, and I was tired of living in my mom's house. Can you blame me?"

"I . . . suppose not."

"There's also the matter of all the training I put myself and my elementals through. There comes a time when you want to see the results of your hard work.

I also want to see how I compare to the finest warriors of the kingdom. This is an opportunity to scout my future rivals in a nonhostile environment. I can't pass that up."

Everly smiled eagerly at the thought of meeting so many challengers. "There's also a possibility I might meet someone like me. A transplanted soul. It's very unlikely that I'm the first soul to ever navigate to this place from Earth. It'd be nice to meet a fellow traveler. I'd love to compare notes with them."

"But wouldn't such a person be a rival?" asked Carter.

"Not necessarily. We might have a lot in common. Besides . . . "

"Besides?"

Everly began grinning so hard from excitement that she could feel the corners of her mouth begin to stretch and ache from the strain of maintaining it. "What if they *were* my destined opponent? The hero meant to save the world from *me*? Wouldn't that be *incredible*, Carter?"

She closed her eyes and pictured it. A figure in gleaming silver, wielding a pristine white blade, and fearlessly charging at her.

"I can see it now! My fated enemy draped in righteousness and fury, chosen by the heavens to strike me down! Can you imagine how much *fun* it'll be fighting them to the death? God, I'm so revved up by the idea that I can hardly stand it!"

"Hrrr."

"What?"

"It's just that when you speak that way, I realize I don't understand you very well at all, great one."

"Ahhh, poor Carter. There's really nothing to understand. A dark lord needs to be opposed by a hero. It's like you were saying about magic—there's a balance to these things. Some people need a lover to complete them, but villains just need their *heroes*."

"Is that so?"

"It really is. I didn't just come to this world looking for power. I came here looking for *completion*. I know they're out there somewhere. I don't know who they are yet—I don't even know if they're human—but they're here. And they're waiting for me, just like I'm waiting for *them*. And on the day we meet, every-thing will finally make sense."

"What do you mean?"

"I mean that I'll finally understand myself. That's something we both have in common, Carter. I've never once truly understood why I'm like this. It's a fun way to live, but it's also very confusing. But once I defeat the hero, I'll finally be complete. Everything will finally make complete sense."

"Ahahaha! That sounds like complete madness! Oh, majestic one, please stop!" Carter choked out as laughter consumed him.

He stopped laughing when a sudden nauseating horror filled his mind. He could feel things *crawling* beneath his skin, tiny insects and arachnids that were chewing on his nerve endings, making him shriek hysterically at their unwanted contact with his inner flesh. In his desperation to be rid of them, Carter bit savagely into his own arm, hoping that by stripping the skin free from it, the bugs would bleed out and leave him alone.

However, the moment he tasted his own blood, the madness left him. He looked up fearfully and saw Everly making steady eye contact with him while wearing a furious expression.

"Don't *ever* laugh at my dream, *Skiddz*," she said quietly. "I would never laugh at yours. Treat me fairly."

"I . . . I'm sorry, master. It won't ever happen again," Carter wept.

"Be sure it doesn't. We're having *such* a nice day."

Later, as they continued their way silently down the road, Everly reviewed her relationship with Carter.

Should she get rid of him? It was tempting. She hadn't even *wanted* the goblin. Eris and Titania had begged her to take him in. But what had *she* gotten out of it? What had Carter ever done for her? She'd made him special, given him more knowledge and power than any other goblin who'd ever lived, but how had her generosity been repaid?

With cruel mockery. With laughter.

No, he hadn't just laughed.

He'd laughed *uproariously*.

Maybe it was her fault for growing so comfortable in his presence that she mistakenly believed she'd befriended him. She'd never before talked to anyone about the things she *really* wanted. Not even Eris and Titania. Sure, they loved and empowered her, but with them she could never be certain that it was of their own free will.

Weren't they her servants by their very nature? Such beings couldn't possibly understand what she wanted from life. They weren't with her by choice but by design.

Carter had been different. Sure, Everly had given him a lot, but his decision to serve her was entirely his own. He was an actual person, like her. She thought he'd be her Alfred. Her number two. Her trusted confidant.

Instead, he'd mocked her.

Mocked the future ruler of this world.

That wasn't right.

Perhaps she shouldn't have settled for terrifying him with an illusion. Maybe she should have cracked his tiny mind in half. Or caused all the gases in his body to violently expand until his torso exploded. Or just incinerated him with a good ol' fashioned bolt of lightning.

No. That was an overreaction. She was overreacting.

She just hated being laughed at. She would explain it to him later. He'd understand.

But she didn't feel like speaking with him right now.

God, she was in an awful mood. She was now in a truly, *truly* awful mood.

She dared the next bastard to show up. She *dared* the next bastard to show up and give her a reason to unload on them. *Go ahead. Please, go ahead. Whenever you're ready.*

Whenever you're fucking ready . . .

Everly, Eris suddenly said to her. *There are many riders approaching on horseback. Dangerous, focused minds. And there are two among them who possess true power.*

Is that right? Everly asked her.

She wondered who they could be.

"Carter. Hide," she ordered him. Without a word he vanished from sight.

A few minutes later, thirty or so soldiers in spotless white armor came riding down the road. Riding behind them in rolling cages were dozens of battered-looking women and children.

It was strange. They didn't look particularly dangerous. Typical farming stock from the looks of them. Everly wondered what they'd done to elicit such cruel treatment.

"And what have we here?" a melodious voice asked. Everly looked away from the prisoners and saw a young woman, barely older than she was, astride a massive white charger. She was wearing silver decorative armor with a skirt. An unusual look for what she now realized was some sort of high-ranking temple knight.

"Hello," the girl said. She was very pretty, but something seemed off about her.

Everly's instincts told her to avoid this one for now. She'd be annoying to deal with.

"Hello," Everly replied without breaking her stride.

Sarah was confused. She was very confused.

Who was that strange girl? Why was she dressed like a boy?

Why did she *walk so arrogantly* in front of a paladin?

Why did she wear a sword on her hip?

And why was she ignoring Sarah?

Were people allowed to do that?

Were people allowed to ignore her?

No. No, they were not.

Nellie ignored her. Nellie's mind had turned inward and closed itself off from the world. She stopped talking after a while, stopped moving, stopped being fun.

Nellie was *boring* now.

How had that happened? Did it matter?

Poor Nellie.

But now there came this girl, and she seemed more fun than Nellie ever could be.

Sarah wanted to know her.

Sarah wanted to speak to her.

Sarah wanted to *collect* her.

But instead, the girl was walking away. Walking away as though Sarah weren't a paladin and a Godwell who could do whatever she wished, wherever she wished, whenever she wished.

This was very confusing.

What can she possibly be thinking? Sarah wondered to herself.

Then, like the slow movements of a slithering snake approaching its prey, she sent out tendrils of her powerful mind to probe the thoughts of this fascinating new toy and learn everything she could about her—

Sarah's head snapped back as blood poured down her nose.

"Uh. Uh-huh? *Ahahaha* . . . " she said to herself with a delighted smile running her tongue over her lips and teeth.

"Is something wrong, my lady?" Bandon asked her, before his remaining eye widened in surprise.

She's bleeding? She can BLEED? What the hell am I seeing? he asked himself.

"I can't hear her," Sarah said with a jittery grin.

"What?" Bandon asked in alarm.

"I said I can't *hear* her, Bandon."

Bandon looked to where Sarah pointed. Some ponytailed young girl dressed in rumpled male traveling clothes. No one consequential by the looks of it.

"I want that. Bandon, I *want* that," Sarah said excitedly.

"My lady, we need to finish our delivery for the mine. The transport that will take our volunteers to the north is on a strict schedule. You don't have time to pick up any new toys."

"I don't care. I want that. Bandon, I *want it.*"

"My lady, the instructions we were given were—ow."

Bandon fell to the ground and landed painfully on his back after Sarah swatted him away. Next Sarah turned her horse around and eagerly raced after her new friend.

Where is she, where is she, where is she?

That was an excellent question. Where *was* she?

The girl had disappeared. Vanished as though she'd never existed.

Sarah couldn't find her. She couldn't *feel* her. She was nowhere to be seen.

Sarah searched as thoroughly as she could and even dismounted to look through the brush, but despite her efforts, she couldn't locate her new toy.

It was *very* frustrating.

After a while, one of her knights approached her and said, "My lady, Sir Bandon regretfully says that we've wasted enough time here, and we really must depart."

Sarah punched a hole through his breastplate and tore out his heart.

She hadn't meant to. He'd been *mean*.

Then she sighed, mounted her horse, and rode back to her men, leaving the dead knight behind her. A pair of riders broke off from the main group to go collect the body.

"Feeling better?" Bandon asked her as they continued north.

"I wish it had been you." She pouted.

"No, you don't," Bandon said before kissing her on the forehead like a doting uncle.

Sarah smiled. Bandon was fun.

But she still wondered who that fascinating girl had been.

Let's meet again one day, she sincerely hoped.

CHAPTER TWENTY-EIGHT

Sloth

The demon king of sloth was floating down a dirty river on his back. He didn't have any arms or legs, and he was also missing quite a bit of his skin and hair. Gobs of it. *Gobs.* All he could see was the bright blue sky above him, filled with clouds and birds without a care in this world, and he was thinking . . . just thinking . . .

I want to burn this fucking planet into ash. Just toast it into utter black nothingness.

Sloth detested this wretched world he'd been summoned into. He much preferred Earth, with its wonderful food, remarkable technology, and myriad conveniences, especially its soft beds in climate-controlled rooms. But his kin required him to resume his duties of kingship in this boring little world, and thus he'd allowed himself to be summoned back.

Sadly, the fool charged with receiving him had utterly blundered. *Why* hadn't he been summoned to the lands directly controlled by his siblings? He couldn't understand the reasoning behind it. Clearly, the man had just been stupid. That was what came of raising humans to demonhood.

It clearly muddled their minds beyond repair. He'd have to have a word with Pride and see to it that practice was ended.

Once he'd been summoned, Sloth had tried to adapt to his circumstances and make things work out. Unfortunately, this land's inhabitants kept trying to *kill* him. His incompetent summoner had somehow deposited him on the wrong continent! Here a local religion of light reigned.

Their clerics had quickly detected his unnatural presence without realizing who he was or the extent of his power. In their ignorance, they'd sent forth a few common warriors to dispatch him like he was a common imp.

Their efforts failed, of course. But that hadn't stopped them from being persistent. No matter how much of a mess he made of his assailants, the assassination attempts kept coming.

It was wearing away at him.

Sloth wasn't aware of anything he'd done to justify this level of sustained hostility to his presence. After all HE HADN'T ASKED TO COME HERE. Now it had come to this. He was reduced to being a crippled freak, about to die in what he was certain was the river the local town used to dispose of its sewage.

Sloth was feeling pissed. Truly, *truly* pissed.

Earlier.

Sloth had spent the previous four months hiding in various remote locations, barely keeping ahead of the temple's exasperatingly persistent killers. The last one had been much stronger than the earlier fools and had succeeded in drawing some of his blood. It had been a close call, leaving him shaken and paranoid, unable to decide how to proceed.

In his darkest moment, when he feared he'd never return to his dear siblings, hope finally appeared. His new human friend Claudia arrived before him and said she had arranged to have him *taken care of.*

Ha. What an amusing choice of words.

They both agreed that the village he was hiding in was now under too much scrutiny for him to remain any longer. If he wanted to avoid unnecessary trouble, he was going to have to go west to the reclamations.

The reclamations were huge areas of land that had once been part of this continent's ancient empire. After its collapse, they lay there for centuries, untouched and undisturbed, until the growing population of the kingdom mandated a westward expansion. Once again, manifest destiny had taken root in the heart of man, and now was the time for ambitious citizens of the kingdom to pull up stakes and go forth into the wilderness, to build a new life for themselves in the wild.

It all sounded a bit too much like *Little House on the Prairie*, to Sloth's way of thinking.

The call wasn't just for settlers either. Guilds of brave adventurers were also going west to claim the secrets of the ancient ruins for themselves. People were making fortunes by discovering old magic and technology thought lost to time. It was a golden age of exploration and discovery. The reclamations were a perfect place for Sloth to escape from unfriendly eyes and arrange his escape to the demon continent.

Sloth had to admit that Claudia had done an excellent job of selling him on the prospect of peace and safety. By the time she'd finished explaining her plan, he was psyched to begin.

"Perhaps I'll masquerade as an adventurer," he said, imagining himself as the suave, dashing figure he would surely become. It sounded kind of fun. Any profession that allowed you to drape a mantle over your shoulders in public was one worthy of pursuing a career in.

Claudia smiled sweetly at him and said, "Now, don't get too carried away, great devourer. There will be some difficulty as well. But I think that if anyone's capable of meeting the challenge head-on, it's you."

Oh, Claudia. What a sweet and helpful girl she was. Meeting her had been the luckiest break Sloth had been given in years. She'd even seen his true form, but rather than scream in horror as most did, she accepted him for what he was and vowed to assist him however she could. She'd practically bent over backward to help him safely escape his pursuers.

Such a kind, wonderful soul.

If only he'd killed her on the spot.

When the day came to leave, Sloth was given a trunk filled with clothing, funds, and the prospects for a happier future. He ate breakfast with Claudia one last time and surprised the girl by giving her a firm hug before boarding the carriage that would take him west. Claudia blinked and stared at him, surprised by the sudden physical contact.

Sloth was a little embarrassed himself, but . . . hell, he'd just been feeling so emotional! If they ever saw each other again, he'd be at the head of a massive army of demons, destroying her country and enslaving her people. But even so, he'd make certain Claudia would be spared.

After all the time they'd spent together, she'd become dear to him.

Sort of.

Well, he valued her more than most humans, anyway. That had to count for something, right?

It was silly to expect any sort of emotional depth from Sloth.

He was a *demon*.

Sloth waved farewell one last time, and Claudia in turn gave him a lovely smile with tears running down her cheeks.

And that was that.

In the time he'd spent with her, Sloth learned Claudia was a very capable young woman. Sure, she enjoyed dressing elegantly, and adored pretty things and frivolous gossip, but behind her mask of superficiality lived a sharp and observant intellect. A very pragmatic one too. When it came to finding effective solutions to life's problems, Claudia preferred keeping things simple and direct.

Claudia's gifts as a mage were telepathic, and they allowed her to play with the minds of other people as though they were her dolls. That meant the maids who served in her mansion frequently had their memories altered and erased. She liked to customize them to her liking and make them as loyal and obedient as could be.

As such, her maids always flawlessly followed her every command, felt no fear in the presence of danger, and never asked questions. Not even when they once discovered the estate groundskeeper being baked in the kitchen oven, skin crispy as a holiday turkey with an apple stuffed in his mouth.

Sloth did enjoy his snacks.

Sloth found the magic used by the inhabitants of this world fascinating. He very much wanted to examine Claudia's spirit elemental and gain a better understanding of how its abilities worked. Sadly, Claudia had declined his request. Her elemental wouldn't have survived Sloth's examination and was far too rare to risk losing. Sloth was disappointed to miss out on the opportunity to experiment, but he'd been a guest in her home, so he hadn't pressed the issue.

Another thing about Claudia that Sloth didn't learn until sometime later was that one of her gifts was called [**Remote Viewing**]. And that ability was exactly what its name described. It let her watch anyone she wished from a great distance away, with no chance of being discovered.

Because she was an extremely ambitious person, Claudia enjoyed using this ability to not only steal precious secrets but also to gather sensitive material for the purpose of blackmail. She'd even used her ability to spy on a certain prestigious academy of imperial magecraft.

By psychically auditing their classes, she'd stolen heaps of practical knowledge from them and used it to greatly increase her own personal power.

Of course, the thing Claudia was most proud of, the one that would make her a feared name in the future, had nothing to do with spirit magic. It was a mechanical skill she'd acquired from the tinkerers' guild, a recently developed innovation for mining that involved combining detonative devices with automated clocks.

On Earth, these splendid devices were known as "time bombs."

It was a very practical tool. Claudia knew that in terms of magical power, Sloth towered over her like a giant. By nature, a demon king's mind was extremely powerful. Did that mean he was immune to her skills? If he was, then challenging him directly would have been a very silly thing to do.

No, if she wanted to get at Sloth—you know, *really* take him out—it would have to be at a moment of utter vulnerability. Like if he was in a carriage. Asleep from boredom. Thirty miles outside town, where there were no witnesses to connect her to the deed and no one who would try to help him.

Sloth had often been accused by his siblings of being an overly sound sleeper, but even he couldn't ignore the thundering *BOOM* that shattered his eardrums and sent him flying from the splintering carriage, minus his arms and legs and most of his skin.

As Sloth lay facedown on the dirt road with smoke rising from his freshly detonated body, the tip of a boot appeared and nudged him onto his back. A handsome young man in a white mantle (cape!) that covered him from his shoulders to the tops of his fine leather boots looked down on him, smiling.

His face had a familiar look to it.

"Is this him?" he asked someone standing beside him. He waited for an affirmative response before turning back to the injured demon.

"Greetings, oh great beast of sloth! It's an honor to finally meet you! My name is Sir Aiden Vae-es Belsar, and I've come to deliver a message. Your beautiful but heartbreakingly disloyal friend Claudia, coincidentally my adorable younger sister, must regretfully inform you that she can no longer support the foul fiend whose existence threatens the safety of the kingdom. Sadly, that means you must vanish from this world."

"H-hhhhghhhhh!" Sloth squelched in reply. Claudia had a brother?!

Sloth's head rocked back violently after Sir Aiden suddenly punted him under the chin.

"Watch your language, monster! I'm just the messenger! Let's please keep this civil! Now, listen: Claudia is a lovely person, but she's a *horrible* winner. Her message goes on for ages, crowing about how smart *she* is, and how stupid *you* are, and how anyone with a brain would have seen her betrayal coming."

Sloth had to admit, the knight had a point.

"From what I can tell, you seem like a nice enough fellow, unholy abomination though you are, so I'm going to spare you all that," Sir Aiden continued. "Now, I'd slit your throat to hasten your death, but honestly, you look *gross*, and I don't want any of your demonic gunk getting on my dagger. Luckily, a solution has presented itself to me."

He gestured to his men and gave them their orders. Two of them approached Sloth. One of them cut a slit into his torso and then reached in, rummaging around the foul opening until he produced a large bloodred gem, which he meticulously cleaned with a cloth before placing in Sir Aiden's hand.

"Ha!" the young knight happily crowed as he held the jewel up to examine it. "A blood shard from an actual demon king! It's about time we got our hands on this! Goodness, my fingers are *tingling* just from holding it! The power contained within this must be amazing! How delightful!"

Aiden turned his gaze back to Sloth and gave him another dazzling smile. "You sure made us play a long waiting game, my friend. Finding the perfect moment to strike was *agonizing*. No worries, though. We forgive you."

He then looked at his men and tilted his head in the direction of the river.

"Get rid of it," he ordered them.

His underlings grabbed Sloth beneath the ruined stumps of his arms and began dragging him to the riverbed.

"This is farewell, Sloth!" Aiden continued. "Be at peace knowing that life will go on without you. You'll quickly be forgotten, but that's okay! No one wanted you here to begin with!"

No one had wanted him here to begin with?

Was that true?

What a remarkably cruel thing to say to someone.

Sir Aiden's men tossed Sloth into the filthy waters of the river and let him float away, knowing he'd soon submerge and drown. As Sloth stared at the sky, he thought about the knight's words.

Sloth wasn't a bad person, was he? Maybe a little self-absorbed, but surely not evil? He made practical decisions based on how they'd affect him, but wasn't everyone guilty of doing the same? And hadn't he made a vow not to kill people at random, despite the pleasure he received for doing so? That was self-denial, wasn't it? Didn't that automatically make Sloth a good person?

But look at him now. One more turd in a river overflowing with them. And miles away, Claudia was laughing at him because she'd gotten everything she wanted and even found a way to tie up a loose end.

He'd get her for this.

He'd destroy the entire Van Belsar family!

Sloth would take his revenge, and it would be a lingering, terrible thing. Did these savages not realize who they were dealing with? Sloth was one of the seven great evils that eternally plagued the mortal races! He was the damnation of this world! What sort of games were these fools playing at? Did they really think there would be no consequences for this outrageous behavior?

Did they really believe they would escape their punishment?

They would soon learn otherwise.

You're going to suffer for this, Claudia. Aiden. Whoever else . . . You're going to lose EVERYTHING. Just wait . . .

Still, having vowed all that, it sure would have been nice if a solution to his current problem would neatly present itself. He really might drown here. He was already up to his eyebrows in this horrid water . . .

Oh, hey. Look at that. A giant spider. A huge furry arachnid with a glowing X on its forehead.

Coming right for him.

Sloth sighed.

Honestly, what a *terrible* day this had been.

Just the worst.

CHAPTER TWENTY-NINE

The Beast Below

It was perhaps a testament to how thoroughly terrible Sloth was feeling that day that he didn't immediately die of a terror-induced heart attack at the sight of the arachnid. He knew this terrible world was a ridiculous fantasy setting, so coming across a giant spider was just an inevitability, right?

That was just how it went. Wanted to be an adventurer? Earn that big-time adventurer money? Wanted to search the mysterious catacombs for eldritch lore? Or find out why the tavern owner's cats hadn't left the cellar in so long?

Well, friend, if that was where your interests lay, then at one point or another, you were going to fight a giant spider.

And weren't giant spiders just such a reliable old fantasy trope? No writer had to put any great thought into these abominations to make them terrifying. Loads of people were scared to death of ordinary smaller spiders on principle alone! They were furry in all the wrong ways, alien looking with those eyes and chittering mandibles, and something about the way they skittered just made the hairs stand up on your arms, right?

Of course, there was also the fact that many breeds of the horrible things were extremely aggressive, filled with deadly venom, and could move faster than an eyeblink.

Yep, take all that natural awfulness and then make the creatures big enough to make a leisurely meal of you, and that's an honest day's work done right there.

But was this giant spider big enough to eat Sloth? Was it big enough to consume one of the seven beasts?

Uhhh, yes. Yes, it was. Not that he cared anymore.

It was true that only a few moments ago, Sloth had been determined not to die. He'd been fighting mad and ready to wage war on this obnoxious world! But that had been back in his days of naive innocence, when the future seemed bright and full of exciting prospects for young quadruple-amputee demons slowly drowning in a stream of filthy water. Back when he thought things like vengeance mattered.

But then the world had sent a giant spider after him, and he'd finally gotten the message. And the message was, *Go fuck yourself, Sloth!*

The big brown beast gently lifted Sloth out of the river and carried him to the shore. As the water ran down his skinless flesh and his many awful wounds, he couldn't help but howl in mind-searing agony. But not for long because the spider quickly brought him around, bared its vicious finger-length venom-dripping fangs, and bit him in the shoulder.

Sloth gave one final scream of fear, and then he—began tripping balls.

Holy shit. Holy shit.

Holy shit.

Spider venom is supposed to either paralyze you, kill you outright, or start breaking down your internal organs so that the spider could begin ingesting your innards. Sloth had never thought it was something that could also utterly bliss you out to the point that you'd be feeling *nooooo* pain.

Sloth found the sensation incredible. In his previous life, he'd been a middle-class teenager with a hardworking single mother supporting him, so he liked to think he knew a thing or two about raiding a medicine cabinet for old prescription meds or buying a few party favors with money filched from her purse; but man, this spider bite taught him how ignorant he had actually been.

A dilettante. A mere beginner.

*Keep your stinky weed, normie scum! REAL players got melted on arachnid neurotoxins! Excuse me—*magical *arachnid neurotoxins!* he thought sagely to himself.

With a huge grin on his face, he hung loose and happy as the spider carefully webbed him up and tucked him away on its back before scampering off into the dark. He sang tunelessly as it carried him away, happy as could be.

When Sloth came to later, he saw they were now in some sort of sewer, just beneath the town whose name he hadn't yet learned. Water flowed quietly beneath him, making soothing, rippling sounds that helped him to relax.

As soon as the spider had returned to its massive lair, the first thing it did was pull off what remained of Sloth's ruined clothing. Then, gently, it vomited an acidic fluid over his burns and rubbed them into his wounds, while carefully sloughing off all his dead skin.

At first, Sloth thought the monster was just tenderizing him before having its meal. After a bit, he realized it was giving him a sort of antiseptic bath, like a mother with a sunburned child. Oddly enough, it made him think of his own childhood in the abyssal realms, when he'd been an infant in the arms of his true mother, Lilith.

Had he ever told her how precious their time together had been? He hoped he had. People should let the ones who mattered to them know how important they were. Life was never a certain thing, and you never knew when the bomb stowed beneath the carriage you were riding in would detonate.

Later, Sloth was surprised to learn that the spider didn't eat people. Was that a disappointing discovery? No, of course it wasn't. Okay, maybe a little. Whatever.

Instead, the spider subsisted off a population of enormous rats that made their homes in this surprisingly spacious sewer. Vicious rats the size of fat little bulldogs. Every night, the spider crept from the web and disappeared for about an hour before returning with a fresh catch.

It was generous with its meals too, though for Sloth to have any, the spider had to vomit acidic fluid all over the meat to tenderize it enough for Sloth's sensitive toothless mouth.

Mmmm, sewer-rat slurry, spiced with spider puke. It's yum-yum-yum, until you're done-done-done.

The spider spent most of its time repairing the web, patrolling for food, and doing other spidery things Sloth couldn't account for. Despite being a repulsive monster, it actually made for a considerate and ideal roommate. It was quiet, clean, and quick to dispense its narcotic bites whenever the pain from Sloth's injuries flared up.

Sloth, for the most part, spent his time in the web slowly healing and just . . . hanging out.

Life in a spider's web really wasn't bad at all. When the air was chilly, the spider covered him in silk and wrapped its legs around him, letting him nestle in its warm grip. Sloth could hear its heart beating in a soothingly steady cadence that lulled him into a deep and restful sleep.

A demon could get a lot of thinking done in the safety and comfort of that nest, letting his mind drift and explore. Without even realizing it, Sloth was roaming the area in his astral form. The relaxation and awareness normally required to reach this state of enlightened being were easily achieved simply by being immobilized in a high corner of the ceiling with nothing to stare at but the wall.

Being narcotized all the time certainly helped too.

In his spirit form, Sloth could see the people walking about on the streets above. He could see the townsfolk shopping at the markets, children playing, cats chasing dogs, lovers holding hands. He even learned the name of the town: Bremburg.

He could see *everything*.

Soon, Bremburg became Sloth's chief source of entertainment. He delighted in watching families interacting with each other, friends and neighbors cheerfully insulting each other, rivals fighting with their fists in the streets before fleeing the town watch, and the occasional illicit love affair. This was good. This was very good.

It was as if the people of this place lived their lives for Sloth's entertainment. He never got bored observing them, and there was always something interesting to watch! Their triumphs, their tragedies, their joy, and their sorrow. It was all for him. Their lives existed for him alone.

During this quiet time as Sloth's body slowly healed, he pondered his own nature.

Sloth meant you didn't move, right? Allegedly nothing could be achieved by a slothful person because of their sheer laziness. Their lack of effort and care eventually devolved to the level of a mortal sin because a slothful person characterized life itself as not being worth their effort.

For them, nothing mattered in the slightest.

But what if that wasn't true? What if being an agent of Sloth simply meant you didn't *have* to do anything? From Sloth's perspective, the world came to him, so he didn't have to lift a finger to get everything he ever wanted. All he needed to achieve success was wait for it to come his way.

Maybe the world just didn't get what being slothful was really about . . .

There in those dank, dark sewers, Sloth—bereft of his body and limited in his options—realized that he wouldn't have to make any special efforts to begin facilitating his vengeance. Why make any great effort? That idiot knight had claimed Sloth wasn't wanted in this world.

What utter idiocy! Sloth belonged *everywhere*.

To be one of the seven beasts meant being *more* than a simple thought in the shadows, experiencing dark apotheosis. Sloth was greater than any meager mortal king; he was a kingdom unto himself! An empire of one! There were no walls that could keep him contained; he was everyone and *everything*.

The real sin was defying him. The real sin was asserting yourself against him. If a kingdom was greater than any one man, then surely that meant Sloth was greater than any man who ever lived! The logic was absolute! The needs of the many existed for him alone!

Sloth couldn't stay in these sewers. He had too many things to enjoy at his leisure. Or perhaps he had too much leisure to enjoy? Whatever the wording, this pleasant little half-life of his couldn't continue down here forever. All the glorious new knowledge he'd gained of himself, this wonderful feeling of exciting self-discovery, didn't mean much if he remained so vulnerable and weak.

The spider could only keep him going in this wretched state for so long.

There was a world out there waiting for him to trod over it. But first he needed feet to trod with.

He needed healing. And he knew how to get it.

But first he needed bait . . .

The most powerful healers in this kingdom were affiliated with the Temple of the Holy Will. They were a typical collection of generic fantasy Roman Catholic knockoffs who trained all the crusading "holy" classes like priests, paladins, clerics, and monks. The typical roles played at a tabletop by some of the most rigid people you know.

"I'm sorry, Tina, but I can't use the gem of Vordmare to cleanse the werewolf's curse because you stole it, and stealing is *wrong*."

"Scott! The werewolf is about to eat Mikey! He'll die if you don't use it!"

"But stealing is *wroooooong!*"

Anyway, the strongest healers in this country were considered living treasures by the temple. People came from all over the world to request their help.

With such talent, they could easily regrow limbs and purge a body of sickness and disease. One of them was exactly what Sloth needed to complete his recovery. However, those wonderful healers would surely be defended tooth and nail by an army of fanatical believers. They rarely left their church strongholds.

Like Sloth, they preferred to let the world come to them.

In order to acquire one of those saintly gems for his personal use, he first had to lure them out. And the only thing that could tempt such people into willingly exposing themselves to danger would be a challenge to their faith and skills.

And what could possibly be more challenging than a plague?

My apologies, oh good people of Bremburg. But the Kingdom of Sloth demands sacrifices, the demon thought to himself. *Time to take one for the team, guys.*

CHAPTER THIRTY

Welcome To Bremburg

Shift over, Fred?" the captain asked in a genial tone.

"Yes, sir!" Fred called back with a smile.

For eight years, Fred had worked as a watchman in Bremburg, and each night, at the end of his shift, the captain would always ask him if he was finished for the day. It'd become a routine as familiar to him as the path of his daily patrols.

"Well, we'll be seeing you at eight sharp like always, then?"

"As always, sir!"

"Good man, Fred. Good man."

Fred *was* a good man. He really was. He knew he should be humble about acknowledging this, lest it border on sinful self-regard, but he couldn't help it. He had a life that many would rightfully envy: a beautiful wife, a wonderful son, and an easy job that paid well. Clearly, he was someone who had the favor of the gods.

Clearly, he was a good man.

Thomas had a case of the summer chills, and Helen was concerned.

Wasn't that just like a mother?

"I want to take him to the apothecary, Fred," she said, shortly after he arrived home. "He's been so quiet and sluggish. He went to bed earlier in the day, and now I can't get him out of it. I've never seen him like this . . . "

"He'll be all right, dear," her husband said. "Heh, it figures we'd get through the whole of winter unscathed, and then he'd catch the chills in the middle of summer. That's just the gods flipping our skirt for a laugh."

"That may be so . . . " Helen said uncertainly.

"It is so, love. Don't worry about it. He'll bounce back soon enough. Now, why don't you come over here and share some of that worry with your husband? I had such a trying day at work! Feels like my shoulder could pop out any moment now."

"Oh? Sounds like you need a closer examination, then. Should I get out my tools?"

"Oh, ho-ho, I certainly hope you will!"

Fred smacked her firmly on her bottom, laughed at her playful shriek, and followed her into their bedroom. Fun ensued.

Later that night, he returned to his son's room and stood over his bed, watching him sleep. Was life meant to be this good? Was it possible for one man to be this happy?

He'd have to put in an extra shift at work to pay for a visit from a healer. He didn't mind. He loved his family. For their sake, he'd make any sacrifice.

Oh, the gods were so good to him.

And why wouldn't they be?

He was a good man.

"Watchman! Hey, Fred! Fred! I need you over here!" someone shouted during his morning patrol.

It was Bill Thimble, normally a cheerful old baker, fat and content, who'd been known to share a sweet treat or two with a hungry watchman doing a hard day's work. Not so much today. Today he was flushed and angry, with odd swollen red marks on his pale scalp that made his bald head look unbearably itchy.

"How can I help you, Bill?" Fred asked.

"You c-can start by getting that fool out of my shop!" Bill said, so agitated that he stumbled on his words.

An old man had wandered into the bakery, barefoot and shirtless. His torso and limbs were covered in infected welts that leaked clear fluid across his chapped skin. He had an uneven beard that should have been white but had been colored pink by the erupting pus sliding down his boil-infested chin.

"Bastard just walked into my shop and started spitting on all my wares," Bill said. "What in the world is happening here, Fred? All the damn rodents running around unchecked, and now all these dirty freaks wandering the streets."

The big man reached for a cloth in his pocket and began dabbing at his sweaty brow. "There's sickness everywhere."

"You don't look so well yourself, Bill," Fred said warily.

"Don't I know it? But my hired help's all down with fever too. If I didn't come in myself, no one would be here to mind the place."

"Sounds like an ordeal."

"It is. It really is—"

"I SEE YOU! I SEE YOU!" the old man screamed rapturously inside the store, before slamming his hands on the wooden counter and running outside. He blinked, dazed by the brightness of the sun, and quickly covered his eyes. He stopped when he saw Fred and Bill and smiled at them. Fluid poured down his pants leg and flowed over his dirty feet.

The old sod had just pissed himself.

Disgusting.

"Friend, you need to stop this right now," Fred said sternly as he reached for his truncheon. He pointed the club at the man in warning. "I don't want to hurt you, but I won't allow this nonsense to continue on my streets."

"He calls," the old man said. "He calls! Why don't you hear him? He says the most wonderful things! He would share his blessings. He would share his love!"

The old man began crying, tears running down his filthy face, even as his grin grew wider and wider, splitting the sores on his cheeks and allowing even more awful yellowish fluids to run freely down his skin.

Fred was utterly repulsed. "Keep back! I won't warn you again!"

"Share his love!" the old man screamed, then ran toward Fred, his arms raised. Before Fred could push him away, he licked him across the face, which caused him to accidentally inhale the revolting fluids directly into his nostrils.

Fury exploded in the watchman's head. "Dirty bastard!" he screamed in outrage. He brought his club down with vicious force against the old madman's head, rejoicing in the feel of it smashing into his warped skull.

With the old man now collapsed at his feet, Fred kicked him in the ribs, leaving him wheezing on the pavement, before stomping on his head until he was unconscious.

"You like that, bastard? You like that?!" Fred shouted over and over.

"Gods, Fred," Bill said, after hurriedly grabbing a kettle of hot tea from his shop and pouring it on a cloth to give Fred something to clean his face with. "What is happening in Bremburg? These wanderers are turning up everywhere. Are people going mad?"

"Hell if I know," Fred said grimly. "Starting to feel like a damn plague—"

"Oh no, don't you say that word," Bill cut in. "That's impossible in this land! We're faithful! The Cathedral of the Heart is a two-day ride from here! We're supposed to be safe!"

"Well, I don't know what to say, then," Fred said glumly. "But *something's* going on."

As the weeks went by, there were more and more of them.

Men and women of various ages, children as well, all covered in blistering sickness, running amok. They were increasingly agitated and violent, breaking things, taking things, forcing their way into people's homes, preaching their mad gospel.

All of them seemed so very happy.

Droves of them. A crowd. A mob.

An *infestation*.

Helen had grown beyond worried.

Something was wrong here. So terribly, terribly, wrong.

Thomas had gone to sleep early in the afternoon, but he hadn't yet awakened. Every time she tried to get him up, he mumbled that he was still tired and refused to move. The evening was swiftly approaching, and he hadn't been out of his room in hours.

His skin felt damp and clammy to the touch. Odd patches of red infection were showing up on his chest and arms, and his eyelids had been glued shut by an awful gummy fluid leaking from within them.

Her little boy was sick. Very sick, despite what Fred had said, and she couldn't do anything to help him.

They'd tried taking him to the apothecary a week ago, but the poor man was overworked beyond his capacity to respond to every request. More and more people showed up at his small clinic, desperate for help, overwhelming him.

Two days ago, Helen had seen a naked man shoving tufts of grass into his mouth and laughing in delight as he bit down on his tongue. It had been the apothecary. He was no longer concerned for his patients, now that he had been made carefree by madness.

Was it the rats? Was it the spiders? Could they be carrying something virulent, and were they now spreading it to the citizens? The creatures were fearlessly attacking grown men and women, gnashing and gnawing and poisoning any they saw fit. They were the new and uncontested rulers of Bremburg. Or was it now *Brem-bug*?

Helen was terrified.

A sudden crash in her son's room drew her attention and had her running swiftly toward the door. When she opened it, her eyes bulged in horror at the unnatural sight.

"Thomas!" she shrieked in fear. There were rats and spiders everywhere in his room. They paused, an undulating mob of quivering flesh, and fur, and *eyes* that seemed to look at her in perfect unison. The revolting mass shifted and moved, forming something, and for a single hideous moment of perfect heart-stopping terror, Helen believed she saw a face looking back at her . . .

It was smiling.

Thomas sat up in his bed, covered in sores and sickness, yet so unnaturally vital. The vermin ran across him, covered his bed, bit and kissed him, but he seemed deliriously happy in their midst. As though he'd been made angelic by their foulness.

"Mommy!" Thomas screamed joyfully. "Come with us! We want to show you something fun!"

"Tommy . . . " Helen moaned as he unhurriedly climbed off his bed and began to walk toward her. "Tommy, no . . . Tommy, stop. Please, please, please!"

"Silly," he said happily as he crawled toward her with a horrible tottering grace. "Mommy's so *silly!*"

"Tommy—"

"SILLY!" he screamed one last time before throwing her to the floor with sudden inexplicable strength. Helen tried to kick him away, but he caught her leg easily and pulled her toward him, then crawled over her body with the revolting ease of an arachnid.

"Tommy—" she whimpered one last time into his smiling face.

"I love you, Mommy." He giggled before biting into her cheek with his rotting teeth.

Fred hadn't been home in two days. He'd tried to be. He *wanted* to be. But after his shift had ended two days earlier, just as he stood at the edge of the entryway of his house, he'd heard Helen screaming. He heard Tommy laughing as well, and he knew that if he tried to help his wife, that if he got in Tommy's way, Tommy would get him too.

Tommy was the head of the house now.

At the sound of his little boy's demented giggling, Fred had pissed himself, just as that old man at Bill's bakery had. Then he ran back to the watchhouse. Not to get help, though.

For safety.

He made it back just in time. The captain ordered it boarded up and all the watchmen armed and ready. The town had gone mad. The infected now wandered the streets, hunting for the healthy, determined to spread their illness, begging everyone to heed the call of their unseen master.

There were only nine watchmen left. Nine out of twenty.

"It's hell," Fred said, after someone wondered aloud what was going on. "That's all. A devil has come here, and he's brought hell with him."

"Shut your mouth, Watchman," said the captain. "We're men of faith! Don't believe that nonsense for a moment. This is a plague, plain and simple. Not one we've seen before, but certainly something the temple can deal with."

The captain was a veteran of the wars and an imposing figure of a man. Even though he was half past his fifth decade, he could still dominate younger men with ease due to his incredible strength.

"Fred might be right," Thompson opined. He was a young man, beginning his first year on the job, but he was a veteran as well. He'd come with glowing recommendations for his service out west and in the summer campaigns. "I've seen things like this before, out in the reclamations. *Virilations*, they called them. Spirits that spread illness from person to person. Unclean things."

"Enough, Thompson," barked the captain. "This is not the heretical west nor the rebellious south. Things like that don't happen out *here* in civilization. Unfortunately, however, plagues sometimes *do*. Until we see proof of an actual possession—"

"What do you call those freaks out there?" Fred yelled, his anger erupting due to the captain's patronizing tone. "You didn't see what became of my boy! You didn't hear his voice!"

"From how you described things, I don't believe you saw what became of your boy either," the captain replied coldly, before turning to face the others. "Now listen. We're going to break for the stables just after dawn. These infected people seem dazed by the light of day. Under its protection, we'll mount up and race for our salvation. As long as at least one of us makes it past them, we can alert the cathedral, and then hopefully they'll deploy aid to the town."

"We won't make it," Fred said blankly. "We'll die trying or join their numbers. It doesn't matter. Nothing matters."

"In which case, you're more than welcome to stay here, you mewling little *shit*," the captain growled. "Honestly, Fred. I thought you were a better man than this. I thought you had some steel in you."

"To hell with you! How would any man act if his family—"

"Your family may yet be saved if we succeed!" the captain roared, anger finally overtaking his patience. "But you've already decided that success is impossible, haven't you? Well, *I* haven't given up yet! Neither have *they*," he said, gesturing toward the other watchmen.

"I've got a family too, and I mean to see them through this, Fred! And if you impede our chances in any way, you worthless coward, I swear I'll see you dead for it! Now make your choice, man. Help us or *piss off*."

Fred bit down on his tongue and nodded. Tears streamed shamefully down his cheeks.

"Good man," said the captain. "Good man."

But was he really?

They made their move two hours after dawn, giving the daylight enough time to cover the entire village.

It did not go well.

In their lurching multitudes, the infected came for them. The watch's attempt to escape by horseback had been anticipated. Of the nine of them who remained, by the time they reached the stables, only three were left.

They'd been waiting for them.

"Fred! Fred, no! What are you doing? Help me! Help me!" the captain screamed as the infected brought him down.

Fred sneered at the panic he heard in his leader's voice. Not the big man now, was he?

It hadn't helped that Fred had cut the tendon of the captain's leg from behind. He didn't know where the urge had come from, but hadn't it been a good one? Now he stood there and watched. And listened. And laughed. Oh, the things they did to the captain.

It looked like fun, so he decided to join in.

Good times. These were good times.

Good times for a good man.

Behind the revelry, unnoticed through the screams and laughter, Thompson raced away on a horse.

Later, Fred made his way home, walking casually down the dirt road, the same path he always took on foot. It had been a long couple of days. He'd be glad to get some rest.

He came through the front door, a sickly smile now fixed on his pale face. Vermin covered his feet, almost knocking him onto his back with their mass. The contact they made was beyond revolting, and it was all he could do to keep down the vomit that nearly surged up his raw throat.

His house now smelled of sickness and decay. It was a repulsive stench that clung to the surface of everything it touched. He didn't care.

"Honey!" he called out cheerfully. "I'm home."

"That's wonderful, dear," his wife's beautiful voice called out from the hall. "Thomas and I are in our room. Why don't you lie down for a bit? Come join us."

"Yes." Fred nodded to himself. "Why don't I?"

And there they were, on the bed. He couldn't quite make out their features in the shadows. And they felt so cold to touch! But when he lay on the mattress, his boy happily rested his head on his father's chest, and his wife stroked his hair and shoulders lovingly, and he knew that there wasn't any place in this world he'd rather be.

He didn't mind when the hunger overtook them and they bit into him with their flaking red maws. He loved his family. For their sake, he'd make any sacrifice. No screams from him. No screams from the loving family man.

Oh, the gods were so bountiful with their blessings.

Didn't that make him a good man, after all?

Tearing down the streets, his face buried in his horse's mane, Thompson rode as though a demon were chasing him. The fierce young mare he'd chosen was more than up to the challenge, knocking down anything that dared approach them, pushing past them with wild ferocity.

Gaining a lead of a few minutes, Thompson made his way to the town's gate, and after a few frenzied moments spent unbarring it, and a close call while remounting, he raced out unto the forest path, screaming "Plague! PLAGUE!" to any who would hear it.

He screamed his warning until his throat ached. Until he could scream no more.

Within an hour of his escape, a messenger bird was sent to the cathedral.

CHAPTER THIRTY-ONE

The Quest

Ah, the summer campaign! What a thrilling time to be alive! It was finally that precious time of year when the great nobles of the great kingdom of Winstead would set aside their numerous irreconcilable differences to join hands and march south to kill foreigners and take their stuff.

Hurrah for patriotism! Hurrah for war! Hurrah for crimes against humanity!

What exactly was the summer campaign and why was Everly so excited to join in? You don't *know*? If that's so, then please allow this humble narration to take the time to inform you, oh curious audience! Because it really is an interesting story. It goes a little something like this:

Centuries back, the Kingdom of Winstead had once been a far larger country. The ancestors of the reigning royal family had been forced to flee to this continent to escape being persecuted in their homeland after losing a terrible civil war initiated to overthrow them.

After they established themselves here in what had once been the center of the old empire, they immediately began making friends with everyone they met and became the source of all happiness forever.

Hurrah!

Ha! Just kidding. No, what they actually did was kill and enslave most of the natives and threaten to do the same to anyone else who resisted their expansion or refused to bend their knees. It was a method not unlike the Roman expansion on Earth. They achieved excellent results and soon became the dominant power on the continent.

Everly found it interesting how the royal family had such a knack for starting pointless conflicts. Some people just had a gift.

The newly anointed kingdom had ruled uncontested for centuries but the people they oppressed never stopped yearning for freedom. Eventually they rose in rebellion and successfully fought for their independence. Which was a great thing for everyone except for the kingdom, which was cut in half after the rising.

The newly freed southern half renamed itself the Oldstead Republic and became a fairly prosperous nation, due to its abundant natural resources and mineral mines. Mines that Winstead felt belonged to them. But then again, Winstead felt that *everything* belonged to them. They were kind of greedy like that.

Oldstead and Winstead rattled sabers at each other for centuries, but nothing much ever came of it until the recent civil war when the republic made the mistake of openly backing the king's brother.

Yikes!

Everly thought she understood their reasoning. The king's brother had a sizable army, and with the support of Oldstead's own military, it seemed like a certainty that he'd be the one to claim the throne. It was just his bad luck that the king managed to convince the Western Temple (and more importantly, the Godwell family) to back his own claim.

That was the game changer that decided the war.

The temple had the hearts and minds of everyone on the continent. By declaring that the king's brother was a heretical would-be usurper, they'd effortlessly turned every true believer against him overnight. Half his army abandoned him, and the rest that stayed were slaughtered by the holy legions, the private armies loyal only to the temple, led by their superhuman paladins and spearheaded by an absolute unit known only as the maiden of the holy sword.

Ohhh, man, thought Everly. *The maiden of the holy sword . . .*

Everly found that title sounded *utterly* badass. She'd heard so many stories about the maiden and her predecessors. It was a generational role passed down through a sacred bloodline from mother to daughter for hundreds of years. If the four paladins represented the pinnacle of human potential, then the maiden was their scalpel. A tool that could heal, but also kill.

But, uh, in a *churchy* sort of way.

The maiden was basically the temple's ultimate assassin/lawman/enforcer wandering across the land wherever she felt she was needed, like the Kwai Chang Caine of paladins. But whenever the temple sent forth its armies, she was always at its head.

Everly heard her body count during the war had rivaled the Mountain Splitter's. She supposed that made the maiden her god's favorite little monster?

Whatever. I could take her.

Because Oldstead had backed the losing side, the Western Temple passed an edict accusing their leaders of apostasy and declared that, in the eyes of the faithful, their nation no longer had any right to exist. So the king followed that up by ordering them to reunify with Winstead and once more become a single godly nation.

Oldstead responded by rejecting the temple, evicting every single priest from their lands, and creating their own state religion. They also told Winstead where to stick it.

Oh, boy, the old men in charge sure didn't like hearing *that*.

Which brought us to the summer campaigns. You see, this continent had the ugliest, coldest winters you can possibly imagine, north or south. The winters in the southern half were particularly brutal, due to the proximity of the ocean. In other words, Oldstead was a damn cold place! But that worked to their advantage because the weather made it impossible to wage a sustained campaign during the cold season.

For the first five years, the war against them consisted of gradually taking territory from them bit by bit before having to fall back for the winter and then returning and repeating the same process in the spring. It sounded like an enormous waste of time and lives.

Things changed, however, with the successful construction of two massive fortifications by the late Duke Rondale, which finally allowed Winstead to maintain permanent garrisons in the south and to finally keep the land they claimed. Since then, although it went at a snail's pace, Winstead gradually penetrated deeper and deeper into Oldstead's territory. Now it was only a matter of time before they were within striking distance of their capital city, Landfrey.

So now there were a lot of noble houses jockeying for the right to lead the first direct strike against the enemy capital and claim the honors (and the loot) that would come with that privilege. It was a great time to be a citizen of the kingdom. Everyone was puffed up with confidence and patriotism. Good feelings and a solid sense of national pride flowed every which way you turned.

But if you lived in Oldstead, you were essentially hanging on by the skin of your teeth. Resources would be tight, most of the men and boys would be conscripted, and an unceasing feeling of imminent doom would slowly encroach upon you.

The citizens knew what was going to happen to them. Sure, a few of their nobles would lose their lives, possibly their political leaders as well. But the real idiots in charge, the men who ruled from the shadows, they'd escape punishment. They always did. And that meant the ones who'd absorb the brunt of Winstead and the temple's wrath would be them, the commoners.

They would be beaten, violated, murdered, and stolen from. Once their defensive line was breached, defeat and all the horrors that word entailed would be their reward for living on the wrong side of a line on a map.

It sounded like a real tough break. Just another reminder that life was a complete lottery.

Perhaps the moral of the story was to try to be born with wealthy parents in a bigger country, if possible? It had done wonders for Everly.

"Majesty, there are riders swiftly approaching," Carter said, interrupting her introspection.

He'd been contrite since his earlier misstep. Very polite and eager to make amends for his mistake. He'd been so sincere that Everly just couldn't stay angry at the little guy. She told him so too, but he'd still been a little wary of her since that day.

She supposed she couldn't blame him for that. She'd been just as surprised as him to discover that she *hated* being laughed at. But wasn't that a useful thing to learn? Now they *both* knew something interesting about her!

"More of them, huh?" Everly mused aloud. "I wonder what's going on?"

They were getting closer to the border, so she wasn't surprised by the sight of soldiers on the move. So far, though, she hadn't seen the colors or sigils of any notable house. Just a bunch of temple warriors in their drab white tabards.

"Perhaps it's a deployment of some kind, mistress," Carter offered. "Those men, despite their professional demeanors, were very tense. I believe a battle will soon begin nearabout."

"Whoa, you think so?" she asked him eagerly. "Shoot, that would be interesting. But wait, you don't think that redhead in the silver armor will make an appearance, do you? Ugh, that would be annoying."

"I meant to ask why you so thoroughly avoided her gaze," Carter said. "I was surprised when you had Eris mask your presence from her."

"Well, let's just say I've got a sensitive nose, my friend," she told him with a worldly nod. "And that chick smelled nuttier than a pecan pie."

"Master? I'm sorry; I don't understand that reference," Carter said apologetically.

"Oh, sorry. That's an idiom from the world I came from," she said sheepishly. "It means she was noticeably problematic. More trouble than she was worth. Cuckoo. *Crazy.*"

"Mentally unwell?" Carter asked.

"Yeah, but not in that fun and quirky way that they are in Hollywood. She smelled like blood, and she smiled too widely. Some people are best avoided."

"I see. If she is that large a potential concern, then why not simply kill her and negate any risk?"

"Carter! Come on. You can't just kill people because they're annoying," Everly said, shocked by his callousness. "You should only kill them when it's thematically appropriate. Or really funny. You know, it's got to be done in a way that doesn't kill immersion. Otherwise, that's just—"

"Crazy?" Carter asked carefully.

"*Exactly,*" she said, happy that Carter was so quick to catch on. "Exactly. It's got to suit the scene. If you're just killing because you feel like it, instead of in service to a dope-ass narrative, then your brutality lacks panache! Remember, ours is not the way of *petty* villainy! We're artists!"

"Right . . . of course. Artists . . . "

At that moment, the new arrivals caught up to them. Everly turned to look at them and smiled in recognition. It was those adventurers from a few days ago who'd gone out to investigate the emergence of her tower. The ones who'd viciously torn into one another like disagreeable house cats.

Their leader, the cleric Bryce, gave her a polite nod, but that annoyingly flirtatious rogue, Eric, trotted right over to her and gave her an unwelcome smile.

"Well, *hello* there again," he said cheerfully. "Bet you didn't think you'd see me again so soon, huh?"

"Well, I *was* sincerely hoping otherwise, but I guess wishes are for fishes," Everly replied in an equally cheerful voice. "What brings you lot back so soon? I thought you were investigating the emergence of a mystery dungeon or whatever."

"Tch. That was a total bust." Eric glowered as he dropped from his saddle to walk his horse alongside her. "Those yokels must have been chewing on fermented grass clippings. There was no mile-long tower to be seen anywhere."

"Awww," Everly said sympathetically. "Well, at least you got to visit the countryside. That counts for something, doesn't it?"

"You're not wrong there," Bryce said. "We were on our way back to our guildhall, cursing our bad luck, when the temple announced that they were going to commence a holy cleansing. What are the odds of coming across an event like that at random?"

"A holy *what?*" she asked him, intrigued by his choice of words. "Are they about to purge some unbelievers? Shoot, that'd be interesting to see."

Guyner, the heavy knight, looked at her in confusion. "*Why* would that be interesting to see?"

"I appreciate dynamic visuals," she told him. "Nothing more classic than holy figures rebuking the unclean and all that. *Purge the wicked! Purge the wicked!* All those whips and chanting monks? I'm down."

Bryce coughed suddenly as though he were trying to clear his throat. "I served for four years as a temple cleric before becoming an adventurer. I can assure you that we're not in the habit of randomly flogging the citizenry and accusing them of heresy."

"Really? So, there are no sudden purges? No sweaty old men in white robes ordering voluptuous and sexy women to be burned as witches for tempting the faithful into sin? No naughty nuns with paddles?"

"What? No! No, there are no naughty nuns with paddles. Wh-where are you getting this nonsense?"

"Nowhere, I guess," she said sadly.

Man, why does the internet exaggerate everything?

"So, why does this cleansing have everyone so hyped up? It must be a big deal if they're sending so many people."

"It really *is* a big deal!" Eric said excitedly. "The holy order is marching on the town of Bremburg. Apparently, some manner of unholy presence was detected there by a temple seer. It's been spreading illness and death and other such unsavory things."

"What exactly is an unholy presence?" she asked.

"A demon," Bryce said somberly. "For a call of this magnitude, a greater demon must have physically manifested itself in our realm."

Everly was flummoxed. "Isn't Bremburg just a boring little town bordering the next county? What could possibly attract the presence of a greater fiend?"

Guyner shrugged. "Who knows? I never want to be accused of understanding the thought patterns of a demon. But the randomness of its behavior aside, this is still a fantastic opportunity for us."

"How's that?" she asked him.

"Heh, nobles really are sheltered. Adventurers who manage to get in the good graces of the temple can receive access to some *very* lucrative quests, my lady. Trust me, these religious types pay extremely well."

"Ha! They ought to since they're exempt from taxes." Eric snorted.

Bryce frowned at his choice of words but held his peace.

"So, what are you guys going to do?" Everly asked next. "Are you just going to show up at Bremburg and hope they put you to work?"

"That's pretty much it," Bryce said. "We'll get some consideration, though, because of our guild ranking."

"What's that?"

"Mid-stone," he said proudly. "All of us. And with just a few more successes, we'll qualify for high-stone."

"I'm sorry, Bryce. I have no idea what any of that means."

Mid-stone? High-stone? What the heck was any of that? Why couldn't they just use a letter ranking system from *F* to *SS*, like every other *isekai* fantasy out there? Everly hated it when writers tried to be clever with established tropes. It just meant they were trying to be smarter than their audience.

"It's easy to understand," Eric said. "Guild rankings start at the very bottom, which is ash. Then from ash, they go to stone. From stone, it's mountain, and from mountain, it's sky. Each ranking also has three sub-ranks that divide them. Low, mid, and high. So, when we say we're mid-stone, that means—"

"That you guys aren't considered bottom-tier fetch monkeys?" she asked.

"Uh, yeah. It means we're well past being amateurs," Eric concluded while giving her a deep frown for some reason.

"Look down on us if you want, but we're proud of what we've achieved so far," said Bree the mage, finally speaking up after glowering at Everly and Carter in surly silence for what seemed like ages. "Climbing the ranks in the adventurers' guild isn't as easy as asking your daddy to buy you a new dress."

"Are you *sure* about that?" Everly asked her innocently. "I'm pretty certain I could excel at will over there if I felt like it."

"Horseshit. Absolute horseshit," Bree said angrily. "Adventuring's not for the likes of you, little girl. Your clothes are too clean. And I can tell just by looking at you that you've *never* had to kill for survival. You're just another soft country noble in a nation that's already filled with too many of your kind."

"Wow, that's a perceptive eye you've got there, miss," Everly said in a maliciously sweet tone of voice. "I suppose you're right, though. I've never once had to kill to survive. I guess life's just been too kind to me."

She certainly wasn't going to mention those times that she had killed for *fun*. Survival, no. Fun, yes.

And also because those moments were thematically appropriate.

I have to stay true to my artistic vision, y'know, she thought to herself.

"Heh, I knew it," Bree said smugly.

"Can Carter and I accompany you?" Everly suddenly asked.

"What?" Bryce asked in confusion. "Why would you want to participate in a holy cleansing?"

"I dunno," Everly replied honestly. "Maybe I have a complex relationship with religion or whatever? Or maybe I just want to see something interesting. Whatever, let us come anyway. We could be pretty helpful to you. You already know how fast and quiet Carter is, and I'm a deft hand with a sword."

"My . . . lady, I'm not certain I feel comfortable participating in such an activity. My kind are barely tolerated by the temple," Carter said nervously.

"Carter, don't be such a wet tip, okay? We'll be fine. It'll be fun."

"It's *not* going to be *fun*," Bryce said sternly. "Miss, we're flattered by your offer of assistance, but you're simply too young for this. And frankly speaking, using words like *fun* to describe a sacred mission to rescue the innocent says a lot about your lack of maturity. Your offer is declined."

"Uh, what? Are you being serious right now?" Everly asked in surprise.

"Very," Bryce said. "I don't doubt you have some talent, but talent without self-reflection and modesty is a hindrance, not a blessing. I hope you realize that one day. In the meanwhile, we'll be taking our leave."

"Sorry, kid. It could have been fun," Eric said with a shrug.

"Bryce only spoke the truth; don't take it too personally," Guyner said as he followed the other two.

Bree didn't say anything at all as she trotted past. She just smirked one last time and continued her way.

Huh. So *that* was what rejection felt like.

Everly couldn't say she cared much for the taste.

I could make it look like an accident, Everly, Titania rumbled ominously. *It'd only take one shot. Just give me the command, and I'll start compressing them.*

Don't be silly, Sister, Eris said. *Damaging the road would cause a nuisance for other travelers. Let's just wait until they're asleep, and then I'll torture them to death in their dreams.*

"Guys, I love you both so much," Everly said in appreciation. "But there's no need to inflict punishments here. I'm going to Bremburg anyway. If *they* want to run around without my protection, that's their problem, isn't it?"

What could we possibly gain from intervening in the matters of the faithful? asked Eris.

"It's an opportunity to experience genuine combat, babe," Everly told her. "Let's just think of it as warming up before we arrive at the border. And besides, even if the whole ordeal is a waste of time, it'll still be fun to watch."

Is having fun the only thing you care about? Eris asked chidingly.

"Not always. But it's the only thing I care about *right now.*"

Off to Bremburg they went.

CHAPTER THIRTY-TWO

The Golden Wanderer

Hold still, you wretched brat! I swear I'll cut you in half!" the bandit leader yelled as he swung wildly for Everly's head.

Today was a day of firsts for her. It was her first time trying out alcohol, and it was also her first time having a genuine sword duel with a person who wasn't a mental training construct. If she had to be honest, the sword fighting was baller. She was just *nuts* for blade-against-blade combat.

But the alcohol had been *laaame*.

From the way they described it in all those old *Mighty Thor* comics she'd illegally torrented back in the day, mead was supposed to taste like a liquid honey bun that got you buzzed. But the reality was that it tasted more like a cup of sugar soaked in river water and peroxide. It was a complete letdown, although she would have to give it props for making her head feel a little *whirly*.

Everly dodged another swing from her opponent's sword and purposefully stumbled around to make it seem as though she'd nearly lost her balance. Then she deflected the thrust he aimed at her throat and turned the momentum into a clumsy-looking roll after allowing his boot to connect with her midsection. So far, Operation Barely Survive the Fight was going perfectly!

Yes, *all* according to plan.

She was having a pretty good time!

Perhaps it would have been better to say she was having fun with this duel despite the methods she was forcing herself to use. Instead of wielding a massive great sword the length of a human body—y'know, the sort of preposterous, *straight out of an extremely unrealistic fantasy Japanese RPG* melee weapon that made her heart *sing*—she was using a pair of rapiers.

Honestly, that wasn't her ideal method of fighting. Dual wielding looked amazing, but she much preferred using a big sword that she could put a lot of force behind. Looking graceful was cool and all, but Everly preferred to look like an artless thug who used overwhelming force to get by.

There was a term used to describe a certain style of architecture that she'd learned back on Earth: brutalism. She loved that word. It meant "stark, basic, stripped of accoutrement and frivolity." Once she'd discovered that word and learned its definition beyond its utterly metal-sounding name, she knew in her heart of hearts that this was how she wanted her swordsmanship to be described.

But that was a style she would only use in her role as the Empress. For now, while she was still working out the details of when she would present herself to the world, she needed something less flashy. As a seemingly inconsequential person of mediocre talent, she'd decided to fight using something more appropriate for her size.

After all, it would have been extremely conspicuous if anyone saw a dainty young lady running wild with a *Zweihänder*.

That meant she had to use a more acrobatic method of combat, moving gracefully and using motion, momentum, and perfect timing to dance around attacks, as if she couldn't just smash through them and devastate anything before her with sheer might.

She hated it. Fighting like this felt so *embarrassing*. Sure, her captive audience was eating it up, but that just showed how ignorant they really were.

"Dance all you like, girlie. Once I get a solid hit in, it's all over. That'll teach you to meddle where you're unwanted," the bandit said.

Jeez, the utter lack of respect!

If this guy had a shred of talent, he would have seen he was being toyed with. It really irked her that he was too stupid to see just how outgunned he really was.

It just goes to show that playing with an amateur is beneath me.

"Are you going to cry when I kill you?" he asked with an ugly sneer.

"Are *you*?" Everly replied with a plucky grin. Her role for this production was that of an underdog female adventurer who accidentally stumbled upon a tavern robbery in progress, here in this sleepy little village whose name she'd completely forgotten.

It had looked like there was some potential for fun here, so instead of just blowing them all away with a minor application of Titania's power, she instead had chosen to clash swords with these dingleberries while playing the part of the hero.

Oh, what the audience must be thinking right now! *Her? A hero? Don't make us laugh!*

Well, let the narration assure you, it was just for fun and games, okay? Plus, Everly considered this a great opportunity to show off her versatility and range as a performer! There was nothing wrong with occasionally stepping out of your comfort zone, right?

Of course, there wasn't!

Now, to be fair, Everly wouldn't have gotten involved if these goofs hadn't threatened to kill her. She had been on her way to Bremberg but discovered this village along the way and decided she wanted to check it out. You know, do a little sightseeing, chat it up with the locals, get a feel for the region.

Part of the fun of traveling was supposed to be seeing new sights and doing things that you hadn't tried before. One of the villagers had pointed her in the direction of the tavern and informed her it was famous nationwide for the quality of its honey mead.

So Everly strolled in, ordered a mug, and downed it in one gulp.

Ugh.

As she resisted the urge to spray it all back up over the countertop, those four jerks came swaggering in and declared they were robbing the place and putting everyone to the sword. Wasn't that dumb? What was the point of killing someone if they were willing to cooperate? If you killed *everyone* you robbed, then didn't that mean you'd eventually run out of people and places to steal from?

That kind of slash-and-burn approach to villainy was far too shortsighted. Everly felt compelled to let them know. It was like they'd never even heard of conservation.

Their leader didn't appreciate getting talked down to by someone who, from his perspective, was a mouthy teenager. So, he drew his blade and challenged her to back up her bold words with steel. Everly was only too happy to oblige him.

She *liked* settling things with steel.

So that was how their bout had started.

"You won't get away with your misdeeds, you bullying bandit!" Everly said dramatically. "Even if you strike me down, surely another adventurer will catch up with you eventually! Your road will end at the tip of a sword or the end of a hangman's noose!"

"You deluded little dreamer!" the bandit leader said with a cruel laugh. "Time to learn that life isn't like the stories your papa told you!"

Oof. What he'd said had actually stung a little. Neither of her fathers had ever told her any bedtime stories.

"Shut up about people's families!" Everly yelled at him. "You don't even know the particulars of my relationship with my dad! Some of us live complicated lives!"

"You should seek counseling if you're that uncertain about his feelings for you!" the bandit replied as Everly hastily sidestepped a vicious thrust toward her neck and leaped for safety behind the bar counter.

"Why should *I* seek counseling from anyone? *He's* the one who chose to exclude me!" she yelled back as she hurled glassware at her enemy's face.

"Ha! Such an ungrateful child! You'd rather play the victim instead of seeking reconciliation! Brats like you don't know the pressures that come entwined with the word *father*. All you can see are the things *you* missed out on! What about what *he* had to sacrifice for your sake?"

"He didn't have to sacrifice anything! He's rich!" Everly said as she swept his leg out from beneath him.

"Fool! The wealthy have problems too! Many of them struggle with feelings of inadequacy and guilt!" he said from the floor after she kicked away his saber.

"Sounds like a problem for the upwardly mobile!" Everly snarled as she lashed out with the tip of her boot against the bandit's skull, striking him unconscious with her kick.

"Boss!" shouted one of her opponent's henchmen as he drew his own sword and moved toward them. The other two joined him; all three wore ugly expressions of anger on their faces.

"Hey! This was an honorable duel. You were told not to interfere," she said to them. Of course, she'd known they wouldn't follow through on their promise because bandits, by their very nature, were all untrustworthy pricks. But it had been fun playing along when their leader ordered them to stand aside.

"You hit him when he was on his back! That's against the rules of chivalry!" one of them declared.

"What about when he tried to stab *me* in the back?" Everly retorted.

"How's that his fault? You kept spinning around like a top!"

"Don't criticize how I fight! I'm small!"

"Yeah? Well, you're dead *too*, whore!" shouted another.

"Resorting to gendered insults means you can't prove your point logically!" Everly said, irritated by his choice of words.

Honestly, these goons weren't quality villains in the slightest! If he'd called her a bitch, that would have been one thing. Lots of tough chicks got called bitches. For some, it was a point of pride. *Don't mess with so and so; that bitch is mean.*

But *whore*? How did that even come into play? She hadn't even had a chance to become promiscuous yet. She'd been too busy!

He was just trying to be hurtful!

Naturally, instead of responding to the point she'd raised, all three of the underlings came for Everly at once.

It was at that moment that she decided playing the plucky underdog had lost its amusement value. Instead, it was time to play the plucky underdog who'd discovered a hidden reserve of strength that she didn't realize she'd had all along.

Yes, the moment had come for the fabled protagonist's second wind. That moment in an adventure where certain defeat for the hero instead became a crushing victory. It was a very popular trope in *shonen* fighting manga and martial arts web serials.

With a burst of *harada*, Everly caught the first attacker with a perfectly timed thrust that easily penetrated her heart, rupturing it like a water balloon. After that, she performed a spectacular spin that slit her second assailant's throat wide open. Then she ducked low beneath the clumsy swing of their final comrade and rose with an upward slash that caught him at his crotch.

"Hrrrrrgh!" he shrieked girlishly as he clutched at his bifurcated fun bag.

He was the one who'd called her a whore, by the way.

Not that she particularly *cared*. Who held grudges over words? Certainly not her! She was above all that.

Really.

"It *huuuurts!*" he screamed as blood pooled beneath him.

"It'll hurt even more the next time nature calls," Everly said. "Just leaving that out there."

Aww, he sure does look miserable, Everly thought to herself.

Maybe he'd just learned a profound lesson about not resorting to awful slurs just because he had problems controlling his temper? Perhaps he'd now change his ways and be wary of the words he used against others? Maybe, starting at this very moment, he'd become a better person?

"You bitch, you slag, you filthy fucking whore. I'll kill you for this, I'll kill you for this, *I'll kill you for this!*"

Uh, or maybe the painful humiliation he'd just experienced would instead drive him to double down on his hateful rhetoric because changing for the better was just not something that most roving thieves and murderers were capable of?

"I'll cut you open and rip out your *ovaries* by hand!"

Jesus, this guy was a trooper!

"I'll leave your corpse hanging under a sign that reads, *'This is what slags get'*!"

Seriously! Was this guy the Charles Atlas of being a hateful asshole? He had to be! Where did he find the energy?

"And then I'll find your fucking *mother* and set a pack of dogs on her!"

Whoops, now he done goofed.

Everly really *hated it* when people threatened Lyona.

It was uncalled for. It was ungentlemanly. It was *ungracious*.

It also really *pissed* her off.

So, what did she do with him? Did she give him another cut to the groin? Did she slash him thousands of times until he was nothing but slushed bits of gooey red slurry? Did she jump up and down on his head like she was a Mario brother who'd found a snapping turtle by the creek?

No, she did worse than any of that. *Far* worse.

She let Eris play with him.

Teach him not to run his stupid mouth.

The tavern owner ran to Everly and bowed gratefully. "Thank you so much, my lady! That's Jaspar Kreel and the Bogsters! They surely would have killed me and my family if you hadn't intervened. Thank you so much!"

"Eh, *Bogsters*?" Everly asked him in confusion. "These bandits called themselves *the Bogsters*? I'm sorry, what the hell is a bogster?"

"It's a local songbird, my lady. A fat green thing with wings that warbles tunelessly in the evening."

"Tunelessly? So, it doesn't make a beautiful sound?"

"Far from it, ma'am. It sounds like a dying old wretch in his cups vomiting from a window to the street."

"Jesus, why would anyone want to name themselves after something like that?"

"I expect they do it because they're a bunch of wet tips, ma'am."

"I guess so," Everly said.

"Stop it, please! Please, I'll be good! I'll be a good boy! Mommy, not the rake! Mommy, not the *raaaaaake*!" the bandit sobbed behind them.

"Uh, my lady?" the tavern owner asked.

"Yo."

"My lady . . . what did you do to this man?" he asked her hesitantly.

"Who can say for certain?" Everly asked philosophically. "I suspect his many seasons of wickedness have finally broken his fragile mind. Let that be a lesson to us all. The path of criminality may be rife with sweet temptations, but all too soon, such flavors turn bitter."

"I'm sorry, what?" the tavern keeper asked.

"He did a bunch of bad stuff, and now he's crazy forever," she said obligingly.

"Oh. Thanks for clarifying."

"No problem."

"Is that the bees, Mama? *Nooooo, not the beees!*" he said, weeping.

That poor bastard. He had to choose today of all days to mouth off. Eris was *deep* into a recent infatuation with Nicolas Cage.

"Owwww, wh-what? What's happened here?" asked the bandit leader, Jaspar, as he blearily pulled himself back to consciousness.

Wow. He's awake already? He's a lot tougher than he looks.

This time she kicked him in the head twice to make certain he stayed down.

"Ma'am, will you be staying here while we send for the sheriff?" the tavern keeper asked. "There's sure to be a bounty on the heads of these men. A nice profit to be had, for sure."

Ohhhh, a profit! Maybe that could be the motivation for her character?

She could be a roaming hunter of criminals, forever chasing the setting sun; she'd wander from town to town, helping the locals with their troubles and having all sorts of adventures in small-town Winstead along the way, only to move on once the villain of the week had been defeated.

It would be like a classic syndicated television series. *Xena: Warrior Princess*, *Hercules: The Legendary Journeys*, *Kung Fu: The Legend Continues*. Stuff like that.

Everly thought that sort of cover story sounded really cool. But then again, it wasn't as if she needed any money. Not with Titania being able to transmute dirt into gold. Not to mention, if she was going to pose as a bounty hunter, she would literally have to hunt bounties. And that meant fighting incompetent dirtbags like these chumps, repeatedly.

Sure, today had been fun, but constant clashes with trash like this would get very old, very quickly.

As a young professional aspiring to scale the heights of power and villainy, these bums just weren't worth her efforts.

"It's all right, master tavern keeper. I didn't stop these fiends for the sound of clinking coins," she told him.

He seemed surprised by her answer. "I don't understand, ma'am. If not for coin, then what?"

Everly smiled at him and clapped her hand on his shoulder. "Why? Because it was *the right thing to do*. Keep the reward for yourself and your family. You deserve it for what these monsters tried to put you through."

"My lady! Thank you so much!" the tavern keeper exclaimed. "I won't lie, ma'am. Things have gotten a little tight around here. We make most of our coin off traveling soldiers and mercenaries during the summer campaign, but the king's new taxes have been a burden."

It couldn't possibly be because your vaunted honey mead tastes like rancid goat's piss, Everly thought uncharitably.

"Then put it to good use, friend," she said with a smile as she walked toward the exit.

"My lady! Who shall I say was the hero who saved my family?" the tavern keeper called to her back.

"There was no hero here today, sir," she said humbly. There really hadn't been. "I'm just a wanderer who saw an opportunity to make a difference."

"My lady, please! You deserve to be praised!"

Everly had to admit, she was *loving* this! She would have stuck around and had praise heaped on her shoulders for hours if she could, but that wouldn't have been suitable for her current character arc.

"If anyone asks, this deed was performed by . . . uh, Grail," she told him.

"By . . . Grail? But, Lady Grail, your graceful manner reveals your obvious noble blood! Haven't you a family name to share?"

Everly solemnly looked away with a bittersweet expression on her face, as though she were lost in painful memories of the past. "Do I possess a family name, you ask? No. Not any longer, friend. A student of the sword carries only her weapon and her hopes for the future. The past is a place we can only revisit in our dreams."

Having said that, she walked away, leaving the tavern keeper awed in her wake.

Once back on the road, she discussed her performance with the gang.

Why did you use my *name?* Grail asked unhappily.

"I'm sorry! I couldn't think of anything else! Besides, it's a big world, isn't it? There's room for two Grails, isn't there?"

I thought it was flawless in its execution, Everly, said Eris. *Your somber dignity spoke of a history of disappointment and pain, yet also hinted at the strength of resolve you possess to march forward toward your dream. I'm tingling from enjoyment right now!*

"Wow, you really think so?"

Of course I do! Death to ANYONE who dares speak otherwise, oh great one!

"Heh, yeeeah," Everly said in agreement.

I just don't think Grail *is as common a name as you believe it is.*

"I *said* I was sorry!"

Everly, I was a little confused, said Titania. *Why didn't you just kill them all the instant they presented a threat to you? They're weak, aren't they? The weak should bow before the strong.*

"Well, it's like I'm always trying to tell you: There's no fun to be had if you end the game too quickly. Humans can't live a proper life if they base *everything* of value on strength and strength alone."

I don't get it.

"Hey, that's all right. Just let me do the thinking for us both."

Okay. You're better at it, anyway. I don't get all the small moving parts. I prefer to just smash the things that irritate me.

"And you're very good at it! Life is best enjoyed when people stick to what they're good at."

That sounds right.

Good ol' Titania. She never sweated the details.

"I have to say, though, my lady: Why were you fluctuating between a clumsy demeanor and a composed one?" asked Carter, who'd popped back into the real world to accompany Everly on her walk. "I felt like it made it a little more difficult to get a handle on what you were trying to portray."

Carter! How dare you question our master's performance! Eris seethed.

"She asked for feedback, Lady Eris! I'm merely sharing my observations," Carter said.

Why, you ungrateful little goblin! Never bite the hand that feeds you! For your temerity, I ought to build a nest of psychic spiders in your brain—

"Hey, Eris! Ease up! Carter's right. I asked for some honest feedback! Jeez, if you fly off the handle every time someone says something about me that you don't like, you'll be building psychic spider nests all day, every day, for the rest of your life!" Everly said to her.

I mean, I would if you'd just let me, Eris said unhappily. *I just want people to respect you more.*

Oh, man, thought Everly.

Eris had always been a fiery one, to put it mildly, but when had she gone from being defensive of her leader to becoming a full-blown *yandere*? Had Everly not been spending enough time with her? Or had she always been this way and Everly was just now catching on? *Well, I guess the rat room was a small hint.*

Everly refused to be one of those annoying, deliberately obtuse main characters who remained willfully blind to all their servants' personality flaws. If Eris was in danger of becoming a trope instead of a person, Everly was going to have to nip it in the bud right away.

She appreciated Eris's loyalty, but she couldn't stand people who threw temper tantrums over the smallest things they didn't like. As a master of the dark arts and a future dark lord, Everly insisted that those who represented her interests showed dignity and self-restraint.

Pouting brats who constantly flipped their lids just weren't cool. Look at Kylo Ren for god's sake!

"Finish your thoughts, Carter. I insist," Everly said to the goblin.

Carter paused for a moment, uncertain if he should continue or not. Then he shrugged and resumed the conversation. "Well, I understand the need to craft an appropriate public identity, but I was also confused by why you chose to discard your birth name. Everly Vel Belsar is a name that could open doors for you."

"Yeeeah, but I really hate it. Do I really look like a Vel Belsar to you? That's like a name for an old Southern widow claiming a recent drought is the lord's punishment for interracial marriage."

Ohhh, that went hard, said Titania, who enjoyed watching period dramas in the memory palace.

"Just saying what I feel," Everly said with a shrug.

"So, you really intend to set aside your name? You'll now be Grail from this moment hence?" asked Carter.

Hey! Not funny, goblin, growled Grail.

"Nah. *Grail* will just be my traveling name. I'll still be Everly Vel Belsar to those who know me. Or when it's convenient."

"Ah! I think I now understand your aim," Carter said. "You intend to operate under three separate identities! As an adventurer, you'll be Grail, the golden wanderer. Among the nobility and the strata of high society, you'll resume the identity of Everly Vel Belsar! And when the time comes to unleash your power and ferocity against the world, you'll be . . . you'll be . . . Actually, that's an excellent question. Who *will* you be, Majesty?"

Huh? What?

Everly had been busy just wrapping her head around what Carter had just suggested. *Three separate identities?* A hero, a noblewoman, *and* the dark lord? Was that the plan she had come up with? Maybe? Perhaps not quite like that, but she really liked the way it sounded!

Okay, sure, she'd take credit for Carter's idea. There was no harm in it since he already thought it was all part of her overarching plan. After all, part of being a masterful villain was knowing when to just shut up and look like you knew what you were doing.

"I haven't settled on a name yet for the most important role," Everly admitted to him. "I'm getting close, though! It's just got to sound, you know, *metal.* Kind of foreign, but still rolls off the tongue, yeah? I'll get it eventually."

"I'm certain you will. Your creativity seems boundless," Carter said.

"Hell yeah, it is! But, uh, Carter?"

"Majesty?"

"Why 'Grail, the golden wanderer'?"

"Ah! Well, you're very blond, ma'am. It's quite an eye-catching feature. You know how humans are, always defining things by their most basic features in order to better catalog them with their silly, imprecise languages."

"Human language is imprecise?" Everly asked him.

"Oh, absurdly so! They never get anything right the first time, do they? They'll be calling you *the golden sword,* or *the golden heroine,* or *the golden adventurer* everywhere you go by the end of the week. In my opinion, *the golden wanderer* suits you best. Yes, it speaks to an obvious physical trait, but it also highlights the wanderlust that lies at the true heart of your character."

Everly considered Carter's words for a moment and then gave an appreciative nod. He had a point! She was convinced.

"Well, all righty, then!" She decided. "Grail, the golden wanderer, it is! What's she looking for? What's she fleeing from? Who can say what mysteries hide behind her fearless grin? Is Grail the hero of her tale or the villain lying in wait? Stay tuned to find out!"

It's the second one! I think it's the second one! Titania said.

Do I get a say in any of this? Grail asked unhappily.

Everly turned and gave Carter an impromptu high five.

"I love it," she told him. "It sounds like the synopsis of a cheesy eighties French fantasy comic. And I *love* cheesy eighties French fantasy comics! I'm promoting you, buddy! From now on, you're not just my trusty goblin majordomo. You're also a *consultant!*"

"It pleases me to be of service to you, Your Majesty," Carter said humbly as he bowed before her.

I'm being serious. Do I get a say in ANY of this? Grail asked again.

Hmph. I don't see what Carter did that's so special. Eris sniffed.

"No, no, none of that. You're pretty *too*," Everly said to her while thinking:

Ugh, I'm not looking forward to the conversation we're going to have later. Oh, well. I got into this business because I wanted an interesting life, not an easy one.

That was just how Everly rolled.

"SRAAAAAAAACRAWWWWWGH!" screeched a fat green bird as they walked beneath its nest.

CHAPTER THIRTY-THREE

Replacement

The people whose suffering he caused would undoubtedly be upset with him for his excesses, but Sloth didn't care.

None of this was truly his fault. After all, he hadn't been the one to blow himself up! He was simply following through on his plan. It was a good plan too. No, not just good, *great*. Excellent, in fact. He'd put a lot of thought and enthusiasm into it. This was a brilliant gamble for restoring his ruined body, and it was going to succeed.

Sloth had a gift he'd been honing for some time, a gift for controlling vermin. Flies, bugs, rats, whatever. If it was small and repulsive, he could make it do whatever he wished. People as well, of course, but lesser life-forms were just so much easier to manipulate. Less strain on his brain, as it were. He had also recently evolved a fairly nifty skill called [**Remote Viewing**].

To put it mildly, he loved it. It was a gift that brought him much pleasure. [**Remote Viewing**] let him see things that were extraordinary distances away if he knew specifically what it was that he sought. For example, if he knew what someone looked like, as well as their name, he could find them easily.

One prime example was his dear, *dear* betrayer, the gorgeous Claudia Vae Belsar. There she was, back in her home, working on another bottle of wine. Goodness, for such a young lady, she could really put away her drinks. She allegedly was also a skillful remote viewer, thanks to her spirit elemental, but it seemed that Sloth was a cut above her.

She couldn't even sense that he was in the same room as her, metaphorically speaking. She appeared before him, so vivid and real that he was surprised he couldn't smell her perfume.

Oh, he had such terrible retribution planned for her. Sloth couldn't wait to see her beautiful face marred with blood and horror. He'd make those dazzling eyes turn lifeless and dull as her mind was slowly broken by what he intended to put her through. Oh, the games they'd play!

Perhaps he'd eat her arrogant brother in front of her.

Or even better, make her do it herself!

So many, *many* wonderful possibilities. Sadly, their joyous reunion would have to wait.

A great battle would soon be upon him.

Sloth was hardly an expert on the biology of germs, but thanks to [**Remote Viewing**], he could see the nasty little things on a microscopic level. That included the uncountable billions of horrendous viral and bacterial life-forms all around mankind's habitats that could cause devastating illnesses among the masses if they weren't held back by acquired immunity developed over thousands of years of exposure and an intelligent mind that knew the value of basic sanitation.

Evolution was such a remarkable thing!

Sadly, Sloth required a healer. With one of his mana cores removed, his regenerative ability wasn't strong enough to regrow his limbs by itself. He also didn't need a mirror to know that he probably didn't look very appealing to others. There was just something about being blown up and then being given nightly tongue baths by a giant spider that didn't inspire confidence in his personal hygiene.

If he still had a nose, he was certain he'd choke on his own stench.

Yes, he needed all this sorted right away. He needed to be refurbished *badly.* So, to that end, he convinced a colony of little squiggly horrific things that he found floating in a puddle of raw sewage to hop a ride on some rats and roaches and go take a tour of the town above. *Go see the sights of historic Bremburg, meet the people, get some lunch, make a day of it!*

Oh, and while they were at it, they should also multiply, spread, and *infect.*

His new friends took his advice and went out into the day. And just like that, there was a plague going on! And it sure was a doozy!

Now, Sloth was not a medical professional of any kind. He was just an average, everyday, ordinary sort of guy who could whisper action into filth. That didn't make him *special,* even though it obviously did. He couldn't spell "acute encephalitis" with a spellchecker. Brain inflammation? Did that make it combustible? How would *he* know? He was just a layman who happened to be a lord of sin and a king of demons!

But what he *did* know was that his plague immediately attacked the brain and essentially turned their victims into living zombies. Talking, giggling, *trapped helplessly inside their own minds and silently begging for someone to please help them while they're forced to watch what they're being made to do against their own will* zombies.

Oh, those guys became *unsettling*.

They'd wander around, talking to no one in particular, just being disgusting, leaky things one minute, and then the next, they'd snap under the strain of their slowly developing madness and start attacking anyone near them, obeying a maniacal instinct to spread their sickness and see others brought low as well.

Thanks to Sloth's effective delivery system of rats, fleas, and flies, he had the infection spread around town in no time. Once he really got it going, the hardest part had been holding his new servants back long enough for some of the foolish locals to get the hint that they should seek aid.

But to Sloth's immense frustration, they kept hesitating and tried to wait it out. Were they afraid of angering the clergy in case they were wrong? Were they too proud to ask for help? Were they more independent than a Canadian professional wrestler? How the hell should *he* know? What mattered to him was that they were taking too damn long!

The good news/bad news part of the tale was that this was where little Tommy came slobbering along.

Ahhh, Tommy. What an evil little bastard. What a remarkably malevolent literally six-year-old piece of human garbage. His parents shouldn't have been surprised that he'd decided to kill them. Tommy had an absolutely *predacious* mind. Something had gone very, very wrong in that creepy little freak's development.

Where other souls were filled with revulsion and horror at the deeds committed by their possessed bodies, Tommy delighted in them! It wasn't because he was a child who misunderstood what was happening due to youthful ignorance either. He might have just been a small child, but there was wickedness in him at his core. Even if Sloth had never come to Bremburg, that little boy would still have eventually become a murderer.

He was *dead inside*.

Sloth personally found the kid delightful. Although he hadn't originally intended for *quite* so many people to die, he just couldn't get enough of li'l Tommy's antics! Perhaps he'd take the boy with him when he reunited with Claudia so he could give the lad a few pointers.

But first, Sloth would have to assert his dominance over his new favorite toy.

The issue at hand was that Tommy was now roaming the town, going from place to place, searching for survivors, as well as randomly killing his fellow infected. Sloth had been forced to organize his army of sickies to drive him away whenever he appeared and began attacking.

What was supposed to be an idle wait for salvation had swiftly turned into a frenzied battle for survival.

A zombie civil war. And why was that?

Because Tommy somehow knew about Sloth. He could sense the presence of his creator.

And the little twerp was *hunting* him . . .

For his part, Sloth was extremely grateful for the distraction that the little monster provided. Waiting for the temple and its healers to arrive had become tedious. With Tommy to play tag with, the time swiftly passed by, and before he knew it, people began gathering just beyond the gates of Bremburg. Dangerous-looking ones armed to the teeth, but not professional soldiers from the look of them.

Adventurers.

Sloth hated adventurers. As a demon king, he'd had to slaughter more than a few over the years. They were just *such* bothersome people! Some came after him for profit, some for glory; some of them had been downtrodden farmer spawn, angry because they blamed him for the loss of their villages, or loved ones, or whatever.

They always said stupid things like, "In the name of righteousness/the gods/ my dead siblings/parents/girl I never worked up the nerve to ask on a date, I will strike you down!"

Sloth *HATED* heroes. He hated them so much! He'd much preferred it back on Earth, where such high-minded idiots existed only in stories and corporate-controlled media. Why would *any* sensible servant of darkness ever want to be around people like them?

The worst thing about adventurers was their complete unpredictability. One could never assume they were incapable of being dangerous, based on their appearances alone. Actually, the ones to *really* watch out for were the unassuming rookies with bland exteriors, boring personalities, and average physical statistics.

Fuckers like that always possessed hidden reserves of strength inside themselves, waiting to awaken at an inconvenient moment and spur them on a killing spree in the name of justice.

Absolute psychopaths.

No, Sloth was going to have to take precautions against these interlopers. Despite his name, he was going to have to put in some serious work to make sure everything stayed on track.

Damn you all, he fumed. *Damn you for forcing me to make an effort . . .*

The gates of the cathedral opened, and a solemn procession of men and women in silver-enameled armor came trotting out on horseback. A beautiful chant was sung in angelic tones that drifted through the air, warming the souls of all who heard its haunting litany.

It was an ancient hymnal of regret, begging the creator to forgive the transgressions of his unworthy creation, performed so well that it could bring a tear to the eye.

Even Kent was impressed.

With all the power and skill these holy knights possess, being able to sing beautifully too is just cheating, he thought to himself unkindly.

Beside him, his companion and lover, Laurel, shifted on her saddle and was now staring at him as though she'd read his thoughts and had decided he was an idiot. She very well might have. It wouldn't have been surprising.

Laurel, like the grim riders of the cathedral, was a templar. But not just *any* templar; she was the former maiden of the holy sword. An office held by only the most dangerous and skillful member of the temple's knightly order.

As the maiden, Laurel had wielded power that surpassed that of even the elementals—power that could smash any opponent and lay waste to cities, power that she would only use to punish the wicked and proselytize to the innocent with miracles for the spreading of her faith.

Indeed, she'd been the ultimate soldier of the temple. Loved and feared worldwide as Laurel the unyielding. Even the heathens of the Eastern Temple respected her.

That was until she'd met Kent, the insolent thief who had literally charmed her out of her armor and into his bed. It had begun as a standard pursuit to catch and chastise a minor no-name *criminal* who had literally been caught trying to sell boxes of goods that had fallen off the back of a carriage. She had easily defeated the ruffians Kent had with him for backup but was annoyed to see that he'd managed to escape her.

Ordinarily, she'd have moved on to more important matters, but then the idiot started bragging to anyone with ears about how he'd gotten away unscathed. "She might wield the holy sword, but she can't catch *me*!" he crowed to anyone who'd listen.

And there were many who did. There were quite a few people of unsavory character who gladly paid for Kent's drinks upon hearing his tale, happy to see the temple's perfect princess made a fool of by a gutter rat like him.

Driven to protect her reputation, Laurel began a relentless pursuit of the thief, which gradually became an obsession when he *somehow* kept eluding her grasp. No one had ever before made her work this hard!

Throughout her career as the maiden of the holy sword, she'd slain countless monsters and outlaws. She'd brought to justice many arrogant members of the nobility who'd believed their titles and magic exempted them from the rule of law, and she had also single-handedly banished many powerful demons back to the chaotic depths of the void.

But for some reason, some *maddening* reason, Laurel couldn't catch this incredibly lucky, incredibly arrogant *nobody* who somehow always seemed to be one step ahead of her and *always* bragged about it the next day.

It was driving her mad!

When she finally, *finally* caught up to the fool, she had him on his back at the point of her gleaming sword, and despite her steely self-discipline and the years of training that had forged her into the champion of justice that she was, Laurel was sorely tempted to take Kent's head off on the spot.

"Well," she said, tilting his jaw back with her blade as he lay there on his back. He'd tried to put up a fight and had been utterly trounced.

Naturally.

"Have you anything to say? Any jokes? Hmm? Go ahead, thief. I'm listening."

"Um," Kent began.

"Yes?"

" . . . You want to get a drink?"

Was it his dry delivery? Was it her mood? Had Laurel's long pursuit of Kent been about something other than enforcement of the law all along? Did natural twenty rolls exist in the multiverse? Who could really say? All that mattered was that in that place, at that very moment, Laurel's eyes widened due to the fool's sheer nerve.

And then she laughed and said, "Okay. Why not?"

That had been three years ago. Now, she and Kent were inseparable. Their relationship wasn't without consequences. The first was that she'd refused to let Kent return to his criminal ways. She thoroughly dedicated herself to his reformation, forcing him to join the adventurers' guild and dedicate his earnings to the repayment of all the people he'd stolen from in the past.

Which really hadn't taken that long. With Laurel backing him up, Kent was able to take on many dangerous, high-paying guild missions that swiftly had him swimming in gold—more money than he'd ever been able to steal in his entire lifetime as a crook.

It had been humbling.

The second consequence was that the temple had rebuked Laurel for abandoning her sacred duty as the maiden of the holy sword to be with a thief. They ordered her to return her sacred armor and sword, which she did, regretfully. But when they next ordered her to retire to a convent and spend the rest of her life in prayerful reflection of her misdeeds, she rebelled.

She'd originally intended to obey their command, but Kent wouldn't hear of it.

"They can take your toys and your title since that was theirs to give. But to hell with them if they think they own your life too!"

"Kent, you don't understand. My father is seated in the directorship, and my younger sister is training to become a healer. The temple is literally my family . . . "

"*Real* family sticks together," Kent said angrily. "Laurel! I—I'm not saying I'm worthy of this . . . worthy of *you*. The light alone knows what you see in me. But even to a fool like me it's clear as day that your precious father is trying to throw you away out of *embarrassment* and anger. After all the good you've done for the world too! And *despite* all the good you can *still* do! Well, I won't let him! And I won't let you do this to yourself out of some misguided need to earn his approval!"

"You don't know what you're talking about!" she shouted.

"Then correct me! Prove I'm just an idiot who's out of his league! Do anything you want, but don't walk away from me!"

Kent then grabbed her waist, which was an unusually aggressive move from him, considering their usual dynamic. Before she could say anything else, he kissed her passionately. And in that moment, Laurel knew she'd truly found the one for her, that before he'd upended her life with all the chaos and fun he brought with him, she hadn't truly been living at all.

She loved him.

With him at her side, she felt *complete*.

Smiling with affection and somewhat stirred by his boldness, Laurel kissed Kent back. Then she threw him on the ground, and other things ensued that quickly ended his complaints.

That had been a fun night.

The sword and armor, she'd sent back.

Her freedom, she'd kept.

Now Laurel and Kent sat astride their horses as a pair of anonymous adventurers. Their reason for being there was simple. The temple had declared they had a new maiden of the holy sword. The sacred armor and sword now had a new powerful wielder, who would soon begin her first mission.

The town of Bremburg had been overrun with a mysterious plague, and the lone watchman who escaped had warned, with terror and near madness dancing in his eyes, of the locals being possessed and dangerous. Many believed it could be a demonic incursion and a direct challenge to the temple because it occurred so near the cathedral.

The temple would have none of it. The new maiden of the sword was immediately dispatched to oversee the cleansing, healing, and if necessary, the purging of Bremburg. She'd accepted her mission at once, and now rode forth at the head of a mighty force of templars and clerics.

She would not fail. She would bring mercy to the faithful, and anything that stood against her would become ash.

Her name was Fenneth.

She was Laurel's little sister.

"So, that's your kid sister, huh?" Kent asked. "I see the resemblance. Is she as good with that sword as you are?"

"No, she isn't," Laurel said bluntly. "Fenneth is a healer with no experience in combat. What's my father thinking, having her raised to my old office? Is he that desperate to maintain his standing on the council?"

"Well, losing you had to be a blow to his ego," Kent said thoughtfully. "Having his daughter as the temple's top enforcer, especially one as powerful as you, had to be a real feather in his cap."

"Even so, forcing my role on someone as gentle as Fenneth makes no sense. Even with three years of hard training, it would be impossible for her to meet the standards the job requires. He's basically sending her out to be slaughtered—oh, gods, oh, light, not *her*."

"What? What's going on? What's wrong?" Kent asked, alarmed by Laurel's sudden change in demeanor.

"Her," Laurel said darkly. "He's sending *her* out with Fenneth. Oh, Father, why did I never before realize what an absolute fool you are?"

Laurel pointed at a beautiful auburn-haired girl in white-and-silver armor who now rode alongside Fenneth. Kent looked at her, squinted a bit as he tried to recall if he recognized her, then gave up when he realized he didn't.

Then he asked, "Okay. Who is she?"

Laurel frowned deeply at the sight of the other woman before saying, "*That* is my cousin Sarah."

Kent's eyes widened in surprise. "No way! *The* Sarah? Isn't that a good thing? She's almost as famous as you are! If she's backing your sister up, then isn't that a good thing?"

"No."

"Why not? I know Sarah's young, but her reputation is stellar."

Laurel's frown grew even deeper. "For that, all credit must be given to the propagandists who serve the temple. Their ability to hide corruption and distort the truth is without equal."

"What does that mean?" Kent asked her.

"It means that we're going to Bremburg as well," Laurel said grimly. "Even if the threat is minor, as long as that monster rides beside her, my sister is still in danger."

"Oh, boy," Kent said dryly. "No drama like family drama, huh? Or should I say *trauma*?"

"As you say," Laurel replied. Then she gently stirred her mare and began following the procession, leaving Kent to catch up.

Maaaan, Kent thought to himself as he went after her. *What was my bigger mistake? Getting hit by that truck or falling in love with a Godwell?*

Ah, well. Why complain when life was this much fun?

* * *

The spider stirred in its web, suddenly sensing danger. Extreme danger. It grabbed Sloth and hurriedly secured him to its back before swiftly climbing down. Sloth blinked in confusion as he was forcibly pulled back from the [**Remote Viewing**] he'd been enjoying.

The spider circled, agitated, its fangs bared.

"What the hell's got you so worked up?" Sloth asked.

"FOOOOOOOUND YOOOOOU," came the demented, singsong lilt of a little boy as a massive horror of tumorous flesh and malignant muscle waddled down the sewer pathways.

Oh. Tommy.

"Interesting," Sloth said with amusement as the behemoth approached him. "Believe it or not, I was *just* thinking about you."

CHAPTER THIRTY-FOUR

Found Family

Once Everly and Grail arrived at the outskirts of Bremburg, she took a moment to assess the slowly amassing army of temple warriors and adventurers assembling before the town.

"Wow," Everly said. "So these are the mighty defenders of the 'one true faith.' I can't really say I'm very impressed by the size of it."

"More like an advance group of scouts here to set things up before the main strike force arrives from the cathedral," said Grail. Everly had insisted he escort her to the town since the presence of Carter would have drawn unwanted attention.

The body she'd given him was of a stern, handsome-looking man in his midthirties, with his hair cut short, wearing a carefully maintained beard.

In comparison, Everly remained unchanged except for two slight things. Her hair was now raven black, and she was wearing a pair of glasses.

"I don't even get the supposed differences between the two sects," Everly complained. "They both say the same phrases, they both dress in white gear, and they're both obnoxious. How are they not the same exact group?"

"It all comes down to their doctrine," Grail said. "The Western Temple believes that elementals are the servants of the gods and therefore they should be subjugated. The Eastern Temple believes that the elementals *are* the gods and therefore they should be worshipped."

"Huh," Everly said. "So, Titania, does that make you and Eris goddesses?"

I'm not sure, Everly. What is being a goddess supposed to feel like?

"Eh, you know. You feel powerful and far superior to all other beings; you also feel entitled to punish or reward them at your discretion. Mostly you just do whatever you feel like without caring about the consequences for others."

Isn't that how you *feel all the time?*

"Yeah, but I might have some undiagnosed issues."

"Ah. *Might*," Grail said dryly.

"That sounded perilously close to sarcasm," Everly warned.

"Dyeing your hair black I can understand," he said, ignoring her threat, "but why are you wearing that silly thing on your face?"

"Shut up! You *love* it," Everly said as she gestured toward her brilliant disguise. "Glasses are the *ultimate* means of obscuring your identity! Good enough for Superman, good enough for the Empress."

"Isn't Superman your ideological foil?"

"He is! But sometimes in war, we're required to use the methods of the enemy."

"As you say," Grail replied mildly.

"Jeez," Everly muttered as they passed by another pair of templars. "These guys are really giving us some stink eye, huh?"

"Well, you *are* wearing attire better suited for a man and carrying a sword. I'm sure you understand Winstead's cultural mores regarding gender roles."

"That's so stupid," Everly complained. "These guys are *templars*. There are plenty of women serving in their ranks as knights. Two of their precious paladins are chicks! Not to mention their vaunted maiden of the sword."

"It's a religious order, Everly," Grail replied. "The templars prohibit no one from joining them. However, women battling in service to their gods is one thing. For a secular person like you, it's still quite a taboo."

"Pretzel logic like that is why I prefer being agnostic," Everly said.

"Be that as it may, if you wish to remain undetected in their midst, I'd lower your volume," Grail said as they continued past the hard-eyed templars. "The truly devout are renowned for their intolerance of being flippantly mocked."

"Sounds like they need to develop a sense of humor," Everly said airily. "I'm telling you, once we've completed our takeover of the Eastern Temple, I'm making it canon doctrine that people take a day to themselves once a week to just *chill out*. There'd be a lot less religious conflict if people had more time to themselves."

"Interesting. Why would that concern you?"

"I'm interested in more general conflict. I feel like religion really muddies the water too much. Like, would Cobra from *G.I. Joe* ever pass on an attempt at world conquest because it happened on a Sunday?"

"Ah," Grail said quietly. Although he perfectly understood Everly's many pop culture references thanks to the mental modifications he'd been given by Eris, he still found his leader's constant emphasis of them as a frame of reference for *everything that she planned* a little bewildering.

It sometimes felt to him as though she were living her life in a self-indulgent fantasy.

Not that he would ever voice that opinion aloud.

"How do you like the body, by the way? Doesn't it feel good to finally be out under the sun?" she asked him.

"It does, actually," Grail agreed. "I feel . . . strong. Vital, even. Good in a way I haven't experienced in years. It's a strange thing to grow old, Everly. As the years pass, you begin to lose track of so many things that were once precious to you; they fade away so gradually that you don't even realize what you've lost."

"You know, technically you haven't lost *anything*. All your memories belong to someone else," Everly said with a sly smirk.

"Of course I realized that," Grail replied. "The sun that seems so familiar to me and the blue sky we stand beneath—today is the first time I've ever experienced any of it in person. And yet the knowledge and experiences of a lifetime remain within me. I *still* feel renewed. I *still* feel restored."

"Well, good for you, I suppose," Everly said with disappointment.

"You didn't have to do that, by the way," Grail said.

"Do what?" she asked innocently.

"Attempt to provoke me. If you want an argument or a fight, just ask for one. I'm quite used to making attempts on your life, so there's no need to dance around it with petty provocations."

"Hey! *Nothing* I do is petty," Everly said.

"Tch. Your Majesty, you can be very clever at times, but I've spent decades in the capital living in service to the courts of three different kings. You're a guileless child when it comes to playing mind games."

"Uh, what?"

"Frankly speaking, you're a rank amateur."

"Grail. You *know* I could kill you with one firm glare, right?" Everly asked him lightly.

"You could, but that would only prove my point," he replied. "The nasty little games that the nobility enjoy playing are far more convoluted and crueler than anything you can imagine. Everly, do you wish to become a monarch who rules her subjects through sheer brutality? That would be easy enough for someone like you, but in doing so, you'll deny yourself the pleasure of mastering a more subtle form of dominance."

"Ha! Boring! That sounds absolutely *boring*!" Everly snorted. "Court intrigue is the kind of thing that puffy-shirted wimps and coke-sniffing mean girls like to engage in. You've surprised me, Grail. I'd have thought a person like you would prefer the direct approach to doing things."

"Not every issue should be handled with brute force," he said. "Parrying words can be just as much of a challenge as parrying a blade. Knowing what to say and *when* to say it can destroy your opponent as utterly as a thrust to the heart. It's a good mental exercise."

"Hmm," Everly said, as she considered his words. "I don't know if I care for the pretense of sophistication. But I do like the idea of hurting people just by speaking to them. Breaking the will of an opponent through words alone would be a useful skill."

"You've done a fine job of it with young Nalec."

"Him? Oh, please. We instilled some deep-seated mommy issues in that thing. It's just a form of control."

"In the upper echelons of society, practiced casual cruelty will be an immensely useful tool to have at your command. I recommend you continue to develop it."

"Grail! Stop giving me *homework*," Everly said irritably. "God, even my own father never spoke to me like this."

"Your father from which life?"

"Either of them!"

"Then they're both fools who didn't realize your true potential. Just because those two failed to give you proper guidance doesn't mean that I will," Grail said.

"What? Is that what this is?" Everly sneered. "Do you want to play father figure, Grail? Hmm? Do you want me to cuddle on your lap and call you 'Daddy'?"

"Don't overestimate your charms, girl. Women more beautiful than you have dueled each other for my attention," Grail said in a mild tone of voice. "They also had *far* better personalities."

"That has to be a lie!"

"It isn't. But I must admit, even though they aren't my memories, I do . . . miss the feeling of giving guidance to younger people. Of passing on knowledge and wisdom, helping to mold my students into dignified figures for the betterment of society. Who knows? Perhaps I can offer you a similar service."

"Huh?" Everly asked in confusion.

"I suppose what I'm asking, child, is . . . do you *want* me to call you my daughter?"

A strange small smile grew on Everly's lips. "Heh. Well, I suppose we do share the same name now, don't we, Grail?"

"That we do, Grail the golden wanderer."

Everly leaned into his shoulder and took his elbow. "All right, Dad. You want to teach me? I'm willing to learn."

Grail smiled as they walked arm in arm down the road. "Of course you are. No child of mine would ever fail to rise to a challenge."

"You have to get me something for my birthday now," she suddenly said.

"What would you like?"

"The throne of Winstead."

"Hmm. That could take some doing. Well, first we'll need to see how your grades are."

CHAPTER THIRTY-FIVE

Death Flag

This is so *revolting*," whined Sir Aiden Vae-es Belsar as he and the one hundred knights under his command neared the town of Bremburg. He and another man, Sir Casten Meers, sat inside a luxurious stagecoach that he chose to travel in because riding on horseback chaffed unpleasantly at his thighs.

"I mean, it's a *plague*. The very air itself could be dirty and *infectious*! I could *catch* something. Oh, I hope I don't! I couldn't stand the idea!"

"We've got talented healers in our employ, Sir Aiden," the other man said. "There's no need to fear illness."

"Still, this is a cleansing! That means there could be fighting! Oh, what a chance I'm being forced to take!"

"Sir Aiden. You're now a *knight*. Engaging in battle is an expectation of the role."

"Ohhh, knighthood was only something I pursued in order to please my mother. I admit, I *do* look dashing in this armor, but I'm reluctant to wield my martial skills in combat. I'm a lover of life, you see."

"Ah."

"I am!" Aiden insisted. "Oh, I just feel so exposed in such an environment. I feel *endangered*."

"Your house knights will prioritize your protection above all else," Sir Casten said. "There is nothing to be afraid of."

"I'm not afraid! Take that back, you cur! I'm a warrior born!"

"Of course you are. I apologize for misinterpreting your complex emotions," Sir Casten replied.

He wondered if his master would detect his sarcasm, but Aiden had already changed subjects.

"Sir Casten, *why* must mother punish me like this? How could she not appreciate the gift I presented to her? It was the heart of a demon king, which I claimed at great personal risk! No, *perilous* risk! I could have died! She should have been proud of me. She should have loved it! *Why* didn't she love it?"

Aiden rubbed tenderly at his cheek where his mother had slapped him. It had throbbed painfully for two days. He supposed that made him lucky since she'd struck him lightly.

Still, it gnawed at him.

He'd wanted her to hug him.

Instead, she'd deployed a sizable number of Belsar County's knights and soldiers and ordered him to assist the temple in whatever way he could.

"Clean up your mess, Aiden. See that none of this is traced back to us," she'd ordered him coldly.

"B-but, *Mother*—" he'd stammered.

"Leave me," she had commanded in a tone that brooked no disobedience.

He'd retreated from her presence at once.

"Countess Anne did not approve of the risk you and your sister undertook," Sir Casten replied. "When you claimed it was on her behalf, it offended her. She has little tolerance for foolish behavior."

"That's not how Claudia said she'd react," Aiden said bitterly. "Claudia said she'd love it. Claudia said she'd be grateful!"

"Lady Claudia lied to you," Casten said indifferently.

"Hold your tongue, sir!" Aiden shouted. "My sister *loves* me. She would never lead me wrong! She idolizes and adores her older brother as a proper sister should. She is my comfort, and I'll hear no disparagement of her honor! Not even from you."

Sir Casten sighed to himself. "My apologies, Sir Aiden. Clearly, I misspoke. It shall not happen again."

"See that it doesn't," Aiden said primly. "I would hate to be forced to draw my blade against a dear friend of the family."

Your bladework is a greater failure than your miserable attempts to gain your mother's affection, you miserable little shit, Casten thought darkly to himself. *I cannot believe you're Anne's son. How could the Godwell blood be so thin in you?*

Sir Casten had been Aiden's guardian and mentor for most of the boy's life, a position he'd once believed was a sign of confidence and respect shown toward him by his beloved Lady Anne. An opportunity to help guide a man of the Godwell family into maturity.

He'd been honored to accept this sacred duty. No, he'd been *beyond* honored. Grateful, even.

And in the years since then, Aiden had proven himself to be an absolute disappointment.

She knew, Casten thought morosely to himself. *Lady Anne knew. She sensed his unworthiness from birth, but she was too kind to drown him in his bath. Instead, she foisted the needy little fool on me, and it's been sheer misery ever since.*

Aiden was an egotistical, untalented dolt. He possessed his mother's beauty but not an iota of her intelligence or power. His brilliant half siblings Caleb and Claudia both ran circles around him without even trying, but he was too stupid to realize it.

Although he was currently the family heir by right of birth, Casten wouldn't have bet a copper penny on him ever inheriting his father's title. It would almost certainly go to cruel, cunning Caleb.

Heh. It was a shame Caleb didn't have an ounce of Godwell blood in him. Perhaps Lady Anne would have him married into the family. Now *he* was someone with potential!

That boy is death incarnate, Casten thought admiringly.

Given a little more time, Caleb Vae Belsar would probably become the most dangerous human being on the planet. Which was precisely why Lady Anne had sent him away for specialized training. Even *she* was excited by the enormity of his potential. Claudia remained behind, missing her brother, but the countess had taken the girl under her wing to provide her with training of her own.

Claudia would be another great addition to the kingdom. Although she couldn't match her brother's sheer power, she had a subtle way about her. She could manipulate other people as easily as a child played with a doll. Casten suspected that if he hadn't been given Lady Anne's personal protection, even he would be just another toy in her collection.

In her own way, Claudia was terrifying.

Aiden's relationship with her was particularly troublesome.

The idiot is perverse. He lusts for his own sister. He fantasizes about her! Watching him interact with her is nauseating. Seeing his obvious jealousy when she deliberately speaks of other men to rile him sickens me to my core.

Sir Casten was a disciplined man. He never showed his emotions unless someone dared to dishonor his mistress. He was a knight, a warrior, and a privileged servant of the Godwells. He would endure this trial and eventually move past it. His was a core of steel.

It could be worse, I suppose. I wonder how Lyona's little bastard turned out? She's a young woman by now. Heh, that creature is probably the only being in this world who could be a greater disappointment than Aiden.

How could Aiden have bungled smothering an infant in her crib? That disgraceful day, when he'd failed to erase that stain on Lady Anne's honor, had been the day he'd proven his absolute unworthiness. Casten had coached him so carefully and helped him work up the nerve for the attempt. But what had the results been?

Failure. Utter failure.

I really should have just ended them both then and there. Lyona and her brat. Lady Anne would have been upset, but I'm sure she would have forgiven me eventually. Everything I do, I do for her sake.

"My lord," said the coach driver through a slotted opening. "We've now arrived at Bremburg."

"All right, then," Aiden sighed. "Well, let's get this chore over with."

"As you say, sir," Sir Casten said humbly.

"I'm *telling you*, that's her!" Bree insisted.

"Not a chance," Eric said, just as insistently.

"She's dressed the same, she's wearing her hair the same—she's the *same person*!"

"Uh, Bree? Do I really need to point out the difference between black and blond hair?"

"She dyed it!"

"At what salon? There's too much empty road between where we left her and Bremburg. Plus, that girl's wearing *glasses*."

"What the hell is that supposed to prove? Glasses are removable, you idiot!"

"Yeah, but why would anyone as attractive as that want to wear them? Now who's an idiot?"

"Bree, Eric, *stop*," Bryce said sternly. "Please don't embarrass us in front of the templars! This is a great opportunity for us!"

"Yeah, yeah, yeah, that's what you keep saying," Eric said dismissively. "But we've been out here for hours, and so far, they've been ignoring us completely. I'm bored out of my skull."

"Everything bores you," Guyner said. "What are you two arguing about, anyway?"

"See that cute little noble over there?" Eric said, pointing in the direction of an attractive raven-haired girl sitting on a bench beside a stern-looking older man dressed in black and red. "Bree's trying to say it was that girl we ran into on the road."

"Huh," Guyner said. "I don't see how. She's wearing *glasses*."

"*Right?*" Eric said triumphantly.

"You're both such idiots," Bree said.

"Name-calling is hurtful, and only dumbasses do it," Eric said.

"That's about as much logic as I should expect from a cud chewer like you." Bree sniffed.

"Guys! The templars are *staring at us*!" Bryce hissed angrily.

"Well, let them stare! I'm over this!" said Eric in annoyance. "Hey, Bree. Let's just settle it by asking her. What do you say?"

"I'm not going over there," Bree said. "She's obviously stalking us."

"Are you saying we have a fan?" Eric said enthusiastically. "A groupie? A loyal follower? And she looks that good? Well, all righty, then! I call dibs!"

"Absolutely disgusting," Bryce said with disappointment.

"She's a child, you perverse monster," Guyner said disdainfully.

"A pig. You're just an opportunistic pig," Bree said, shaking her head. "The enemy of all women."

"What did I say that was so bad? I'm only eighteen!" Eric said in a desperate attempt to defend himself.

"Old enough for the gallows, I'd say," Guyner said.

"Did your parents fail you, or did *you* fail *them*?" asked Bryce.

"If it walks like trash and talks like trash, it must *be* trash," concluded Bree.

"Damn, Eric. You never did know when to shut up, huh?" asked a familiar voice.

Eric spun around in surprise, then shouted joyfully when he recognized the speaker.

"By the gods, who's this lucky bastard in front of me? Not Kent Surehand!" he said as he gave the other man a tight embrace.

"Like hell it isn't," Kent replied as he squeezed back against his friend. "How've you been man? My jaw dropped when I heard you left the thieves' guild to take up adventuring! Who'd ever figure the Scarlet Tip himself would go legit?"

"*The Scarlet Tip?*" Guyner asked with a raised eyebrow.

"Yeah, that's what we used to call him. See, there was a crotch pox outbreak in the east end of the capital, and *this* relentless brothel chaser ended up with—"

"Stoptalkingstoptalkingstoptalking," Eric said very quickly with a frozen grin on his face.

"What? Don't be embarrassed." Kent laughed. "Remember what we said? This is one of those stories that's going to be hilarious in hindsight."

"Details, please," demanded Guyner with an evil glint in his eyes.

"All of them. *All of them*," echoed the equally diabolical Bree.

"Kent, if he's your friend, then you should stop tormenting him," admonished the beautiful brunette woman who appeared beside the group. "You're doing him an unkindness."

"Ah, sorry, love. You are correct," Kent said abashedly. "My bad, Eric. I fall into old habits when my angel isn't around to keep me honest."

"Your angel?" Eric asked as he turned to look at the newcomer. Then his eyes popped out of his skull. "Ghosts below, YOU LUCKY BASTARD! How did a gutter-born puddle of regurgitated filth like *you* score a woman like THIS?"

"Pure charm and nothing else, bro!" Kent crowed.

"Liar!"

"You wish!"

"Well, all she has going for her are her looks, right? She's probably boring in the sheets," Eric said hopefully.

"YOU WISH! This girl gets me more tangled up than a bundle of old twine! I can barely keep up with her! I *always* wake up sore!"

"GODS DAMN IT, I HATE YOU!" Eric shouted before giving his friend another hug.

"Idiot," Laurel said as she slapped the back of Kent's head.

"Moron," Bree said as she did likewise to Eric.

"We're sorry," the rogues said remorsefully.

"Wait," Bryce said suddenly. "Wait, I know you . . . gods above. Gods above, you're her! You're Laurel Godwell!"

Bryce dropped to a knee before the woman, followed quickly by Guyner, who also recognized that name.

"We're . . . we're *beyond* honored to meet the maiden of the holy sword," Bryce said. "This is . . . that is, I . . . Uh, before I became an adventurer, I served as a temple healer. You are *everything* I have ever admired, my lady. I—I—I . . . "

"Please, please don't humble yourself, good priest," Laurel said. "Nor you, noble knight. My service as the maiden ended years ago. I'm the same as you now, a simple adventurer seeking to contribute to the greater good."

"Really?" Bryce asked. He rose to his feet. "You consider yourself the same as *me*? I'm flattered!"

"Hey, buddy," Kent cut in. "Ease up, will you? The lady's taken."

"Wait, you're really with *him*?" the flabbergasted Bryce asked Laurel. "I mean, *you* . . . with *him*?"

"Eh. Life takes you down strange roads," Laurel said with a smirk as she put an arm around Kent's shoulders and kissed his cheek.

"Fuck yeah, it does." Kent preened.

"Language."

"Sorry, honey."

"So, you're here to help cleanse this plague?" Bree asked curiously.

"Among other things," Laurel said.

"We're also checking in on her sister," Kent said. "It's her first outing as the new maiden of the holy sword. Laurel just wants to make sure she's up to the task."

"Kent! That's private," Laurel said sternly.

"It's okay, angel. We can trust these guys. Any crew Eric runs with are righteous folk," Kent assured her.

"So, your *sister* is the new wielder of the sword? That's very impressive," Guyner said.

"I suppose it is, but I still worry," Laurel replied.

"What do you mean—" Bryce began to ask when the sound of a blowing horn announced the arrival of the main force.

"Well, here she comes," Kent said.

"This is nice. Isn't this nice?" Sarah asked as she rode alongside Fenneth. "Look, Cousin! All these people are *so* happy to see us. Because we're the heroes! You should wave at them. Why aren't you waving? Bandon, shouldn't she wave at them?"

"Mmm," he grunted as he stared at the sealed gates of the town.

"What? Bandon, *I said* Fenneth should wave at everyone! Are you ignoring me?"

"Oh, I'm sorry, my lady. No, of course I'm not, I just . . . feel that something is a bit off."

"What?" Sarah asked. "Something's off? What? What is it? Now I'm feeling curious."

"I can't really say. Something about the gates. It's right on the edge of my memory. I'm sure it'll come to me before long," Brandon said.

"Tch. That sounded so mysterious. Oh, I *really* hate mysteries! I much prefer it when things are as simple as can be," Sarah said. "What about you, Fenneth? How do you feel about mysteries?"

"Cousin, do you *ever* stop talking?" Fenneth asked her as she dismounted from her horse and handed the reins to an attendant.

"What's that supposed to mean?" Sarah asked defensively. "I love people and people love talking. So I love to talk. It's perfectly sensible. Why did you have to ask a question like that? That was *rude*."

"I would say that the greater rudeness was you forcing your company on me during my first official task," Fenneth said disapprovingly. "Unlike you, I take my position very seriously. I'm here to enact the will of the gods. You won't find very many opportunities to abuse defenseless peasants under my watch."

"Ugh, you're *sooooo* serious," Sarah whined. "We're *faaaamily*. I'm just here to make sure you're all right. Isn't that so, Bandon?"

"The gods bless you for your loyalty, my lady," Bandon said.

"Right? *Thank you.* You're not behind the safe walls of the cathedral anymore, Fenny. Anything could happen to you out here. *Anything.* The council just thought I should walk beside you for a bit to make sure everything went smoothly—"

"And how exactly would *your presence* guarantee that, murderer?" cut in a derisive voice.

Sarah jumped, so startled was she by that voice.

Fenneth gave no indication it had affected her. Then she asked, "What are you doing here, Laurel?"

"That's the very question I wanted to ask you," replied her sister.

"Isn't it obvious? I've taken up the sacred duty that you abandoned in favor of your little thief."

"Or, more likely, our father forced you to take it up in order to maintain his position on the council."

"So what if he did?" Fenneth said without emotion. "The fact remains that someone must do it. The faithful need to be defended."

"I've forsaken my title, Sister. But *never* my duty," Laurel said. "I simply realized one day that I didn't need anyone's permission to do the right thing."

"Oh, listen to you go on," Fenneth said angrily as she turned to face her sister. "Another one of your great revelations, I suppose?"

"What's that supposed to mean?" asked Laurel.

"You've always been like this!" Fenneth said with growing resentment. "Doing what your *heart* says, following your *instincts*. You're selfish, Laurel! You've always been selfish, and because of you, I had to give up my calling! I want to heal lives, Sister. Not *take* them! But thanks to you, that's exactly the position I've been put in!"

"Then don't. Give the temple back their sword and come with me. Forcing you to do this is *wrong*," Laurel said.

"I can't just walk away from my life, Laurel! Turning my back on everything I know isn't as easy for me as it is for you!"

"I'm not a murderer," Sarah said unconvincingly, clearly stung by Laurel's earlier comment.

"Why are *you* even here?" Laurel asked her sharply.

"My question exactly," said Fenneth. "Go away, Sarah."

"Hey! You can't talk to me like that!" Sarah shouted as her temper erupted.

"Of course I can. I outrank you. *Go away*, Sarah," Fenneth repeated.

"You outrank me?" Sarah asked, an ugly, dangerous light gleaming in her eyes. "You *outraaaaank* me? Fenny outranks me! Fenny outranks me! Poor, poor me. I have to do what she *saaays*."

Sarah thrust herself into Fenneth's personal space and stood bare inches away from her. "Well, go ahead, Cousin! Give me another order! I *haaaave* to obey you. Give me an order. *Give me an order. Give me a fucking order—*"

Laurel lightly pushed her sister back and now stood face-to-face with Sarah. "She told you to leave, Sarah. *Do it.*"

Sarah grinned nastily, then said, "Big sister's being a big sister. So very, very sweet, isn't it?"

"No more warnings, Sarah," Laurel warned her.

"I've always loved you, Laurel. I dream about you sometimes. Doing things with you. Doing things *to* you. I'm always sad when I wake up because I'm not allowed to play with family."

"I've never once considered you family."

"I've always wondered what kind of wonderful expressions you'd make if I forced you to watch me whip your crying little sister with an oiled lash." Sarah leered. "Would that make you *gaaaaasp*?"

Laurel's expression didn't change when she attacked. Her body didn't give the slightest hint of her intention. One moment the two women were glaring at each other; the next, the steel sword belted at Laurel's waist was drawn and pressing against Sarah's gauntleted arm, which she held out in a block.

When Sarah's gauntlet and the sword collided, a shock wave emanated from their point of contact that threw everyone around them back in a perfect circle of fallen bodies. Only Bandon and Fenneth had the strength to keep on their feet as the two warriors clashed.

Fenneth shook her head and walked away, refusing to participate any further.

"STOP THIS AT ONCE," yelled Bandon of all people. His usual easygoing demeanor had been replaced with alarm and genuine anger. "Godwells do NOT behave like this in public! Lady Sarah, back away. Lady Laurel, you have *no* business being here. Sheath your sword and depart at once."

"I don't take orders from *you*, Bandon," Laurel said in a mild tone of voice as she continued pressing her blade against Sarah's gauntlet.

"Coz wants to play. So I'm *playing* with her," Sarah said with a sneer.

"If you force the issue, I'll have the templars take you into custody. If you resist in any way, it could be considered a heretical act."

"You'd *dare*?" Laurel seethed.

"You have no standing here," Bandon said. "You drew a blade against the paladin of the north! Be grateful I'm not throwing you into a dungeon!"

"I'd like to see you try . . . "

"Stop being so arrogant, girl. Your family name is why you still have your freedom. I see that the thief you ruined your life over has joined you on this little excursion. Do you believe your last name will protect *him* as well?"

Laurel glared at Bandon. She glared at him so angrily that he felt the intensity of it like a gust of burning air. It wasn't a very pleasant sensation. A few tense moments passed . . .

Then Laurel sheathed her sword and stepped back.

"Awww, Laurel got in *trouble*." Sarah laughed. "Hey, have you been slacking in your training? You're slower than I remember."

"Is that right?" asked Laurel. She reached a finger toward Sarah's cheek and gently wiped away a trickle of blood from a cut that now ran across it. "Because I believe I'm faster than you realize."

Laurel rubbed the blood on her finger down Sarah's bottom lip before walking away, leaving her cousin to stare at her back.

"Bitch . . . " Sarah said with widening eyes. "Bitch, bitch, bitch, *bitch, bitch* . . . "

She took an angry step toward the departing Laurel but stopped when Bandon put his hand on her shoulder.

"Not here," he said.

"*Baaaandon.* She cut me!"

"Not. Here," Bandon repeated.

Sarah fumed.

She felt humiliated.

She felt *angry*.

Laurel . . . Laurel, I can't let this slide. I can't this slide at all. No, no, no, no, no.

Laurel had to pay. Sarah *had* to teach her a lesson! But Bandon wouldn't let her! And she couldn't hurt Bandon. She *literally* couldn't! He was covered in monitoring spells. If she did anything to him, her father would know, and then she'd be in real trouble!

It wasn't fair!

She has to pay. She can't do things like that! Not to me! IT ISN'T RIGHT!

But how could she do it? How could she get even?

Then she remembered Fenneth.

Then she smiled.

If this day gets any more intense, my heart is going to give out, Bandon thought to himself.

He was glad he'd been able to intervene before Laurel and Sarah had really begun to throw down. That had been a close call. Too damn close! There was no question in his mind that he would have been the one to take the blame if they'd destroyed the entire area.

Damn rich girls. They never gave any thought to the plight of the working man.

"It's the gates," he muttered unhappily to himself.

Ever since he saw them, they'd been bothering him. But why?

Bandon was a practical man. Meticulous as well. When it came to battle, he always triple-checked everything and then did it once more, just to be safe. He didn't take chances whenever it could be helped. He'd thoroughly read the report offered by the watchman who'd escaped to alert the cathedral.

All the people of Bremburg were afflicted and violent. But they were also full of low cunning.

According to Thompson, the plague victims had lain in ambush and picked off the watchmen one by one as they made their way to the town stable. That meant they were patient. And possibly under the guidance of a leader. Which would probably be the demon responsible for the outbreak.

That bothered Bandon greatly.

Why would a demon cause a mass outbreak? That would only bring swift reprisal from the temple. Which was exactly what had occurred. Which wasn't logical at all, unless the demon *wanted* them to gather like this.

Again, why?

They're ambushers. That's a proven fact. They attack when you least expect it. Watchman Thompson said he barely got the gate open in time to escape—

Wait, what?

They're ambushers. That's a proven fact. They attack when you least expect it. Watchman Thompson said he barely got the gate open in time to escape—

Thompson barely got the gate open—

Got the gate open—

Got the gate open—

Bandon looked at the entrance to the town.

The gates were closed.

Why were the gates closed?

They're ambushers. That's a proven fact.

Ambushers.

The walls surrounding Bremburg were high. It now occurred to Bandon that they could be amassed right now. At this very moment there could be a massive group of them just waiting to attack, and he wouldn't even know it because the walls were high, *and they'd closed the fucking gates . . .*

Ambushers.

"SHIELDS UP! SHIELDS UP! READY YOURSELVES!" Bandon roared.

Sloth smiled.

Then he said, "Go."

"Your lady doesn't look so happy right now," Eric said to Kent as they watched Laurel return to them.

"Yeah. I guess her reunion with her sister went about as well as you'd expect," he said sadly.

"That sounds bad. Be there for her, brother."

"That's what I intend to do, my friend," Kent replied.

"SHIELDS UP! SHIELDS UP! READY YOURSELVES!"

"Huh?" Eric asked. "What did he just say?"

The gates to Bremburg opened. From inside came hell.

Literally hell.

The infected were completely under Sloth's control. All four hundred citizens of the town.

A sizable number, to be sure. But not nearly enough to match the power of the templars.

Which was why Sloth had been using them to summon many of his lesser brethren from the abyss.

Fiends who were only too happy to heed the call of one of their seven blessed kings.

It was a small force for hell. An inconsequential percentage of a percent.

But for the shocked templars and adventurers who'd been caught completely off guard, the infected and the demons seemed uncountable.

"HIIIIIIIIII!" shouted a huge pustule-laden behemoth of glistening muscle and fat that smashed into the adventurers before they could react and grabbed Kent by his shoulders.

"I'M TOMMY!" he squealed.

"Hi . . . Tommy," Kent said slowly. He hoped in that terrifying moment that if he spoke carefully and made no sudden moves, he could distract this creature long enough for Laurel to reach him in time.

She'd done it before.

"You have a funny face," Tommy said.

"Do I really?" Kent asked him.

"Uh-huh."

"Why does it look funny?" Kent asked.

"Because I wanna EAT it!"

"Huh?"

Tommy opened his mouth. It was a cavernous, gaping thing that stretched well into the center of his chest and was lined with endless rows of spikey, shark-like teeth. There seemed no end to the depths beneath his gullet.

Kent smiled and tried to remember better days.

I love you, Laurel.

Tommy then used his teeth to tear into Kent's neck. After his victim stopped struggling and fell limp, Tommy clamped down harder and bit through muscle and sinew to slowly pull Kent's head free of his neck.

Then he swallowed it.

CHAPTER THIRTY-SIX

The Red Knight

All the violence had been quite entertaining so far. Everly had no complaints in that regard.

She and Grail sat shielded on their bench. A clear glass-like dome surrounded them. It had been conjured by Titania and was impervious to harm. Likewise, Eris now blocked their presence from the minds of those who surrounded them.

So, now that they were invisible *and* invincible, there was nothing to do but kick back and enjoy the show. And *what* a show it was! There was so much going on at once that it was hard to keep track of. So many stories being told! So many little lives being lost! Eris assured Everly that she was recording every moment of the battle and would have it edited and ready for a cinematic presentation at the palace in no time.

Everly was already looking forward to it.

It was a shame, though. A situation like this really called for dynamic intervention. Too bad she couldn't think of a reason why she should care. Well, she *could* think of one good reason, but unfortunately, she just didn't have the tools that would allow for it.

Holy magic. Ha! Like I even care. That's stuff's lame anyway.

She wasn't just saying that as a coping mechanism either.

Really!

Everly had quickly become convinced that holy magic was stupid and that only losers practiced it. Her opinion had nothing to do with the fact she was having great difficulty mastering it.

Definitely not. She wasn't such a petty person. She was maturity incarnate.

Who cared if holy magic didn't come as naturally to her as everything else had? That was fine. No one could be good at everything. There was no shame in being a specialist. Didn't common sense teach that it was better to master one skill than to generalize and be a master of nothing?

And it wasn't as though Everly had only one skill to rely on. Her mastery of earth magic had reached a level that was nearly unthinkable. If her targets were unable to shield themselves in time with *harada* or sorcery, she could kill them outright.

She even possessed power over death itself. At her command, the dead would rise. That was pretty cool, right?

She didn't need holy magic in the slightest. She was perfectly complete just as she was. *Everly was okay.* And if anyone dared to say otherwise, well, she'd just have to firmly disagree with them. Extremely firmly. So firmly in fact that a mop and a grout-scrapping tool would be required for the cleanup.

She wasn't being sensitive about this. Everly was not a sensitive girl. In fact, lack of empathy was sort of her trademark.

"Everly, is something bothering you?" Grail asked, after noticing her darkening expression.

"Hmm? Oh, no. Not really. I'm just feeling a little sad over such a big missed opportunity."

"A missed opportunity for what?"

"Well, look at them! They're all getting their asses handed to them, right? I just thought this would be a great moment to step in and play hero. Y'know, I'd cast a bunch of healing magic and buffs and give these losers a much-needed second wind to overcome this demonic tide. A total last-minute rescue."

"Okay," Grail said. "So, why don't you?"

"*I caaaaaan't,*" Everly whined miserably. "Healing magic is too hard! It doesn't work for me."

"Is that right?"

"It is! I've been beating my head against it for months in hypertime! I just can't crack it."

"Is it really so difficult?"

"Oh, it's beyond infuriating. It doesn't work at all like elemental magic. Intent is *everything* with it! To use it, you genuinely have to care about other people. You have to want to help them."

"Ah. So what you're saying is that you lack empathy."

"Don't make it sound like such a personal criticism!" Everly pouted.

"I'm not. I understand that it can be frustrating not to master something right away. In my youth, believe it or not, I struggled to comprehend the basics of *harada.* It was the struggle of my life to—"

"Yeah, yeah. I know, Grail," Everly said dismissively. "I've been inside your head. I'm even going to refrain from pointing out that those aren't *your* memories, since you're trying to be helpful."

"Ah. Well, thank you *so much* for your restraint," he replied sourly.

"Aww, Papa got angwy," Everly said mockingly.

"Such ill-tempered behavior is beneath you."

"I know. That's why it's fun."

"NO! NO! NOOOOOOO!" shrieked a terrified templar as the huge demon before him shattered his skull with a sweep of his club.

"Wow. Did you hear that? *No! No! Noooo!* That extra was really going for a BAFTA, wasn't he?"

"It's not an unusual thing to see a man beg for mercy from an implacable foe," Grail responded.

"Oh? Is that something you've heard often in your career?" Everly asked him.

"During the war? More times than I care to recall," Grail said grimly.

"*Graaaail,*" Everly said as she leaned into him. "Why does it bother you so much to watch them die? They're extraneous! If they were important to the narrative, then they'd be stronger. But they're not. So the least they can do is entertain us on their way off the stage."

Grail was silent for some time before responding.

"That may be so, my Empress. I know I'm not truly one of them . . . but even so, I dislike watching men and women die like this. This isn't honorable combat. This is gross slaughter. Pointless cruelty. Human beings deserve better than to be torn apart by foul mutations and unholy demons."

"What are you saying?"

"Let me intervene."

Now Everly was quiet as she gazed at her servant.

"No," she finally said.

"Everly, why?"

"You're not made for saving lives, Grail. That was someone else, remember? Why do I have to keep reminding you of that? Those are *his* instincts. *His* urges. You're someone else entirely. Someone I like quite a bit. But I won't have you running in being the good boy who saves the day. That's ridiculous. I won't even consider it."

"But . . . but you just said that you yourself wanted to play the hero!" he said.

"So? *I* can do whatever I want. I'm special. You aren't. That's the narrative at work again. Does it bother you?"

"Does it bother me?" he asked angrily. "Of course it bothers me! That's just contrarianism for its own sake! It's pointless cruelty! I thought the great Empress was someone who wouldn't indulge in purposeless slaughter!"

"Graaaail," Everly said as she rolled her eyes. "I haven't lifted a finger against these people. These circumstances have nothing to do with me. Therefore, I'm not obligated to intervene. That's just me being lawful evil. It's cruel, but it's perfectly reasonable behavior."

"It's dishonorable."

"In what way? What obligations do I have here?" Everly asked him.

Grail began to think quickly. "For one thing, these foul creatures are demonic. The miasma they'll spread will harm the land for generations. Which in turn will anger Lady Titania."

He's got a point there, boss, Titania said. *Seeing all these little freaks running around my plane of existence is like finding a bunch of lice on your mattress. I really want to kill them.*

"Thank you, Titania," Grail said. "Furthermore, demons are spiritual beings made manifest through foul incantations. Due to their spiritual nature, however, this is a rare opportunity for . . . *Lady* Eris," he said her name with great reluctance and barely contained hostility, "to enact her . . . *pleasures* on genuine flesh and blood and not merely settle for inflicting psychic torment on her prey."

Oh, Eris said. *Oh, Everly, your dog speaks truthfully! These lesser demons are manifesting themselves through psychoplasmic constructs. I CAN strike at them directly. OHHHH! Everly! Everly! Please let me play with them!*

"Oh, good, you've gotten her worked up," Everly said in annoyance. "Thanks *so* much for that."

"I was only making an observation," Grail said contritely. "Of course, I'm saving my best argument for last. An open appeal to you for aid."

"Say that again?"

"Everly, on behalf of the Kingdom of Winstead, which now suffers under the blight of a demonic incursion, won't you please raise your sword in their defense? You're the *only* one who can stave off this invasion. Without you, this conflict will continue to escalate to catastrophic levels."

"Hmm," Everly said thoughtfully. "So, what you're basically saying is . . . I'm the only one who can help?"

"Without you, there is no hope," Grail said solemnly.

You're their last chance for survival, boss! chimed in Titania.

I want to pull them all apart one by one and feel their blood spraying into my face . . . Uh, and, you know, think of the children? Eris half-heartedly offered.

"Wow, gang!" Everly said. "You guys are really pushing for this, huh? Well, since that's the case, I suppose the only thing I can really say is . . . NOT a fucking chance."

What? Why not? whined Titania.

Everly! These little beasts are brimming with all manner of fluids! Let me burst just a couple! Pleeease? Eris begged.

"I don't understand," Grail said. "Why do you refuse?"

"Because, dummy," Everly said as she elbowed Grail in the side. "You keep trying to appeal to my better nature. I DON'T HAVE ONE! Think of the children? Save the town? To hell with the children! Fuck the town! I'm not invested in any of this nonsense, and I *only* do the things that I enjoy! Sorry, Papa, but you rolled a one with that argument."

Damn it, Grail thought bitterly. *She's such a selfish brat! Why did I swear fealty to her again?*

For the life of him, Grail couldn't remember why. Not that it mattered. He'd done it, and he would live with it because his personal honor still mattered to *him* at least. Still, he had to try to convince her. Not for the sake of the templars, or even the town, but because the world in general would suffer if demons found a way to profit.

Grail cared nothing for Winstead or the temple. But there were millions of uninvolved people who would potentially suffer if he let things stand as they were.

The problem, of course, was Everly. He could tell by the smirk on her lips that she was enjoying this argument and taking sadistic glee in denying his supplication. To use the vernacular of her home world, she was being a "troll." Trolls couldn't be reasoned with. They could only be ignored or appealed to . . .

He didn't dare to ignore her. The leash she gave him only stretched so far.

But *what* in this situation would Everly find appealing?

And then it occurred to him.

Oh. Of course.

He wanted to slap himself on the forehead. It now seemed so *obvious*.

He'd been trying to appeal to Everly's logic.

He *should* have been trying to appeal to her sense of drama. He should have been trying to increase her sense of immersion in the story.

Everly was a role-player. Character consistency was extremely important to her. Since she considered herself a villain . . . she simply needed a villainous reason to intervene.

With that in mind, Grail stood and faced Everly.

Then he knelt before her.

"Hmm?" she asked curiously.

"My Empress," Grail said, as he deepened his voice.

"Yes?"

"Demonic interlopers have appeared. Foolish intruders from some inconsequential layer of the abyss who have dared to attack *your* enemies, without first seeking *your* permission. Such behavior is *unforgivable*."

Everly cocked her eyebrow. "Why would they seek my permission? They don't even know who I am."

"Their ignorance of their crime doesn't excuse them. Furthermore, they have invaded *your* territory. Trespassing poachers who dare lay claim to your prey? Their punishment must be extreme."

Lord Grail speaks truly, Your Majesty! said Eris, who quickly caught on. *Be it heaven or earth, wherever the Empress lays her head is her kingdom. Those who disobey the laws of her kingdom are criminals. ALL CRIMES MUST BE PUNISHED!*

Everly! Everly! They're right. I didn't even think of it that way! These guys are totally breaking the law! Titania said urgently. *We can't let them get away with that! They'll think they can do it whenever they want!*

Everly had begun to blush and grin. She looked to the kneeling Grail, crossed her legs, and twiddled her thumbs as she shivered.

"They must think you're a worthless pig," Grail said. "Trash to be discarded. Human rubbish to be jeered at and mocked."

What a worm they must believe you to be, Eris said. *They must spit at the very mention of your name. What a weak and worthless child. A pitiful fool deserving of naught but scorn. Such a welp should be led around with a firm grip on her hair and beaten with a stick before a crowd.*

"Uhhhh," Everly said as she squeezed her eyes shut and began to twitch.

Hey, Everly. I think one of them said you were a demented pervert and would probably get off on being scolded or something, Titania chipped in.

"*Oh, my GOD*," Everly shouted ecstatically. Then she quickly said, "Uh, we've got to do something! Yes, this isn't right! Something has gone amiss!"

She leaped quickly to her feet and stumbled slightly when her knees nearly gave out, then steadied herself and turned to face Grail. "Lord Grail! These demons have *offended* me with their presence! I am *offended!*"

"So I see, my Empress."

"Yes, yes! Exactly that! How *dare* these inhuman encroachers invade my lands! They're second-rate! No, worse—*sub-rate*! And, for their temerity, they shall *suffer!* I demand their heads be made *separate-ed* from their necks! Grail! I command thee!"

"What is thy command, Great Everly?"

"SLAY THEM ALL."

Everly raised her hand and tapped the kneeling Grail on his forehead. And in so doing, she activated the power she had endowed him with.

This was a feature she bestowed upon everyone she created a body for. After all, what was the point in merely recreating a human body when you could *tweak* it a little? Make it more dynamic, more powerful, more . . . well, *everything*. She'd made them all powerful, but Grail was her favorite creation, so she'd made him the strongest of all.

Grail's body swelled and grew as his muscles and skeleton enlarged. Liquid metal flowed from the pores of his skin and wrapped itself all around him, encasing him in steel plates that slowly grew and expanded until he was covered in red-and-black armor.

The last piece to fall in place was the horned helmet that now protected his head. The light of his fiery, glowing eyes spilled forth from his visor, making his appearance far more demonic than the fiends now racing around the field.

Finally, his weapon flowed into his hand. Not a sword. After a long consideration of the matter, Grail had decided the elegance of a blade no longer suited him. He was a machine of death now, and he would require a weapon that lacked the grace and subtlety that a sword embodied.

He would be straightforward at all times. When his foes saw him coming, they would know what that meant.

The axe he now held was larger than his entire body. He wielded it as lightly as a twig.

"Their blood will flow in a crimson surge. I promise you," the steel-forged monster vowed.

Everly blushed with delight. She held both hands against her cheeks and sighed with pleasure at her dear creation. "Will you really do it?"

"I WILL LAY WASTE."

"Fall back!" Bandon shouted. "Fall back! We're being overrun!"

"HOLD!" shouted a voice that dwarfed his own.

Bandon turned to berate the fool who dared to counter his command but could only stare in numb surprise as what appeared to be a metal statue of an abyssal fiend, a monster standing nearly twelve hands high, leaped ahead of the struggling templars and collided with the demon horde.

The creature screamed as it landed, its voice filled with inhuman anger greater than that of the beasts it was aimed at. It tore into the ears of all who heard it, and even Bandon, a sword king, stumbled upon hearing it.

For the demons, that war cry was an irresistible challenge. They surged toward their attacker, compelled beyond reason to tear its invoker apart.

Instead, it was they who were destroyed.

"INTERLOPERS! THIEVES! INVADERS! THIS WORLD IS NOT YOURS TO PLUNDER!" shouted the steel fiend as his axe obliterated them.

"Then whose?!" shouted a particularly large demon, a goat-headed abomination who stood even taller than the axe-wielding knight. "I claim these mortal lands in the name of the Seventh King! Who are *you* to defy my master?"

"YOUR MASTER IS DUNG UNFIT TO FERTILIZE A PAUPER'S FIELD!" boasted the steel knight. "AND YOU ARE A DOG UNWORTHY OF HEARING MY LADY'S NAME!"

God, YES! Bandon thought he heard a girl's voice yell ecstatically.

"Fool!" screamed the goat demon. "For your insolence, I will feast upon your soul for all eternity—"

Before it could complete its sentence, the knight was upon it. Moving with speed that even Bandon could barely follow, he hewed through the limbs of his opponent and now stood with his boot upon the creature's torso, staring down at it without mercy. Then he raised his axe, before saying, "THE ONLY THING *THE WEAK* SHALL FEAST UPON *IS MY STEEL!*"

"Wh-what? What?" babbled the demon before its head was sundered.

"It matters not!" squealed another demon. "Kill as many of us as you can! Our numbers are uncountable! And your dead are legion! You will fall, mortal!"

The red knight laughed mockingly at his foe's threat. When he next spoke, his voice was quieter but no less menacing.

"Wrong, demon," he said. "I shall win. Because today, the dead *are* legion!"

The red knight swept wide his arms, and his voice rang out in command.

"RISE, WARRIORS! RISE, YOU DEFEATED FOOLS WHO FAILED IN YOUR FINAL DUTY! YOUR SOULS WILL NEVER KNOW REST WHILE THOSE WHO SLEW YOU YET LIVE! LET YOUR GRIEVANCES AND RANCOR STIR YOU ONCE MORE!"

"What's he doing?" Bandon gasped. "What in the name of the gods is he *doing?*"

"LET YOUR GRUDGES LEAD YOU TO BACK TO THIS WORLD!" continued the knight. "LIFE BROUGHT YOU DEFEAT! NOW LET DEATH BRING YOU *VICTORY!*"

At the red knight's words, they began to stir.

First they twitched.

Then they trembled.

Then their eyes *opened*.

The dead began to rise.

Even the dead templars, who by all rights should have been immune to this defilement.

Even the demons who'd fallen before his axe.

"Oh, fuck me. Fuck us all." Bandon trembled. "This is *necromancy*."

Even the demons were astonished.

Then, after the dead fell upon them . . .

The demons were afraid.

CHAPTER THIRTY-SEVEN

Penalty

Tommy wasn't having a very good time right now.

No. No, he was not.

He loved his new body. He loved being bigger and stronger than everyone else. He loved the terror in the eyes of his victims as he approached them, loved toying with them, but above all else, he *especially* loved killing them and feasting on them. Just as he'd done with the adventurer he'd surprised.

Sloth had told him that as long as he was a good boy and obeyed, he'd be able to indulge in such wonderful behavior for the rest of eternity. An eternity of hunting and feeding and fun. So Tommy obeyed his new master. And at first, he'd been having so much fun that he could barely contain his joy.

But that was before the other adventurers recovered from his ambush and began to fight back.

"You nauseating abomination! You fucking goat-sucking piece of shit! YOU KILLED MY FRIEND!" screamed Eric the rogue. He leaped at Tommy's face with his daggers out and slashed madly at his eyes, blinding one and only narrowly missing the other. "You want something to eat, you bastard? I got a meal for you right HERE!"

The pain of losing an eye was horrible! In his anger, Tommy lashed out, hoping to crush the agile little man before he could attack with those awful knives again, but the rogue was too quick on his feet. As Tommy clumsily spun around to find him, intense flames seared at his back as the group's mage struck at him.

"Flames that roar with hell's own vigor, burn the one that I now hate! Roast him, toast him, scorch this sinner! Him, I'll now **[Incinerate]***!"* shouted Bree, as

she raised both palms toward Tommy and poured endless waves of flame at him, filling the air with the scent of him being cooked.

"RAAAAAAAAGH!" screamed the agonized Tommy.

"It doesn't end there, you monster! This is just a preview for your eternity to come!" shouted Bree, who grinned malevolently at the sight of her burning enemy. She hadn't known Kent that long, but he'd seemed like a good man. And he and poor Laurel would've had such a bright future to look forward to . . . This thing *had* to pay!

Her thoughts of vengeance were broken, however, when Tommy forced himself through her barrage and knocked her away with a wobbling swipe of his hand.

"Ahhh," moaned Bree from the ground as Bryce's hand gripped hers and lifted her. Light enveloped his body and flowed into her, soothing away the pain from Tommy's blow and mending any injury she'd sustained.

"The gods saw your courage, Bree. The fight's not over for you yet," he told her.

"Heh. Damn right, it isn't," Bree said.

"I'LL EEEEEEEAT YOU!" Tommy shrieked as saliva, blood, and liquified flesh dribbled down the bottom of his jaw.

"SIT DOWN!" yelled Guyner as he came charging in. Swinging his massive kite, he smashed its steel into Tommy's face with such force that even the tumorous behemoth was taken off his feet and knocked into the dirt.

Before Tommy could recover, Guyner was at him, bashing his face over and over, relentlessly taking him apart.

"Save some for me!" yelled Eric.

"That's my line!" Bree said as she joined the fray.

Guyner merely grunted and continued bashing away.

"The gods would prefer we show mercy . . . but to hell with it. Leave me a piece!" said Bryce as he began smashing his staff against Tommy's limp body.

Soon, all thought of techniques, spells, and prayers fled their infuriated minds. The Brave Quartet had no desire left except to give Tommy the absolute hiding of his life. Their attack soon devolved into an instinctive pack-animal blitz that consisted of stomping him into the earth with their boots, screaming and spitting on him as they did.

Kent hadn't been one of their crew, but he'd been a friend who'd shared laughter with them. Adventuring was a dangerous life, and true comradery was prized above everything else.

When you messed with an adventurer's friend, you reaped a bloody reward.

Tommy was soon reduced to quivering ruin. But the quartet wasn't satisfied.

"Step back, guys," said Bree darkly. "Give him room. I want him to see this coming."

"Bree?" Guyner asked. His adrenaline was up, and now he was having some issues focusing.

"Come on, big man. You know what she's about to do," said Eric as he led him away.

"Ahhh," Guyner said as realization dawned on him. "Right. Ha! Serves you right, you fuck-fold," he said contemptuously to Tommy before spitting in the monster's remaining eye.

"I'll pray for the souls of your victims," Bryce said solemnly to the fallen beast. "But *only* for them."

Tommy wondered what was about to happen. Those mean adults had really messed him up. He couldn't move! He hurt so badly! This wasn't fair! He'd just been having fun, was all. What was wrong with that? They couldn't do this to him! He was just a kid! He was just a little kid! He was innocent! He had to convince them! He had to let them know!

Children were the future!

But before he could say anything, Bree began her final chant.

"My foe is crushed, to my delight. But he still lives, which isn't right! Let doom now fall before his sight! Come crush this pig, oh [Meteorite]!"

What was that? What was a meaty-o-right? What *was* that? Tommy had never heard that word before.

What was it?

Tommy soon figured it out.

It started off as a dot on the horizon and drew closer and closer and closer and *closer*.

Moments before it hit, Tommy wondered if he should have been a better person in life.

BOOM!

[Meteorite] was a rare ability even among the strongest of fire mages. As its summoner, Bree could shield herself and those she chose from the effects of its collision. Since it was impossible for her to know *everyone* engaged in combat, she simply told it not to harm any untainted humans.

The effect it had on the infected plague victims and their demon allies was devastating. The exploding wave of magical fire swept over the field, incinerating their numbers. This, in tandem with the red knight's undead assault, completely changed the course of the fight.

Now the demons were falling back; they retreated in disarray and terror as Grail led the charge against them, followed swiftly by the enraged survivors of the templars, who were now in a religious fervor and fought with such ferocity that even the demons feared their approach.

It was pure chaos.

And Everly was *feeling* it!

* * *

Grail wasn't the only one of the gang in the thick of it. Titania was flowing throughout the field, sending unexpected spikes of stone through the torsos of unsuspecting demons, swallowing them up and suffocating them when they fell, and outright crushing them with landslides here and there.

Eris was also having a great time. She'd manifested herself as a formless black cloud with long tendrils flowing from within it. She floated above the field, snatching any unfortunate demon up and pulling it inside, laughing wildly as she did so.

She reminded Everly of a predatory man-of-war colony ravenously seeking her prey.

However, she wasn't killing her victims.

"Rat room, rat room, rat room, rat room, rat room, rat room, rat room, rat room, rat room, rat room." She cackled madly as she hunted for more toys.

The rat room was always open for business.

And there, untouched by the carnage but delighting in it more than anyone else, sat Everly. This bedlam was her doing, and watching it was more pleasurable than anything else she'd ever known in her life. Unknowingly, she *fed* on the fear and suffering of the participants; the greater the intensity of the conflict, the more power she unwittingly drew from it.

In that moment, everything was for *her*.

Every life, every death, every desperate moment for survival, every slide into the void.

Everything was for her.

In the center of Bremburg, Sloth sensed something had gone terribly wrong.

"Hurry up . . . Hurry up!" he urged his slaves as they brought him another temple cleric.

"Abomination! The gods will smite you for your temerity!" the old priest yelled before Sloth plunged one of his tendrils into his forehead.

"Yeah, yeah, whatever. *Heal me!*" Sloth commanded him.

It had all been going so well. Smooth as could be! Sloth had no idea how the tides of battle could be turned so quickly; he just knew he was now in a lot of trouble, and he had to get out of there.

Over a dozen clerics had been snatched from the templars and were now being compelled to restore Sloth's body. They tried to fight back, of course, but Sloth had been breaking minds since the dawn of time. Mortal resistance was nothing to him. Bit by bit, he was slowly restored.

He just needed a little more time, and then he would be complete.

The gates of Bremburg, which he'd ordered resealed, trembled beneath the relentless pounding of the ravenous dead. It wouldn't hold much longer.

"Bastard, bastard, bastard!" he snarled to himself.

This red-knight aberration. Just who the hell *was* he? A warrior necromancer hadn't stridden the fields of blood in this world for centuries. Sloth had personally witnessed the death of the last one. That battle had been an endless nightmare that lasted for a year and a day before they'd finally dragged the monster down through sheer attrition. Then he'd died from his wounds and been reborn on Earth.

I should have stayed there! I should have stayed there and never returned! To hell with this world! To hell with being a king! AND TO HELL WITH ALL NECROMANCERS!

Sloth *knew* he deserved to be punished for what he'd done to this town and its people. He deserved far worse than death and damnation. But he didn't care. He hadn't gotten this close to succeeding only to be dragged down by some out-of-context nightmare like the sudden appearance of a necromancer.

He was *going* to escape! End of story!

"Hurry up!" he repeated as he slowly drained the healer's life.

Demons. Undead. Chaos. Madness.

Whatever. Sarah had more important things to deal with.

"Whatever's going on, Bandon can handle it," she said to her friend. "And if he can't, well, so? What am *I* supposed to do about it? I like being a paladin, but I've always considered my role more ceremonial than anything else. And anyway, my term of service is almost over. And I've decided not to renew it. I think a more secular career would better suit me."

The body she dragged behind her said nothing.

"What's that supposed to mean? I have a lot to offer the world! I've—I've—I've had unique experiences, and made all sorts of friends, and enjoyed all kinds of adventures! People love me! They really do! And I deserve to be loved! I always try my very best!"

Again, the unconscious body said nothing.

"Well, to hell with *you*, then, Fenneth!" Sarah vented. "Everyone *always* doted on you and your damn sister! Treated you like you were more precious than gold! What about me? I wanted that too! But I always had to *earn* it. I always had to earn it, earn it, *earn* it! YOU WERE LOVED FOR FREE! How is *that* fair!"

It was indeed the maiden of the holy sword that Sarah was dragging behind her. Blood trickled down her head from where she'd been struck from behind.

By Sarah.

"I don't want to do this. I really don't," Sarah mumbled. "It's not *my* fault. It isn't! Your sister attacked me! She attacked me! In front of witnesses too! She should go to *jail*. She should be imprisoned and locked away forever! She's a *maniac*! But even *Bandon*, my Bandon, *my Bandon*, MINE, MINE, MINE, even *he* took her side!"

The two of them were now in a grassy field, removed from the conflict.

Alone.

"She took from me, so it's only right that I take from her," Sarah whispered. "I'm in the right here. I really am."

Sarah let go of Fenneth and removed her gauntlets. Then she knelt over her cousin and slowly ran her fingers down her face.

"Pretty," she said. "Pretty, pretty, pretty."

She looked around to make certain no one could see her.

Then she leaned down and kissed Fenneth's lips.

She giggled delightedly.

"*Pretty*," she said once more.

Then she clamped her hands around Fenneth's throat and squeezed.

Fenneth's eyes popped open, and she began to struggle beneath Sarah's weight. But Sarah held her firmly in place and continued to choke her.

"Look at me. Look at me." Sarah grinned. "Look at me, Fenneth. *Look at me...*"

Everly decided that she was going to have to step into this fight. Everyone was having so much fun that she was starting to feel left out.

It's time! she thought to herself. *This has been a blast to watch and everything, but now it's time to step in and show everybody how it's REALLY done—*

Everly grunted painfully and fell to her knees.

She couldn't breathe.

She couldn't *breathe*!

In her panic, Everly felt her glamour dissipate, revealing her true hair color once more. She grabbed desperately at her neck as she tried to force air into her lungs to no avail. She was being strangled! She was being killed!

For the first time in her life, Everly was completely helpless.

As he raised his axe and prepared to shatter the gates preventing his entry, Grail dropped to all fours and screamed as his very form was disrupted. He felt as though he were being torn apart and was only being held together by the seams.

Around him, his undead legion collapsed back into lifelessness as the power that flowed from him was severed.

Everly, he thought desperately.

Something was happening to Everly.

Titania and Eris shrieked as their connection to the world was slowly torn away from them. Panic flooded the minds of both sisters as they realized their mistress was under assault, but they could do nothing to help her. Instead, they were forced to suffer as Everly did.

She wasn't only their mistress. She was their lifeline. Whatever pain she felt, they endured as well. And as her life was stolen away, so too was theirs.

Everly. Titania sobbed.

Everly, echoed Eris.

On her knees, Everly crawled, refusing to give in.

She couldn't fight back against this terrible force. She couldn't free herself.

But she refused to be afraid.

Kill me, then. Fuck you, whoever you are, KILL ME IF YOU CAN! she ranted manically.

It all would have ended there.

Everly would have died never knowing how or why. Eris, Titania, and Grail would have joined her. And the Empress would never have arisen.

That would have been the story of her life.

But she was spared by one very important fact: Sarah was a hopeless sadist who relished inflicting pain on others to the point of it being a detriment to her.

Killing Fenneth quickly in order to avenge herself on Laurel would have been the smart thing to do. The loss of both her man and her sister in one day would have devastated Laurel beyond all hope of mental recovery. It would have been the end of her.

But Sarah was enjoying herself too much to let her murder of her cousin end so quickly. She had to draw it out. So she made the greatest mistake of her life.

She let go of Fenneth's neck.

Air came rushing back into Fenneth's lungs as she gasped and sputtered.

"Having fun?" Sarah asked her sweetly.

Air suddenly came rushing back into Everly's lungs.

The instant it did, she flooded her body with *harada.*

Now her body was fortified. By using *harada* she could draw out that one breath and make it last for nearly ten minutes. Plenty of time to find out whoever it was that had taken a shot at her.

A sudden image shot into her mind. That of a familiar-looking girl. Someone a little older than her. Beautiful, with auburn hair, wearing a revolting leer on her face.

It was that paladin from before. Sarah, she'd heard someone call her.

Having fun? whispered the vision.

No, thought Everly. *But I'm about to, you absolute cun—*

Everly, I've located her, said Eris.

Show me.

A pillar of red light shot toward the sky. A pillar that only Everly could see, which marked where her tormentor now was.

Everly raced toward it with her fists clenched.

* * *

"Stop this," Fenneth whimpered. "Sarah, stop this."

"I can't. I can't. I wish I could, but I *caaaan't*." Sarah smiled. "If I do, you'll tattle on me. You will, won't you? You'll tell everyone how naughty Sarah's been. But I can't help it! Your skin feels *so* nice!"

"Sarah," Fenneth said. "Sarah, *please*—"

"Sarah, please. *Sarah, please. Sarah, pleeeease*," Sarah moaned as she closed her hands around Fenneth's throat once more.

This was good. This was *so* good. Better than she'd imagined it would be.

"Sarah, *pleeeeeeease*," she said one more time before she clamped down once more.

Then a boot stomped directly into her face and broke her nose.

It hurt. It *hurt.*

It hurt. It hurt.

It hurt. It hurt.

It hurt. It hurt.

It hurt. It hurt.

It hurt. It hurt.

It hurt. It hurt.

It hurt. It hurt.

Sarah had never felt pain before. Not even once. She was completely unfamiliar with the sensation.

In a lot of popular stories, when a person had never felt pain before, they immensely enjoyed it the first time they experienced it.

As it turned out, that was complete nonsense. Sarah did *not* like pain! Who would?!

A hand reached down and mercilessly tangled itself in Sarah's hair before ruthlessly pulling her up, away from Fenneth, to stare face-to-face with the person who'd attacked her.

She looked familiar.

"You should have kept your hands to yourself, *BITCH*," said Everly without humor.

With her right hand holding Sarah in place by her hair, Everly drew back her left fist and then lunged forward with it, making a perfect standing reverse punch as taught in karate. Only, this blow was enhanced by both *harada* and Titania's immense strength.

When her punch hit Sarah's midsection, the paladin went flying away as though she'd been shot from a cannon. When she landed, she didn't just come to a skidding halt. Her body had dug a *furrow* into the ground that stretched the length of a field.

Sarah slowly crawled from the dirt she'd been embedded in, on her hands and knees like a wounded animal. Then she vomited a blood-streaked puddle of fluid on the ground and collapsed onto her back, sobbing in pain as she clutched at her abdomen.

From above, a shadow loomed over her.

Sarah felt something land on her chest.

It was the clump of hair her assailant had been holding when she'd punched her.

Sarah had been *scalped*.

"Why are you doing this?" she asked.

"Oh, I'd quit my moaning if I were you, sweetie," said Everly. "You and I are just getting started."

CHAPTER THIRTY-EIGHT

Fenneth

What unites two souls?

When we think of the term "union," most of us assume it's a union of love.

Love is a powerful force in many worlds, after all.

But there are other forces that are far older. Forces that existed before the very *concept* of emotion.

One of them is the union of *blood*.

Blood can bind your soul more thoroughly than love ever could.

Especially the blood of an enemy.

Here's one example.

Fifteen years ago.

"God damn it. *God damn it!*" Abe Tulido whispered as he cowered in the bathroom stall of a girls' public restroom.

"I knew this would happen one day," he said. "God damn it. I *knew it!* Kids are going nuts everywhere you look! No respect for tradition, the law, the Bible. *It's all gone to shit!*" he ranted.

"Well, they ain't getting me. I'm nearly old enough to retire, and they *ain't* getting me!" He reached toward his ankle, where he kept his peace of mind holstered. A Sig P365.

A small gun with *big* stopping power.

Abe was an assistant principal and damned good at his job. Too good not to be given his own school, in his humble opinion. But whenever the subject of promotion came up, the school board would always slide right past his name. It was infuriating. The lack of respect and the refusal to give a standout employee like him his own kingdom to run . . . It just highlighted the absolute unfairness of the world!

He'd been in the education game for thirty years and was now working for people who'd been elementary schoolers that he'd taught. It wasn't right! It wasn't fair! But that's how life went when you were a man of *principles* in a world that respected nothing. If more people like him were in control, society wouldn't be half as cracked as it was, and that was a damned fact!

Take today, of all days. One of those tik-tokey, or whatever it was called, addicted rich pukes who made up the student body of this sheltered little private school had gone nutso!

It was just like they warned him on the cable news he loved watching. In the midst of a crisis, when the lunatics were running wild, there was only one thing that could stop the *punks* from getting at him. And that was the glorious weight of cold iron in his hand.

"Just bring it, you little junkie scum! Just come and get me. I dare you! Fuckers! *Fuckers!* You ain't getting me! This is *my* school!"

"Mr. Tulido, *please* calm down," said the transfer student he'd been guiding to detention.

She seemed like a nice girl. Pretty too, in a messy sort of way. But he saw that her backpack had a Phish logo on the back, so he'd immediately given up all hope of her being normal.

She *claimed* she'd accidentally missed her bus, but he bet she'd been doping it up at some pot party and lost track of the time in a haze of dirty smoke. And she thought she could just sneak into class like she'd done nothing wrong?

Not on *his* watch!

Normal kids didn't listen to any of that *druggie* music.

They had milkshakes at the malt shop and went to church on Wednesdays, damn it!

He had the stall door closed so she couldn't see his gun. "Don't tell me what to do, kid! I know better than you what's required!"

"Why'd you drag me in here?" she asked. "Why are you so afraid? What did code eleven mean when they said it on the intercom?"

"Code eleven means there's someone armed on the premises," he snapped. "It means one of you *degenerates* is going hog wild! I knew this day was going to come. You kids are too politicized! You're a bunch of blood-crazed whack-a-doos! Well, you ain't getting me! I swear to god, you ain't getting me!"

"Sir, when you talk like that, you don't make me feel very safe," the girl said.

"Grow up, kid! Time to stop being a snowflake and put on your grown-up pants!" Abe said. "I got something for any punk who comes at me . . . Just try it, just you fucking *try it* . . . "

"*Okaaaaay*," the girl said as she stepped away from his stall.

Suddenly, voices cried out in pain.

Oh, great god almighty, that was just down the hall from the bathroom!

Next, a gunshot rang out!

Abe's chest tightened in fear as tension seized his body. "Stay away, stay away, stay away, stay away!" he moaned fearfully.

"Mr. Tulido, stay here, *please!*" the girl said. "I'm going to go see if anyone needs help!"

What? That stupid little cow. She was going to alert the attackers to their presence!

THEY'D COME FOR HIM!

"Nnnnnnn," he said. But before he could tell the brat to stay put, she went racing out the door.

"Bitch. Stupid *bitch*," he said hatefully.

What if she'd been in on it? What if she was *one* of them? Was she really a transfer student? Maybe she'd been scouting out the place for her no-good buddies!

Fuck them! They wouldn't catch him unawares.

Abe left the stall, then pointed his gun directly at the bathroom exit. The instant that door opened, he'd open fire on the next maniac he saw.

Just like John Wayne and Dirty Harry.

"Make my day, you *punks!*" he said as he cocked his weapon.

Things happened on the other side of the bathroom door, and then a girl was dying.

Breene hadn't meant to do it. One moment she was holding the other girl's heavy sword while her back was turned. The next, the attacker turned around, and before she'd realized what she was about to do, Breene had run her through.

For some reason, the other girl seemed pretty pleased with the result. She kept chattering away in a perfectly conversational tone, as though she weren't slowly bleeding out.

"Mortal wounds sure freakin' hurt, though," the psycho continued while grimacing in pain. "Nice sneak attack, by the way. Your character class must be assassin."

"I wasn't trying to hurt you," Breene said, as tears began to leak from her eyes. She wanted the other girl to understand it had been an accident. "I just wanted to get that sword away from you. Wh-when you turned around, I panicked and—and—*and*—"

"Hey, hey, don't be like that," the attacker insisted. "Feel a little pride in yourself, okay? Your instincts took over. And you know what? They were the *right* instincts. If it helps, I'm okay with what you did."

"You are?" Breene couldn't believe her ears. Who could possibly be okay with something like this?

"Yep. No grudges here," the other girl assured her.

Breene sat beside the other girl against the locker, paying no attention to the blood now staining both their school uniforms. "Aren't you on the student council? Why'd you *do* something like this?"

"Hee-hee! It's a *seeeecret*," the other girl said with a knowing smirk.

"You seem like a nice person. Couldn't you have talked to someone?"

"Probably, but they wouldn't have said what I wanted to hear."

"Aren't you scared of dying?"

"I think I'm more afraid of living in a world that doesn't need someone like me in it," she replied after giving the question a moment's thought.

"That's selfish. You have a family. You had friends."

"Yep. I'm a very selfish person," the dying girl said in agreement. "I always do whatever I want."

She shivered in pain. She was feeling a lot colder now. So very cold. She seemed surprised when Breene held her hand and regretfully said, "I really am sorry for killing you. I wish we'd met sooner."

"You seem pretty cool. I wish we'd met sooner too," the other girl said, as though she were surprised by this development.

She closed her eyes and slumped against the locker.

A few moments later, she died.

Breene didn't release her hand until the medics arrived. Before they helped her to her feet, she gave the body a hug.

Blood was now all over her. But she didn't care.

She wondered if that other girl had ever been hugged in her life.

The first responders asked her if she was okay, if she needed treatment, if she was injured anywhere. Breene shook her head and said no. She was okay. She was doing a lot better than the dead girl was, anyway.

One of the paramedics laughed as if she'd made a joke. The sound of it startled her.

Breene felt so out of contact with reality.

An officer approached her, wanting to take her statement, when Breene suddenly remembered poor Mr. Tulido cowering away in the girls' room.

"Hold on, sir, please? Just a second! There was someone with me. I need to let him know that everything's all right."

The officer protested, but Breene had already taken off. She jogged over to the bathroom entrance, pushed it open, and said, "Mr. Tulido? Mr. Tulido, everything's okay now—"

Bang-bang-bang-bang-bang-bang!

* * *

Abe was ready. Oh, boy, was Abe ready! He'd been born for this. Society was collapsing, the world was slowly going to hell, and chaos reigned in the once peaceful land of America, but he was a righteous man *with a gun*, and he wasn't taking one step backward!

NOT A ONE!

The door opened, and just as he feared, one of the maniacs stepped inside. A lunatic whose school uniform was covered in blood. She must have been on a killing spree! And she somehow knew his name!

"*Mr. Tulido*, everything's okay now," she hissed with a demonic smile on her youthful face, no doubt anticipating adding his blood to the mess on her clothing.

It was all right now, was it? Why? Because now it was time for her to kill *him* just like she'd undoubtedly slaughtered her earlier victims? To hell with that!

Abe Tulido opened fire and emptied his weapon into the girl's body. The bullets tore through her forcefully and knocked her gracelessly to the floor. One of them had gone through her head and made a terrible mess of it.

Serves you right! he thought with satisfaction. *Teach you to mess with a veteran of the ROTC!*

He exited the bathroom with his gun still pointed at the twitching body. To his surprise, he saw police officers and medics staring at him with bewildered expressions on their faces. Well, how about that? It seemed help was closer than he'd realized.

"I got her!" he told them triumphantly. "I got her ass!"

One of the policemen began slowly approaching him.

"Uh, am I going to get a medal?" Abe asked hopefully before the nightstick came down on his skull.

And that was the end of Breene Collins, a new girl in school who'd made a new friend and a new enemy all in the same day and who'd only tried to do the right thing.

Her blood poured from her wounds, but as it did, it intermixed with the blood of the other girl, Kerri.

The blood of an enemy was a powerful force in some schools of magic.

Kerri's soul was no longer connected to the Earth. As it fled her body and drifted into the greatness of the multiverse, seeking a more appropriate home for itself, it didn't notice that it was now tethered to Breene.

Two souls. Two enemies. Bonded by blood.

Two equals.

Bonded by fate.

Breene opened her eyes in confusion.

What was happening now? Why was it so hard to think?

She felt herself being cradled in a warm embrace.

It was nice.

"Congratulations, Lady Celia. She's so beautiful," said a voice she didn't recognize.

"Thank you. Laurel will be delighted to learn she now has a sister," said the smiling woman who held her.

"Have you and your husband thought of a name?" the other voice asked.

The woman kissed the baby gently on her forehead and beamed lovingly at her.

"Fenneth," she said warmly. "We're naming her *Fenneth.*"

CHAPTER THIRTY-NINE

Punishment

So, sweetie. How did you do it?" Everly asked Sarah after she forced the mewling paladin to her feet.

"Wh-what?" Sarah asked her.

"How did you *do* it?" Everly repeated. "How'd you do it? How'd you do it, Sarah? How. Did. You. Do. It?"

As she asked, she punctuated each word with a vicious slap across Sarah's face.

"Let go of me," Sarah yelled angrily. She lashed out with her hands and scratched Everly across her cheek, which startled her attacker into releasing her.

"Oh, what the hell," Everly said disgustedly as she ran her fingers across the wound. "What kind of technique is that? Quit fighting like a girl."

"Shut up!" Sarah said. "Shut up, shut up!"

"You gonna make me?" Everly taunted her. "I don't think you are. I think you just want to sit there and *baaaawl* like a little baby."

"Fuck you!"

"Ha! You try so hard to be tough, don't you?" asked Everly. "You really rely on your reputation to carry you. But it's not enough, is it? Paladins are supposed to be warriors, aren't they? *Fighters.* But you don't look like a fighter to me, Sarah. You look like a victim. You look *soft.*"

"*Shut up.*" Sarah trembled. "You shut your fucking mouth. You shut your fucking mouth!"

"You look like a *doormat;* did you know that?" Everly continued. "Something I get to rub my dirty feet all over and not even think about for the rest of the day . . ."

"I SAID SHUT UP!" Sarah screamed. Now she came at Everly in a fury, swinging her powerful fists with blinding speed, delivering blows that would have killed anyone else if they could only connect.

"There it is," Everly said encouragingly. "Look at you go! That's much better than before."

Sarah didn't respond to her taunts this time. Her eyes were narrowed, her face was frozen into an expression of animal frenzy, and spittle began to drip down her jaw.

Kill this bitch, kill this bitch, KILL THIS BITCH—

No one had ever treated Sarah this poorly. No one had ever mocked her this badly. No one had ever truly *injured* her. The hate she'd felt for Laurel that sparked her attempt to kill Fenneth was nothing compared to what she now felt for this smirking insect.

Didn't she know who Sarah was?

She clearly didn't.

Didn't she *care?*

She clearly did not.

Well, Sarah would *make her!*

For her part, she was enjoying watching Sarah losing more and more of her composure; Everly found her opponent to be more than a little contemptible.

She'd heard all about the great paladins of the temple, of course. Everyone had; they were practically a national treasure. One-man armies, the mightiest warriors of the faith, the chosen of the gods, blah, blah, blah.

They got a lot of good press, didn't they?

But why?

Sarah was strong for sure. Durable too, obviously. She was definitely something more than merely mortal—that was a fact. But it didn't matter. Not in the slightest. Because as fast, and strong, and tough as she was, there was one terrible flaw holding her back from being an actual threat.

This chick couldn't fight.

She couldn't fight for *shit.*

She moved on pure animal instinct combined with her amazing physical prowess. But that was all. There was no refinement to any of her attacks, no sign of any kind of training. All Sarah relied upon were her incredible natural abilities.

Everly found that disgusting.

Utterly disgusting.

Natural talent could only get you so far in life. It didn't mean anything without hard work and practice. Without self-discipline, and the willingness to be humbled, you'd never have anything but your *potential.*

To Everly, Sarah was an absolute waste of space. Someone who got by in life by dominating those weaker than herself.

A silly little schoolyard bully.

These were also characteristics Everly shared. She wasn't a hypocrite; Everly *knew* that she herself was also bullying scum. Dominating the weak was *fun*, after all. But the difference between her and Sarah was that Everly had *earned the right*.

She'd put the work in. Lording it over everyone else was her just reward for a job well done.

But this sad little creature?

She was a *poseur*.

"Okey dokey," Everly said. "I think we're done here."

"We're done when I SAY we are—" Sarah said before being cut off when Everly stopped playing with her and began preparations to *really* cut loose.

Everly knew the world she now lived in possessed conventions not dissimilar to certain genres of popular entertainment on Earth. One of them that she particularly enjoyed was developing and naming her own magical attacks.

Techniques specific to her alone.

Signature abilities that only *she* could perform.

Naturally, in her enthusiasm for the subject matter, Everly had overdone it. She hadn't created only one signature attack.

She'd created *three*.

And they were ridiculous.

Everly called them "the three sorrows." Each one was such an escalation of violence and destruction that she knew she could only call upon them on certain special occasions.

They were *that* awesome.

To hell with the wizarding world and its unforgivable curses. Until he could fire off multiple *avada kedavras* like he was spraying a crowd with shots from a Gatling gun, that snake-nosed dork Voldemort could just sit his ass down and let the professionals work.

Naturally, possessing such forbidden power appealed greatly to Everly's sense of showmanship. Signature attacks like hers were a staple of video games, light novels, American comic books, and manga. She especially liked the manga versions because those involved shouting your attack's name before releasing it.

Everly had never done that before. But here, in this moment, with this appalling little paladin who possessed absolutely *no sense of style*, she knew the time had come.

And in that moment, she felt a speech coming on.

"You depraved false paladin. You wrap yourself in righteousness and believe yourself shielded from the consequences of your cruelty. You trample over the dignity of your victims and delight in abusing the trust and authority invested in you. But the shadows *see* you, Sarah Godwell."

Everly raised her hand, which she began shaking forcefully to make it seem as though it were trembling and she was struggling to control it. As she did this, she also began fortifying her body with massive amounts of *harada*.

"A wicked power now arises within me!" Everly continued dramatically. "It demands I bid thee *welcome*, Sarah! It recognizes you as one of its own! The darkness that now surges throughout my being demands that I CLAIM YOU!"

Now Everly began drawing deeply upon Titania's power of earth. She wove it intricately around the *harada*, slowly combining the two powers.

"ITS SEARING BLACK FLAMES WILL CONSUME YOUR VERY SOUL!" she shouted. For the last part, she used Eris's ability to project a fiery dark aura around her body.

Because that part just looked *cool*.

"Receive now the first of the three great sorrows! Destroy everything before you, [Sundering Strike]!"

Everly often wondered if she should shorten the name of the attack to [Sunder]. "Sundering strike" sounded good, but it was also a little unwieldy. A single-word attack might have been preferable because its bluntness would better suit its abrupt, devastating nature.

Oh, well, she'd already said it.

Too late to take it back.

Oh, shoot! she suddenly thought. *A cape. I should have added a cape to Grail's look. His armor and axe are AWESOME, but a cape would have really completed the set! Arrrrrgh! Why am I just now realizing this? Do better, Everly! Do better!*

[Sundering Strike] was a power that obliterated everything before it. It was an attack that disrupted the earth, the air, and the spirit. Anything within Everly's field of vision would be hit by it, whether on the ground or beneath it, whether in the sky or sea.

It hit *everything*. She would have called it the [Raging Demon Strike], but she respected the great Akuma-sama far too much to rip off the name of his trademark attack so haphazardly.

To differentiate it from her spiritual sensei, she developed [Sundering Strike] as a weapon technique that would ordinarily be channeled through her sword; but Everly didn't consider Sarah worthy of that great honor. So she instead channeled it through her open palm and struck it against the paladin's chest.

There were three things that saved Sarah's life that day. The first was that Everly hadn't bothered putting her full power behind the blow. The second was that she'd used her open hand instead of a closed fist. And the third was that she hadn't added Eris's ability to the mix, like the recipe called for.

If she'd done any of those three things, the four great paladins of the Western Temple would have had their numbers reduced by one.

Even so, Sarah *flew*.

Like a bird.

Like a spirit.

Like an *angel.*

But when she landed, she was a half naked, mangled, broken thing.

"Woooooow," Everly said, genuinely impressed by the other girl for the first time that day. "*Wooooow*, you really should have died! What are you *made* of?" she asked.

"Graaaaah," Sarah moaned.

Well, that wasn't a helpful answer.

Whatever, she'd figure it out during the autopsy.

Before Everly's eyes, the paladin's skin began to heal, her broken bones and torn muscles knit themselves together, and her twisted limbs snapped themselves back into place, accompanied by a hideous popping sound.

Everly was enthralled.

"Sweeet," she said. "A genuine healing factor! That's awesome! You can just go on forever, can't you?"

"Please don't," begged Sarah.

"What? Don't be silly!" Everly said with a mischievous grin. "This is a great opportunity for us both! Now I get to finally cut loose on someone who can take it, and *you* get to see how much you can take before the pain drives you insane! Err, *more insane*, in your case, I'd say. Well, come on. Get up! We're burning daylight!"

"Get away from me!" Sarah cried.

"You see, your mouth and your body language say *nooooo*, but your earlier attempt on my life says *yeeeeees*, so you can understand my confusion, right?"

"I wasn't trying to kill you! I swear I wasn't!" Sarah said tearfully. "It was Fenneth; it was her. I was trying to kill *her*." She wept as she pointed at the unconscious Fenneth.

"Huh?" Everly asked in confusion. She stepped over to the girl and gazed upon her.

She was . . . cute. She was really cute. Everly briefly wondered what color this Fenneth's eyes were.

Oh, well. Plenty of time to find out later.

"And just who exactly is she supposed to be?" Everly asked out of curiosity.

"Th-that's my cousin!" Sarah said. "That's the maiden of the holy sword!"

"Holy *shit*." Everly whistled. "You really tried to kill the maiden? God, you really *must* be *cracked*. Did someone pay you to do it? Are you in league with the demons? Is this a church conspiracy? Come on! Out with it."

"Noooo," Sarah whined. "*Nooooo, nooooo*, I'm not with them. Never!"

"Then why'd you do it?"

"Her sister . . . her sister . . ."

"What did her sister do?"

"She *scratched me.*"

Everly paused, uncertain if she'd correctly heard that. "Uh, come again?"

"Her sister scratched me! She made me angry!"

"Are you fucking serious?" Everly asked her in a flat tone of voice.

"It was an attack. It was an *attack!*" Sarah yelled with her eyes shut.

"Oh, for god's sake," Everly said, as she shook her head in disappointment. "You . . . you are really . . . ugh. I don't even have the words right now. You are *such* a loser."

"No, I'm not!" wept Sarah.

"Uh, yes you *are.*" Everly insisted.

"It's hard!" Sarah shouted. "It's fucking *hard,* okay? No one *ever* sees anything from my perspective! Everyone always tells me I'm wrong, or I'm stupid, or I'm crazy, and I'm fucking sick of it!"

"You *are* wrong, you *are* stupid, and you are *definitely* fucking crazy," Everly replied without sympathy.

Enraged, Sarah leaped at her tormentor, only to be easily punched back down.

"You're a slow learner too." Everly frowned.

"You can't do this!" Sarah said as she climbed back unsteadily to her feet. "You can't!"

"I think you mean I *shouldn't* do this," Everly corrected her.

"What?"

"If I *couldn't* do this, I obviously wouldn't be able to," Everly explained helpfully. "But because I'm doing it, then it's obvious that I *can.* Do you understand now? You shouldn't be making an appeal regarding my *capacity* for violence. I'm clearly very capable of it."

To demonstrate, she slapped Sarah across the face before the paladin could react, causing her to spit blood.

"See? It's easy for me! Now, what you *ought* to do is make an appeal for *mercy.* Not that *I can't do this.* But rather, *I shouldn't.* 'It's wrong. I'm weaker than you, I'm injured, it isn't right, spare me.' That sort of thing."

"It *isn't* right! I *am* injured!" Sarah said. "Spare me!"

"See? You're already doing a better job of getting your ideas across!" Everly cheered.

Then she brought her hands together and clubbed Sarah across her face, sending her sprawling back into the dirt.

"Now let's discuss my capacity for mercy," Everly suggested.

On her knees, Sarah tried to crawl away.

Everly clucked her tongue at the sight of it. "Oh, what are you doing now? A turtlecrawl? I don't get it, sweetie. This isn't the story of the rabbit and the hare; it's the bull moose and the termite. Do you even understand why I'm doing this to you?"

"Nooo!" Sarah sobbed. "No, no, no, I don't."

"That's a shame. If you can't admit your faults, then you'll never learn from this."

"Learn? *Learn?*" Sarah shouted hysterically. "You arrogant bully! You . . . you posturing nobody! Who are *you* to teach *me* a lesson? Do you really think y-you'll get away with this? How *dare* you! I'm a Godwell! Do you hear me? *I AM A GODWELL!*"

In response, Everly grabbed the other girl by the tattered remains of her white cloak. Then she forcefully swung Sarah over her head and smashed her painfully into the ground. Then Everly did so again, and again, and again.

From the dirt, Sarah wheezed painfully. "Hhhhhhrrrrrrrrr."

"Heh, *puny Godwell.*" Everly snorted.

Who loved the classics?

She did!

Still, it was past time she ended this farce.

Everly held out her hand and made a gesture. A large pile of dirt gathered in on itself, coalescing and merging, then began glowing as she used Titania's power of the earth to transmute it.

Within moments, a massive sword appeared and floated into Everly's waiting hand. She then placed her boot on Sarah's chest, pinning her to the ground while she pointed her weapon at her throat.

"Sarah Godwell, false paladin of the temple faith," Everly said. "You now stand accused of the high crimes of sucking at your job, picking a fight you couldn't possibly win, whining like a little punk when you lost, and worst of all, attempted murder of a potential *waifu*. The sentence is *death*. Have you any final words?"

"Nononononononononono!" Sarah whimpered.

"Let the record show that until the very end, the condemned was an utter pussy willow," Everly solemnly said. "Now, in the name of Her Imperial Majesty, which is to say *meeee*, I will now carry out this grave duty. May the gods you believe in, but who probably don't exist, now have mercy on your soul."

"NOOOOOOO!" Sarah cringed as Everly raised her blade.

"Stop right there!" shouted another voice.

"Huh?" Everly said as she turned her head, only to find that a sword was now inches away from her neck.

"Release your weapon and step away from my cousin, or I swear I'll *kill you*," Fenneth said fiercely.

A grin slowly dawned on Everly's face.

This girl. She had *beautiful* light-brown eyes.

They reminded her of a pair she'd seen before.

"Okay," said Everly as she dropped her sword and stepped away. "*Well*, then . . ."

CHAPTER FORTY

Everly

So, what happens now?" Everly asked Fenneth as she stepped away from Sarah with her hands up. "Are you going to arrest me? Take me into custody? Have me strip searched? *Ohhh*, are you going to do it personally? Do I get to strip search you next? We could turn it into a tickle *fiiiight*."

"Silence!" Fenneth blushed. "I—I *am* placing you in custody for assaulting a temple paladin. By royal decree and temple law, *none* may lay hands on a defender of the faith."

"Really?" Everly asked. "That doesn't seem to jibe well with what *she* was about to do to you."

"I had it handled!" Fenneth said.

"I think you mean *she* had *you* handled. Oh, *no*," Everly said as she suddenly stepped into Fenneth's personal space, brushing aside her sword as she did so, causing Fenneth to nearly stumble back in surprise before Everly caught her.

"Look at your poor neck," Everly murmured as she gently ran her fingers along the bruises around the other girl's throat. "It's like your cousin vandalized a work of art. You really should just let me kill her."

"S-stop that!" Fenneth said. "Hey, back off! I'm fine!"

"Do you *feel* fine?" Everly asked doubtfully. "An experience like that can really shake some people up."

"I'm more used to it than you think," Fenneth said stubbornly. "Now back up, I said! Flirting isn't going to get you anywhere."

"Are you suuure?" Everly wondered. "You seem like you like it."

"No, I don't!"

"You *do*. You *liiiiike* me," teased Everly.

"Shut up!" said Fenneth angrily. "God, you're too cocky! Why would I be into anyone as full of herself as you?"

"I dunno. They're *your* loins," said Everly dismissively.

"Get on your knees right now!" ordered Fenneth.

"Woo-hoo! *Now* we're talking!" Everly said eagerly.

"It's so I can bind your *hands,*" Fenneth said after furiously blushing again.

"God *DAMN*, who knew church girls went this hard?" said Everly appreciatively.

"Raaagh!" Fenneth growled in frustration. "*Dios me salve! Esta chica es demasiado salvaje.*"

"Blah, blah, blah," replied Everly. "*Deja de luchar y bésame, estúpida.*"

"*Chinga tu madre, pendeja! No soy estúpida!*" shouted the incensed Fenneth.

When they realized what they'd both done, they stared at each other, stunned.

"*¿Tú hablas español?*" asked Fenneth slowly.

"*Soy mala en eso,*" Everly replied, just as slowly.

"Yeah, your pronunciation really sucks," agreed Fenneth.

"I only learned enough to be annoying to strangers," Everly admitted.

"You really are a bitch, aren't you?" Fenneth asked her.

"It's been suggested before." Everly shrugged.

Then they freaked out.

"Oh, my god. OH, MY GOD!" Fenneth shrieked. "Are you fucking with me right now? Am I having a stroke?!"

"You?! What about *me*?!" Everly screamed. She began jumping up and down excitedly and grabbed Fenneth by her hands. "Where are you from?" she demanded to know.

"I—I was raised in the temple with my sister," Fenneth said.

"No, dummy, where are you *from*?" Everly repeated.

"Oh! OH! Uh, my dad was from Pittsburgh and my mom was from Rosorito!"

"I have *no* idea where that is!" said Everly gleefully.

"Of course you wouldn't, you privileged little snot!" Fenneth said cheerfully.

"I was from Brookville!" Everly told her.

Fenneth paused. "New York?" she asked her.

"Duh, where else?"

"No freaking way," Fenneth said. "*No freaking way.*"

"What? What is it?" Everly asked her.

"That's where *I* lived too. My dad got a new job and transferred there. What school did you go to?"

"Saint Julian's of the Holy Grace," Everly replied. "Heh, it's funny. Saint Julian was the patron saint of—"

"Murderers," Fenneth concluded for her. "Holy *shit*."

Now Everly's eyes began to widen. "Noooooooooo way . . . "

"I was a transfer student. It was only my second day there," Fenneth said. "I was late because I was getting blazed behind my dad's garage, and then the *wildest* thing happened . . . "

"That's why we never hooked up," Everly said in wonder. "We had never even met before! God, I used to *dream* about those eyes," she said as she stroked Fenneth's cheek.

Fenneth quickly grabbed Everly's hands and pulled her close. "What's your name?" she asked quietly.

"Everly."

"Everly, can I ask you a question?"

"Sure. Yeah, anything," Everly replied.

"Everly . . . were you on the student council?"

"Yeah. Yeah, I was."

"What . . . was your position?"

"I was the treasurer."

"Oh." Fenneth nodded. "Oh, I see. Yeah, that makes sense," she said to herself.

"Why's that?" Everly asked, when suddenly Fenneth's haymaker came whistling in at what felt like a million miles an hour and connected forcefully with her jaw, sending Everly spinning ungracefully around like an unbalanced dreidel before she landed on her rump.

"Ow! Fenneth, what the fuck—" she whined when Fenneth's boot caught her in the face.

"YOU CRAZY FUCKING, BITCH!" Fenneth screamed as she kicked at Everly over and over again. "*Maldita perra loca!* What did I *ever* do to you? YOU! RUINED! MY! LIFE!"

"Knock it off!" Everly screamed. "Come on, stop!"

This was so weird! Everly *knew* she had a field of *harada* surrounding herself. She could also *feel* Titania's power within her. Fenneth's kicks should have been as inconsequential to her as a gentle spring breeze.

And yet, for some reason, they *hurt*. They hurt *a lot*. And if she took too many more of them, she was going to be seriously injured.

Fenneth was *strong*.

"I SAID STOP!" Everly roared as she caught Fenneth's foot in midstrike and swept the other one from beneath her. She then mounted Fenneth at her waist and used her leverage to pin her arms down, leaving them staring at each other with their faces only inches apart.

"What is your *problem*?" Everly angrily demanded.

"*Puta!* I swear I'm going to kill you!" Fenneth growled at her.

"Hey, honeysuckle, if memory serves, then didn't you *already* get to do that?" Everly laughed at her. "If anything, wouldn't you say it's *my* turn?"

"You don't even know what you did, do you?" Fenneth seethed.

"Don't know or don't care? Take your pick, gorgeous."

"You got me killed!" Fenneth yelled before suddenly headbutting Everly.

While Everly was stunned by the surprise attack, Fenneth shifted her weight beneath her and rolled to her side, reversing Everly's pin. Now it was Everly who was trapped beneath *her*.

"You got me killed and stole me from everything I ever knew and everyone I ever loved!" Fenneth yelled at her. "You got me trapped in this weird-ass world where the music sucks, the food sucks, and everyone's either a grimdark psycho or a self-serving bastard! I hate this place! *I hate you!*"

"Naaah, *you like me*," Everly smirked at her.

Fenneth stared at her. She stared at her for a long, long moment . . . and then she let her go.

Then she sat on the ground, huddled to her knees, and said, "No, I don't. You're horrible. You're just too selfish."

Everly lay there and considered the other girl's words for a moment. Then she sat up beside her and wrapped an arm around her shoulders.

"Yeah," she agreed. "You're right. But I told you I was, remember?"

"You did," Fenneth admitted. "But you're still horrible."

"You'll get used to it. I'm irresistible," Everly assured her.

"No, you're not." Fenneth snorted.

But she didn't resist when Everly leaned in and kissed her.

It was a quiet moment they shared.

Sarah had *no* idea what was going on.

CHAPTER FORTY-ONE

Two Conversations About Death

Hmm," Everly said to herself after their kiss ended.

"Hmm?" asked Fenneth. "What do you mean by that?"

"Oh, nothing. Nothing. It just felt a little . . . unpracticed."

"Excuse me?"

"Well, there wasn't a lot of technique behind it," Everly said. "It was good! It was good! Honestly. You're like a talented ingenue. There's *potential* there. I'm sure you'll grow into it; I shouldn't even worry about it."

"Okay, sure." Fenneth frowned. "Or maybe the problem is that you're a little *too* practiced?"

"Oh? Go on," said Everly.

"No need; I think I made my point," Fenneth said.

"Are you slut shaming me right now?" mused Everly. "Because I have to admit, if that's what's happening, I'm really into it. Do it some more."

"Gross. No," Fenneth said as she stood up and stepped away from Everly.

"Oooh! Now you're *kink* shaming me. Damn, you're more fun than I thought," Everly purred.

"You get entirely too much pleasure out of being yourself." Fenneth sniffed.

"Fenn! Keep being mean to me! *Pleeease?*" moaned Everly.

"Don't call me *Fenn*! I hate that nickname," said Fenneth.

"Too late! You're Fenn now!" gloated Everly. "See?"

"Damn it!" cursed Fenn. "How did you do that?"

"I'm the main character. I have privileges," said Everly with an unbearable level of smugness. "Oh, well. I guess if we're done making out, I can get back to killing your asshole cousin."

"I'd prefer you not do that," Fenn said.

"Yeeeah, a lot of people I kill probably think stuff like that," Everly said indifferently.

"Have you really killed a lot of people?" Fenn asked her.

"Haven't you? Aren't you, like, god's favorite little ninja?" replied Everly.

"This is actually my first battle," Fenn admitted. "I was trained as a healer before."

"That's cool," said Everly, who didn't understand why anyone would ever want to willingly become a healer. "Well, just think of it as reverse-healing some-one. I've reverse-healed loads of people. It's fun."

"It's demented," Fenn scoffed.

"And fun too," repeated Everly.

"Haven't you ever felt the weight of a life in your hand before?" Fenn asked her.

"I sure have," Everly said.

"What did it make you feel like?"

"God."

"Jesus Christ!" Fenn exclaimed.

"No, god," Everly corrected her.

"Blondie, you might actually be fucked in the head," Fenn said with some concern.

"In the throat once, in a bathroom stall."

"Huh?"

"Nothing."

"Gross."

"It was a *joke*." Everly snickered. "Are all holy maidens of the sword so uptight? You didn't seem like this before."

"Yeah, because we knew each other *so well* for the three minutes we had before we died."

"How *did* you die, anyway?" Everly asked out of curiosity.

"Poorly," Fenn replied.

And that was all she would say on the matter.

"I still have to kill Sarah, though," Everly said.

"Why? Why is it so important to you that she die?"

"The math demands it!" Everly said.

"What?" Fenn said it flatly.

"An excellent question!"

"Will you *answer it*?" Fenn said in exasperation.

"Fine!" said Everly with enthusiasm. She then began gesturing wildly as she spoke.

"You see, Fenn, the problem with sparing Sarah is that I'm only two-thirds complete with her punishment. For the sake of mathematical clarity, I obviously have to kill her. It's not just because I'll enjoy doing it. It's for the *math*."

"I think you need to explain," Fenn said in a skeptical tone.

"Well," Everly began. "Have you ever heard that phrase 'bad things come in threes'?"

"I have."

"Good! Then you already understand. I'm a bad thing! But since there's only one of me, I'm required to commit three bad acts. For Sarah, first I broke her mentally when she realized she couldn't beat me. *Then* I broke her physically when she stopped resisting. And *now* I'm going to break her *permanently* by killing her. One-third times three equals three. As you can see, my argument is perfectly sound."

"Everly?"

"Yes, Fenn?"

"One-third times three equals *one*."

Everly froze as though she was paralyzed with shock. Then she turned to face Fenn and vigorously shook her head. "Nah, that can't possibly be true. One-third of three is *one-third*. What have they been teaching you in that temple?"

"Uh, apparently they've been teaching me *math*," Fenn replied. "One third of three is one. One plus one plus one, yes?"

"Huh?" Everly said as she stared at her fingers. "That can't be right! If that's true, then what have I been doing all this time?"

"Clearly, you've been following the algebra of insanity," Fenn concluded.

"No!"

"Definitely."

"Really?"

"I'm afraid so."

"Well, shoot," Everly said. "Clearly, this contradicts my vision of myself as an unparalleled genius. And now that Sarah has witnessed how stupid I *actually* am, that's really just more motivation for me to kill her. Death silences all whispers."

"Does that mean you're going to kill me too?" Fenn asked her. "I mean, now I know how stupid you are as well."

"Nah, we're smooch buddies," Everly said with a flip of her hair. "It'd be rude to snuff out someone who's been tonguing it with me."

"In that case, I forbid you from killing Sarah," Fenn said decisively.

Everly smirked. "Hey, babe. I'm a wild stallion, okay? I don't take orders from ponies."

"You're actually a *mare*," Fenn corrected her. "Stallions are male, you dork."

"So even biology *dares* to oppose me," Everly muttered darkly.

"That would appear to be the case," Fenn said apologetically.

"Well, that hurts my feelings!" Everly declared.

"Should that matter?"

"It should! My feelings are awesome!"

"Your self-confidence is terrifying," Fenn said. "The belief that you can do anything is self-destructive. Everyone has limits, Everly."

"That's like the opposite of everything they ever taught us in school." Everly smirked. "Ever since kindergarten, they told me I could do whatever I wanted and become whatever I wished if I only tried hard enough and believed in myself. As the resident god-cop superhero, shouldn't you be encouraging my dreams?"

"What do your dreams entail?" asked Fenn.

"World conquest, self-deification, and destroying anyone who annoys me," Everly answered promptly.

"Yeah, that's a hard no from me," Fenn replied.

"Oh, don't be like that," Everly said. "Being a villain is great! It's like eating ice cream every day without getting cavities. You'd like it!"

"I doubt it."

Everly stepped closer to Fenn and put a hand around her waist. Then Everly began gently guiding her around the field in a pseudo-tango as they continued to speak.

"Don't knock it until you try it, Fenn," Everly said.

"Why would I ever deliberately want to be a bad person?" Fenn asked her.

"Because being good often demands sacrifice," Everly said. "Being bad only requires you to sacrifice someone else."

"So, instead of preserving lives, you think it's better to just take them wholesale?"

"It's easier, and it's more fun. Plus, there's the absolute and inescapable fact that some people simply *have it coming*. Like Sarah! She tried to kill you, silly! And she seemed to be well practiced at it. Ask me honestly and say you would have been her first victim."

"Of course I wouldn't have been," Fenn replied. "But there was never any proof before. Her men always lied to cover for her, and the council wouldn't deign to hear any accusations without evidence. But now *I* can give personal testimony, and she can finally be punished."

"Or we could just skip the preamble and punish her right now," Everly said as she dipped Fenn down and then pulled her back into her arms.

"That's vengeance, not justice," said Fenn.

"Nah, it's just murder. I don't take extra steps."

"All the more reason that someone *should*."

"Babe, she's rich, she's famous, and she's a Godwell. Do you think your big, perfect family will let themselves be humiliated by letting one of their own be put on trial?"

"I wouldn't let them interfere," Fenn said with determination.

"God, do I want to kiss you again or slap the stupidity out of you?" Everly wondered.

"Shut up!" Fenn snapped. "Where'd you learn how to dance like this, anyway?"

"I have perfect muscular control and an eidetic memory," Everly bragged. "I can copy any dance technique I've ever seen. I'm kind of like the Taskmaster in that regard."

"Who?" Fenn asked.

"*The Taskmaster*," Everly repeated. "The infamous Marvel Comics mercenary who can duplicate any physical feat that he witnesses, from Daredevil's acrobatics to Captain America's skill with a shield. The only feats he can't copy are those that are beyond an ordinary human's capabilities, like Spider-Man's agility or the Hulk's strength."

"So the only people he can copy are the ones who can't really do anything interesting beyond hopping around and throwing stuff?"

"Yeeeeeah," Everly said reluctantly.

"Taskmaster kind of sounds like he sucks, Blondie."

"He does not! He dresses like a pirate!"

"Pirates aren't cool anymore."

"God, it's like I hardly even know you!"

"We don't know each other at all!" Fenn said with annoyance.

Everly kissed her again.

Fenn enjoyed it, but Everly's personality still irritated her. "Hey, enough already," she said as she pushed the other girl away.

"What did I do wrong?" Everly asked with a wounded expression on her face. "Shakespeare himself wrote, 'A kiss taken is sweeter than one given.'"

"Yeah, well, Shakespeare would have gotten his ass knocked out where I grew up," Fenn said. "All joking aside, I'm taking Sarah in. That's the end of the discussion."

"Oh, yeah?" Everly sneered. "And how are you going to stop me, Altar Girl? The kisses *were* sweet, but I'm starting to feel stifled."

"Are you really?"

"I sure am." Everly nodded. "I don't think I'm ready for a relationship right now. Skynyrd sang it best: Everly's a *free bird*."

"So, are you going to kill me to get to her?" Fenn asked.

"You don't think I will?"

"I don't."

"Why? Because you're *so* interesting?" Everly asked mockingly.

"I think I am," Fenn said with confidence.

Everly considered her words for a moment. Then she reluctantly conceded. "Ugh, you might have a point. Can I really wipe out the only other living soul in this world who knows how good a McGriddle tastes?"

"I think it would haunt you," Fenn said.

"Damn right, it would," Everly agreed. "Fine! Keep your stupid cousin, then. She's going to try to kill you again later, though. Crazy people don't learn."

"Well, I'll have to be sure to kick her ass instead," Fenn replied.

"You *do* hit pretty hard," Everly said.

"I'm a *very* mighty warrior," Fenn said humbly.

"How'd she get the drop on you?"

Fenn said nothing.

"Hey, *come on*," Everly said. "How'd she sneak up on you? We're friends here; don't be embarrassed."

"I killed a big demon when they rushed out of the town gate," Fenn said with some reluctance.

"Cool, cool, go on," coaxed Everly.

"It was the first time I ever killed anything personally, though. So, ugh, its blood got in my eyes, and when I was trying to wipe them clean, Sarah hit me from behind."

"Oh, wow," Everly said. Then she began to snicker.

"It's not funny," Fenn said.

"Yeah, no, it's actually *very* funny." Everly giggled.

"No, it isn't!" Fenn insisted. "She was going to kill me!"

"Oh, *now* you're upset about that?" Everly laughed.

"Okay, wow, you are *definitely* a smug bitch, Blondie," Fenn said with a glower.

"You *love* it."

"You *wish*."

"Fenneth! Lady Fenneth!" a man cried out. Everly and Fenn looked away from each other to see a young knight a few years older than they were, surrounded by dozens of guards, swiftly approaching them.

Everly was about to dismiss them as irrelevant when she recognized the stylized *B* embroidered on the cloaks the soldiers wore. The symbol was that of Count Van Belsar, the ruler of Belsar County.

Her father.

A mischievous smirk slowly grew on her face when it dawned on Everly who the young knight in command must be. "Well, holy *shit*," she said with a giddy anticipation that had been percolating away within her ever since she'd been an infant.

This had to be Aiden. Her idiotic older brother.

He'd grown handsome and strong, and he didn't look bad in the fancy-looking armor he was adorned with. But beneath the superficial veneer of disciplined professionalism he exuded, she smelled *weakness*.

Aiden was bigger, stronger, and more experienced. But he was still the same loser he'd been as a little boy. Everly could *feel it* just by looking at him.

And who was that now walking beside him? A little older, a little wrinklier, but still the same imposing, stone-faced bastard he'd been in her infancy. That stuck-up house knight who'd threatened Lyona into silence on the night Aiden had tried to kill Everly.

Casten Meers.

Well, what do you know? Everly thought gleefully. *Krampus has come early this season.*

Just outside the gates of Bremburg, Laurel slowly came to.

Her sore body ached mightily where the stampeding demons had run her down, crushing her beneath their weight. She could only remember walking toward Kent and his friends when a sudden surge of inhuman bodies flooded onto the field.

She'd tried to fight back, but she'd been so surprised by their sudden appearance that she hadn't drawn her sword in time. Before she could react, they were on her, stomping, punching, kicking, and preparing to tear her apart.

How was she still alive?

Suddenly, a scabbard appeared before her. She immediately recognized it as her own.

Reacting instinctively, Laurel unsheathed her weapon and leaped to her feet. She wouldn't be taken by surprise this time!

"Easy, warrior," a deep voice said to her. "There's a lull in the fighting. You're safe for now. I personally rescued you. But do not offer me thanks."

Turning toward the voice, Laurel was shocked to see a massive nightmarish figure in red-and-black armor, topped with a horned helmet, standing before her. She'd never seen anything like him before and was instantly wary of the massive axe he held.

"What are you?" Laurel demanded of him, "Man? Demon? Or something else entirely?"

"I don't truly know myself," the red knight answered. "I give it no thought. I exist. I have a *purpose*. That is enough."

"And what *is* your purpose?"

"I serve the future master of this world," he said. "All shall kneel before her or die."

"Is that a fact?" Laurel said. "Well, I may have something to say about that!"

"I certainly hope that you do," replied the knight. "It would bring me considerable pleasure to cleave your head in twain and leave your body to rot beneath the sun."

"Many have tried, monster," Laurel said without fear.

"I know. I was one of them."

"Take off your helmet."

The giant figure began to diminish in size, shrinking until he stood barely taller than her. The steel surrounding his head retracted and moved away from his head until the handsome bearded face of a black-haired man with gray eyes looked at her.

His features were striking, but she didn't recognize him.

"Where do you know me from?" she asked him.

"The war. Where else?" he replied.

Ah. The civil war, then. That made sense. The temple had supported King Septus during that awful conflict and had dispatched her to aid in his victory. She'd killed many rebellious citizens of Winstead during the three years she served in that bloody conflict. She'd also made many implacable enemies.

This man appeared to be one of them.

"The war feels like a lifetime ago," she said to him. "I was a girl back then. Why do you still bear hatred for me?"

"It didn't become hatred until recently," the red knight said. "Not until I learned that you abandoned your role as the maiden of the holy sword. Before then, I resented you, but I still *respected* you. You weren't just a soldier; you were a warrior of the faith who believed her acts were in accordance with the wishes of her gods."

A frown began creasing his brow, and an edge of bitterness slowly crept into his voice as he continued to speak. "You killed so many good men, Laurel Godwell. Proud warriors who fought for the king they believed in and for the good of the realm. Conner would have been a fair ruler. His reign would have brought stability and peace to the land, as well as prosperity to its people."

"That wasn't my concern," Laurel said harshly. "King Septus was the older brother, and Prince Connor was an apostate who tried to open Winstead to the Eastern Temple and its heresy."

"That is a lie spread by Septus and his minions," the knight said angrily.

"Believe what you want; it's the truth! The temple council showed me the evidence. Furthermore, Conner could have surrendered at any time and ended the war. He *chose* to fight. Any lives I was forced to take were due to his selfishness!"

"So you were just following orders, like a good, obedient doll," he said mockingly.

"An honorable warrior obeys their leaders. If you don't understand that much, then you had no business fighting in the first place," Laurel said.

"Yes, yes, you're right. An honorable warrior *does* obey their leaders," the knight said. "At least until their orders become inconvenient. Isn't that right, Laurel?"

"What are you talking about?" she asked him.

"You *left* the temple to be with your lover. Isn't that so?" the red knight asked her. "You, the fierce, unrelenting Laurel who ended hundreds of lives because your leaders commanded it, decided on a whim to disobey them and live with some thieving simpleton, because when your orders got in the way of *your interests* . . . they really began to chafe, didn't they?"

"No," Laurel said in denial. "No, it wasn't like that."

"That's *exactly* what it was like," the red knight said. "I could accept that you killed my friends and fellow believers in freedom because you believed you were doing the right thing. But upon learning that your resolve was so *weak* that it could be shaken loose by a childish infatuation, I could hold back my hatred no longer!"

He pointed an accusing finger at her as he continued.

"*Why* did my friends have to die? Why did my king have to die? Why did his son have to suffer? You didn't have to fight at all, Laurel, if your beliefs were so flimsy! So many lives could have been spared, and the destiny of this kingdom would have been changed for the better! But you *did* fight for a cause you didn't believe in, and then you *spurned* that cause for a new life with your precious new lover! And for that, I can never forgive you! Because of you, *MY FRIENDS DIED FOR NOTHING!*"

The red knight's eyes blazed with hellish light as he yelled, and his grip on his axe tightened. For a moment, it appeared there would be violence between the two of them, but before it could occur, he calmed himself and regained his composure.

"What do you want from me?" Laurel asked him.

"I want you to feel as I felt for so many years. Broken. Despondent. Bereft of hope. I want you to suffer for your sins, Laurel Godwell. And then I want you to die," he told her.

"We can settle this here and now, monster," she said.

"No. Not yet," he replied. "My master may have some future use for you. Until then, I'll simply settle for the sight of your face when I tell you the awful news."

"What awful news?" she asked.

"Your lover, the thief, is dead. A monster attacked him, and his friends failed to save him."

"No . . . " Laurel whispered. "No, you're lying. You're lying!"

"To you? Never." The knight laughed. "Unlike you, I maintain my honor. No, your lover *is* dead. He was *eaten alive*. I observed it with my own eyes. And Laurel? He died whispering your name."

A long moment of silence passed between them.

"Could you have saved him?" she asked.

"Yes," he answered cruelly.

"Why didn't you?"

"For this very moment."

"RAAAAGH!" she screamed as her sword slashed through his neck, sending it falling to the ground.

The deed was done, and she then collapsed to her knees and wept.

Then a voice interrupted her.

"Silly woman," said the jeering head of the red knight. "I can never die by the blade of a mortal. I'm no longer a mere creature of the flesh."

"Noooooo!" Laurel screamed. "NO, NO, NO!"

"Oh, yes." He laughed. "I return now to my master's tower, far from where you can reach me. On the day we next meet, your life will end. Look forward to it!"

The red knight continued to laugh at Laurel's screams of fury as his body dissolved into the soil. Soon, he was gone, and the sound of his mockery faded into the wind, leaving Laurel by herself.

"I'll find you," she vowed. "I swear I'll find you! You and your master both! I WILL HAVE JUSTICE!" she screamed. "*I will have justice!*"

Then, once her anger began to fade, grief replaced it.

"Kent," she whispered. "*Kent . . .* "

Then she left to look for her lover's body.

"Grail?" Everly asked. "I just felt something. Did you return to the tower?"

Yes, Your Majesty, he replied in a deeply satisfied voice.

"What's got you feeling so pleased?" she asked him.

Nothing, Everly. It's a small matter.

"Well, if you say so. Is the mastermind still in town?"

I believe so. He appears to be awaiting your challenge.

"Oh, he wants a one-on-one, does he?" Everly asked eagerly. "Well, if that's the case, then let's *go!*"

"Who are you speaking with?" asked Sir Aiden in bewilderment.

"Nonya," Everly promptly replied.

"What?" he asked. "Who is that? Is she a spirit user?"

"Uncle, no. Don't," Fenn cut in. "She's mocking you."

"What?" Aiden sputtered. "How *dare* she!"

For her part, Everly stared at Fenn in surprise.

"Hey, did you just say he was your *uncle?*" she asked.

CHAPTER FORTY-TWO

Kneel

Yes?" Fenn replied. "Through our mothers. Well, his mother is my grandmother. Why?"

Everly blinked at that description.

"His mother is your grandmother?" she asked in a mild tone of voice.

"Yeah, it's complicated," Fenn said dismissively. "She's youthful."

"She's *youthful?*" Everly asked incredulously. "Fenny, there's—"

"*Bzzzzz,*" Fenn said as she held up her palm while making a buzzing noise. "Nope, nuh-uh, incorrect, stop. I'll let you have Fenn, but that's where it ends. No Fenny."

"Aww, but *Fenny* sounds cute," protested Everly.

"I've made my ruling," Fenn said firmly. "Fenny dies here and now."

"*Fine,*" Everly said with a roll of her eyes before correcting her sentence. "She's *youthful?* There's being a young mother, and then there's getting knocked up while watching Nicktoons. What's up with that?"

"I told you, she's *youthful.* We don't discuss it."

"Sounds freaky," Everly said.

"It's not!" Fenn protested. "Anne's less like a grandmother and more like a cool big sister. I admire her a lot. I wish Sarah would take after her more."

"She's her granddaughter too?" Everly asked.

"Yep. She shares a lot of her gifts, but not an ounce of her self-control."

"Oh, now that you mention it, I do see a similarity in personality between Wesley and Sarah," Everly mused.

"Everly, my uncle's name is *Aiden,*" Fenn said.

"Yeah, but doesn't he look more like Wesley? Look at that dour little chin! That's the chin of a Wesley, if ever I saw one. I always thought so, anyway."

"I beg your pardon?" Wesley asked angrily.

"Everly!" Fenn snapped. "Knock it off."

"Fine," Everly sighed. "Killjoy."

"I beg your pardon?" Aiden asked angrily.

Now it was Fenn's turn to wear a puzzled look. "Have you met my uncle before?"

"Oh, way back in the day, when we were kids," Everly said with a wave of her hand. "*Way*, way back. But, hey, look at him now! Look at you, Eric—"

"*Aiden*," he corrected her stiffly.

"*Aiden*," she said without skipping a beat. "You look so handsome and grown! Oh, you're just like Mama's little man, aren't you, buddy? Come here!"

Before Aiden could move, Everly had her arm around him in a headlock and began roughly tousling his hair.

"What are you doing?" Aiden said in alarm. "Unhand me at once! Stop this! Sir Casten! Sir Casten, help!"

"Release my lord at once, girl," Casten said immediately. "Your familiarity is unwarranted and deeply offensive. This man is the heir to Belsar County and is of the Godwell lineage. You will end this behavior *now*."

"Hey, I'm just playing with him!" Everly protested. "This little chode and I *have history*. I remember you too, Duckworth. Still playing babysitter, huh? Is that a mark of confidence in your abilities or a subtle way of keeping you away from anything of importance?"

Sir Casten froze in place. Terrible anger flooded throughout him, directed at this mocking girl's words. He could barely articulate which he took more offense at: her referring to his lord as a *chode* or her cruel but accurate assessment of the role assigned to him by the countess.

A desire to teach this brat a lesson now sparked inside him. The girl grinned merrily at him, as though she knew the effect her words had but didn't care in the slightest.

The arrogant little *bitch*.

"Hey, Andy. I've got a question," Everly said to Aiden. She lowered her head so he could more easily hear her. "If Fenn and Sarah are your mom's granddaughters, and you're only a few years older . . . I mean, jeez, your mom's had at least three kids, yeah? I bet there's more, though. So now I'm wondering: What did her first husband die from? Old age or exhaustion?"

"What?" Aiden sputtered. "What did you just say to me?"

"How's *your* dad doing, by the way? With a wife like that, I bet he has a limp. Hey, does he wear any clothes, or does he just walk around naked, carrying a saddle on his front for her convenience?"

"Stop impugning my mother!" Aiden shouted.

"I wonder what her difficulty setting is," Everly mused. "Well, with all those kids, it's probably *easy*, am I right?"

"Hey, that's uncalled for, Everly," said Fenn in annoyance; she lightly pushed the other girl back to free her uncle from her grip.

"I'm not being disrespectful!" Everly said. "It's a compliment! This Anne person must be cooler than an icebox. Huh, Andy?"

"What? Why an icebox?" asked Aiden.

"Because that's where all the meat goes."

"God damn it, Everly," Fenn groaned as the soldiers surrounding them immediately drew their swords.

"MEN! Seize this wretch at once!" Aiden bellowed.

"Wait, my lord. One moment," Sir Casten said. "Lady Fenneth, did you say this girl's name was Everly?" he asked.

"Yes," Fenn replied. "She's a, um, wandering adventurer who provided me some assistance today with an important matter."

"'*Some assistance*'? Is that all we meant to each other?" Everly asked her while making a wounded expression. "That's awful! Has anyone ever told you what a cold fish you can be sometimes?"

"What could she have possibly assisted you with?" Aiden demanded. "More importantly, why aren't you over there?" he asked, pointing toward the gates of Bremburg. "Both of you should be fighting! You're making the Godwells look incompetent!"

"Well, in Fenn's defense, this psychotic paladin bunny *was* trying to give her a perma-ouchie while she was trying to do her job, Andy," Everly said. "But hey, now that you've brought up the fight, why aren't *you* guys participating? I didn't see anyone flying Van Belsar colors on the field. Pretty suspicious if you ask me."

"I wasn't asking *your* opinion, you commoner slattern!" Aiden yelled.

"Wooo, that's dirty talk. You said a dirty word." Everly giggled.

"Do I have to teach this preening sow some manners myself?" Aiden said angrily.

"Well, you don't, but I'd *really* like you to try," Everly said smugly.

"Lady Fenneth, is it true that Lady Sarah assaulted you?" asked Sir Casten.

"I'm afraid so," Everly said.

"I was *asking* Lady Fenneth," Sir Casten said coldly.

"I know, but I was feeling left out," Everly said.

"Would you *please* remain silent?"

"Would that please you?"

"Greatly."

"Pass."

Sir Casten approached Everly and looked down at her, looming in a threatening manner over the much smaller teenager with his hand held just above his scabbard.

The threat implied was obvious to all.

"Wow, you're *tall*!" Everly said admiringly.

Well, it was obvious to *most* of them, anyway.

"Lady Fenneth said your name was Everly. What's your full name, girl?" asked Sir Casten quietly.

"I ain't got one," she replied.

"Is that right?"

"Yeah. Because my mom didn't raise a *fool*. Get it?" She smirked.

"You don't seem to understand the situation you're in, child," Sir Casten said menacingly. "You've forced your lips on a daughter of the Godwell family."

"You were *watching* that? Dirty, dirty, *dirty*!" Everly blushed. "Did you like what you saw? I bet *Aiden* did. Oh, he's putting out some *vibes*. I'd better not get my hand stuck in a sink around him!"

"You've also manhandled my lord, and if I'm hearing this correctly, you assaulted Lady Sarah!" Sir Casten continued icily. He then drew his sword and pointed it at Everly. "Worst of all, you've slandered the name of Countess Anne. Are you too *stupid* to understand the consequences of your behavior?"

"A dead retainer says what?" replied Everly.

"Huh?" asked Sir Casten.

"No, *what*," repeated Everly patiently.

"What?" he asked.

"*There* we go," Everly said happily.

Then she slapped Sir Casten across the face, delivering the blow with such force that his neck broke from the strain, leaving his head bent at a hideous angle.

"Lyona says hello, dickhead," Everly said to the newly made corpse. "Uh, but she's not the one who called you a dickhead. *That* was all me. You heard that, right? Wait, you didn't? Oh, you're dead now. Well, that's fine too."

"Everly!" shouted Fenn in anger. "What the hell have you *done*!?"

"Assassin! *Assassin!*" shrieked Aiden. "Protect me! Cut her down!"

"I didn't do anything illegal," Everly calmly said to Fenn. "I just disciplined a rogue retainer. Can you believe the nerve of that man? Waving around his sword and threatening his lord's daughter? What a loose cannon! Thank goodness I was around to set him straight."

She paused and reconsidered her words. "Er, or make him crooked? His neck? Oh! Do-over! Do-over! Thank goodness I was around to *snap him out of it*. Huh? Huh?" she said as she nudged Fenn's side. "Because I snapped his neck?"

One of Aiden's knights rushed at her from behind. Everly calmly stepped to the side, easily avoiding him, then seized him by the back of his neck and brutally slammed him to the ground with such impact that his head spattered against it, crushed like ripe fruit.

"Uh-oh!" she said. "It looks like we had another rogue on the payroll. What is Daddy *thinking?*"

"EVERLY!" Fenn shouted. She rushed at the other girl in an attempt to tackle her to the ground. Everly, however, had learned her lesson earlier about how potentially dangerous Fenn could be. Instead of directly engaging her, she conjured a stone wall from the earth to impede her. Then she summoned three more and slammed them all together around Fenn into a tight binding enclosure that left only her head exposed, with no room for her body to move.

"You are *precious*, babe," Everly said fondly to the other girl. She reached out her hand and scratched Fenn affectionately under her chin. "I'm going to need you to stay out of this, though. It's got nothing to do with you."

"That was Anne's personal knight!" Fenn yelled. "Do you have any idea what you've done?"

"Well, he may have been her personal knight, but between him and me, it was also pretty *personal*," Everly said indifferently. "Sorry, but he threatened my mom. I make a list when people do that. Then I cross it off."

"You killed him over a mere threat?" Fenn said in astonishment.

"*Babe*, I kill when there's not enough chocolate in the cupboard," Everly said. "I really feel as though you haven't been listening to me when I speak. It's got me worried about our future. I mean, you're *so* pretty, but you're *so* stupid. Are you really meant for a job like yours when there's someone like me running loose in the world?"

"Everly, stop! For god's sake, you can't behave like this!" said Fenn.

"Can, will, did, *doing*," Everly corrected her. "Oh, speaking of which, I seem to recall *this* little shit once urging Sir Casten to cut me and my mother down. Wasn't that how you put it, Andy? You even called me a *bastard* when you said it. *That's such a mean word*, bro. It really tore at my heart. Is it cool if I tear at yours too?"

Everly took a single step toward Aiden.

"Stop her! Stop her, I said!" he cried.

"Put away your swords, or *you're all dead!*" Everly suddenly yelled, all traces of humor gone from her face and voice. "My name is Everly Vel Belsar, daughter of the lord you've sworn yourselves to! Pointing a weapon at me is a betrayal of your oaths! Kneel before me and apologize!"

The knights stood there, confused and unsure of how to react. Everly gave them no time to rally themselves.

"I SAID KNEEL!" she commanded. With Eris filling her words with power, Everly's command was impossible for them to resist. As one, they dropped to their knees.

"*My lady!*" they all shouted as one. "*Please forgive us!*"

"That's *so* much better," Everly purred with satisfaction. "Now, what was I doing before? Oh! I was admonishing my dear older brother for his rudeness. Poor, poor Andy. Why are you so afraid? It's *me*, your adorable little sister!"

Everly walked to her cowering brother and gently helped him to his feet. "Brother, Brother, Brother *dear*. Now *this* is what they mean when they speak of delayed gratification! I've let you linger on the periphery of my mind for so long, knowing I'd eventually get back to you when it was convenient for me. And look! It's *so* convenient right now! That's some real kismet right there, wouldn't you agree?"

"Everly?" Aiden whimpered. "You're that bastard Everly?"

"Big *brooo*," Everly said chidingly. Then she grabbed his chin and began squeezing it so tightly that his teeth loosened in his jaw. "What have we *said* about that word?"

"Everly! Everly, stop!" Fenneth said desperately. "Everly, please don't do this. He's my uncle! He's your brother!"

Everly smiled sweetly at Fenn's pointless little words.

"He *was* my brother," Everly said. "*Now*, he's about to become a finger painting."

"Everly, if you care about me at all, you'll stop this RIGHT NOW!" Fenneth shouted.

"Okay," Everly said mildly.

Then she began squeezing Aiden's face even harder.

"*Glllllllllllrhghgh*," Aiden moaned in agony as his teeth popped free one after the other, leaving cracked and bloody nubs of calcium to fall from his mouth on a stream of bright red saliva.

"EVERLY!" Fenn screamed.

"That's my name; don't wear it out."

Everly smiled as Aiden's jaw began to powder beneath her grip.

Suddenly, a massive pillar of unnatural green light shot upward from the center of Bremburg, which then formed strange black clouds that darkened the noon sky.

"Ohhh, something marginally more interesting has begun to occur," Everly said with delight. Then she tossed Aiden to the ground, having lost interest in him. "Oh, that's right. I was going to go fight the demon boss. Heh, look at me getting lost in nostalgia. I'm a silly thing, aren't I, Fenn?"

"You're a *monster!*" Fenneth said it with intense loathing. "How could you do that to your own family?"

"It's easy," replied Everly. "All you have to do is grab his chin and squeeze. You want me to give another demonstration?"

She reached a hand toward the wounded Aiden, who immediately squealed and tried to backpedal away before slipping onto his backside and weeping in pain and misery.

"Leave him alone!" Fenneth screamed.

Everly's hands trembled. She had to clench them tightly into fists to keep from grabbing Fenn's head and doing something messy and fun.

Fenn was so resolute.

So unyielding in her principles.

So unwilling to back down before a superior opponent.

So *helpless* to do anything to stop her . . .

"Oh, man." Everly blushed as she looked at her and shivered. "You're too much, Fenn. You *really* are. But maybe you should slow down before I do something crazy, okay?"

"You're going to pay for this, Everly. I swear you will," Fenneth vowed.

"Pay for what?" Everly wondered. "Fenn, these knights are *mine* now. Aren't you, boys?"

"*Yes, my lady!*" they all said at once.

"See?" Everly continued. "They'll echo anything I say. And I say executing a couple of traitors who took a swing at me was a righteous and legal action. And anyone who's ever met Andy will believe them when they say that he was a clumsy fool who broke his own face tripping over his silly feet. Now play nicely, and I'll let you keep Sarah. Keep threatening me, and I'll only let you keep her *head*. Okay?"

Fenneth said nothing in reply. But she did continue to glare angrily at Everly.

Everly smirked and snapped her fingers. Fenn's prison broke away, surprising her and causing her to tumble to the ground.

"Silence is complicity, sweetie. That makes us partners. Don't forget!" Everly said as she offered a helping hand to her.

Fenneth slapped Everly's hand away and stood on her own. "To hell with you," she said as she carefully helped Aiden to his feet. "Does he have a horse?" she asked one of the kneeling knights.

The knight ignored her and said nothing.

"It's all right; you can answer her," Everly said to him.

"He and Sir Casten came by coach," the knight said blankly.

"Go retrieve it for her," Everly ordered him. "She, Sarah, and Andy can scurry away to Belsar County in comfort. The rest of us will remain here and deal with the demons."

"At once, my lady!" the knight said respectfully as he rose to his feet and ran to obey her command.

"Oh, I *like* him," Everly said with a smile. "It's great when the pretty ones are obedient. Isn't it, Fenn?"

"Stop talking to me," said Fenneth coldly.

"If you insist," Everly replied with unfeigned indifference.

After the carriage arrived and her wounded (Aiden) and psychologically shattered (Sarah) relatives were loaded up, Fenn boarded it while saying nothing.

But she did, however, continue to stare hatefully at the other girl, who, in turn, didn't seem to notice that she was leaving.

After she was gone, Everly addressed her new followers.

"All right, men," Everly said to her father's retainers. "The dangers before us are now obvious! These demons have clearly been up to something! Undoubtedly, their sinister machinations are serving some sort of fiendish purpose, and it's up to us to put an end to it! So let's go take care of it. Make me look good, boys, and I'll make *you* look good! Have we got a deal?"

"*Yes, my lady!*" they all echoed at once.

"Heh, cool. Okay, let's do this!"

With Everly leading their formation, the knights began to march on Bremburg.

In their wake, Sir Casten continued to lie where he fell.

Soon enough, the flies discovered him.

CHAPTER FORTY-THREE

Titania

So, what did you guys think of Fenn? She seemed kind of nice, right?" Everly asked her servants as she and her mentally dominated knights continued their march to Bremburg. "A little vanilla for sure, personality-wise, but she had other attributes that made up for it."

Such as? wondered Eris.

"Dat *ass*." Everly smirked. "Shorty was thicker than a Chicago deep-dish pizza, what-whaaaat?"

Isn't pizza an Earthen food item? Titania asked her.

"It sure is." Everly nodded. "Quite a tasty one as well."

Does that mean you wanted to . . . consume her flesh?

"Say it correctly," Everly said.

Sorry, Titania said. *Does that mean you wanted . . . to eat dat up?*

"Sho 'nuff." Everly snickered. Then after a few moments of deafening silence, she said, "Okay, I'll stop."

Thank you, said Grail.

I felt very uncomfortable hearing that, Carter confessed.

You just haven't gotten used to her yet, Titania said.

Should anyone have to get used to that? Grail wondered.

"My ears are burning," Everly said.

I sincerely doubt that's true, Grail said.

"Heh," Everly laughed to herself.

Regardless of Fenneth's notable physical attributes, I don't believe there to be a point in beginning any sort of long-term relationship with that irritating girl, said Eris. *She clearly opposes the rightness of your actions.*

"Yeah, all those goody-good vibes did kind of dampen my enthusiasm," Everly admitted. "Still, she's dynamic! And who among us has never been tempted by a preacher's daughter?"

I haven't, said Eris.

Me neither, echoed Titania.

Although I find their various cultures fascinating, the idea of lying in sexual congress with a human woman is repugnant to me, Carter said apologetically.

"Really?" said Everly in surprise. "Wow. Watching *Goblin Slayer* convinced me that gobbies were a bunch of horny devils that went nuts at the sight of a naked woman."

That sounds like a lurid pornographic fantasy concocted by a demented mind.

"Ouch! So, you're saying you don't even find *me* cute?" Everly asked him.

I find you utterly fascinating, oh great one, Carter said quickly.

"That didn't really answer my question, bud."

Everly, leave the goblin alone, said Grail. *Only a petty narcissist needs constant assurances of her value.*

"But *Daddy*, I *am* a petty narcissist." Everly pouted.

Are you going to kill Fenneth? Grail asked her.

Everly frowned.

Grail, she'd begun to notice, was a very perceptive fellow who could easily cut through to the heart of the matter. Her preamble was no defense against his insightful nature.

It was sort of annoying.

"It's on my mind," she admitted. "Fenn did promise to be a future buzzkill, after all. I'm not sure I want that hanging over my head like some sort of emo sword of Damocles, y'know?"

I'm surprised, Everly. I thought you relished the idea of having an opponent who was your moral opposite.

"That ain't *her*." Everly scoffed. "I want to fight a *hero*. Fenn's just a feather in the wind. She doesn't have any dreams or aspirations. She just does what she thinks she's supposed to instead of what she *wants*. How can I possibly acknowledge someone like that as an opponent? Even that Sarah idiot has a better worldview than her."

Aren't you just guessing? What could you know about her in the short time you were acquainted?

"I know she whines far too much." Everly grunted.

I think she's got you there, Grail. Titania chuckled.

What do dreams have to do with anything? asked Grail.

"Are you kidding me? Dreams are *everything*!" replied Everly. "If you haven't got something to aspire to, then what's the fucking point of being alive?"

I can understand the value of having a goal to work toward, but there does come a time when you should settle for what you can realistically attain versus what you desire to achieve.

"Bullshit." Everly snorted. "Spitters are quitters, Grail."

Contextualize that vile phrase in terms of this conversation, please.

"A dream is not a mere achievement, old man. To qualify as a dream, your heart's desire has to be *unobtainable*. Anything you can accomplish in your life-time isn't a real dream; it's a mere goal."

Everly. That's utterly absurd.

"And that's the nature of a dream!" Everly said with a manic laugh. "Absurdity brought to life! Like a mouse that wants to be a dragon. Or Sarah thinking she could kill the likes of me!"

Speaking of Sarah, cut in Eris, *how* did *she manage to harm us?*

Was she the one who inflicted that attack? Carter asked. *It was terrible! Even the tower was shaken to its foundations! I thought I was about to be cast off bodily into the astral realm!*

"It couldn't have been," Everly said. "If she had that level of power, she would have used it during our fight. Instead, I stomped on her like a bug. She didn't have a clue about what I meant when I asked her how she hurt me."

This means that she's either an excellent liar . . . Eris began.

"She isn't," Everly said.

Or that you weren't her target at all, Grail concluded.

Lady Fenneth was the sole focus of her ire, said Carter.

"Shit!" cursed Everly loudly after she realized the implication.

Oh, said Grail. *That isn't good at all.*

This could be trouble, agreed Carter. *Measures will have to be taken.*

Whoa! Wait, no. Huh? Sorry, everyone. I don't get it, said Titania.

My sister, Everly's life appears to be directly linked to Fenneth's. Eris sighed. *If she dies, then so will our mistress.*

Oh, no! Titania said. *That sounds awful!*

Where would we be without your gifted insight? Eris asked her sister sarcastically.

Did I really help? Titania asked.

I . . . thought so? said Carter slowly.

Like the sun's rays breaking through a cloud of confusion. Such is the level of your perceptiveness, said Grail.

Oh, my! said Titania with some embarrassment.

When did you both become such boot-licking sycophants? Eris asked the two of them in annoyance.

When I realized that I prefer the continents in their current placement, Grail said without shame.

Lord Grail speaks truly, Carter said. *One should tread carefully when question-ing a titan's ability to reason.*

Why do you fear her so much? I'm the one who delights in destroying minds.

Yes, but your cruelty is calculated and thus predictable, said Grail. *Your violence lacks spontaneity.*

Excuse me? Eris said angrily. *I dare you to say that again!*

Lady Eris, haven't you ever heard the phrase "beware the nice ones"? asked Carter.

Ridiculous! You're both a pair of fools! Everly, correct this misperception of me!

"Oh, I'm not dipping my toe in this water. No sir, no how," Everly said.

What are we even talking about? asked Titania.

"Nothing," said Everly.

The topic eludes me, said Grail.

I was distracted by recollections of that overweight squirrel outside Anders, said Carter.

Hey, he was fat, wasn't he? said Titania. *I was the one who pointed that out!*

Nothing escapes your eye, praised Grail.

You're VERY good at noticing things, said Carter.

"Someone *had* to be feeding him," Everly decided. "No way he got that big on his own."

Eris harrumphed loudly but said nothing else.

Skewer

So, what are we going to do about Fenneth? asked Eris. *Her very existence has become dangerous to us. We must remove her before it's too late.*

What do you suggest, Lady Eris? asked Carter.

My recommendation is that we remove her mobility and place her in safe storage like we did with Alec, Eris said. *We'll better protect ourselves by limiting the chances of her coming to harm.*

A sensible precaution, Carter agreed.

I'm against it, Grail said. *Keeping Alec alive in such a manner is a necessity for controlling the choir of seers. But doing this to an innocent girl is an unfathomable cruelty.*

Grail, if you wish so badly to die, then I recommend you quietly end your own life, Eris said harshly. *But do not think that the rest of us wish to join you in oblivion. Fenneth is a time bomb. Letting her roam free is a risk we cannot take.*

Grail, I kind of like Fenn too, but . . . I don't think I like her enough to want to die when she inevitably gets herself killed, Titania said reluctantly. *She's too high-minded. Even I can tell that. A tree that doesn't bend with the wind is eventually broken by it. I think Eris is right.*

It is the most logical decision we can make, Carter said. *Emotions mustn't factor into it. Our duty is to our Empress.*

Exactly, Carter, Eris said with a pleased voice. *For Everly's sake, we'll deal with this problem at once. Titania, go intercept that carriage and bring Fenneth to us. They shouldn't be too far along. Once we have her, we'll—*

"It's the strangest thing," Everly cut in. "I *know* I'm the one who leads here, and yet my precious followers seem to be making decisions *for* me instead of asking for my permission to act. But that can't be right! Because such behavior would greatly anger me, and they should know better than to do that. Hmm."

Everly, our intention is not to offend you! Eris said at once. *We're just concerned about your future! Fenneth's very existence is a threat to you.*

"*Nothing* is a threat to me," Everly said firmly. "*I'll* be the one who decides how we proceed. Let's leave it at that and focus on our objective here."

But, Everly! Eris said in frustration. *It's not just you who will suffer if you allow things to proceed like this! We're all devoted to you; can't you spare us an ounce of consideration before making this choice?*

Everly sighed in disappointment.

"And *now* you're arguing with me," she said. "I understand. I do. I keep warning you to stay in line, but I never really follow through, do I? That's what comes of affection. Of *spoiling* someone. You can never imagine a day will come when your pet treats disobedience as the norm. What a fool I've been."

Everly thrust her hand forth into the air . . . and *through* it. Her arm appeared to vanish from her fingertips to her elbow. She'd inserted it into a kind of circular void that hung in the air before her. As soon as she did so, Eris began to panic.

Everly, what are you doing? Everly, please stop! Everly—grkk!

"There you are," Everly said. Then she pulled her arm back from the opening into nothingness she'd created and pulled someone out. Wriggling at the end of Everly's grip around her throat was a young pale girl in a white gown.

"Everly! Everly, please! I can't breathe!" the girl said in a panic as she clutched at Everly's iron grip. "What did I do? Forgive me!"

"Surprised I could do that, aren't you?" Everly asked her in a mild tone of voice. "I figured I could. If I could pull the tower itself into this world, why couldn't I also make an opening into it? It's so easy. *Everything's* getting easier, Eris. I'm not complaining about that. I rather enjoy it."

"Everly, why are you doing this? Why have I done to so offend you?" Eris asked.

"Why am I doing this? The answer is simple, Eris. I've grown *tired* of your behavior. I'm tired of your stubbornness and your lack of self-control, but most of all, I'm tired of your *disobedience*. It's so very, very annoying. I've spoken to you about this before. More than once, in fact. I've even threatened you over it, but you still refuse to change. Is it because you don't take me seriously? Is it because you don't believe I'd ever punish you?"

Everly's grip tightened. "It's been like this for years. I keep trying to gently guide you into the servant I want you to be, but your refusal to listen has become a glaring issue. And now . . . now you're giving *me* orders? ORDERS?!"

A manic light began to gleam in Everly's eyes as she spoke. "I just can't take it anymore, Eris. It *bothers* me. *You* have begun to bother me. Your approach to life is just so simplistic and *stupid* . . . You've become a creature of the moment. It's like you have no capacity for patience, and now your bad manners have begun to fray at my affection for you."

"I wasn't giving you orders! I swear, I wasn't!" Eris moaned.

Everly, please, she didn't mean it, Titania said.

"Quiet," Everly ordered her.

But, Everly, my sister doesn't mean to—

"I said *be quiet*," Everly said.

Titania silenced herself.

"Eris, this is it. This really is it," Everly told the girl as she continued to throttle her. "With my full authority, I command you: *Never* argue with me again. Take no action without my permission. Make no decisions without first consulting me."

"I didn't mean to anger you." Eris sobbed.

"You never do, do you? And yet here we are, you fucking disappointment," Everly said. She then released her grip on Eris's neck and let her drop to her knees.

"Wow, I'm so glad I got that off my chest," Everly said. "That was a real weight on my shoulders, for sure. Return to the tower, Eris. Don't speak to me again for the rest of the day. I want you to sit in a dark room by yourself and think of ways you can make amends for your misdeed. Now get lost."

With that said, Everly and her knights walked past her crying servant without a backward glance given.

Was that really necessary? Grail asked her at once.

"Tch, now you as well?" Everly muttered. "Seems like everyone thinks their opinions suddenly matter today."

Eris loves you more than the rest of us combined. She's completely devoted to you.

"I know," Everly said indifferently.

Then why treat her that way?

"It's common sense, Grail. If you let a dog run wild, then whose fault is it when it ignores your commands?"

Is that what we all are to you, Everly? Grail asked bitterly. *Mere dogs? Fit only to obey?*

"What if you were? Would that really be such a bad thing?" Everly asked him. "There are dogs who've had more joyful lives than any human being who ever lived. I think it's mere pride that keeps most people from admitting they'd be happier as a pet."

I'm not your pet, Everly.

"Of course, you aren't." She smiled. "I respect you *far* too much to demean you in such a manner. And neither is Eris. I love her *so* much."

You do? Titania asked.

"Of course I do! She's literally a piece of my soul. Being forced to chastise her almost makes me feel empathy," Everly assured her. "But Eris isn't like you, Titania. *You're* so intelligent and wise."

I am?

"Oh, yes, without a doubt. You heed my words in all matters and never question me. That's why I favor you over all others. If only Eris were as diligent and respectful as you are."

She . . . does question you too often. I've always said so! I'm always saying Everly's right about everything, so let's just do as she says!

"And that's why I love you, Titania," Everly said warmly. "Unthinking compliance is just another term for *personal growth*. Now, hopefully, Eris will take this final lesson to heart and learn to apply herself as you do. I wouldn't even say no to you . . . personally correcting her behavior if you feel it's called for."

What? I mean . . . okay? Yeah. Yeah, I can do that. I can help her become better.

"Awesome sauce," Everly said. "Titania, that's the kind of behavior that's going to mark you as a future leader. Just you wait and see!"

Thank you, Everly!

"Think nothing of it."

I can't listen to any more of this, Grail said angrily before vanishing into silence.

"Gosh, what's gotten into him?" Everly smirked.

I don't know. Grail can be so moody at times, can't he? said Titania.

"It's a darn shame. He's a good person, otherwise," Everly said with a sad shake of her head.

He should practice more unthinking compliance!

"He really should," Everly agreed.

Outside the gates of Bremburg, the remains of dead adventurers, templars, and infected humans lay everywhere. Everly was surprised to see the corpses of the demons had simply vanished from sight, leaving behind nasty streaks of oily residue as they evaporated.

"Why didn't they leave any bodies behind?" she asked Titania. "Remember the spider? He didn't evaporate after we killed him."

These were conjured demons, Titania informed her. *Summoned from the abyss and given temporary bodies. Their true forms exist elsewhere. The old priest, on the other hand, was inside his actual body when he was destroyed.*

"Ahhh." Everly nodded. "That makes sense. I thought for a moment there we were dealing with a plot hole."

Nope! Everything remains consistent with the premise! Titania said cheerfully.

Titania really was an ideal servant. Sure, Carter had knowledge of the world, and Grail was too much fun to toy with, but there was something about Titania that Everly found absolutely delightful. She really did enjoy being around her.

It was a shame she had to set her against her sister like that. Titania and Eris made a very effective team. Perhaps too effective? The real issue was Titania's willingness to be led around by her older sister. Titania was gradually becoming more and more powerful.

It simply wouldn't do to have her listening to anyone other than Everly. Which was why she'd had to intervene when Eris began giving Titania orders that Everly sensed Titania was perfectly willing to obey. She hadn't actually been angry with Eris; she'd just been nipping a potential future problem in the bud.

Although, if she were being perfectly honest, squeezing the air out of Eris for just a few moments sure had felt good. Everly loved her, naturally, but come on! She'd had that coming for years.

You could only indulge someone's nonsense for so long before you had to respond. Clearly, getting away with her shenanigans for so long had caused Eris to develop a little too much confidence in herself.

There was nothing wrong with confidence of course. As long as it didn't keep you from feeling fear.

That was what Everly thought.

Eris hadn't been wrong about Fenneth, though. This was an issue that wasn't going to go away by itself. But despite her whimsical nature, Everly wasn't stupid. She knew exactly how to handle it. Or she thought she did.

Okay, she didn't.

But she was sure she'd figure it out. She was a clever person.

But first, she wanted to deal with this issue in Bremburg.

It needed . . . closure. Finality. She'd already gotten this deeply involved.

May as well finish things up.

The surviving adventurers and templars had pulled back to the outskirts of the town, leaving their dead behind. Everly stared at the remains that surrounded her and considered her options for the battle ahead.

Should she raise the dead to fight for her? That wouldn't be a bad choice. It never hurt to approach a dangerous situation with as much backup as one could muster. She didn't know how effective her father's knights would be; they seemed well trained, but she didn't sense much in the way of magic or sword aura among them. Just a few minor talents surrounded by ordinary men.

Then again, Grail had already made such a dynamic impression when he led his undead force into battle. Although he'd been emulating her, wouldn't others mistake Everly for a copycat? Oh, that would be so irritating!

On the other hand, there were undoubtedly dozens of infected and demons left standing, and killing them all by herself might take a while. She wasn't interested in such a prospect. Demons were revolting, and the infected were nauseating. They were both gross.

Really, what sort of choices were those?

She'd be fine of course. Nothing in their ranks was a threat to her. The problem was that the knights she'd stolen from her brother weren't nearly as durable as she was. They'd undoubtedly suffer heavy losses in the fight. Not something she'd ordinarily care about, but she'd made such a big show of marching them out here that she'd feel embarrassed if too many of them died.

What to do, what to do, what to do? she thought to herself.

In the end, she decided a saturation bombing was what was called for.

First, using geokinesis, she tore a gigantic section of rock and soil free from the earth and lifted it into the sky high above Bremburg. Then she began tearing small portions of it free and used [**Transmutation**] to change them into edged weaponry—spears, daggers, swords, even axes.

It didn't take long before there were thousands of weapons now hanging in the air. Beneath them, Everly next opened a massive rift into the astral realm. It was similar to the one she'd used to pull Eris bodily into the world, but this one was many, many times larger.

It was into this hole in reality that Everly dropped all her newly made toys.

I don't get it, boss, Titania said. *Why forge all that steel if you're just going to throw it all away?*

"I didn't throw them away," Everly corrected her. "I'm letting them build momentum. I really need to introduce you to a game called *Portal*."

It sounds fun.

"It really is. How many pointy things would you say I made?"

I stopped counting after three thousand.

"Cool," Everly said with satisfaction. A short while later, she said, "It's been about two minutes, I think. That should be plenty of time for terminal velocity to have set in."

So, what happens now? Titania asked.

"Now we open the gates of Babylon," Everly said with an unpleasant smile.

With a wave of her hand, she reopened the gateway.

About a hundred feet above Bremburg, an outpouring of deadly weapons fell faster than the speed of sound.

What followed swiftly in their wake were screams of pain.

Leaving her knights behind, Everly entered the town, fascinated by the results of the destruction she'd rained down upon its occupants.

The dead were everywhere.

There was so much blood.

Perhaps she'd overdone it?

Nah. It had been so cool.

Walking carefully, she eventually reached the town square. Seated in its center, surrounded by dozens of dead temple clerics, was a gravely wounded man with black wings sprouting from his back, which had been made into a gory pincushion by the various bladed objects now embedded in him.

"Hey," she said to the dying demon.

"Hey," he responded slowly to the monstrous human.

"I like your wings," she said.

"You killed everyone in this city," the demon said in disbelief. "They could have been healed. They could have still been saved."

Everly looked around the murdered town of Bremburg. He seemed to be correct. Except for him, all the remaining infected were now dead with a sword or worse jutting from their body.

"Eh, sounds like work," she said with an indifferent shrug.

"What kind of salvation is that?" he asked her.

Everly smiled.

CHAPTER FORTY-FIVE

Wings

Let me take a look at you," Everly said as she approached the demon. Following a lazy wave of her hand, the rubble and discarded weaponry that separated the two of them floated into the air, removed from her path.

When she was closer to him, she ran her fingers admiringly across his large black wings. "Dazzling," she said earnestly. "What an amazing sight you would have made if I hadn't clipped you beforehand. I wish I could have seen it."

She knelt then and gently lifted his head with her hands cupping his chin. "You're pretty too. And yet . . . you're missing something. A finishing touch that would truly mark how splendid you are. But what can it be . . . ?" she asked herself.

Then she snapped her fingers. "Oh! I know!" she said.

She placed the first two fingers of her right hand beneath each of his eyes. Then she began to dig down, using her fingernails to painfully peel away at the skin beneath them, digging two bloody furrows beneath his eyes from which blood poured, making it appear that he was crying bloody tears.

Everly sucked in her breath and beamed in delight at her work. "Goodness! Now you're *perfect*," she said dreamily.

"Who are you?" he whispered.

"Beauty," she replied.

"Why *Beauty*?" he asked.

"It's a quote from an old story. 'T'was beauty killed the beast,'" Everly said. "You know what? I *recognize* you. Earlier this year, just before the snow finished melting, that silly old demon priest was trying to summon you, wasn't he? I guess he succeeded after all."

"You had a hand in that?" he asked.

"I was trying to prevent it. Looks like I took the L on that one, eh? But things didn't turn out so bad. I got to prevent your dastardly scheme or whatever you were trying to do. I guess I turned out to be the hero of this little tale after all."

"I only wanted to go home," he said.

"What's your name?" she asked him.

"Acedia," he replied.

"Pretty. What does it mean?"

"Sloth."

"Oh, *shit*, look at that!" Everly said gleefully. "I bagged a big one, didn't I?"

"A meaninglessly destructive victory. My mother's blessing guarantees my return from death. Even if I don't know where I'll end up, I'll still return one day."

"Demons have mothers?" Everly asked him. "That's interesting. I thought you were all mutated elementals?"

"That's the first generation," he said.

"Which one are you?"

"I'm of the second."

"Which generation is everyone else on?" Everly asked out of curiosity.

"We don't keep count."

"Hmm," Everly said thoughtfully. She then took a seat in the rubble beside Sloth and leaned back on the ruined stone wall. "What does eternal life feel like? I suspect I'll attain it for myself one day, but I'd love to hear the opinion of someone who already has it. Is it as cool as it seems?"

"It's horrible," Sloth said bluntly.

"Why do you say that?" Everly wondered.

"People. People make it awful. No matter their gender, species, or beliefs, intelligent mortal life finds a way to make everything it touches into a sewer."

"Oh," Everly said. "So, you're saying humans ruin everything?"

"Not just humans." Sloth grunted. "Any creature that possesses the spark of intelligence will eventually choose to rebel against the natural order. I've seen it happen a million times."

"Where does it all lead?"

"Self-destruction."

"Always?"

"Always."

"Hmm," Everly said to herself. Then she asked, "Do you think they had fun?"

"Fun?" asked Sloth.

"Yeah, fun. Do you think all those dead fools had fun destroying themselves and everything around them?"

"I have no idea," he answered.

"I think they must have," Everly said. "Think about it. Does it make sense *not* to destroy the world if you were ever given an opportunity to do it? Now that I know reincarnation exists, I'm quite certain that all life is essentially meaningless."

"Ah. Nihilism. How *very* edgy." Sloth snorted.

"Ha!" Everly laughed in response. "I'm just saying. Make a good choice, make a bad choice, so what? Who cares? You'll still end up somewhere. Nothing we do really affects anything. You may as well seek what brings you joy."

"What if what brings you joy brings harm to others?"

"Then someone should stop me."

"Like whom? A hero?"

"*Exactly*," Everly said happily. She then beamed such a warm and joyous smile at Sloth that even he was momentarily taken aback.

"You're a strange one, aren't you?" he asked her.

"I don't think so," she said. "I'm just being true to my nature."

"You killed my prime servant," Sloth said to her. "An innocent child who rescued me from a humiliating end. Who nursed me back to health and gave me an opportunity to restore myself. He even tried to protect me from your storm of swords."

"He didn't do a very good job." Everly smirked.

"A spider's body makes for poor shelter," Sloth said. "You also killed all the remaining humans."

"Don't you feel the least bit hypocritical criticizing me over that?" Everly asked with a raised eyebrow. "I wasn't the one who made them into slaves and put them in harm's way."

"They could have been healed," Sloth insisted.

"Maybe some. But certainly not all of them. Probably not even *most*. Your nasty little plague did too good of a job. Anyway, I was in a hurry, and they were in the way. Life happens."

"What a self-serving point of view," he muttered.

"Ha! I *like* you," Everly said. "You know, you could be a keeper."

"What?"

"I'm offering you a choice," Everly said. "That's not something I do very often. Oh, I like to make it *appear* as though there are multiple options, but that's mainly just me having fun. You, however? I like you. You and I could have some fun together."

"No," he said resolutely.

"What? You haven't even heard my pitch," Everly said.

"I don't need to," Sloth said. "I won't ever turn against my family."

"Loyalty is *so* hot." She winked. "Throw a little of it my way, and I'll make you a *real* king. I'll give you these lands to rule in my name, delicacies from across the world, and silk sheets to lie on. I might even toss a harem or two your way if you *really* impress me."

"What kind of ego must a mortal possess to try to tempt an archfiend?" Sloth asked her in a daze. "It's usually supposed to go the other way."

"The old must make way for the new," she said cheerfully.

Sloth surprised himself and laughed. He laughed long and hard, and although the force of his laughter caused his wounds to tear and ache, he didn't stop for a long while.

"I think we *could* have had fun," he said. "But I'm already a king. It's a throne I never wanted, but it's mine all the same. You and I are enemies. Here's my promise, though. I won't be complacent in death as I normally am. I will return to life with all due haste and seek vengeance against you."

"Oh? Really?" Everly asked him.

"Yes," he replied. "Whatever heights you reach, I swear to tear you from them. I'll destroy everything you build and hurl you screaming into ruinous collapse. If circumstances demand I name myself a hero to do it, then I will become mankind's light."

Everly took his hand and gazed into his eyes. "If you come at me bearing wings, I'll tear them off your shoulders and force you to crawl in the dirt like a maimed fly. Your meals will consist of scraps from my plate. If you're a good boy, I'll let you sleep on the floor beside my fireplace. But if you're *bad*, I'll make you weep."

"I'll rip that arrogance from you in bloody swaths when I have you flayed," he vowed.

She inched closer to Acedia and held his face between her warm hands. "I'll make you love me and then drive you mad with denial," she promised him, wearing an alluring smile.

"What's your name?" he asked her.

"I'm not *telling*," she said with acidic sweetness.

"What's your *name*?" he desperately repeated.

"If you want to know, come find me. I'll tell you if you put up a good fight."

"What's . . . your . . . ?" His head drooped to his chest, and his body lay still and cold.

Everly kissed his forehead and then fondly patted his cheek. As she stood and prepared to leave, she paused. Then she made a swift gesture. One of the swords that had pierced the demon's body slowly floated toward her waiting hand and landed on her palm. With it, she made two precise cuts across his chest, forming a large x. Then she reached into the incision and pulled out a large red gem.

"This will work nicely," she said to herself. "Thanks for your help. I hope you find me soon."

She then made her way back outside, where her father's knights awaited her.

"The job is done, men!" she told them. "T'was a fierce clash of steel and heart, a thrilling duel for the ages! In the end, we stand triumphant! Once more, mankind stands tall and hell slinks away to the abyss to lick its wounds and curse the righteous. You can go ahead and praise me now."

The knights all began mindlessly cheering their lady's victory.

Everly happily preened before them and drank deeply of their affection. "Yes, yes, yes, I was *wonderful!* Sadly, however, it's not yet time for me to claim sole credit. Today, *you people* are the *real* heroes."

That was a line she'd borrowed from a great American. And it was a good one.

"Which is to say, you raced in to finish the demons off before they could regroup, and you took down their leader," she informed them. "Here's the proof," she said as she approached their leader and handed him the gem she'd removed from Sloth's body.

It was Sloth's remaining mana core. She'd been tempted to keep it as a trophy but decided it would be better to use it as part of her cover story.

"All shall be done as you command, Lady Everly," he said with a bow.

"Great!" she said. "Oh, but there's one little thing we need to get out of the way first. Boys, I'm going to need about twenty or so of you to go into town and kill yourselves, if you don't mind."

The knights continued to stare blankly ahead.

"I know I said I'd try to keep you from harm, but my story doesn't really work without a few casualties, yeah?" Everly continued. "A bunch of household knights walking unscathed from a brawl with demons would call the whole thing into question. You don't mind, do you?"

"We'll do anything you say, Lady Everly!" one of them cried out.

"The honor is all ours!" another one yelled.

"Let us DIE for you!" another said. "LET US ALL DIE FOR YOU!"

"Boys, *boys*, stop!" Everly said shyly. "Thank you so much. But I only need twenty! I'll let you decide among yourselves. Thanks again!"

Everly turned her back on the arguing knights and walked away. How sweet of them to fight so passionately among themselves for the right to die for her convenience. From the sounds of clashing blades now ringing to her ears, it appeared a few of them were now killing each other for the privilege.

She really was something special, wasn't she?

It sure seemed that way.

Sadly, she still had one little issue to wrap up before she could declare total victory. It was something she had to do personally. She didn't really want to, but she was management. The big decisions couldn't ever be left to an underling.

Besides, if you wanted total commitment to the cause from your servants, you had to be willing to show them the depths of your own resolve. Kings were crowned by war but forged by murder.

The best ones did the deed themselves.

Oh, well, she thought to herself. *Dessert wouldn't taste half so sweet if we didn't eat our veggies first.*

Keeping that in mind, Everly headed out to finish the day's last chore.

Only One

Count Van Belsar and his family were gone by the time Fenneth's carriage arrived at their estate. They'd apparently been summoned to the capital for an emergency conference called by the king, leaving the house steward to oversee things.

Fenneth immediately took charge and had Sarah confined to guest quarters, with her legs clasped in iron. Then she personally began emergency treatments for Aiden's ruined face.

It was difficult work. And emotionally trying.

There was hope for Aiden. Everly had splintered and destroyed entire portions of his face's skeletal structure, but a sufficiently powerful healer would be able to restore what he'd lost. The question of his mental recovery, however, was one that wouldn't be easily answered.

He might never recover from the trauma he'd been dealt.

But that was a problem for later. In the morning, she'd send a messenger after Countess Anne to inform her of what had occurred. Then she'd contact the temple to let them know she and Sarah were both safe and to warn them about Everly as well.

She'd tell *everyone* about Everly. Who she was and what she was capable of.

It had to be done.

The kingdom needed to know that a monster walked freely within it.

Later that night, Fenneth slept uneasily in the room she'd been provided. She was tired and desperately needed to rest, but anxiety and anger over the preceding day's events made it so difficult.

Just when she thought she'd finally pass out, a voice spoke to her from the dark.

"Dreaming about me?" asked Everly in awry voice.

Fenn jumped to her feet at once and reached for the lamp placed on the table beside her bed.

"Don't," Everly warned her. "Leave it off. For your sake."

"What are you doing here?" Fenneth demanded from her.

"What do you mean by that? I can't visit my friend on a whim?" Everly replied. "Fenn, this is my *birthplace*. It's a place of great significance! One day they might even turn it into a historical landmark. 'Over there,' they'll say! 'That's where they pulled her out of her mother.' Too bad they didn't keep the towels and sheets. Those would be collector's items by now."

"Everly, you have no business being here! Get out!" Fenneth shouted.

"Sorry, that's where you're wrong, Fenn," Everly said sadly. "Business is *all* that's brought me here. Unresolved issues. Loose ends, you could call them."

"What do you mean?"

"I realized that I made a mistake. I let my name get out earlier than I wanted it to. So I had to correct it."

"What did you do?" Fenneth asked quietly.

"I had a conversation with Sarah. We came to an agreement about a few things. Now we're good."

"What about Aiden?" Fenneth asked.

"Well, here's the *thing*," Everly said reluctantly.

Fenneth lit her lamp.

"Oh, my god," she whispered.

From her chest down, Everly was covered in blood. Soaked in it. It had begun pooling below her seat, staining the floor of the bedroom.

She looked like an absolute horror.

"I *told* you to leave that off," Everly chided her.

"Jesus *Christ*," Fenneth moaned.

"Nope. Just me again," Everly said. "I really had no intention of doing that. I didn't *care* about him. I just wanted him to keep his mouth shut, right? But when I woke him up to talk, he gave this silly sort of *squeaking* reaction, and well . . . it triggered a response from me."

"What?"

"You know how with cats, if you slowly drag a shoestring across the floor, they just lose it and attack? Kind of the same deal. He had it coming anyway, but ahhh, what am I even saying? A nice girl like you wouldn't understand a predatory mindset."

"He was your brother, Everly. He was your *family*," Fenneth said.

"There are all kinds of creatures where such distinctions are as meaningless as thanatology," Everly replied. "So, we shared a common point of origin? Okay, so what? Honestly, you must not have known him that well, Fenn. He'd have done the same to me in a heartbeat. In fact, he *tried* before. He just didn't realize that in this case, the female was by far the deadlier of the species."

"Why are you still here, Everly?" asked Fenneth.

"I think you already know," Everly replied. "I'm not going to apologize for what I have to do. This is survival, and if we're being honest, Fenn, you weren't living much of a life anyway."

"You're going to *kill me*?" Fenn asked in horror.

"Afraid so, yeah," Everly said. "I don't really want to, but . . . what choice is there? The rules of the game clearly state that it's you or me. And, well, I like you, Fenn . . . but I *love* me. So there we have it."

"What are you even talking about?!"

"I figured it out on the walk over here. What I had to do. It's obvious in hindsight. I realized it when you gave me that little beating earlier. We're *vulnerable* to each other, Fenn. You can hurt me. But I can also hurt you. It's a link. But it's a link made only for us."

"What does that even mean?"

"It means this world really is too small for the two of us. I'm special, Fenn. And I think you're special too, but you haven't yet realized it. We're on opposite ends of a pendulum meant to keep each other in line. Even worse, if one of us dies, the other one dies too. *Unless*—and mind you, this is just a guess on my part—one of us dies by the other's hand."

"Everly, that is absolutely psychotic!" Fenneth shouted. "You say if I die, you'll die, so your big solution is to *kill me?* How does that make any fucking sense?!"

"It doesn't! Which means it does! That's how these kinds of puzzles work, Fenn," Everly said. "Sometimes you have to go with instinct over logic. And besides . . . leaving you alive just isn't an option."

"Why not?"

"Fenn, this is *my* story. Not yours! This life is what I've always wanted for myself! You just . . . stumbled into this accidentally. You said it yourself—you hate this place! Well, I *love* it! It's all I've ever dreamed of! And it isn't fair! It isn't fucking FAIR to risk losing everything for the sake of, what? *You?* Some nobody? Some fucking *background character*? Does that make *any* sense?"

"You'd really kill me over this?" Fenneth asked her.

"Of course I would. How could I not? That's what separates me from the herd. *Resolve.* The willingness to swing the sword. I won't let your drab existence deny me my destiny."

"You sound like a fucking cartoon character," Fenneth said.

"Yeah. I do," Everly said sadly. "Stupid, right?"

Before Fenneth could respond, Everly ran across the room with a surprising burst of speed and put her hand through the other girl's chest.

Then she gripped her heart and squeezed.

"Gahhh," Fenneth gasped.

"I'll remember you. I won't let you be forgotten," Everly said quickly. "I promise. I promise this is what's best. Just close your eyes. None of this was ever real. It wasn't your life—it was *my* dream. Sleep, Fenn. *Sleep*. None of this was ever real . . . " she whispered.

Fenneth couldn't scream. She couldn't move. She could only cry silently and shudder.

Then she lay still.

Everly held her carefully. Then she lifted her body and carried her back to her bed.

"Only one of us," she said quietly. "That's the way it had to be. I didn't make this rule. I just had to follow through on it. Only one of us. It's not my fault. It really isn't."

She pulled the covers over Fenn's body and stepped away.

Everly was still alive. Wasn't that something? Of course, it was.

Still alive.

It had been a test. That was all. A test. She'd passed. She made it.

"Still alive," she whispered.

She looked at Fenneth's face and then gazed at her own reflection in the mirror attached to the guest vanity.

Her own smile seemed hollow to her. Why were her eyes so red? Ridiculous. She wiped away at them, staining her face and hair with fresh blood as she did.

She breathed deeply.

Just a test. Just a test. And Everly had passed it.

"Kill your heart and only good things can happen," she said to herself.

She climbed out the window and let herself drop to the ground below. Then she walked away from her crime.

Just a test.

She'd won again.

Everly always won.

That was a good thing, wasn't it?

About the Author

J. V. Simms was the author of the Empress and My Eyes Glow Red series, originally released on Royal Road. When he wasn't writing, he spent his time avoiding his cat, who was likely seeking vengeance for her most recent trip to the vet. Simms lived in Indiana and was always better than his nephew at Minecraft. That's in writing so it must be true.